THE
SIRENS

Also by Emilia Hart

Weyward

THE SIRENS

A NOVEL

EMILIA HART

ST. MARTIN'S PRESS
NEW YORK

First published in the United States by St. Martin's Press, an imprint of St. Martin's Publishing Group

THE SIRENS. Copyright © 2025 by Emilia Hart Limited. All rights reserved. Printed in the United States of America. For information, address St. Martin's Publishing Group, 120 Broadway, New York, NY 10271.

www.stmartins.com

Designed by Jen Edwards

All emojis designed by OpenMoji – the open-source emoji and icon project. License: CC BY-SA 4.0

Water texture © ganjalex/Shutterstock; shell, coral, and seaweed illustrations © SpicyTruffel/Shutterstock

The Library of Congress Cataloging-in-Publication Data is available upon request.

ISBN 978-1-250-28082-4 (hardcover)
ISBN 978-1-250-39021-9 (Canadian & international, sold outside the U.S., subject to rights availability)
ISBN 978-1-250-28083-1 (ebook)

Our books may be purchased in bulk for promotional, educational, or business use. Please contact your local bookseller or the Macmillan Corporate and Premium Sales Department at 1-800-221-7945, extension 5442, or by email at MacmillanSpecialMarkets@macmillan.com.

First U.S. Edition: 2025

First International Edition: 2025

10 9 8 7 6 5 4 3 2 1

For Katie, who inspired this novel,
and for Jack, who believed I could write it

The Ocean has its silent caves

—NATHANIEL HAWTHORNE, "THE OCEAN"

HISTORICAL NOTE

In 1788, a fleet of eleven British ships landed on a shore almost ten thousand miles from England. The ships carried convicts whom the overburdened British prison system could no longer hold. A significant minority hailed from Ireland, which had been under British colonial rule for centuries. Exiled from their homelands, the convicts were put to work to create a new penal colony called New South Wales. Over the next eighty years, British authorities transported thousands of convicts to New South Wales and the nearby colonies of (as they were then called) Van Diemen's Land, Brisbane, and the Swan River Colony. In 1901, these and other surrounding colonies united to become Australia.

The First Australians, Aboriginal and Torres Strait Islander peoples, had thrived on the land for millennia before the arrival of those ships. It is estimated that over 250 languages—reflecting distinct nations with distinct cultures—were spoken in Australia prior to 1788. British invasion was devastating for Aboriginal and Torres Strait Islander peoples. Their lands were taken from them. Many lost their lives to colonial violence and imported disease. Following 1788, First Nations peoples were subject to racist policies that aimed to "assimilate" them into white Australian society, an attempt to deprive them of their language and culture as well as their land. The effects of this are still felt today.

This is a painful legacy and one that is not mine to write about. Nor is it my place to write about the enduring agency of First Nations peoples and their conservation of language, culture, and connection to Country. I would encourage you to seek out their stories. The Australian Institute of Aboriginal and Torres Strait Islander Studies, accessible at aiatsis.gov.au, is a good place to start.

ACKNOWLEDGMENT OF COUNTRY

Comber Bay is a fictional place, inspired by my treasured memories of staying with family in Batemans Bay, on the South Coast of New South Wales. I would like to acknowledge the Walbunja people, the Traditional Custodians of that land, and pay my respects to Elders both past and present.

PART ONE

PROLOGUE

She breathes in time with the sea.

In.

The waves crash against the rocks, frothing through the mouth of the cave. Icy on her toes, her shaking thighs.

Out.

The tide sucks away, leaving offerings in its wake. A glistening rope of seaweed. Pieces of shell, pearled as bone.

She grits her teeth but the pain rips through her—a bright, shocking thing—and the next breath is a scream.

Another contraction, her cry swallowed by the thundering waves. She knows she is safe in her dark cave, with its slick rocks and its steady drip of salt. But the sea is hungry and it must be fed.

She places a shaking hand between her legs, feels the baby's skull with its bloodied caul.

Now.

She lifts the fabric of her dress, bunching it into her mouth, biting down hard on the cloth, her body gathering itself together. One more push and she howls, her body split open until it is empty, spent, and the child is in her arms. She touches the tiny starfish hands; the half-closed eyes; the shell-pink lips.

She allows herself this one, precious moment. And then she rises, trembling, her child mewling at her breast.

Below the entrance to her cave, the sea churns over the rocks, waiting.

1

LUCY

MONDAY, 11 FEBRUARY 2019

HAMILTON HUME UNIVERSITY

BROKEN HILL, NSW

AUSTRALIA

900 KILOMETERS INLAND

It's the scream that wakes her.

The room smells of must and sleep. She can feel the rapid beat of a pulse, the tender cords of a throat. Fingernails rake at her hands.

A gray dawn filters through the slats in the blinds, and in its light Lucy sees Ben below her, his eyes bright with fear. A blood vessel has burst in his left sclera, forming a red star. She stumbles back from the bed.

"Lucy," he splutters, one hand clawing at his neck. "What the—"

The words choke out of him, his voice strangled.

Strangled. Her hands on his neck, the bulge of his eyes.

She'd been strangling him.

He sits up in bed, switches on a lamp. She bucks away from it like an animal. There is movement outside, in the corridor. A knock at the door.

"Ben, mate? Are you all right? I thought I heard—"

She moves slowly, as if through water. Her pulse hammers at her throat. The knocking intensifies; Ben is coughing now. Calling for help.

The press of the door at her back. She grasps the doorknob with sweaty fingers, uses it to ground herself. The door is already unlocked, the faulty dead bolt jangling. She wrenches it open, pushes past Nick, Ben's roommate, and runs down the corridor up the flight of stairs to her own room.

Once inside, she leans against the door, breathing heavily as she struggles to process what just happened. Her dorm room is pin neat as always, the books in careful piles on her desk and bedside table. But the bedclothes are rumpled, the air stale. Her sheets feel damp, as if she's sweated through them.

She tries to draw the events of the evening back to her. Not willing to face the canteen, she'd skipped dinner, soothing her anxious stomach with ginger tea in her favorite mug brought from home. Then she'd put on a podcast and settled in for an early night, hoping the distraction would vanquish thoughts of Ben and what he'd done.

There'd been a dream, she remembers now: cold water licking her skin, stones digging into her feet. The scrape of rock against her skull. A man's hot breath in her face, his fingers digging into her flesh—fear warring with the desperate need to fight, to survive—

And then she'd woken to find herself straddling Ben's chest, her hands clawed tight around his throat. Horror sweeps through her, numbing her fingertips, her lips.

She'd been sleepwalking. Something she has never—not once in her life—done before.

She looks at her hands, watches them tremble. Had she *wanted* to hurt Ben—to kill him, even—after what he'd done to her? Or had it been the dream, which lingers still like a bad taste in her mouth—the gnaw of fear, that primal need to fight, to survive? It was as if some limbic part of her brain had directed her to his room, a puppet led by its master.

A panicked glance out of the window tells her that the sun is rising now, turning the sky pink. She sees a dark blur of movement in the quadrangle: a uniform with neon lettering. A campus security officer. Ben—or his roommate, Nick—must have called after she fled.

She imagines what he'll say: *I woke up, and she had her hands on my throat—she was trying to kill me.* Her thoughts whirl; she tries to slow her breathing, but finds that she can't. The panic rises and rises, an awful heat in her blood.

There'll be an investigation, she's sure of that. She'll be suspended, possibly even expelled. God, could they get the actual police involved? Could she be arrested—charged—with assault?

Everything she's yearned and worked for. Gone. She pictures Ben: bruises blooming around his throat, the gouge marks from her nails in his flesh. *She* did that. Even if she doesn't remember it, even if she wasn't *awake*.

But who would believe her, especially after what happened?

After all, they've already taken his side.

Sweat dampens her armpits, the urge to flee rising inside her.

But where can she go? She can't go home to her parents. That would mean telling them that she, Lucy, their *good girl*, attacked some- one. And, worse, it would mean telling them *why*, telling them what Ben had done. No, she could never. But then, who? Who will help her, provide refuge while she works out what to do, how to fix things?

And then the answer comes to her. She changes quickly, scrabbles inside the small cupboard for an overnight bag. Underwear. Clothes. Wet wipes. Moisturizer. Laptop. Laptop charger. A notebook. She packs with shaking fingers.

She opens the drawer of her desk, retrieves a battered postcard, runs a fingertip over the address scrawled on the back.

Cliff House, 1 Malua Street, Comber Bay.

There's only one place she can go, one person who might under- stand.

The road stretches on endlessly in front of her, merging with the hori- zon. Around her there is nothing but empty gold scrub, miles and miles of it. Dusky pink corellas—her mother's favorite bird—burst from a withered tree as she passes.

There are no other cars. She is alone.

She reaches to the passenger seat for her iPhone, wedges it between her thighs as she calls her sister. After several rings—Lucy holding her breath in the silence between each one—the phone clicks.

"Jess?" she says, hope catching like a burr in her throat. But then her sister's prerecorded voice comes bright and terse down the line.

"Hi, you've reached Jess Martin. I'm unable to come to the phone right now—"

"Fuck," Lucy whispers as she hangs up.

Her eyes well with tears, blurring the landscape in front of her.

She tells herself that it's all right. That Jess will answer eventually, that she'll know how to help.

Won't she?

2

LUCY

Lucy's phone rings a few hours into the drive. She pulls over into a lay-by, relief thudding through her. For a moment, she's sure it'll be Jess, calling her back.

But the caller is her friend Em. Em, with her haywire curls and salon-sharp nails, who'd been expecting her in their 9 A.M. class. Em, who has already texted her five times.

Lol did you sleep in

Can't believe you've left me to face a Monday morning lecture on my own. Harsh

Seriously though are you OK?

Hey—I just saw Nick. He said you attacked Ben?! Lucy, what's going on?

Call me.

Lucy wipes her eyes with the back of her hand, takes a long, shuddering breath to compose herself.

But it's no use. Already, her face burns with the memory: of how trusting she'd been, how foolish.

She and Ben had slept together just before the beginning of the summer holidays—the night before everyone left campus last December. Right away, it was clear that it meant more to her than it did to him: she'd read it in the practiced way he removed her bra, the ease with which he slid inside her. She can still remember every sensation, every whispered sigh. As if she'd known, even then, that it would never happen again. After all, how could someone like Ben— Ben with his beautifully muscled shoulders and dark glossy hair—be interested in someone like Lucy?

But then, he'd surprised her. He'd texted her over the break, sending links to cat videos and Twitter memes. Once, they'd even spoken on the phone, comparing notes on the books they were reading (he bought *In Cold Blood* on her recommendation; she read *Joe Cinque's Consolation* on his). It had felt so easy, so natural, that she was worried they were falling into friendship territory. That she would never again feel his fingertips on her thighs, his lips against her ear.

And so, just days before the start of their final year, she'd plucked up her courage and asked him if he wanted a picture.

She'd never done anything like that before. For a start, no one had ever asked for one; and why would they? Who would want to see Lucy without her clothes on?

But she thought of Ben's sigh as he sank himself inside of her, the way that he kissed the tender flesh above her collarbone. Like he didn't see the rivulets of cracked skin between her breasts, across her rib cage. He was different, she could feel it. He was safe.

It felt like her heart ceased to beat as she waited for his reply, the minutes stretching on and on. First the blue ticks, then those thrilling words: *Ben is typing*.

That depends, he'd replied. *On whether it's a picture of you.*

Again and again she'd adjusted the lighting, hoping the soft glow of her bedside lamp would hide the worst of her skin. She must have taken dozens, in the end. How badly she'd wanted to be beautiful for him.

She'd been happy with the picture she'd chosen: the dark glimmer of her eyes, the wet shine of her lips. The way the lamplight gilded the curve of her breast; the rest of her robed in silky shadow.

Wow, he'd told her. *You're gorgeous.*

And she'd stared at the photo through new eyes and thought that maybe, just maybe, he was right.

She'd been so excited to get back to uni, to see him again, to pick up where they'd left off. But he avoided her eye in their Tuesday afternoon lecture, and rushed to his next class before she could say hello. The strange thing was, other people seemed to be avoiding her, too: her classmates fell back when she passed, murmuring to each other; a Red Sea of gossip.

She'd thought it was because people knew about her and Ben, that they were an item, or becoming one. She'd let herself feel a twinge of pride.

How wrong she'd been.

It was Em who saw the TikTok video first, who sent her the link. *I'm so sorry*, she said. *But if it were me, I'd want to know.*

The shock of her own body in the video was magnified by the sick horror of its soundtrack: "Monster Mash." It was all there, visible, even beneath the cruel distortion of the filter. The crusted white flesh on her torso, the silver streaks across her breasts, the insides of her wrists.

But the worst thing was the look on her face—the soft melt of trust.

Lucy flicks the indicator on before she pulls back onto the road, even though there's no traffic—just a lone truck creaking up ahead. Her palms feel clammy on the steering wheel.

This is why she has to get away. Why no one will believe that she didn't mean to hurt Ben—that she'd been sleepwalking, in the midst of a nightmare. That she hadn't known what she was doing.

He hadn't meant for it to happen, Ben said when she confronted him. Yes, he'd shared the picture with some friends on WhatsApp, but that was just something they always did. He'd never expected—he couldn't believe!—someone would be so cruel as to put it on TikTok.

He was sorry.

Lucy swallows, remembering the caption, the comments.

Tfw your friend's girl is a literal gorgon

Hideous

Talk about a graveyard smash

Perhaps naïvely, she'd been surprised how little the university was willing to do, how dismissive they'd been.

"Isn't it a crime?" she'd asked the student welfare officer, a fortyish woman with multiple rings in each ear. "Sharing an intimate image without consent—I looked it up. I want to make a report to the police."

The woman had winced, sliding a box of tissues toward Lucy, even though she wasn't crying.

"I'd ask that you think long and hard about taking such a step," she'd said. "I understand that you're upset—truly, I do—but everyone makes mistakes. Something like this could really derail Ben's life. As a mother of a son myself—"

Furious, Lucy had risen from her chair and walked out.

Hadn't Ben derailed *her* life? Since the discovery of the video, she'd spent most of the week in her room. In lectures, she'd sat as close to the exit as possible, leaving before the others rose from their chairs, before a hundred heads could swivel to stare at her. The post had been removed for violating TikTok's policy, but she had no doubt that people had taken screenshots; that it circulated still, via Facebook and WhatsApp and Snapchat. The previous day, she'd ordered a coffee from the campus café, and the boy serving her squinted with recognition before blushing a deep red.

It felt like the whole world had seen it. Like it would follow her forever.

At the welcome assembly two years before, the university chancellor had told them to look around at the students sitting on either side of them. "This is the best journalism course in the country," he'd said. "We have alumni working everywhere, from Sky News to the *New York Times*. The majority of journalists working at the *Sydney Morning Herald* and *The Age* studied at Hamilton Hume. Remember that, during your time here. The young man or woman sitting next to you isn't just your course mate, but your future colleague."

It was a phrase Lucy couldn't get out of her head. All of her future colleagues had seen her disgraced. How could she possibly have a career after this?

But despite her fury, the meeting with the student welfare officer had got under her skin, planted seeds of doubt. What if the police dismissed her, too? Then she'd be out of options. Besides, Ben's father was an employment lawyer, at a fancy firm in Melbourne. "The kind who represents the employers instead of the employees," Ben had told her, with a sneer in his voice. He hated his father, he said, for "greasing the capitalist machine." But Lucy doubted that hatred would prevent him from asking for help if he needed it. That's who she'd be up against, if she made the report.

For three days, she'd faltered, unsure of what to do. And then this morning she'd found herself with her hands wrapped around Ben's throat, like her body had made the decision for her.

Well. She can hardly tell the police about the video now, not after what she's done.

She needs to focus on getting to Jess. On staying awake: another twelve hours to go. Her sister recently moved to Comber Bay on the South Coast. Lucy's never been there, and she only has the address because Jess sent her a postcard for her birthday in September; the same postcard that now rests on the dashboard. A cliff looming over the sea, sunset etching shadows in the rockface. Garish font announces the location as Devil's Lookout, Comber Bay. It's touristy, tacky—which is strange, not like Jess at all. She normally makes her own cards—if she remembers to send them, that is.

Happy birthday, Lucy, it reads. *I know I've been distant the last few months, and I'm sorry. I'd love to see you, though, and catch up properly. Let me know if you ever want to come and stay—it's lovely here. Anyway, hope you have a great birthday. Love always, Jess x.*

But for Lucy, it was too little, too late. She was still hurt by how cold Jess had been the last time she'd seen her—over a year earlier, the Christmas before last, in 2017.

She had just begun to think that it might be in reach, the bond they'd shared when Lucy was younger, now frayed by years of distance. She had gone to stay with Jess in Sydney for a weekend over the previous school holidays. It had been Jess's idea, and Lucy was nervous: she felt like such a child in the passenger seat of her sister's car, hugging her backpack tight as Jess asked hesitant questions. Was school OK? Did she still go to choir practice? Did she still want to be a journalist?

Was she happy?

By the time they'd arrived at Jess's poky flat in Marrickville, exhaustion thudded behind Lucy's eyes and homesickness swelled under her ribs. But her sister had obviously worked hard to make the place presentable—fresh linens were folded on the sofa, and the zigzag patterns in the threadbare carpet suggested recent vacuuming. She'd even made Lucy's favorite meal: vegetarian chili, which tasted strongly of burned garlic.

The awkwardness remained until after dinner, when Jess had thumbed through her collection of records and produced Nick Cave's *The Good Son*.

"Dad *loves* this one," said Lucy, as the melancholic piano of "The Ship Song" filled the room.

"I know," Jess said, grinning. "So do I."

In an imitation of their father's dramatic singing, they'd ended up standing on the sofa, arms flung wide as they bellowed the words. But soon they were singing in earnest—they both had good voices, deep and rich for their small frames—and half waltzing, half spinning around Jess's cramped living room, sending piles of books and art materials everywhere. Lucy had felt the years melt away: she might have been five years old again, balancing on her older sister's feet as they danced to the Wiggles.

By the time the song had ended, a neighbor was knocking angrily on the wall and Lucy was winded. Her sister's eyes glittered and for an embarrassed moment Lucy wondered if Jess might be crying. Perhaps the reminder of their dad was painful for her—over the years,

Lucy had sensed a tension between her father and her sister that she didn't quite understand.

But when Lucy asked if Jess was OK, she'd just smiled and said she was going to make them each a hot chocolate, "with a bit of Baileys, but don't tell Mum."

They spent the rest of the weekend exploring her sister's favorite markets and galleries. They laughed over a drunk tourist in Circular Quay and joked about getting matching tattoos when Lucy was older. The special language they'd had when Lucy was small—how she treasured the memories of her big sister singing and drawing with her—seemed to be returning.

Jess even began to call Lucy after the visit—weekly on her mobile, rather than saying a quick hello after her irregular conversations with their mother. But just as suddenly the phone calls stopped, and then that Christmas Jess had spoken to Lucy so little that she had spent the festive meal swallowing down tears.

And so when the postcard with its paltry apology had arrived on her birthday, Lucy had kept her response brief and cold.

Thanks for the card, was all she'd texted. *Birthday was good.*

She'd ignored the invitation to visit. She couldn't face another rejection.

But now she has to put all of that aside. Jess is the only person she knows who sleepwalks, who might have some insight into why this is happening to her, how she can deal with it.

Lucy had even seen it once, when she was about five or six and Jess was home, making one of her rare visits from art college. She'd been woken by a roaring sound, which she'd first taken for a monster before she realized it was the thundering of the kitchen tap.

Gripping the banister with two hands, she'd made her tentative way down the stairs, across the corridor and into the kitchen, her stubby arms too short to reach the light switch.

Jess had stood rigid in front of the kitchen sink as water poured from the faucet. Fear had bloomed in Lucy's chest at the open, unseeing eyes, but still she'd crept to her sister's side, tugged on the unresponsive hand. Her sister's eyes were so vacant that Lucy had run back to bed and hidden under the covers.

Later, when Jess had returned to Sydney, Lucy asked her father about what she'd seen. She remembers the new tightness to his face, sudden as a curtain-fall. His hands trembling as he poured cereal into her bowl. He'd covered it with a laugh, a tousle of her hair.

"Not bewitched, Goose," he said. "Some people—like Jess—walk around when they're asleep. It's nothing to be frightened of, I promise."

When she's halfway to Comber Bay, Lucy lets herself stop at a motel off the highway. The neon VACANCY sign blinking overhead makes her think of *Psycho*. The woman on reception lifts her eyebrows in surprise, no doubt expecting a long-distance truck driver rather than a five-foot-two girl with a buzz cut. But she takes Lucy's cash and clanks a brass key on the countertop. Judging from the forest of others hanging behind the desk, Lucy is one of the only guests.

Inside, the corridors smell of ancient carpet and cigarettes, and the walls are lined with vintage advertisements for Bushells tea and Victoria Bitter beer. There's a vending machine from which she buys a bag of chips and two KitKats, deciding not to check the sell-by dates. Next to the vending machine is one of those mounted singing fish, all rubbery fins and greenish scales. Lucy shudders at the memory of the dream that accompanied her sleepwalking the previous night. There are only fragments, but they are enough. Brine in her nostrils, sharp hands on her skin; sharp rock against her skull. She doesn't want to remember more.

The room smells stale. The curtains are drawn, the floral pattern—a match to the bedspread—furred with cobwebs. She opens them, revealing the highway, the horizon pink with dust. A truck rumbles past, its tires whining. She feels a lick of fear at the hours of driving that face her tomorrow, imagines her eyelids drooping, her hands faltering on the wheel. Imagines the crumple of metal, the music of breaking glass.

She cannot be tired in the morning.

She must sleep.

But she can't escape the memory of Ben's vulnerable throat in her hands, the knowledge of what she might do—who she might hurt—when she's unconscious.

She must stay awake.

She sinks onto the bed, wincing at the bite of the springs through the thin mattress. She needs to listen to something, a distraction. A podcast. True crime is her preference, but anything of an investigative bent will do. The soothing drone of a familiar voice, a puzzle for her brain to solve until her thoughts become slow and dulled, exhaustion winning out.

Lucy had been fourteen when she'd listened to a podcast for the first time, *Serial*. Sarah Koenig's voice had woken something in her, had shaped the plastic of her young brain. Enthralled by the question of innocence or guilt, she'd raced through the episodes, the need for an answer burning inside. It was intoxicating, like the first sip of an alcopop. Chemical-sweet and dangerous.

She'd known then that she wanted to be a journalist. She wanted to be the one speaking into the microphone, unraveling a story like a spool of knotted thread. She wanted to be the one to fight injustice with the only weapon that matters: the truth.

That had been the plan, anyway.

Will they even let her finish her degree now, after what she's done?

Even if, by some miracle, they do—does she want to go back?

She's not sure she can face it, the humiliation. It was bad enough, knowing that everyone in the lecture hall or the cafeteria or the uni bar had seen her like that, exposed and wanting. What will people say, once they know she's attacked Ben? Even if she told the truth—that she was sleepwalking—they'd still think she was insane. Unhinged.

There's something else, too. Something that goes to the heart of who she thought she was, the plan she'd laid out for her life. The reason she pursued a degree in journalism in the first place.

It's the doubt that has simmered inside her since the meeting with the student welfare officer, the way she discouraged Lucy from contacting the police. From telling the truth. She's felt like a religious zealot having a crisis of faith. What use is a weapon people are too afraid to touch?

Now, she scrolls through her podcast app, unsure whether she wants something new and distracting, or familiar and comforting. And then she remembers.

She'd downloaded the episode a few months ago, after her parents told her where Jess was moving to. *Comber Bay.* There'd been an instant spark of recognition at the name. Every Australian with a passing interest in true crime or mystery has heard of it. Comber Bay is infamous, uttered in the same breath as the discovery of the Somerton Man and the disappearance of the Beaumont children. The sleepy town on the South Coast is like a real-life Hanging Rock.

It's funny, the way some cases are forgotten, yet others live on in the public consciousness, the victims somehow immortal. Of course, the mystery itself—an unsolved puzzle, luring hacks and sleuths—is part of it. But with Comber Bay, Lucy suspects the appeal is deeper. It's one of the handful of cases she can think of where the missing (or the victims, if the serial killer theories are true) are men.

The series is a multi-episode special of a podcast she likes, hosted by an anonymous Australian man with a soothing monotone and a meticulousness she admires. "Comber Bay: Australia's Bermuda Triangle." Clever name. No wonder it's amassed so many listeners.

She presses play on "Part 1—Devil's Lookout." As the ominous theme music plays through her earphones, Lucy wonders again why Jess has moved somewhere so infamous. Although she doubts her sister is interested in true crime—Jess is an artist: she cares about feelings, sensation, beauty. She barely reads the news.

In a picturesque seaside town two hundred kilometers from Sydney, a disturbing mystery remains unsolved . . . Between 1960 and 1997, eight men disappeared from its sandy shores. Samuel Hall, Pete Lawson, Bob Ruddock, William Goldhill, Daniel Smith, Alex Thorgood, David Watts, and Malcolm Biddy. Though the victims differ in age, profession, and social class, they all have one thing in common: no trace of any of them has ever been found.

As she listens, Lucy takes her tub of medicated cream from her backpack and opens it, grimacing at the hated chemical smell. She rubs it into the silver cracks and whorls that cover her shins.

Did the men drown, like the twenty swimmers who have so far perished at Queensland's notorious Babinda Creek? Or were they murdered by a killer who has evaded detection—and justice—for over thirty years?

She locks the window—the panes are thin enough that she can still hear the rhythmic whoosh of the highway—and the door.

Could some natural phenomenon be responsible for the disappearances? And what of the strange case of Baby Hope, found abandoned at Devil's Lookout in 1982?

We'll explore all of that and more in this two-part series, "Comber Bay: Australia's Bermuda Triangle."

Before she gets into bed, she moves the chair out from under the scratched desk and wedges it under the door handle. She hopes it will be enough.

3

MARY

Waves slapped against the dock, the spray icy on her cheeks. Her sister's hand brushed hers, the fingers warm and soft. Mary tried to clasp them in her own but was prevented by the bite of steel shackles at her wrist.

She looked into wide-set eyes, innocent in their blankness. Love formed a fist around her heart.

Mo dheirfiúr.

My sister.

"Please," Eliza whispered. "Tell me. What can you see?"

Mary swallowed. She could still taste dust from the road. The light had seared her eyes since they were pulled from their cell at Kilmainham, with its scurry of rats and its drip of water on stone. In the cart, the landscape had rushed past, the green gold of it so bright it lodged hard and painful in her throat, with the knowledge that she might never set eyes on it again. She was not the only one who looked away: the other women crossed themselves when they passed through the places where the fighting had raged two years before. The places where burned-out cottages mouthed the sky; mud walls already strangled with green, or else still blackened from fire.

At these moments, Eliza said nothing, a veil drawn across her

20

face, and Mary knew that though her sister could not see the land with all its wounds, she could smell the cinders in the air, could still hear the echo of musket fire. She knew she was wondering what might have been, if the rebellion had not failed. If the English had lost their hold on the land.

It seemed safer then not to look, to keep her gaze fixed on the grime between her toes. She'd learned not to make eye contact over the last long months, in the cold stone jail cell, where the male prisoners poked black fingers through the bars, reaching for them.

Until now, Eliza had not asked her to tell her what she saw, had not asked her to perform her sisterly duty.

Since babyhood, Mary had painted pictures for her sister with words, brought the world to life inside her mind. Walking through sun-dappled woods, she'd pluck crunchy red leaves from the ground and lift them to her sister's nose. Together, they'd breathe the scent of peat and earth, of things ending and beginning. She had traced the shape of the distant hills in her sister's palm, had told her it was the red-breasted robin who chirped so, the black hooded crow that screamed.

But she did not know how to show Eliza this. More than that— she did not want to.

"We are standing at a dock, in a crowd of many others," she whispered, trying to keep the trembling from her voice. "Packed tight together, like closely woven cloth." She remembered this, the feel of flax beneath her fingers. Her father smiling as she spun the fibers to ready them for the loom, just as he'd taught her.

Mary swallowed. She did not tell her sister of the other women's faces—for they were all women, with deadened eyes and hollowed cheeks—and how their fear mirrored her own.

"The sea is before us," she continued.

"I can smell it," Eliza said, nodding. "What do you think it would feel like, to touch it? Would it sting, like the water in the stream at home?"

Mary thought of the little creek near the village, the forbidden burn of it on her skin. Human hair, tangled with green fronds of duckweed.

Byrne's hair. His face, still and slack in the water. The heart-swallowing moment when she'd thought—when part of her had prayed—that he was dead, that the wet thud of the rock against his skull had killed him. But that would have meant the rope around both their necks.

They had been lucky, the judge had said, frowning across the courtroom as Byrne spat his disgust at the sentence. Assault meant only exile.

Only. Such a small word for it. For never seeing home again—the little cottage with its ripple of blue flowers, the sweep of hills to the horizon. The silver light on the stream.

For never seeing Da.

"Yes," she lied, for the sea was nothing like the stream. It was gray and furious, lapping at the rocks as if it would eat the land. It stretched as far as Mary could see, a murky gold line in the sky.

"And the ship?" Eliza asked, sounding smaller now. She had heard the lie in her sister's voice. She had an ear for lies, Da always said, as she did for a wrong note.

Mary did not know how to describe the ship. She knew only that it was the biggest thing she had ever seen. Its sails billowed like huge wings while its mast seemed to pierce the clouds. Mary could see at least three decks, the wood tarred and shining. There were some very small windows—from here, scarcely the size of a fingernail.

It looked as though it would be very dark inside.

"Mary?"

And then Mary's eyes settled on the figurehead.

"There is a woman," she said. "At the ship's prow. She is not of flesh and blood but wood and paint, larger than three men put to-gether. Her hair tumbles down her back in carved knots, her eyes are brightest blue. And instead of legs, she has . . ."

She paused. Now she wished she had not seen the figurehead, that she had not begun to describe it to her sister.

Someone pushed her from behind and she stumbled. They were being taken to the shore's edge: she could see little boats waiting for them in the water below. Mary and Eliza and the four score women around them would be taken to the ship in these and then there would be months of fear and darkness before they arrived in a strange land with a name that was foreign and frightening on her tongue. *New South Wales*. Far, far away from their little village, their goat with her soft eyes. From Da.

"Mary?" Eliza's voice was high and thin with fear. "What does she have instead of legs?"

Mary pushed back against the crowd, grasping for her sister's hand, even though the irons chafed her wrist.

"A tail," she said, yelling now to be heard over the other women's shouts. "She has a fish's tail."

"She's a merrow," Eliza said. "From the *tír fo thuinn*, the land beneath the waves. Just like in Mam's story."

Mary did not answer. She did not want to think of Mam, and what had happened to her. Not now, when fear already bloomed inside her belly.

As the crowd pushed them closer to the dock, to where the little boats bobbed in wait, she turned her gaze from the figurehead. But she could not forget the painted woman with her curved tail; the green scales discolored by rust.

4

LUCY

Lucy stares at the shimmering road, willing the bright lines on the tarmac to vanquish the ghostly images from her dream. The dock, wreathed in mist and human desperation. The ship with its masts piercing the heavy sky, the proud swell of its bow. The mermaid figurehead with her painted, watching eyes.

The dream had an ugly vividness to it, a corporeality. This, like the sleepwalking, is horribly new.

Though, she recalls now, there had been a time in childhood when she often dreamed of water. She doesn't remember much. A sun-dappled surface far above her head. A feeling that she was drowning, but somehow safe, that a liquid membrane protected her from the outside world. This was when she started school, when she had first begun to grasp that she was different. A child who couldn't wash her hands, take a bath, go for a swimming lesson. Was it any wonder she longed to submerge herself in water like other children, to be normal?

Gradually those dreams stopped, replaced by more typical nightmares. Bloodied pearls of teeth in her palm. Trying and failing to outrun something, her legs weighted and stumbling. An exam she hadn't studied for. The details fading as the day progressed, sleep remaining a place of safety, a refuge.

24

This is not like that. The remaining fragments seem to burn, splinters in her mind. She can still feel the clammy press of a hand in her own, the unfamiliar words in her mouth.

Muh dri-four.

Waking in the night, the thin motel sheets twisted, she'd breathed the words into her iPhone, watching bleary-eyed as Siri produced a translation.

Mo dheirfiúr.

Irish.

My sister.

How could she have dreamed in a foreign language? A language she has never read, never heard?

Willing the dream to fade, she focuses on the road, on the map blinking on her phone screen. Six hours of driving to go. She can do this. She takes a sip of warm service-station Coke, turns the podcast up louder, letting the mystery of Comber Bay distract her.

Danny Smith was the quintessential Aussie lad. A faded photograph from 1980 shows him at the beach—the same beach from where he'd later vanish—leaning against a surfboard. Stripes of zinc cover his cheekbones like war paint. A mullet brushes his shoulders. He wears Speedos and a necklace made of shells.

His friends described him with the usual phrases. The life and soul of the party. The boy next door. Everyone's mate. A lady-killer.

He was a surf lifesaver, a strong swimmer who knew the beach like the back of his hand.

But early one morning he took his towel and went down to the water, never to return.

Lucy imagines a wave closing over the man's body, white jaws snapping tight. She doesn't think much of the serial killer theory—it seems unlikely that a murderer would operate over three decades. Besides, it's not as if there's any proof: no bodies have ever been recovered. Though that in itself is strange, she supposes, if the men did drown. A detail from another true crime case sticks in her mind—as they decompose, human corpses gradually fill with gas, causing them to float and wash ashore. Odd, then, that none of the Eight—as the podcast refers to the missing men—were ever found.

After brief explanations of the circumstances of the other disappearances, from the Vietnam vet who vanished in 1966 to the itinerant surfer last seen in 1997, the host turns to the natural phenomenon theory teased at the beginning of the episode.

But if criminology can't provide the answer, perhaps science can.

Researchers have suggested that the area's unusual tidal patterns might be to blame for the disappearances. Whirlpools are formed when fast-moving tidal currents, traveling in opposing directions, meet, forming a dangerous vortex that can suck vessels into the deep. A whirlpool or other tidal anomaly might also explain other local events, including a nineteenth-century shipwreck, and, more recently, the discovery of an infant child at a cave in Devil's Lookout—according to some theories, the sole survivor of another, smaller shipwreck.

Whirlpools. Lucy thinks of the *Odyssey*—Charybdis, frothy maw stretched wide as she lies in wait for her prey.

As she gets closer to Comber Bay, Lucy pulls over to check her iPhone for directions, noting with a surge of panic that there are more texts from Em, and a couple of missed calls from the university's administration office. There's a voicemail, too. She doesn't listen to it, doesn't open the texts from Em. Nothing from Ben, she notices. A tiny pulse of disappointment is followed by shame.

During those long, languid weeks of the summer holidays, the chime of her phone—the possibility of another message from him— had been enough to send her heart thudding. But that was before.

She opens their WhatsApp conversation, rereads the message he sent the day before she woke to find herself in his room.

Lucy, I can only apologize for what happened. I never intended for that photograph to be made public in the way that it was. I see now that I should not have shown it to anyone without checking with you first, but because you didn't explicitly tell me not to, I did not realize that I didn't have your consent. Obviously, I had no idea that it would end up on social media. I hope you can forgive me for making such a stupid mistake.

Rereading the messages now, she's struck by his tone, the wheedling self-justification. She wonders if his lawyer father helped him craft it, helped him spin a narrative that he'd done nothing wrong by showing his friends the photo, that he is as much a victim as Lucy. He wasn't sorry for what he'd done, she realizes now, but for the fact that he'd been caught. That, for a brief moment, she'd held his future in her hands.

Except it's her own future she's thrown away.

She pulls back onto the road.

She has to focus on getting to Cliff House and Jess, who seems to be ignoring Lucy's texts and calls. Nerves tick inside her. What will Jess say, when her kid sister turns up on her doorstep without warning?

Again, she thinks back to that Christmas, after Lucy had finished high school. The last time she saw Jess.

She'd got her exam results and they were brilliant: more than enough to get her into the Bachelor of Communications at Hume, the preeminent journalism degree in Australia.

She'd expected to feel elation; triumph, even. But her mood had been dulled by hurt as she'd waited and waited for Jess to call. But there'd been nothing—not even a text to say congratulations.

Her parents, at least, had been proud, in spite of their reservations about her career plans. They'd doused the kitchen with the contents of a dusty bottle of champagne unearthed from the garage. For a moment, the old arguments were left aside.

"Can't you do something more socially responsible?" her mother used to ask, when Lucy spoke of her admiration for Nellie Bly and Veronica Guerin, for Christiane Amanpour and Susan Sontag. "Something that actually *helps* people?"

Easy for you to say, Lucy would think, resentment glowing in her chest. Her mother was a therapist: every morning, she got into her rusted blue hatchback and drove fifty kilometers to Bourke, the nearest

27

large town. There, Maggie Martin worked for an outreach center run by a charity set up to support deprived rural areas. Lucy knew—not because her mother ever told her, but because she'd read her profile on the charity's website—that her expertise was in substance abuse, depression, and self-harm.

In the evenings, her mother came home with her mouth and shoulders sagging, as if her job produced its own kind of gravity. She rarely smiled before starting dinner, normally a meal of an elaborate nature and an obscure provenance, the ingredients for which sorely tested the capabilities of the local supermarket. Coq au vin, home-made gnocchi, lamb tagine. Cooking seemed to loosen something in her, to relax the tendons in her face and smooth the lines from her forehead. But the relief was short-lived: every morning, she would drag herself back to the car and begin the long drive again, martyr-like.

"Christ, Mum, I'm not going to be the next Rupert Murdoch," Lucy would say. "I *do* want to help people. By finding the truth. Getting justice."

And I want to enjoy my job. Not like you.

"Sweetheart, the media ruins people's lives. *Especially* women's lives," was her mother's favored response. "Look at Lindy Chamberlain. Monica bloody Lewinsky."

"But it's women I want to help. What about the #MeToo movement? It's the truth that matters. It's the only thing that does."

"I used to think that, too, once," her mother would say as she filled the kettle—a signal that the conversation was now over. "But then I grew up. And one day so will you, Goose."

She still isn't sure what made her mother come around. On her eighteenth birthday, Lucy had come home to find her mother hurriedly hanging up the phone, cheeks flaming. "Jess says happy birthday," she said. Lucy had swallowed down hurt that her sister hadn't asked to speak to her, hadn't wished her a happy birthday herself.

But since that night, Maggie has held her tongue on the subject of Lucy's career. And perhaps it was wishful thinking, but Lucy wondered if Jess had talked some sense into her mother, persuaded her to support Lucy's ambitions.

Perhaps she did care, after all.

She'd consoled herself with the thought in the lead-up to Christmas, even began to look forward to her sister's arrival. Her father had strung the deck with fairy lights, and her mother had spent weeks on the Christmas pudding, so that the whole kitchen filled with the treacly aroma of spice and fruit.

Jess had arrived on Christmas Eve. She'd looked good, in a long maxi dress and fringed shawl, her black hair flowing. It had seemed for a moment, the four of them opening presents to the strains of "Last Christmas," that everything would be OK. Perhaps Jess had just been busy, with a new art project, a new boyfriend? Perhaps she would explain, even apologize?

But when she and Jess had sat side by side at the festive table, their arms brushing as they reached across each other to spoon food onto their plates, Lucy felt it: that chill of distance. Jess asked her no questions, and when Lucy inquired how everything was going back in Sydney—her painting, the flat—she responded in brief, perfunctory sentences.

Lucy wondered if she'd imagined the fun they'd had a few months before, dancing to Nick Cave. Maybe even her treasured childhood memories of her sister were just stories she'd told herself. Had Jess really balanced her on her knee and sang her lullabies? Had they spread butcher paper and crayons all over the kitchen table, drawing otherworldly forests and undersea caves?

It seemed almost impossible to believe. It still does.

The drive into Comber Bay is tinted green by gum trees that swoop low and close over the road. She winds the window down and breathes in the rich air: the tang of eucalypt, the heady sweetness of wattle. Cicadas hum, and she catches the throaty music of a magpie's call, the familiar sounds reassuring.

She's almost forgotten she's near the coast until the bush falls away on one side and the bay comes into view, stopping Lucy's heart in her chest. She checks her rearview mirror before slowing down to get a better look. It's breathtaking: a green tangle of scrub, brightened by red flashes of banksia, gives way to the sandstone haunch of the cliff. And then the sea, bright and unreal as a painting. She's never seen so many shades of blue: gleaming turquoise near the breakers; further out, a blue so dark it's almost black. Lucy shivers, thinking of the world beneath the spangled waves.

The coastline curves around, so that she can see the cliffs on the other side of the bay, honeycombed with caves. Devil's Lookout. It's the same view she's seen already, on Jess's postcard, but the photographer hadn't quite captured the eeriness of the cliff face. In person, the caves look deeper and darker; one in particular, closest to the waterline, is large enough that she can almost imagine a demon lurking there, surveying the sea below.

A prickle starts at the base of Lucy's spine. Maybe it's the knowledge of what the water would do to her skin. She imagines the waves lapping at her like tongues, stripping her of flesh until she is nothing but bone, gleaming white.

Or perhaps it's the podcast; the thought of all those missing men, presumed drowned. But with the prickling fear there's a strange pull, too. Lucy struggles to tear her gaze from the bright waves, mesmerized by the way they curl over the shore. A part of her wants to get closer, to feel spindrift on her face, slick rock beneath her palms.

It must be the tiredness, she decides, suddenly giddy. She needs to stop driving, to rest. She checks her phone again: still nothing from Jess. Well. Her sister won't be able to ignore her for much longer.

The main road overlooks the beach, a boundary between bushland and sea. A car park faces the water, a few sedans with surfboards or fishing rods strapped to their roofs. She's surprised it isn't busier; the sky is so bright, a burnished blue dome. But then it's the school term, and a weekday.

Opposite the car park is a strip of shops with faded awnings—a general store advertising everything from the *Sydney Morning Herald* to fishing tackle, a post office. There's an ice cream parlor and a fish-and-chip shop, both empty. A café, too, its windows dark, a few chairs and tables jumbled outside.

Strange that somewhere so notorious can look so normal. And it seems an odd place for Jess to live—it's even smaller than their hometown, Dawes Plain, and her sister has always seemed such a city person, talking of Sydney pubs, the latest exhibition she'd seen at the Museum of Contemporary Art or the National Gallery. Things Lucy and her parents had never experienced and couldn't understand. She seemed to make a point of wearing the city like a cloak, preventing them from getting too close.

And yet, Lucy can see the town's allure. There's a beauty to it all—the tangled bush, the rolling waves, the endless sky. Like the place wants to swallow you whole, and you want to let it.

Lucy slows down again after she passes the shops, scanning the rest of the town—a couple of homes, a neat redbrick church—for the turnoff to Malua Street. She's past the beach now, the road taking her through the dark canopy of trees. And then, on the left-hand side, a sign—if it can be called that. The letters etched into the red plank of gum give it a distinctly unofficial feel. The road, too, feels unofficial: more of a dirt track, really. Lucy tightens her jaw as the car shudders over the rocks, branches of the overhanging trees scratching at the windscreen.

She passes a house near the turnoff and the road banks to the left. Lucy squints ahead, seeing the intermittent flash of blue through the gums. The track grows steep, the Honda struggling up the incline, and Lucy catches a whiff of brine through the open window. At last, Cliff House comes into view, flanked by scarred tree trunks.

It's old, Federation style, the wood weathered pale as bone. Bigger than she'd expected—two stories. A wraparound veranda sags in front, thick with gum leaves from the trees that arc above. An old real estate sign wilts near the letterbox, the wood half rotted. The word *SOLD* emblazoned across it looks fresh and new by contrast, and

Lucy wonders whether the house was on the market for a long time before Jess bought it. Perhaps it was uninhabited, even abandoned: one of the windows is covered with plastic, as if it was previously broken. An old bird-feeder swings emptily from a tree, reminding her of her mother. She swallows down a burst of homesickness.

The house is a far cry from Jess's Sydney terrace. She'd believe she had the wrong address, if it weren't for the car parked to the left of the house, a teal-colored Ford that Lucy recognizes from Jess's last Christmas visit.

She wonders now if Jess has had some sort of breakdown—if that had prompted the move to Comber Bay. She tries to remember what her parents told her about this latest development in her sister's life: it had been late last year, not long before the arrival of the postcard on her birthday.

"How's Jess?" Lucy had asked them during one of their weekly FaceTime calls. "Do you think she'll come home for Christmas this year?"

Her parents had exchanged a glance. Some unspoken understanding seemed to pass between them, and when they turned back to the camera it was her mother who spoke. Her father, meanwhile, looked down at his lap, a new crease forming in his forehead—something Lucy had noticed before, when her older sister was discussed.

"I don't think so, sweetheart," her mother said. "She's actually—well, she's moving. She's managed to buy a little house, down on the South Coast. A place called Comber Bay."

"Comber Bay? What—where all those people have disappeared? Why on earth would she want to live there?"

"Who knows, but that's Jess for you, isn't it? A mystery to us all." Her mother had sighed before changing the subject.

Lucy unbuckles her seat belt, exhaustion settling over her like lead. She needs a wash, something to eat. And yet she feels oddly as if she might cry. Her heart constricts. What if Jess is annoyed—unhappy—to see Lucy, angry that she's disturbed her in her coastal hideout? Part of her wants to reverse the car down the drive and go home, to Dawes Plain.

But then she picks up the postcard from the dashboard, turns it over to read the message again. *Let me know if you ever want to come and stay.*

Surely she wouldn't have sent that if she didn't mean it?

The thud of the car door is eerily loud amid the quiet rustling of the bush, and Lucy half expects Jess to appear at the window. But the panes are empty and dark.

Lucy frowns, takes a few steps toward the house. From her vantage point at the house's left, she can see the whole building. She gasps. Now the name—Cliff House—makes sense.

Where you'd expect a backyard, there's nothing but lichen-stained rocks tumbling to the sea below. Through the brush, she can make out the white sliver of the beach, the blue gleam of the ocean. Her breath rasps in her ears, impossibly loud, until she realizes it's not her own breathing she can hear, but the sea, thundering against the shore.

Hugging herself, she turns away from the cliff edge, back to the house. The steps leading to the front veranda creak under her weight. There's a gust of wind, followed by a glassy, almost melancholy sound. A set of wind chimes hangs by the door, scattering greenish light across the faded wood.

The handle of the screen door is gritty under her fingers. She opens it and knocks on the wooden front door, tentatively at first, then louder. The house shudders, and she strains for the sound of her sister's footsteps. But there is nothing, no one.

Could she be out, after all this?

"Jess?" she calls, her voice clumsy with disuse after the long drive. "It's me, Lucy. Are you there?"

She pulls her phone from the pocket of her jeans, sees that the battery has run down to 7 percent. She has a sudden, awful image of her phone charger, still plugged in next to the motel nightstand. *Fuck.*

She dials Jess's number yet again.

A dial tone, and then—alien-sounding against the roar of waves and distant calls of gulls—the electronic burst of a ringtone.

It must be Jess's phone, ringing from inside.

Lucy's pulse slows a little. She's home, then. She'll come to the door, she'll let Lucy in.

But there's no answer, no movement from inside the house. Just the insistent, eerie ring of the phone.

"Jess?" she calls again, knocking harder on the door this time. She turns the doorknob, expecting to feel resistance, for it to be locked—but to her surprise, it swings open.

5

LUCY

TUESDAY, 12 FEBRUARY 2019

The house smells of oil paint and linseed. It's dark, the curtains and blinds drawn, and strips of pink-green light pattern the floorboards.

"Jess?" Lucy calls, mouth dry. There's no answer—no sound at all, but for the hum of the fridge and the gentle groan of timber in the wind. She shuts her eyes, gut slippery with the thought of the drop outside. She shakes her head, gropes for a light switch. There's a jangling sound; her fingers have brushed a set of keys that hang on a hook next to the door. Jess's keys, phone, and car are here—why isn't she?

Lucy surveys the room. The sight of her sister's belongings—last viewed in the tiny Sydney flat—is jarring. In Marrickville, there'd been a bohemian charm to the old velvet couch, the tendrilled spider plants and half-melted candles. But here, her sister's shabby furniture adds to the overall sense of dilapidation, of decay. Intricate orange wallpaper, faded to a sickly rust, peels from one wall to reveal bubbling damp underneath. Tarp covers what appears to be a hole in the floor, and Lucy wonders if the house was damaged in a storm.

The chaos isn't helped by the clutter of art and art supplies: Lucy guesses the living room doubles as a studio, another difference from Jess's life in Sydney, where she'd rented space in a warehouse for creatives. Wooden easels jostle in each corner, canvases line the walls. The scratched dining table, which Lucy doesn't recognize, is littered with newspapers and dirty crockery. Glass jars glint at her—from the bookshelves, the dining table, one balanced precariously on the arm of the sofa. Some of the jars are filled with muddied-looking water, others bristle with color-logged paintbrushes, reaching like bruised fingers.

All of it is disconcerting—it's as if her sister has become so absorbed by her work that she no longer honors the routines of daily life. But it's the enormous canvas on the easel that pulls Lucy's heart into her mouth. That actually frightens her.

She's seen her sister's artwork before, of course. It lines the walls of their parents' farmhouse, jostling for space with her father's sketches of Australian birds. There's a self-portrait, her sister's face rendered in aqueous greens and blues. The shimmering surface of a pool, bright turrets of coral visible beneath. So she's familiar with the lush application of paint, the galaxies of color.

But this? This is different.

The painting is enormous, almost as big as the wall behind it. Her sister has painted two female figures, their backs turned on the viewer as they wade into a raging sea. The brushstrokes are frenzied, lavish, and Jess has done something to make their skin gleam, as if it's lifting from the canvas. Lucy feels sure that if she were to reach out and touch the girls' hair—pale, like her own—she would feel each whorl, each strand under her fingertips.

Both girls are nude, their legs swallowed by furious splatters of paint. Blue green, purple, black, foamy white.

But it's what the figures seem to be walking toward that makes Lucy's heart stall. The proud masts, the winged sails, diaphanous in the light. The figurehead at the bow—wooden curls tumbling over pert breasts, tail curved and glimmering like the body of a snake. A mermaid.

It's the same ship from her dream.

Lucy's eyes skitter around the room. To the left of the painting on the easel, another canvas, darker and murkier, is propped against the wall. She makes out the bright gleam of eyes, stark white against a background of deepest blue. Lines of lighter paint slowly come into focus, forming crouched bodies, packed tight together.

She shudders, looks away, her gaze falling on the painting further left.

Here, her sister has painted the inside of a ship. She can see the coil of rope, cracks of light in the ship's wooden shell. Blue dusk here, pink dawn there. The light falls on female faces, revealing the ghostly outline of a cheek, the limned curve of an ear. Metal glints around wrists and ankles; cheeks are nothing but dark hollows.

In all the paintings, two women are featured, their hands clasped tight together. The face she recognizes from her dream, here repeated twice: the same high cheekbones, the same flaxen hair. One pair of eyes blank and unseeing, the other piercing right through Lucy's chest.

Mo dheirfiúr.

My sister.

She can't bear to be in the same room as the paintings, looming with their violent colors.

She stumbles through the door into the kitchen, leans against the counter. The giddiness has returned. The kitchen doesn't help. It reeks of cat food and the peeling cabinets are painted avocado green, clashing luridly with the yellow wallpaper. Here, too, is a feeling of damp, as if the sea weights the very air. She reaches a tentative hand to the wall in front of her and finds that it is moist, almost springy.

This place would have been outdated when her parents were young; she can't picture her sister living in it now. And yet, the signs of her are everywhere, from the MCA calendar pinned to the fridge to the wizened apples in the familiar wooden fruit bowl, a castoff from their parents.

She opens the pantry to find instant noodles, tinned tuna, and Coco Pops. No proper food, her mother would say. Hunger tipping into nausea, Lucy plunges a hand into the near-empty box of cereal, licking crumbs of chocolate from her fingers.

She pours herself a glass of water, then leans her elbows on the sticky counter, massaging her pounding temples.

She had guessed that Jess had also been stalked by something in her sleep, something that dragged her from her bed at night. She'd seen it with her own eyes, as a child. But for her to have *painted* something that she, Lucy, has dreamed about . . .

Surely, they can't have had the same dream?

Lucy thinks of the grisly cave of the ship's hold, the girls with their frightened eyes. Are these the scenes that await her come night-fall? She thinks of the ship, imagines the darkness of its belly. The press of other bodies against hers.

She runs her fingers through the bristles of her hair, straightens up, then grips the edge of the counter. She's overreacting. Her sister has merely painted women aboard a ship; Lucy has dreamed about a similar-looking ship. That's true. But there could be a million explanations for this. Maybe Lucy *has* seen some of these paintings before, on Jess's website or online? Or perhaps Jess told Lucy about them, on that last strained Christmas visit?

That has to be it.

If only Jess were here, to reassure her. Tears of frustration burn in Lucy's eyes. God, where *is* she? Could she have had some kind of accident?

Lucy thinks of the cliff, that sheer drop. Imagines Jess lying in-jured on the rocks below, or perhaps swept out to sea . . .

She tells herself to stop, that she's jumping to conclusions. Invent-ing stories where they don't exist.

She needs to calm down, to think of the facts.

She pulls her phone from her pocket to check the time, swears when she sees it's dead. She's hundreds of miles from home, alone on the very lip of the world, with no way of contacting anyone.

Then she recalls the ringtone she heard from outside the house. She needs to find Jess's phone.

She starts looking in the living room, although the disorder of it frightens her. There's something too personal about it, crouching on the hard wooden floor and rifling through the crinkling sheaves of paper, like she's touching her sister's thoughts. She moves aside books, a manila file, old newspapers, but finds nothing but a scrawled grocery list. *Frozen peas, bread, milk, coffee.* The ordinariness is such a contrast to the squalor around her, the strangeness of her sister's art.

She climbs the rickety staircase, planning to continue her search upstairs. She's also desperate for the toilet, even though her head throbs with dehydration, her mouth furred and stale.

The bathroom is cramped, the tiles cracked. Toothpaste spots the mirror above the basin. There's a strong smell of urine; an amber pool of it in the toilet bowl.

"Ugh," she says, flushing it away. The seat is up, too—a dark hair curled on the rim. She slams it down and rushes to unbutton her jeans.

It's only as she flushes again that it occurs to her: the puddle of urine, the seat left up. The hair. The toilet looked as if a man was the last person to use it.

Lucy frowns. Had her parents mentioned that Jess was dating someone? Their contact with her is irregular enough that they probably wouldn't know either way.

The only man they'd ever mentioned was Max, Jess's childhood friend. Lucy even met him, once. One Saturday a few years ago in the supermarket at Bourke, where her mother had dragged her on an unsuccessful mission to source cardamom pods for a chicken biryani. Lucy remembers a tall, fair-haired man, shirtsleeves rolled up to reveal tattooed forearms—the gray petals of a rose, stem fanged with thorns.

He'd looked startled, skittish even, when her mother approached. As Maggie peppered him with questions, Lucy saw his gaze flicker to the scabbed skin of her shins, then dart away. Afterward, on the car journey home, her mother sighed.

"I don't know what happened between those two," she said. "They used to be so close."

At the time, Lucy wondered if anyone had *ever* been truly close to Jess, ever truly known her. She's often felt that an invisible boundary exists between her sister and the rest of their family, like Jess has conjured some protective force field. It seems impossible that anyone might have breached those walls.

Lucy crosses the hallway into the bedroom. It's large, and, thanks to the lack of seventies décor, the nicest room in the house. An open window overlooks the sea: curtains billow in the wind, the tide pounding so loudly on the rocks that it might be happening inside her head.

She leans over the unmade double bed to close the window, her fingers freezing on the latch. She can see the cliff from here, lit up by the setting sun. It occurs to her that the house is situated just above those sinister caves cut into the cliff face. Devil's Lookout. Something catches her eye, flickering in the wind. It's a snake of rope, protruding from the cliff face; running parallel with shallow steps cut into the sandstone. Her stomach flips.

She thinks of the unlocked front door, the ringing phone she's yet to find. Could Jess have walked down those stairs, could she have fallen?

She slams the window shut and locks it, turns on the light. Lucy can see nothing out of the window now, nothing but the wan stare of her own reflected face.

This room is messy, too. Clothes carpet the wooden floor, many of them old and paint-splattered. A faded dress hangs limp over the back of a cane chair, sand glittering in its folds. There is a plate on the unmade bed, wiry bronze hairs that must belong to the as-yet-unseen cat.

There's no phone on the bedside table, and no sign that anyone lives here other than Jess. No boxers in the chest of drawers, no men's shirts in the wardrobe. Whoever Jess's boyfriend is—if he exists—he's made no lasting impression on the place.

There are none of Jess's paintings here, Lucy notices. Nothing on the walls at all, in fact, other than a small framed drawing of a fish. It's neat and scientific, not Jess's style, and yet there's something familiar about it. Moving closer, she realizes it's a sketch of her father's: the same precise, controlled lines he uses to capture the birds that he gives her mother every year for Christmas.

Here, he's drawn a lionfish, fins fanning out like propellers, banded spikes sprouting from the ridges on its back. It's beautiful, but somehow eerie. Threatening. There's something odd about the paper, too. It's feathered with tiny cracks. Someone must have crumpled it into a ball—as if they intended to throw it away—before smoothing it out again.

She swallows a sudden pang of longing for her parents, turning toward the bed to continue her search for the phone. It's then that she notices the white cord twisting from behind the bedside table and into the lumpy mess of pillows and duvet. She springs forward, moving one of the pillows, and there it is: Jess's iPhone. Plugged into the wall socket and fully charged.

A rush of relief, tailed by fear. Where would her sister go without taking her phone—or, for that matter, her keys?

She swipes up to make an emergency call, rehearses in her head what she'll say to the operator.

But no—she's being ridiculous, surely. Jess has probably just gone for a walk to the local shop. She could be back any moment. Lucy's been listening to too much true crime, and it's impairing her judgment. Not to mention the sleep deprivation, the dreams. The shock of seeing the paintings, the mermaid figurehead with her coiled tail.

She removes Jess's phone from the charger and plugs her own in instead.

Soon it buzzes with notifications—more texts from Em, three missed calls from the student welfare office, two new voicemails. Nothing, of course, from Ben. He might be talking to the university—or the police—even now.

Her heart lurches with fear but her mind feels numb, unable or unwilling to contemplate the thought.

She puts her phone on flight mode, sinking onto Jess's bed.

For the first time since Monday morning, she covers her face with her hands and sobs.

6

MARY

Mary had not known thunder could be so loud.

There were storms back home in Ireland, of course. She could re-member the night sky cracking open with lightning, a smell of seared things in the air. The trees would bend like dancers at Lughnasa, the wind raking its fingers over the thatched roof. A fug of sweat and breath would fill the cottage, along with the goat's frightened whinny, and she and Eliza would cover their ears at each growl of thunder, until Da, teeth clenched in a smile, would place the fiddle in the crook of his neck and play. After a while, the sisters would slowly take their hands from their ears, joining their voices to Da's music. Both sang sweetly, but it was Eliza's voice—like her heart, Mary sometimes thought—that was purest. All through the village, she was known for it. *The girl who sings but does not see*, they called her.

Those storms had frightened Mary. But home in the cottage, with their song fighting the shrieking wind, they'd been dry and warm. And safe.

This was different.

They had been taken aboard the ship so quickly that Mary couldn't even be sure of where they were. All she knew was that they were below deck, enveloped in a dark heat, as if they'd passed through an animal's rib cage and come to rest in its guts.

There were at least four score women and girls, two to each coffin-sized berth. Their irons had been removed, but chains clanked against each bunk, ready to ensnare them again. The wood was hard against Mary's spine, with not a slick of turf or straw to soften it. The air was thick with whimpers and prayers, the ripe tang of so many bodies packed tight.

Now, as the ship bucked on the waves, she gave thanks that she shared a berth with Eliza. It was so dark that she could see only the pale globes of her sister's eyes.

They had been in the hold for two days now, perhaps three, and not once had Eliza asked Mary to tell her what she saw.

She must have known that darkness had closed around them, that Mary had entered a world that Eliza was all too familiar with.

She tried and failed to put the thought of Da out of her mind: his face at the trial when the judge uttered that first awful word—*guilty*—and then the second—*transportation*. The way he had crumpled into himself.

"*Mo chailíní!*" he'd shouted, arms reaching for them as if he could wrest them from this fate. "*My girls!*"

But they'd been lifted away, the prison guard's arms tight around Mary's ribs. She'd squeezed her eyes shut, not wanting to look upon her father's face and know it was for the final time.

Mo chailíní!

Guilt surged inside her.

There hadn't been time to say goodbye. To say that she was sorry.

They were not supposed to have been at the stream that night. It had been Samhain, when the veil between the human world and the spirits' stretched to its thinnest point. Da didn't like them to go out at night; he liked them snug and safe, he said, in the pallet bed separated from his own by a curtain of old cloth. Nor did he like them to go to the stream, other than to gather water during the day. Even then, they were to take care to balance the heavy wooden bucket so that not a drop spilled on their skin.

Once, when Mary was very young and the memory of Mam was still strong in her mind, she had put her hand in a pail of water, just to see what would happen; if it was as dangerous as Da said. The water seemed to dance on her skin, fizzing and bubbling with joy, just as she remembered from before. But later, when her flesh cracked and peeled, she'd cried with fear at what she had done. Da had taken her hand in his and brought it to her lips, made her promise not to do it again. All that was over, he said. They'd left it behind when they came to Armagh. He would not see his girls endangered again.

For Da believed that water threatened not just their skin but their souls. And on Samhain night especially so. They might find the midnight washerwomen, their long spindly hands rinsing the shrouds for those who'd die on the morrow. Or else be set upon by an *each-uisce*; the shapeshifter who lurks at the water's edge, disguised as a horse, ready to drown those who dare to mount it.

Da was from Ard na Caithne in Kerry, where they'd been born, and where the wild ocean ate the shore. He knew all the dangers of the sea, of *tír fo thuinn*, the land beneath the waves.

It was Eliza who had first disobeyed Da, some months before Samhain. She had taken Mary's hand in the night and whispered of an adventure, refusing to say where she was leading them. Mary had slipped over rocks and tree roots, while Eliza, sure-footed in the dark, had danced easily ahead, humming to herself under her breath.

The girl who sings but does not see.

"We shouldn't be here," Mary said, when they reached the stream, a bright ribbon in the dark. "Da wouldn't like it."

"Da worries too much," Eliza had said, stepping closer and closer to the edge, where water churned against the bank.

She had convinced Eliza to come home, only to wake the next night to the sound of the cottage door creaking softly open. She had known, then, that she would have to follow her sister to keep her safe.

Gradually, a compromise was formed: they would sneak to the stream in the secret dark of evening, but they would never let the water touch their skin.

Mary grew to treasure their nights together. Sitting on the grassy rocks by the stream's soft burble, they talked as they never did at home in the cottage, with Da in earshot. They talked of the future, the things they'd do. Mary told Eliza how she planned to marry—how she longed to birth a child and hold it in her arms, and never let it go. At those times, Eliza said nothing. "What will you do?" Mary had asked. "When you're grown?"

"Find Mam," Eliza had said.

The words had hurt so much that Mary turned her face away.

Now, she wondered whether Byrne had been there all those times—whether he'd followed them on other nights, whether he'd spent months learning their habits, listening to the secrets of their hearts. Had he been biding his time until Samhain, when Da would leave them to their own devices? When the festival, with all its raucousness, might provide a cloak for his misdeeds?

If only they'd stayed at the cottage that night. If only Mary had not said the things she'd said, to drive Eliza into the dark and its dangers.

I'm sorry, Mary wished she could say to Da now. *I never meant for this to happen.*

"Tell me a story," Eliza whispered. Her voice had a dry sound, like summer grass. It had been hours since they had been given any rations, and those had been only foul-tasting biscuits, tarry in their mouths.

"What story?"

"The story of Mam," Eliza said. "Mam, when Da first saw her."

Mary didn't like this story, didn't like to think of Mam. But still, it was something she could do for Eliza. It was too dark for her to describe the women surrounding them, to say who was marked with the pox and who had seen too many summers. Far better for her to tell Eliza how Da had fallen for Mam.

"Da was at sea one morning, on his currach," she began, striving to be heard above the roaring swell. "He was watching the waves, waiting for the silver herring to leap from the sea. But none came, and as the red light broke over the water, he turned back to land, his heart heavy as his belly was empty.

"But then he heard something—a note purer than birdsong, softer than morning dew. He turned. It was then that he saw the woman: she sat on a rock near the shore, singing just for him. Like she'd been waiting. The rising sun set her hair alight, her skin glittered with wet. Her eyes were round and dark as a seal's; her hands soft and warm as summer air—"

But the words caught in Mary's throat like thorns.

All she could think about was Da, and how she and Eliza had abandoned him, just like Mam had done. Now he had no one.

How Mary wished she could pull the past back to her as if it were string, could undo the knot of it.

"Rest your voice," Eliza said now, her words soft and soothing, as if she were the first-born twin. "Try to sleep."

Mary closed her eyes against the blackness, feeling her sister's warm body pressed against hers. She tried to pretend that she was home in the village, on her pallet that smelled sweetly of straw, the air full of the goat's nickering and Da's soft snores. But the sea was too loud, crashing against the ship like hands that would tear her apart. The thunder roared and the women screamed. Mary squeezed her eyes tighter still, focusing hard on the picture of home in her mind, as if she might travel there in her dreams.

7

LUCY

Lucy is woken by the screech of a cockatoo outside.

It's only just dawn—her phone says 6 A.M. There's something liminal about the pale light and the eerie call of the sea through the window, a sense of being outside time. Perhaps that's why the dream seems closer, a room she's only just stepped out of.

Each time, she remembers more and more, as if that other world is lapping at her heels.

Darkness, pressing against her nose and mouth. Women's voices crying and praying. The feeling of another hand in hers, so powerful that now her body aches with the lack.

Mo dheirfiúr.

My sister.

For a moment, the dream is more solid, more real, than the bed with its lumpy pillows, the watery sunlight arcing across the duvet. The only link is the sound of the sea: the rhythmic roar and suck seem to have followed her.

She must have fallen asleep moments after lying down. With a chill, she realizes that she's done nothing to protect herself—she hasn't wedged a chair under the bedroom door handle; in fact she's pretty sure she left the front door unlocked, worried that Jess would be unable to get inside without her keys. So she can't even be sure that she *hasn't* been sleepwalking.

Raising herself onto an elbow, she calls out tentatively in case Jess has come back in the night. But there's no answer: only the wooden house creaking around her.

Perhaps Jess had found Lucy in her bed and, not wanting to wake her, had gone to sleep on the sofa? The idea of her older sister just downstairs, of no longer being alone, is so comforting that she can't bear to break the spell of it.

But she's thirsty and needs the bathroom; she has to get up.

Tentatively, Lucy swings her legs off the bed, flinching at the cold touch of the floorboards. In the early morning light, she sees tracings of sand on the rich wood; notices a dark bloom of damp on the ceiling. It's as if the house longs to be reclaimed by the sea.

In the cramped bathroom she inspects her reflection, suddenly nervous at the prospect of seeing her sister. The sight makes her grimace: her eyes are ringed with shadows and her forehead gleams with an oily sheen.

The old longing—to fill the sink with water and splash it over her face—returns.

The aquagenic urticaria was diagnosed when she was still a baby; she can't remember a time when water wasn't a threat. Over the years she has reached a kind of acceptance, aided by strict routines and rituals. She keeps her hair short, she uses wet wipes instead of showering—though even that small amount of moisture can trigger an attack. She does not think of how it might feel to swim.

But sometimes, the question she tries so hard to suppress bubbles to the surface. When she sees her mother wash her hands at the kitchen sink; when she sees her father delight in the rare gift of rain.

Why me and not them?

She is about to leave the bathroom when she hears the thud of the front door closing. *Jess.* She's back.

Relief pounds through Lucy's body, followed by nerves. She runs a hand over the bristles on her scalp, wishing she was cleaner, that she'd changed into fresh clothes. But it doesn't matter. They're sisters, after all.

My sister.

Heart lifting, she opens the bathroom door.

"Jess? It's me—Lucy. I tried to call—"

There's no answer, but the creaking stops, as if Jess has paused.

Lucy pads down the stairs, rehearsing what she'll say. How she'll unknot everything that's happened, everything that's driven her here, now.

Really, it boils down to two simple sentences.

I need you.

Help me.

But once downstairs, she gasps in shock.

There's a woman standing in the kitchen. But it isn't Jess.

8

LUCY

"Who the fuck are you?"

The woman's voice is as sharp as her body. She's short but wiry, the sinews on her arms like vines. With her blazing eyes and dark cloud of hair, she makes the kitchen—with its moldering fruit and dirty plates—feel dead, tomblike.

She holds a tin of cat food in her hand, raising it like a shield.

Lucy blinks.

For a wild moment she wonders if she's seeing things: if her mind is now conjuring full-scale apparitions. But she registers the lines clustered at the woman's mouth, the chipped red polish on her toenails, the threads of silver in her dark curls. She's real.

"I'm Lucy—Jess's sister. Who are *you*?"

The woman hesitates for a moment, then frowns.

"You do look like her. Sorry—I'm Melody, from number two," she says, stooping to spoon cat food into the bowl. "You startled me. She, ah, didn't mention you were coming."

Lucy could be imagining it, but there's a hint of confusion in Melody's voice, of hurt. She has the uncomfortable impression that Melody is as surprised to learn that Jess *has* a sister as she is to find her at Cliff House.

"I thought you were one of those sightseeing ghouls," Melody continues. "There've been loads of them since that podcast. Ryan Smith found someone camped out in his garden shed a few weeks back, poor bugger. Gave him the fright of his life."

Lucy arranges her face into a blank expression, calculating that it might be best to feign ignorance of the podcast.

"Come on, the Bermuda Triangle thing? Jess must have mentioned it, living here of all places."

"Only vaguely," Lucy offers. "Speaking of Jess," she continues, "did she say when she'd be back?"

"Thought she'd have told you that," says Melody, rinsing out the tin at the kitchen sink, and there's the hurt in her voice again. "But she did look pretty frazzled yesterday when she came round. It was so early, too." She looks as if she's about to say something else, then seems to think better of it. "She asked me to feed Dora Maar. Must have forgotten you were coming."

Lucy swallows.

"But she left the door unlocked," she says. "And her phone in her room."

"I wouldn't worry about the door." Melody says. "She told me she'd do that, so I could get in to look after Dora. As for the phone, well ... Stress does funny things to people, doesn't it? She's been working so hard, poor woman. Think she just needed to get away for a bit, before the big day. She didn't say how long."

Heat pulses in Lucy's cheeks. For a sudden, awful moment—remembering the way she'd found the toilet, her suspicion that a man had used it—she thinks her sister is getting married.

"The big day?"

The frown returns.

"Well, the exhibition, of course. Next Friday. Isn't that why you're here?"

She swallows, letting the words sink in. Jess is hosting an art exhibition. A show. And she hadn't mentioned it to Lucy.

Perhaps that makes sense, given last time. Years ago, when Lucy was fourteen, one of Jess's paintings was being shown at a swanky gallery in Sydney's Inner West and she'd invited Lucy and their parents for the launch. Lucy remembers the long drive, turning her face away from the blue glimmer of the harbor as they drove over the bridge.

The gallery had been crowded, thronged with Jess's arty friends. Her mother had patted her hair self-consciously as they were greeted by Rebecca, a tall woman with blue cropped hair who would become Jess's gallerist. Her father, immune to social anxiety, had vigorously shaken hands, kissed cheeks, as though all these people were here not for Jess, but for him. He told anyone who'd listen that he'd been the first to put a pencil in his daughter's hand, to recognize her talent.

The three of them had been drawn to Jess's painting at the same time, as if it exerted a magnetic pull. *Tomb*, read the title card. *Oil paints and mixed media.*

A glimmering red orb, suspended in darkness. A darkness that was textured and layered, hints of blue and violet revealing themselves the longer you looked. Lucy didn't really understand what it was meant to be, what the crimson circle signified. Glancing toward her parents to see what they made of it, she saw her mother reach for her father's hand and squeeze his fingers tight. Looking back at the painting, she noticed for the first time the hieroglyphs of a tiny skeleton inside. Only then did the painting's title make sense.

There had been plans the following day for brunch, for a trip on the ferry to Manly Beach. Instead her parents bundled her into their car and began the two-day drive home without explanation. Afterward, there had been fewer phone calls between Jess and her mother. When they did speak, her mother took the phone into the bedroom and shut the door, speaking in an angry whisper that, try as she might, Lucy couldn't make out. Once, she'd picked up the extension in the living room to hear Jess say, "I'm not apologizing, and I'm not going to censor my art just because it makes you uncomfortable," before her mother realized Lucy was listening.

"Yes—yes—of course I am," she says now, forcing a smile. "So excited for her. Can't wait." She doesn't want Melody to see how little she knows of her sister's life. "Sorry. Still half asleep. Need a coffee."

"I'll get out of your hair." Melody wipes the rinsed tin with a tea towel before tossing it in the recycling bin. Lucy notices with discomfort—and a twinge of jealousy—the ease with which she moves around Jess's kitchen. "I get up early, to open the shop. The general store on the corner. Pop in later, if you need anything."

She picks up her handbag from the counter, then hesitates.

"Hang on—if you're here, you can take care of Dora Maar. Cat food's in that cupboard over there, but I think you're running low."

Melody puts the handbag on her shoulder, then opens and closes the front door behind her.

Lucy sighs, leans against the kitchen countertop. There's a scratching at the window over the sink, a tawny flash of fur.

"Hi," she says, leaning over to open the window as a yellow-eyed tabby slinks its way inside. "You must be Dora Maar. Funny name for a cat, huh?"

Dora Maar ignores Lucy's outstretched hand, hopping elegantly off the countertop and picking her way over to the bowl of cat food next to the fridge.

As she watches Dora lap at her food bowl, her pink tongue darting in and out of view, Lucy processes her conversation with Melody.

Yesterday morning, Jess had asked Melody to look after her cat. Then she'd gone somewhere to get away, to calm her nerves before her show. Which is next Friday. Nine days away.

Lucy thinks again of the show they'd attended in Sydney. She remembers how nervous Jess had seemed—encased from throat to fingertips in a clinging black dress, sleeves billowing like wings. There'd been a jumpiness to her, as if at any moment she might abandon the whole endeavor, suddenly fly away.

That was years ago; Jess is far more successful now. Lucy's read the profiles in the art magazines—the full-color spread of her posed in her old Sydney studio. And this would be a solo show, so there'd be no other artists to compete with, no one else to share the pressure. Would that make her more nervous, or less?

Perhaps that's why the house is in such a state. Perhaps Jess had felt overwhelmed by the mess, the proximity to her work; perhaps, having finished her paintings, she had to get away from them.

Lucy boils some water in the kettle, taking a pot of instant noodles and a near-empty jar of coffee from the cupboard. An odd breakfast, but better than nothing.

The problem, she thinks as she stirs her noodles, is that she simply doesn't *know* Jess well enough to assess if this is unusual, out of character.

She'd wanted to ask Melody so many questions. They'd been there, formed and waiting, on her tongue.

Did Jess say where she was going?

Do you know if she has a boyfriend, a man in her life?

Do you know if she still sleepwalks?

But she couldn't bear to reveal the distance that has grown between them. She thinks back to Melody's awkward demeanor around her, the way she'd seemed surprised to learn of Lucy's existence. Had Jess really not mentioned her at all?

She takes a sip of too-hot coffee, swallowing the ache in her throat. The caffeine makes her jittery, and suddenly the chaos of her sister's house overwhelms her. She needs to do *something* useful, something to distract herself from the sinking sensation she has of being abandoned and alone. She had pinned so much hope on Jess. In hindsight it seems irrational that just because her sister sleepwalks, she'd be able to help Lucy pick up the shattered pieces of her life; to undo what happened with Ben.

What had she expected? That her older sister would somehow reach back into the past and stop Lucy from putting her hands around his neck that night, from sending him the picture in the first place?

When Lucy has drained her coffee cup, she rises from the dining room table, surveying its cluttered surface. She'll clean the house, she decides, so that it's perfect for when Jess returns—or at least, she thinks, looking at the tarp that covers the floorboards, the mold-blistered wall, as perfect as it can be.

Before she gets to work, she retrieves her AirPods from the bedroom and presses play on the second episode of the Bermuda Triangle podcast.

Part 2, the presenter announces as she dons an ancient pair of rubber gloves foraged from under the sink. *The Tide.*

The morning of Friday, 5 February 1982, began like any other. As the sun rose slowly in the sky, the three fishermen—David Li, Ryan Smith, and the skipper, Robert Wilson—launched the fishing trawler Marlin *from the Comber Bay Marina.*

The sea was flat, the dawn was cool, and the men busied themselves with the tasks they'd performed many times before, that their fathers and grandfathers had performed before them. In the shadow of Devil's Look-out, they cast their nets in the silver water, trawling for the coppery-scaled flathead that grace the tables of the region's restaurants. Miles below them lay a rusted shipwreck from two hundred years earlier, as well as the hopes of the families of five men who had so far disappeared from the town.

Perhaps they sometimes wondered if their nets might dredge up the belongings of the missing men, or even their remains. One of the fishermen, Ryan Smith, had lost his brother Daniel to the phenomenon just a year before. No doubt he longed for some evidence, some clue, as to his brother's fate. For closure.

But the tide had other plans.

Gingerly, Lucy retrieves filthy bowls and mugs from the sink. She sets the dirtiest ones—crusted with food or paint—to soak. She fills the sink with hot, soapy water, relishing the heat as she plunges her gloved hands into the suds.

Soon, she is barely aware of her own actions. Her body works on autopilot: scrubbing, rinsing, drying. There is only the podcast, only this new mystery, unfurling in her brain.

It was the skipper who heard it first: the noise that came from Devil's

Lookout. At first, the men thought it was an injured bird, but gradually they came to recognize the sound. After all, humans are hardwired to respond to the cry of an infant. Deciding to investigate, the men motored as close as possible to the cliff face, as close as the perilous reef would allow.

Later, in newspaper interviews and on radio stations, his colleagues would describe the courage their skipper displayed as he removed his heavy waterproofs and boots and jumped into the sea.

"He saw it before we did," said Ryan Smith, in an interview with the South Coast Examiner *the same week. "Bobby always had the best eyesight. We were still looking around like a couple of stunned mullets and he was already swimming as fast as he could toward the cave."*

The cave Wilson swam toward, the largest of the cave system in Devil's Lookout, is a deep recess in the rock. It is so close to the waterline that it can flood during high tide. Accessing it from land is extremely dangerous: adventurers can either scale the steep stone staircase cut into the cliff face, or traverse the slippery, rocky passage from the beach, a rite of passage for local teenagers. Access by sea is also difficult, given the danger posed to marine craft by the reef, and the resultant whirlpool effect some scientists theorize could be responsible for the disappearances. When the events of that day became known, journalists, police, and conspiracy theorists alike would puzzle over these details—in particular that the cave was almost inaccessible, other than by sea.

Before Smith and Li knew it, their skipper had disappeared from view, seemingly swallowed by the frothing waves. They began to fear that Comber Bay had claimed its sixth victim.

But to their relief, Wilson reappeared, swimming on his back this time, with a pale bundle clutched to his chest. Li and Smith initiated the man-overboard procedure and threw him a life ring, which he fitted around his waist, still holding the pale bundle close.

Only when Wilson was safely back on board did his colleagues realize what he had been carrying, the magnitude of what he had just done.

"It was a tiny baby," said David Li to South Coast Radio. "And Bobby had saved [their] life."

Lucy's hands still. A bubble of detergent flutters past, catching the early morning sunlight. All of this happened at Devil's Lookout, the same cliff face she can see from the kitchen window. The bright day has turned the sandstone a deep gold; the frayed guide rope shivers in the gentle breeze. She cannot see the waves that thunder over the rocks at the cliff's base, but she can hear them. Being here, so close to where the events took place, sends a thrill across her skin.

A court order prevents the identification of the child's name or gender. What we do know is that an extensive search for the child's mother returned no leads. No one came forward to claim the baby, and investigators made little headway in establishing what had brought them to the cave in Devil's Lookout.

Was the child abandoned after birth? If so, what became of their mother? At the time, due to the child's age, authorities expressed concerns for the mother's health. Perhaps she feared coming forward: after all, child abandonment was and remains a criminal offense, carrying a significant prison sentence. There was little understanding of maternal mental health in the 1980s, and thus little likelihood of leniency.

Or perhaps, weak and unwell after giving birth, the child's mother perished: another of Comber Bay's victims.

Some theorized that the child had somehow survived the shipwreck of a small boat, but this, too, provided more questions than answers. How did the child end up in the cave? Had someone left them there before they succumbed to drowning? Was the child's presence in the cave owed not to abandonment, perhaps, but the last sacrifice of parental love?

In the years since, divers have searched the reef below, including the centuries-old shipwreck. No wreckage of another vessel has ever been found.

The newspapers called the child's discovery a miracle; a bright spot in the town's catalog of horror and pain. A local paper dubbed the infant Baby Hope and called for residents to donate nappies and formula.

Mr. Wilson and his wife, Judith, volunteered as foster parents, an arrangement made permanent when they later adopted the baby.

For a time, the couple were lauded as heroes. Robert and Judith Wilson had lived in Comber Bay all their lives. The pair, both in their midtwenties, had been married for three years. They had met at a dance put on by the local Baptist church, where Judith's father, Douglas, originally from England, was the minister. After marrying, they moved to a small house not far from Devil's Lookout. Both regularly attended community events and church services.

It's hard to know what soured the mood against them—whether it was a neighbor with a grievance, or just the local rumor mill in overdrive. Perhaps it was the misogyny of the era, seen also in the media frenzy around Queensland woman Lindy Chamberlain, who claimed her infant daughter had been taken by a dingo during a camping trip to Uluru. Chamberlain would eventually be convicted of her daughter's murder: she served three years but was later exonerated.

Whatever the cause, tides have a way of turning. And so, the tide turned against the Wilsons.

In April 1982, the now-defunct tabloid, Yes! Magazine, *published an article which claimed that, according to an anonymous source employed at a local doctor's surgery, Mrs. Wilson had been three months pregnant in August 1981. It suggested a new theory for the mystery, one that, in the words of the article, the police had not sufficiently explored: that Mrs. Wilson had been the child's biological mother all along. The tabloid hypothesized that Mrs. Wilson might have given birth to the child and then, suffering from postpartum depression, left it in the cave before confessing her actions to her husband. In this version of events, Mr. Wilson was not a hero but an accomplice who had sought to cover up his wife's crime by staging the dramatic rescue from Devil's Lookout.*

Little evidence was presented for the inflammatory claim. But the papers were quick to draw parallels between Judith Wilson and Lindy Chamberlain. An op-ed from the time blamed increasing numbers of women in the workplace for the rise of the "callous mother," despite the fact that Wilson was a homemaker and Chamberlain a clergyman's wife. The laser eye of the Australian media, until now focused solely on Lindy, turned its gaze on Judith Wilson. Tabloids obtained and published personal photographs of Mrs. Wilson—including one depicting her in a revealing black swimsuit, taken on Devil's Beach, just meters from where the child was found.

Eventually, the police were forced to issue a statement that their inquiries had uncovered no evidence that the Wilsons had any prior connection with the child.

But for the Wilsons, it was too little, too late. The fallout was huge. Mr. Wilson lost so many customers that he was forced to close his fishing business. Judith's parents, the Reverend and Mrs. Michaels, returned to their native England.

The couple sold their home and left the area. At the time, locals believed they might have emigrated to England to be with Judith's parents, or perhaps traveled to New Zealand. Our researchers have been unable to locate them.

It is not known what became of the child rescued from Devil's Lookout— the infant the media dubbed Baby Hope, the bright spot in the town's darkness.

One wonders how the townspeople remember Baby Hope now—the victim of parental neglect, or media hounding? Only one thing seems clear: on 5 February 1982, the tide brought Comber Bay a chance of redemption. Then that chance was lost.

In 1986, with the disappearance of Alex Thorgood, the tide would take its next victim.

The presenter's voice fades into the eerie theme music. Lucy removes the rubber gloves and wipes her hands on a tea towel to remove any excess moisture. Boiling the kettle again, she makes another coffee in one of the newly pristine mugs.

In the living room, she sits on the sagging sofa, feeling strangely winded; her mind still full of what she's just heard. Dora Maar slinks inside the room, looking up at her quizzically. Lucy lifts her onto her lap, closing her eyes at the soothing hum of the purring against her chest.

She takes a sip of coffee, but her insides feel cold.

It's the thought of the caves. Even in the cheery sunset colors of the postcard Jess sent her, there had been something disturbing about those hollows etched into the sandstone. To look at them is to know immediately their darkness, to know the rust smell of water bleeding into rock, to hear the sea sluicing its way inside.

A child—*a baby*—alone in a cave, for God knows how long. It's unimaginable. She shudders to think of a small, fragile body at the mercy of the creeping tide. She takes another sip of coffee.

And how sad, that the couple who had adopted the child had come under such horrendous scrutiny.

Typical, of course, that the woman—Judith Wilson—had been the focus.

Does Jess know about this aspect of Comber Bay's history? Does she know that lives were lost, forever changed, mere meters from where she lays her head at night?

She must, Lucy decides, reappraising her earlier assumption. After all, her sister has always been attracted to the macabre. Lucy read an interview she gave once to an art magazine, where she said that she was drawn to the morbid, to the "gristle and viscera" of the human experience. Even now, in her late thirties, she's still a Goth.

It's different for Lucy. She'd go mad living here, she thinks. It's not so much the darkness of it, but the lack of answers. It's one thing to immerse herself in true crime, to devour reams and reams of investigative journalism. But living inside a mystery, the way Jess has chosen to do, in this house that crouches on the edge of a cliff?

The not knowing—it would send Lucy mad.

When she's finished her second cup of coffee, Lucy tackles the mess in the living room. She sorts the books and papers into piles, eventually revealing the scrubbed surface of the dining table, puzzling at her sister's eclectic reading tastes.

There are glossy tomes on art, as she'd expect; but stranger choices, too. A faded book about surrealism called *A Wave of Dreams* seems to have originally belonged to a Sydney library—looking at the inside cover, she sees that the last person to check it out was a C. Hennessey in 1997. There's also a tome on Irish mythology, and a copy of the *Odyssey*, frilled with Post-it notes. Her attempt to slide one book from underneath the others sends the whole pile crashing to the floor, knocking over mugs with dregs of tea and glasses with sludges of paint in the process.

She swears under her breath as she searches, fruitlessly, for a mop to clean the wet mess of tea and paint; settling in the end for an old flannel.

God knows how her sister can live—let alone *work*—in these conditions.

She pictures her own room at the university with an ache of regret. Her neat stack of notebooks, the corkboard above her desk with the carefully pinned index cards and one of her father's drawings—a fairywren—for luck. Her mother had taken her stationery shopping before her first term, and she'd felt so hopeful, choosing the perfect shades of highlighters, ballpoint pens that wouldn't smudge. Hopeful and relieved—at last, her parents had accepted her path of study.

The first year had gone so well. Not just academically—she'd loved immersing herself in the course, in modules on digital media and ethical communication—but socially, too.

She'd made friends: principally Em, who sported a new manicure every week and was unabashed about her ambition to become the Carrie Bradshaw of TikTok.

It was Em who had encouraged her to pursue Ben. She'd caught the way Lucy's eyes lingered on the dark-haired boy who sat in front of them, who answered the professor's questions with a confidence Lucy found hopelessly alluring. One day when they were to be sorted into pairs for an assignment, Em had moved seats so that Lucy and Ben were grouped together.

The piece, authored mostly by Lucy, garnered full marks, for its "incisive yet sensitive" study of the forgotten victims of a recently convicted serial killer. The celebratory beers at the university bar were Ben's idea, "his shout," he'd said. Em had helped Lucy choose her outfit, a black jumpsuit accompanied by a swipe of Em's bronzer on each cheek.

Over the long December break, she'd lain in bed and revisited her memories of that night, delicately, as though they might dissolve under close inspection. His face, flush against hers. The froth of beer on his cupid's bow, the wiry perfection of his eyebrows. The heat of him through his shirt. She'd read and reread his texts, imagining him there, lying next to her.

At first, Lucy had kept her body angled slightly away from Ben's as they leaned against the bar, frightened by her desire for him even then. But as the bar filled with more and more students, as the music thumped louder and louder, their bodies were pushed closer together. When Daryl Braithwaite's "The Horses" played over the speakers, the place erupted and, like everyone else, they'd flung their arms around each other and sung along.

He'd led her outside, away from the scrum of other students, the pulse of drunken conversation, the sticky floor. No witnesses but the night sky, sugared with stars.

"You have a pretty voice," he'd said, touching the tip of her nose.

Later, in his dorm room, he had opened her slowly and carefully, like she was a gift.

She had given into it then, the desire that had so frightened her. And how freeing it had felt: like she was fully inhabiting her body for the first time.

But as soon as he'd sent that photograph to his friends, that feeling had gone. He had destroyed it.

Perhaps the sleepwalking was a reaction to that loss, somehow? Desire morphed into rage. Her body acting of its own accord, taking back what was hers, when her mind had exhausted more reasonable options. But she can't think of it as anything other than a threat—to others, and to herself.

She thinks of Devil's Lookout, that golden staircase to the waves.

She imagines herself, in thrall to some dream world, opening the back door and stepping onto the veranda. Four paces to the railing, maybe five. And then . . .

Lucy hugs herself.

Even though she's sitting on the floor, the tide only a murmur through the house, she has a feeling like vertigo. As if she's on the cliff now, teetering on its very edge.

9

MARY

The other women's voices seemed to Mary one awful, endless sound, like a creature had stowed away with them in the hold. The moans and cries and whimpers melted together, pulsing with the waves.

Everything was louder in the dark.

How she hated it, this blackness. When the night was at its deepest—when no light shone through the cracks between the floorboards above—she no longer knew where her body ended and the darkness began. Sometimes, she was grateful for the cramping hunger in her belly, the rawness of her skin. It reassured her that she still existed.

It was Eliza who taught her how to tell the women apart, how to navigate this world of dank wood against her body, of creaking ropes and sloshing bilges.

"You must learn their voices," she whispered, lacing her cold fingers through Mary's. "Each has a difference, a tell. Start with those in the berth above us."

Mary listened, and realized Eliza was right. Slowly, different voices emerged, like a river splitting itself into smaller streams.

"That is Bridie," Eliza whispered, as a woman laughed when the ship pitched, upending the slop buckets. "I think she must be very beautiful. That laugh—rich as the pouring of ale into a glass."

Mary recognized the laugh, realized that she'd noticed its owner before: had seen the fingers of light pick out the fire of her hair, the milky curve of a cheek.

"Yes," she told Eliza, squeezing her hand. "She has red hair; I have seen it."

Together, the sisters listened, learning the rhythm of each woman's voice. For the first time, Mary noticed what Eliza must have always known, that a voice had valleys and crags, telling you of sadness or delight. You could almost feel it under your fingers, like it was land.

This was how her sister knew things before they were said. The secret hurts and joys.

And so when Bridie told of the crime that had seen her transported—the Englishman she and a friend had robbed on the road from Cork to Dublin, the coins that shone in the grimed palms of their hands—Mary heard something else beneath the swagger, beneath Bridie's insistence that she'd do it all again, "just for the look on his fat English face." She heard regret. Grief.

In the berth next to theirs was a woman called Sarah, with lilting Leinster vowels. She was traveling with her young daughter, Annie, and spoke in a high, uncertain tone, so that everything she said sounded to Mary like a question.

Her husband had died two years before, she told them, fighting in the rebellion. "I tried, God knows, to make ends meet," she said. "Laundry, linen for weaving. I thought of stealing, I'll own it now. But I had my girl to look after, didn't I?"

Mary didn't need Eliza to point out the way Sarah's voice thickened as she told of how a man had tried to buy what she wasn't willing to sell, and then had accused her of stealing from him. "When I said no, he called me *whore*."

The story reminded her of what Da had said, when she and Eliza got their first blood. It had happened to Eliza first; the crimson wings on her shift made Mary scream, terrified her sister was dying. Later, over bowls of stew that Mary had burned, distracted by worry, Da had told them that the blood wasn't something to fear. Mary felt a shameful heat in her cheeks at the glisten of tears in his eyes. Under the table, Eliza's fingers had searched for Mary's. ("He was thinking of Mam," Eliza said later, in the scratch of blankets, Da's snores washing over them. "It would have been up to her, to explain such things.")

"You're becoming women," he'd said into his stew. "From now on"—his hand tightened on his spoon—"I don't want either of you going anywhere alone. Not the market, and certainly not the stream. Do you understand, so?"

Mary and Eliza had both nodded, but for her part at least, Mary hadn't understood. Not then. Da had made becoming a woman sound like something dangerous.

The oldest voice came from Aoife, the woman who shared the berth above with Bridie. Sometimes, the buck and lurch of the ship pushed her half out of the berth so that her hair hung down the side, crinkling against Mary's nose. It smelled of dead, bleached things spat from the ocean. But her voice was all forest, rasping against Mary's ears.

Aoife was from the Blasket Islands. Unlike Bridie and Sarah, she would not say what she had done, why she was there. All her words she saved to hiss curses at the sailors, the captain they'd glimpsed briefly when they were brought on board. Mary had been struck by the slightness of him, how the rich navy cloth of his uniform swamped his thin body. He made her think of an animal that has been born a runt and bares its teeth all the fiercer for it.

"Fool," Aoife had said. "Carrying so many of us. Four score women on a ship. Have you ever heard of such a thing?"

"What do you mean?" Mary asked.

"A woman on a ship. Bad luck, so."

Bad luck or not, the hold buzzed constantly with women's voices like angry wasps. Everyone sharing their stories. There was pain, but laughter, too. Relief in speaking, in hearing your own voice and recognizing it.

It didn't matter that the ship tossed the women together as it foundered over the waves. That flesh knocked against flesh and hair knotted with hair. Talking—telling stories—was a way of keeping yourself separate from the mass of hair and limbs. It was a way of keeping yourself human.

"Humans are born to storytelling," Da used to say. "Does the goat tell stories? The blackbird, or the sheep? No. Sure it is God's gift to us and us alone."

But, Mary thought now, some had more of the gift than others. Da's tales had a way of warming your belly so that, even on a biting winter night, you didn't feel the cold.

Eliza said that Mam had told stories, too; about the merrow who dwelled in the *tír fo thuinn*. But Mary did not like to think of that.

The story Eliza begged to hear again and again was of Da first setting eyes on Mam—the red water in the dawn, the dark pools of her eyes—but Mary preferred the story of their birth.

They'd been born sixteen summers ago, by the sea in Ard na Caithne, County Kerry, at the very edge of the land. In a little cottage, Da used to say, not far from the rocky sweep of shore where their parents had first met.

"Your mam swelled tight and round as a drum," Da's story went. "The moon was so high and bright in the sky, bright enough that its white shadow swam in the water, so that there might have been two moons that night. Twin moons, for twin girls."

At this point in the story, he would always pause to smile at first Mary, then Eliza, drinking in their faces as though he still couldn't quite believe the miracle of them.

"Mam pushed and pushed, in time with the waves beating on the shore. You, Mary, came first—slipping into my hands like a wriggling fish; with eyes as big and dark as your mam's and your hair seal-slick against your skull. Eliza, now—you took a little longer, as though you couldn't quite bear to leave your mother's belly. And you scared us, so you did; for your little mouth was blue as a winter berry. The cord had become wrapped around your neck and my heart raced as I cut you free."

Da would pause again here, his gaze distant somehow, and Mary wondered if he was thinking of Eliza's sight; whether, if he had cut the cord quicker, it might have been saved.

Da would finish the story with Mam cradling a baby to each breast, the four of them warm before the hearth. When she was younger, Mary wished that they were all still there, curled safely together in the cottage. That Mam had never left them.

Eliza liked to speak of Mam, liked to tell Mary her memories in exchange for Mary's own, in the same way they might compare treasures gathered in the woods.

"Do you remember how the sea tasted?" she would ask. "Do you remember Mam taking us deeper and deeper? Do you remember the story of the merrow?"

Mary would shush her sister, looking around to make sure that Da hadn't heard.

"It was dangerous," she'd hiss. "What Mam did. Taking us into the sea. You know how the water hurts us. You know what happened to her."

They'd been five years old when Mam drowned. Mary remembered waking in the old cottage, to the beat of the tide and the call of the gulls, and a strange sound she hadn't heard before. A sort of keening, of the kind a woman might make in *caoineadh*, lament. But it was no woman—it was Da, sitting in front of the cottage with his eyes on the shifting waves, calling out for Mam.

Mary would never forget the sight of him, his shoulders slumped, turning a length of sodden fabric in his hands. At first, Mary did not recognize it, but then she saw the intricate stitching at the hem, noticed its color: lichen green. Da was holding Mam's cloak.

Mam went into the sea, he told them, and did not come out.

She was gone.

Not so long after that, Da packed up their little house, leaving even the fishing nets and the boat behind. He bundled Mary and Eliza into a donkey-led cart and took them north to Armagh, where he'd heard that a man might make his fortune in the linen trade.

Those first months in the new place were hard: Da struggled to make the flax yield, and more nights than not his eyes glowed and his words slurred from too much *poitín*. These were the only times he spoke of Mam: sometimes with tears and sometimes with rage, and Mary realized that he was angry with his wife for drowning, for putting herself in harm's way.

"I begged her not to go near the water," he said, again and again. "I begged her to stay ashore, where she was safe."

Over the years, Da's anger became Mary's own. She locked her memories of her mother deep inside her heart. It was easier, she learned, to be angry than to be sad.

10

LUCY

WEDNESDAY, 13 FEBRUARY 2019

Her phone rings, cutting through the dream, a rope she grasps to pull herself to wakefulness.

Lucy opens her eyes and sees only darkness so heavy that she thinks it hasn't worked, that she's still there, in the roaring black cave of the ship.

The phone stops ringing, leaving her in silence, but for the pound of the sea.

She imagines this must be how it feels to be in water, fighting a current. Clinging to reality even as the dream world surges around her.

She knows what she dreamed. One of the paintings downstairs—white eyes in the darkness, the tangle of grimy limbs. The blue-black and ochre swirls of paint—the very texture of fear—had come to life in her mind. Pressing against her nose, her eyes.

She can still taste it, that animal tang of terror.

The paintings have fevered her mind. Her thoughts are like fish, flashing bright then darting away from her.

There's a circle of mist on the windowpane. As if she had stood there, nose pressed against the glass, looking down at the black sea.

The pane rattles; she sees now that the catch on the window is loose.

She is *sure* that she locked it before she went to bed. She had wedged the chair under the door and closed the window, pulling tight to make sure it was secure.

She must have tried to open it in her sleep. Cold fear washes through her. What if she'd succeeded? What if she'd—

Her horror is interrupted by the chirp of a text, a blue square of light. She picks up her phone, her thoughts reeling. Could it be a text from Ben?

A new fear overwhelms her. She imagines cold, distant sentences: *I just wanted to let you know that I will be pressing charges against you for assault . . .*

But the phone won't unlock: there is no response to the pad of her thumb on the home button. And then she realizes that it wasn't her phone ringing that woke her, but Jess's. Her body thuds with relief.

The screen shows the time: just after 10 P.M. She can see the preview of the text, from someone called Rebecca Waters. The name is familiar: of course, Jess's gallerist. The tall, blue-haired woman her mother had found so intimidating four years ago.

Hey, sorry to call so late . . .

But that's all she can see without unlocking the phone.

She sits up in bed, drawing the coverlet tight around her. Dora Maar, dislodged from her position at Lucy's side, meows in protest.

"Sorry, kitty," she murmurs, caressing the soft nap of fur between the cat's ears.

She bites her lip, staring at the phone screen, belly shifting with guilt.

It feels wrong to even consider such a transgression. But despite Melody's reassurances that Jess had told her she was going away, there's still a flicker of doubt in her mind. If she can get into Jess's phone, then she can read Rebecca's message. Just in case it holds some clue to her sister's whereabouts.

But if she's honest, there's another, darker reason. It stings that Melody, her sister's neighbor, knows so much more about Jess's life than Lucy does.

She thinks of the night they spent at Jess's flat, dancing and singing together; later, the warmth spreading through her belly as they shared hot chocolate and confidences.

"So," Jess had asked, she remembers now, "do you have a boyfriend? A girlfriend?"

"You're worse than Mum," Lucy had said. "She keeps asking if I need her to buy me some condoms or dental dams. I think she hopes it *is* a girlfriend."

Jess had laughed softly, and the sound had emboldened Lucy. She'd scarcely been able to believe she was there, on her big sister's squashy velvet couch, surrounded by the charming clutter of plants and canvases and mismatched furniture. How many times had she imagined such a moment? She'd nestled closer to Jess and leaned forward, intending to put her mug down on the mosaic coffee table.

"What about you? I mean—how old were you, when you first . . . you know."

Jess stiffened, the sudden movement causing the mug to tilt in Lucy's hand, spilling hot chocolate all over the woven rug.

"Sorry, sorry," she'd said, "I'll get a towel."

"It's fine." Jess had smiled stiffly. "Leave it, I'll fix it in the morning. Anyway, I should let you get to bed—lots planned tomorrow."

She stood and switched off the lights, leaving Lucy alone in the quiet dark.

Before they stopped completely, her sister's subsequent phone calls had been one-sided. Jess had asked so many questions about Lucy's schoolwork and study plans that there hadn't been room for her to ask anything in return. Indeed, Jess seemed bent on concealment, from the trick-mirror imagery of her paintings to her uniform of sweeping, shrouding black. Her older sister had drawn a veil down over her life, a veil that Lucy longed to lift.

Lucy sometimes wondered whether something awful—unspeakable—had happened to Jess. Something that she kept buried, locked away inside the fortress she presented to the outside world. She thinks now of Jess's sleepwalking: Could it be the reason for the distance she's created around herself, her protective force field?

Did Jess hurt someone, like Lucy has? Or did someone hurt her?

The phone feels suddenly white hot in Lucy's hands, its temptation so great she might be holding a piece of her sister's consciousness. Here, she thinks, is a way to lift the veil, to see her sister as she really is. The gristle and viscera of her, to use Jess's own words.

Lucy holds her breath as her fingers move across the screen. She starts with Jess's own birthday, even though that feels like a long shot. Surely her sister wouldn't be that naïve.

It doesn't work. She tries her mother's birthday, then her father's. Nothing.

"Fuck," she says, voice rising in frustration. Dora Maar leaps off the bed, startled.

She enters her own birthday.

20 09 99.

The phone unlocks.

For a moment, all Lucy can do is sit there, throat narrowing with pain. The thought of her sister tapping her birthday into her phone multiple times a day—*thinking* of her multiple times a day—is too much. The screen in front of her blurs as she opens iMessages and reads the full text from Rebecca, the gallerist.

Hey, sorry to call so late but just checking if you got F's email? I need your OK re courier. Bec x.

Lucy opens Gmail and sees that most of the messages are from Rebecca—and someone who seems to be her assistant, Freya—with the subject line "The Sirens."

Lucy opens the most recent one, from the day before yesterday.

Hi Jess,

We are so excited for your show!

    Rebecca has asked me to touch base re: arranging a courier to collect the works next Wednesday PM, so they can be hung in the space on Thursday (21 Feb). Just checking that this is all OK with you?

Best,
Freya x

Lucy opens the PDF at the bottom of the email chain.

It's an invitation, bordered with tendrils of dark green seaweed, the brushstrokes swirling and dancing over the page—designed, Lucy is sure, by Jess herself.

Nesbit & Day

invites you to a private viewing of THE SIRENS,
*an exclusive showing of new original works by groundbreaking
young artist and winner of the Mosman Art Prize, Jess Martin*

FRIDAY, 22 FEBRUARY 2019

6–8 P.M.

THE ROOKERY, BATEMANS BAY

RSVP TO REBECCA.WATERS@NESBITDAY.CO.AU

There's an image at the bottom of the invitation that Lucy recognizes from the largest painting downstairs, the one of the women facing the sea, the ship in the distance.

It's a close-up of their hands, pale and clasped tight together.

The panicked tone of Rebecca's text hasn't eased Lucy's worries. Again, she thinks back to her conversation with Melody that morning.

She's been working so hard. Think she just needed to get away for a bit, before the big day.

She tries to reassure herself. The exhibition is still nine days away. And, from the emails she's read, everything is mostly ready: the paintings just need to be collected from Cliff House and taken to Batemans Bay, arranged in the gallery space.

Perhaps, as the artist, it's easier to overlook that sort of logistical detail. Maybe that's *why* Jess left her phone behind; maybe that's the sort of stress she wanted to escape from.

Lucy decides to give it a few more days, until Saturday. If Jess still isn't back by then—well, then she will let herself worry.

She should put the phone down, she knows. She shouldn't pry any further.

And yet, the urge to scroll through her sister's life—to learn something, anything about her—lingers. It wouldn't hurt to check her call records, would it? Just so she'll know who to ring, if Saturday comes around and there's still no sign of Jess.

But the records are sparse. Apart from the calls to and from Rebecca and their parents, the only others are from a private number.

Her finger hovers over the icon for Tinder. A man was definitely the last person to use that toilet before Lucy arrived. What if it wasn't a boyfriend, but someone Jess has a more casual connection with? A stranger, even?

But to her relief, Jess's profile still lists her location as Sydney—she hasn't updated it since she moved to Comber Bay. The bio is spare. *Artist*, it reads. *Carrington, cats, martinis.* She pouts in the profile picture, lips painted vivid red, stark against the pallor of her skin and the jet fall of her hair. In all the pictures, Jess wears long sleeves, a high-necked top, so that only the skin on her face and hands is visible.

All the matches are at least six months old—from before Jess moved here. Lucy doesn't feel right about looking through the conversations. She closes the app.

She scrolls past Google Maps, banking. Another messaging app that Lucy's only vaguely heard of—she has some notion that people use it for sexting—but when she opens it, it's blank.

She looks through Jess's camera roll instead, wanting to get inside her sister's head, to see the world through her eyes. Loads of Dora Maar. A few photographs of her paintings, in different stages of completion. She recognizes a series of the huge canvas downstairs, the two girls holding hands as they walk into the sea.

Further back is a photo of the beach, here in Comber Bay. Jess has captured the sun sparkling on the waves, the great blue sweep of the sky, but these are in the background, out of focus. In the foreground of the picture is a stone cairn with a brass plaque.

This cairn was erected on 20 October 1981 by the Comber Bay Historical Society to commemorate the sinking 180 years ago of the convict ship Naiad, *wrecked off the coast of Comber Bay with the loss of approximately 100 lives.*

May they rest in peace.

Lucy's heart jolts. Fragments of the dream return to her. She remembers a ship's hot belly, the scrape of iron on raw skin, the stench of unwashed flesh.

Convicts. Of course. Moments reorder themselves into a pattern she understands. The terrible splendor of a courtroom. The cold bite of iron on a wrist, the dark womb of the ship. A journey to a foreign, frightening place.

This is what she's been dreaming about.

A Google image search for *naiad convict ship* brings up a blurred thumbnail—a lithograph—and her heart beats faster when she zooms in.

The ship's figurehead.

It's a mermaid.

Her pulse races.

She can hear a voice—not her own voice, but she somehow knows the shape of the words, as if she's held them in her mouth.

There is a woman, at the ship's prow. . . . Her hair tumbles down her back in carved knots, her eyes are brightest blue. And instead of legs, she has a tail. She has a fish's tail.

Lucy tries to order events in a way that makes sense, tries to construct a story she can understand.

Six months ago, Jess moved to Comber Bay. She read about the shipwreck and was inspired to paint its victims. When Lucy arrived in search of Jess, her graphic paintings gave her nightmares.

But that's not what happened. Lucy's first dream about the *Naiad* was two nights ago, at the motel—before she'd seen her sister's painting. How is that possible? Has Jess been dreaming of the *Naiad*, too? Is that the inspiration for her paintings—even for moving here, to Comber Bay?

She picks up her sister's iPhone again, opens the Notes app. Perhaps Jess will have recorded the details of her dreams here, as Lucy has started doing in her own Notes app?

But Lucy finds nothing; the contents of the app are entirely mundane. Grocery lists, drafts of emails to her gallerist.

"Fuck," Lucy whispers, the word echoing in the dark cavern of the room, reminding her how alone she is.

Wait.

Jess used to keep a journal. Her parents told her, Lucy remembers, because she asked for one herself, on her ninth birthday.

Her father had caught her mother's eye over the kitchen table.

"Just like Jess," he'd said, in a sad way that Lucy hadn't understood.

In the end, Lucy's efforts at journaling had faltered. She'd gathered that she was supposed to use a diary to record *feelings*, rather than observations. Facts. (Her mother had laughed when she'd announced one morning that she planned to interview everyone in her fourth-grade class and record whether they preferred *The Lord of the Rings* or *Harry Potter*.)

But Jess—she's the opposite, isn't she? An artist. It's no surprise she'd keep a journal.

Lucy checks the bedside-table drawer. Hand cream, tissues, the furred yellow disc of a cough drop. A packet of condoms, unopened. But no journal.

She opens the battered wardrobe in the corner of the room, wrinkling her nose at the musty smell. An old running shoe falls onto the dingy carpet, the sole caked with mud. Jess's clothes always make Lucy think of great winged bats: black dresses with long, fluted sleeves, the odd pair of navy wide-legged trousers.

She crouches on the floor as she parts the dark skirts. The base of the wardrobe is crowded with more shoes, the abandoned snakes of old tights and socks—a shoebox looks promising, but in the end contains only some yellowed tissue paper.

There is nothing under the bed but furred ropes of dust, a pair of underwear, a chocolate-bar wrapper. Lucy wants to disinfect her hands. She's amazed that Jess has managed to generate such squalor in the few months she's lived here.

She sits back on her haunches, frustration building in her chest. As she surveys the room, her gaze falls on the one place she hasn't yet looked.

There is a cupboard built into the eaves, where the ceiling lowers. At first, the door doesn't budge and she worries that it's locked, but eventually it swings open, releasing a smell of decay that clings to the roof of her mouth. Lucy's heart sinks as she coughs from dust: this cupboard probably hasn't been opened in years; it's unlikely Jess will have made use of it.

But still, curiosity nags at her. Pulling up her T-shirt to cover her mouth and nose, she shines her phone flashlight into the dark recess. Gradually, shapes form into stacks of papers, boxes, the rusted spears of fishing rods. Shining the flashlight on the pile closest to her, she discovers old editions of *Birdwatch* magazine dating from the early eighties. She can't help but smile: her mother, a devoted ornithophile, has subscribed for years.

She wonders about the house's former occupants, wonders why they left this stuff behind. Reaching out a tentative finger, she traces the spines of the magazines: the latest edition is from 1982, the year that Baby Hope was discovered.

That makes sense. Cliff House must be the closest dwelling to Devil's Lookout. Lucy wouldn't be surprised if whoever lived here at the time was inundated with media requests, perhaps even interviewed by police investigating the child's abandonment. Perhaps, like the Wilsons, the former occupants had found the scrutiny too much to bear.

In any case, there's clearly nothing belonging to Jess in here. Perhaps her sister keeps her diary downstairs, or perhaps she's taken it with her?

Lucy shines her phone into the shadowy space one more time before closing the door. Something familiar—so familiar it seems utterly out of place—catches her eye. The yellow crest of her old school, Dawes Plain High, peers at her from behind the closest stack of magazines.

Crouching to get a closer look, she sees that it's a schoolbag. JESSICA MARTIN, announces her mother's neat, distinctive writing in white permanent marker. Lucy grunts, shifting on her side, groping for the backpack. She drags it out, wincing at the awkward angle of her arm.

It's half rotted, the navy canvas veined with ancient mold. Lucy wrinkles her nose. It's such a weird thing for Jess to hold on to for all these years, to bring with her when moving from Sydney to Comber Bay. Lucy only left high school two years ago, and she gladly let her mother donate her own (pristine) backpack to the charity shop the week after her final exams.

The zip is rusted, and when at last she opens it, the smell from the inside is even worse—briny and rotten. She pulls out an old plaid shirt—yelping when she sees its fur of mildew—and flings it to the other side of the room. A plastic pencil case, full of colored markers, a portable CD player with some weird Goth CD inside. And, strangely, a wad of bloated paper that she realizes is an old map of New South Wales, folded many times.

And then there it is. A padlocked journal with a swirly pink cover—Lucy remembers the brand. Groovy something, it was called. The clasp is broken, and Lucy opens the journal to read the first page.

11

JESS'S DIARY

1998

7 February

February is the worst month. Christmas long gone, my birthday, too. Everyone's angry, tired from the heat. The kind of heat that makes you wish you were a lizard, cold-blooded and small, able to take shelter in the shadow of a rock.

There's no air-conditioning in my room, just the fan that stirs the air like soup. At least it drowns out the sound of Mum and Dad bickering. Sort of. I can hear enough to know that it's about me. Again.

After all, I'm the only thing they ever seem to fight about.

Mum walked in on me in the bathroom the other day. I forgot to lock the door, I was so anxious to wipe the sweat from under my arms and between my breasts. I could feel the moisture doing its work already: worming its way into my skin, cracking into a hundred silver rivers. I had the light off—I don't like seeing myself in the mirror—and I guess that's why she thought there was no one in there. She opened the door and screamed. Not exactly the reaction you want to the sight of your nude torso, even from your mum.

Later, she knocked on my bedroom door.

"I don't know how you can read in this light, Jess," she said, pointing at the drawn blinds blocking out the harsh summer glare, leaving only the lava lamp's glow. I love my lava lamp, its shimmering waves of green. It's peaceful, like how I imagine underwater to be.

I rolled my eyes and she sat on my bed, moving aside the pile of clean laundry she'd told me to put away earlier.

"We need to talk about your skin," she said. She took my hand in hers, played with the hem of my sleeve.

"Sweetie—I know you like to cover up," she said, her voice gentle and horribly calm-sounding. Her therapist voice, I call it. "But it's so hot outside. If you wear too many clothes, you'll sweat, and then, well . . ."

"I know," I said. "Frankenstein."

"Oh, sweetie," she said again, squeezing my fingers. I wished she wouldn't. I was worried I'd cry, and then where would we be?

"I'm sorry about before," she went on. "I didn't know you were in there and it gave me a fright—"

I snorted.

"Come on, Jess," Mum said. "You know I didn't mean it like that. Your father and I, we think you're so beautiful."

Like that was supposed to make me feel better. Every child is supposed to be beautiful in the eyes of their parents. But Mum literally screamed when she saw my naked flesh.

I pulled my hand away.

"I'm not ashamed," I lied. "I just like dressing this way. It's cool."

"OK, sweetheart," she said. But I could tell she didn't believe me.

Anyway, now they're yelling. I've turned Rosetta Stone up on my stereo but I can still hear it.

Mum's cooking dinner (paella, so we know she's upset) and the sound of her chopping vegetables filters down the hall with their voices.

"I *know* that's what we said," she's saying, her words punctuated with the thud of the knife on the cutting board. "But that was years ago. And we can't go on like this. *She* can't go on like this. We need answers."

"I'm not taking her back there," Dad says, and then the argument descends into furious whispers.

I know who they're talking about, of course. The skin specialist I saw as a kid, Dr. Becker. He had a weirdly shiny face, like sweaty cheese. Mum and Dad would take turns driving me to Bourke so that I could sit on his examination table while he looked generally confused.

They stopped taking me after Dr. Becker asked if he could write a paper on me for some medical journal. Since then it's just been me and a big tub of Vaseline.

It's easier if I deal with it on my own.

I guess I'm good at doing that.

———

20 February

We did self-portraits in art today. Mr. Hennessey said mine was "unique." He leaned over my shoulder, said he liked the way I'd painted myself in blues and greens. That I had a different way of looking at things.

I've always wondered what Mr. Hennessey would smell like up close. He's so different to the other men around here, the farmers with their crinkled eyes and big meaty hands. His nails are lined with paint instead of dust. It turns out that he smells of soap and coffee. And something else—a strange, sweet smell. Musky and male.

"What made you decide to use those colors, those loose brush-strokes?" he asked. "It's . . . unexpected."

I looked down at the jet stubs of my nails, the black top I wore under my school blouse, the sleeves stretching all the way to my knuckles. I knew what he meant. Most Goths don't see themselves in color.

I wanted to tell him that I long to take the paintbrush in my hand, dripping with blue, and swirl it over my ruined skin. To hide the silver cracks and flakes with patterns of cerulean and cobalt. To make myself beautiful.

But the classroom was silent, the only sound the scratching of bristles on canvas, the slosh of turps in a jar. The fans whirred overhead, rustling paper. The other kids were half splayed out on their desks, cheeks flushed, lethargic in the heat. But I knew they were listening.

"Dunno," I said, and he nodded and moved on to the next person, Shelley Peters, who'd painted herself with yellow plaits and crimson circles for cheeks, like a child's cartoon. "Talk me through the choices you made here," I heard Mr. Hennessey ask her, making thoughtful noises while she prattled on. I felt the blood in my cheeks, and I gripped the paintbrush hard, working furiously. Idiot. I'd thought he was giving me extra attention, like he was telling me—in his understated way—that I was different than the others. Special.

But then, when the bell rang and everyone rushed to scrub the paint from their hands and pack up their work, he asked me to stay behind.

"You're talented," he said, shuffling the sheaf of papers on his desk. Charcoal and ink drawings, other students' names scrawled at the bottom. I wondered what his own art looked like. "Anywhere else, and I'd be recommending your parents enroll you in weekend classes at the local art school, but this being Dawes Plain . . ."

"There isn't one," I finished for him, and we grinned, our eyes meeting. I looked away quickly, my gaze landing on his arms. His shirtsleeves were rolled up, revealing the fine blond hairs on his forearms. I wanted to paint them.

Not for the first time, I wondered what he was doing here: this wasn't the kind of place people like him moved to. It was the kind of place they escaped.

"How would you feel about some extra lessons?" he asked. Something leaped inside my stomach. "One on one, after school. Do you think your parents would mind?"

"Anything that keeps me from devil worship," I said, gesturing at the black leather choker around my neck—which was unfair of me, as Mum and Dad aren't exactly religious. But it made Mr. Hennessey laugh, so it was worth it.

"It's settled, then. Here, after school, next Monday."

I can hardly wait. To learn from him, to get better and better. But I do feel sort of bad about it. There was a time when art was mine and Dad's thing. He was the one who taught me to draw. Some of my earliest memories are of sitting on his knee, his hand guiding mine on the page. "Now, draw what you *see*," he'd say, pointing at a stumpy tree or a vase of dried flowers or whatever it was we were looking at, "not what you *think* you see."

Dad's pretty good, still, though he doesn't draw as much as he used to. But every Christmas he gives Mum a framed picture of a different bird to line the hallway with. There are dozens now, and they're becoming increasingly obscure—the earlier ones are things like cockatoos and kookaburras, but last year he gave her something called a lemon-bellied flycatcher, whatever that is.

It's sweet, how he spends ages beforehand shut up in his study, leafing through her *Birds of Australia* book for one he hasn't done yet. "You'll have to move on to *Birds of England* next," I said once, which made him shudder.

But as good as Dad's bird pictures are, I don't think there's much more he can really teach me. He only ever draws wildlife: birds and plants and butterflies. ("Can't draw a face to save myself," he says.)

I want to do more. I want to draw people, to capture them completely with my paint and canvas. To tell their stories.

What story does a bird tell?

Later

Holy fuck.

My heart is pounding so hard, my hands are sweating so much I can barely hold the pen.

When I got back from school, I kept thinking about Mr. Hennessey. About next Monday. About his words. *You're talented.*

But there was something else, something itching at my brain.

It was something Ms. Entwistle had said about genes in biology. I was wondering if my gross skin was hereditary, and if so, why I had it and no one else. Maybe a grandparent had it? I wouldn't know, Mum and Dad never talk about any grandparents, or any other family. (I never thought that was weird until kindergarten, when everyone started going on about "my nan this" or "my pop that." It had been normal to me that we spent Christmases just the three of us, that no envelopes containing five-dollar notes arrived for my birthday. That there was literally no one else.)

That got me thinking about all the stuff I didn't know, stuff they hadn't told me. I thought that if I told them about what I'd learned—about genes and genetics—then it might open some kind of door, that then they might tell me about their parents and grandparents and siblings.

Our family.

Mum had just put dinner on the table—something she called a cassoulet, but which looked indistinguishable from a stew—and Dad was already shoveling it in his mouth. They both looked tired: there were blue shadows under Dad's eyes, and Mum's lips were pale and pursed, as if with the effort of holding in all the confidential things she'd heard at work. I hate it, the way she listens to other people's problems all day and comes home to pretend we have none of our own.

"Can you curl your tongue?" I asked.

Mum frowned for a second, but then her features lightened.

"Yep," she said, sticking her tongue out in a neat pink roll.

"Dad?"

Dad shook his head.

"We're eating, Jess."

"Come *on*."

"Mike?" Mum prodded.

He swallowed his mouthful of food and stuck out his tongue to show the bluish underside, then folded it, just as Mum had done.

"Happy?" Dad said, eyes already back on his plate.

"Mm," I said, but my mouth had gone dry.

"You all right, sweetie?" Mum said, giving me a sharp look. "You're a bit pale. Is it that time already?"

Normally, I'd have killed her for bringing up periods at the dinner table, in front of Dad, but instead I said, "Yeah, actually, is it OK if I go lie down? Not feeling great."

"Of course," Mum said, her head tilted with concern. "I'll bring you a hot-water bottle later."

I just nodded, scraping the chair back abruptly.

"Thank your mother for dinner," Dad said as I half sprinted from the kitchen.

"Thanks, Mum," I managed.

I dragged myself down the hall into the safety of the bathroom, leaned my pounding head against the cool tile of the wall.

"The ability to curl one's tongue is genetic," Ms. Entwistle had said, rapping her ruler on the blackboard to wake those who had dozed off in the stuffy classroom. "If you can't do it, that usually means one of your parents can't, either."

Mum and Dad can both do it.

But I can't.

So that means one of them can't be my parent.

---

21 February

The sleepwalking is back.

It hasn't happened since I was a child—I'd almost convinced myself that it never would again. But last night it returned.

I was awake for ages, tossing and turning—the sheets seemed to cling to my legs, like the tendrils of some great vine, ensnaring me. The skin behind my knees and in the insides of my elbows itched and itched.

Thoughts jostled in my mind. The tiny blond hairs on Mr. Hennessey's arms, Mum and Dad looking at me across the dinner table. The ways I'm different from them, the ways I'm the same.

I only remember bits and pieces of the dream, like broken shards. The warmth of a hand in mine, a cold wind on my skin. Water, its lap and suck. A reflected face that wasn't my own.

When I opened my eyes, I was standing on the bank of the dam. It was still early; dawn licking the horizon gray. Turning, I saw the glint of eyes in the paddock, the faint outline of the house behind me.

My hands shake even now, just writing about it. The dam is deep—ten feet, at its center. And, thanks to my skin, I'm the only girl in Australia who doesn't know how to swim.

What if I hadn't woken up?

Thank God Max was at school today.

He sloped into English five minutes late, interrupting Mrs. Clark's monologue about *The Tempest*, his trousers slung around his hips as though he couldn't be bothered to properly get dressed. When he sat next to me there was the familiar green stink of weed.

I couldn't help but smile. Max up to his old tricks. Maybe the world hasn't been turned on its head after all.

I've known Max since we were five years old. We met on the first day of kindergarten. The other kids pulled faces when I walked in: the rains had come the day before, and I'd flung myself into a particularly shiny puddle before anyone could stop me. Mum had done her best with the Vaseline, but tendrils of cracked skin snaked out from the hem of the blue gingham uniform. I'd scratched at it in my sleep, and dried blood had formed cratered scabs on my shins. Even the teacher averted her eyes.

At lunch, as I sat in a shady section of the quadrangle, my knees drawn up under my uniform, Max made his way over to me. This skinny blond kid with buck teeth and ears that mushroomed from his head. I guess, in a way, he owed me. If I hadn't been there, it would've been him getting the weird looks.

He sat down and opened his schoolbag.

"I got an Etch A Sketch for Christmas," he said, producing the toy with pride. "Want a go?"

We've been inseparable—joined at the hip, as Mum says—ever since.

Now, I leaned over to whisper in his ear.

"Meet me at the greenhouse at lunch," I said, and he raised his pale eyebrows, then nodded. Wordlessly, he pulled up his shirtsleeve before draping his arm across my desk so that I could draw on his skin. He keeps telling me I should become a tattoo artist after school. "Fuck art college," he says. "Just move to Sydney and buy a tattoo gun. You'd make a fortune."

I could still see the faded marks of last week's design, a repeated pattern of thorns and roses. Today I had something different in mind. I pulled two pens—green and blue—from my pencil case and, when Mrs. Clark wasn't looking, covered his milky skin with scales. Tiny, delicate ones, almost like teardrops.

There was no time to talk after class, and I spent the next lesson longing for Max, longing for him to take a thoughtful drag of a joint and then tell me everything was OK, dissolving my fears like one of his smoke rings. When at last the bell rang, I practically bolted out the door. I don't think I've ever been so keen to get outside, into the heat. The sky was searing blue, and as I walked across the quadrangle I could feel little beads of sweat popping out on my skin under all my layers. (Now I'm covered in scabs, of course. My fingers itch to pick them off.)

I walked past the squat brick classrooms and the rusted metal drinking fountain, then the chalk-smeared tarmac gave way to scrub. Up ahead was the greenhouse. Water restrictions mean it's now just a storage shed, but the name's stuck.

The contents of the greenhouse—old bicycle wheels, cracked hockey sticks, ancient shin pads that smell of feet—spill out onto the dried grass, a cornucopia of rubbish. It sounds gross but there's something weirdly beautiful about it: the harsh sun glinting on the rusting spokes, the view that stretches out beyond. Paddocks and hills, blonde as a girl's hair, meeting the sky in a hazy line.

Max was already there, leaning against the back wall of the green-house, joint dangling from his lips, nodding along to his headphones. I'd never tell him this, but with his gold curls and wide green eyes, he looks almost angelic. I guess he lost the buck teeth and mushroom ears somewhere on the way to puberty.

In some lights, he's even a little good-looking—or at least, he has a face I wouldn't mind drawing. Another thing I'd never tell him.

"So," he said, slipping his headphones round his neck so that I could hear the tinny whine of The Cure, "what's up?"

I took the joint from his lips, pressed it to my own.

"That bad? Fuck."

When I told him, he stood for a while, brow furrowed. In the distance, a magpie burbled and there was the soft thwack of someone hitting a football, followed by a cheer. I brushed a fly from the tip of my nose.

"Are you sure that's right? What the teacher said." Max is good at science, though he pretends not to be. I shrugged.

"I think I read that it was a myth," he offered, taking the joint back from me.

"I dunno," I said. "But a part of me wouldn't even be surprised. I mean, it makes sense, right? Neither of them has the bloody Flakes."

That's our nickname for it, my skin condition. Max says it sounds cool, like a band. I think it sounds like a type of washing powder.

"I wouldn't worry about it," he said, blowing a pungent ring of smoke toward me. "For what it's worth, I've always thought you look loads like your dad."

"Really?"

"Yeah," he said, taking a step closer to me. As well as pot, he smelled of too much Lynx deodorant and Wrigley's chewing gum. "It's the ears. This little bit here"—he pinched the top of my left ear between his thumb and forefinger—"it's kind of pointy. Like an elf's. Your dad's is the same."

"Ow," I said, stepping away from him, though it didn't actually hurt. But my ear felt hot where he'd touched me, and my cheeks burned.

He'd broken our new, unspoken rule. Even a year ago, I wouldn't have thought twice about leaning my head on his shoulder, or punching him in the bicep. But now, the space between us felt different, charged somehow. I guess that's why the drawing started—the tattooing, as we call it.

It's become the only safe way to touch each other.

It makes me sad, sometimes. And scared, too. Scared that I'll lose him, or that maybe, in a way, I already have.

"You OK?"

I nodded, even though I wasn't really. I almost told him about the sleepwalking then, but I didn't know how to find the words.

Now, I don't know what to think. Maybe Max is right. Maybe there is some kind of rational explanation, some way that it all makes sense. But another, louder part of me feels like something is wrong, like my parents are keeping something from me. And the more I try to ignore that feeling, to swallow it down, the more it grows and grows, swelling like a parasite in my gut.

12

LUCY

WEDNESDAY, 13 FEBRUARY 2019

Lucy's chest feels tight. Around her, the room seems to expand and contract. Her pulse drums in her ears, keeping time with the roar and crash of the waves outside.

She resists the urge to throw the diary across the room, as if that will somehow obliterate what she has read. Is Jess—for, unthinkable as it is, this is the only explanation that would make sense—not their father's daughter?

But she just can't imagine her mother having an affair. Her parents adore each other, to a degree that Lucy finds embarrassing. They're old now, older than her friends' parents—Lucy, a surprise baby, arrived in their early forties—and yet she still sometimes walks in on them canoodling in the kitchen.

She remembers going to get a glass of water one night when she was in high school, finding them swaying gently to a song on the radio, spotlit by the yellow moon coming through the window. For a moment, before they saw Lucy standing there, they'd looked like a couple from an old film. They'd burst apart, transforming into her graying, middle-aged parents again, but Lucy had felt a wistful ache as she padded back to her room. Even before what happened with Ben, she couldn't imagine someone loving her like that, wanting to hold her like that. Not with how she looks underneath her clothes.

That's the other thing.

I could feel the moisture doing its work already: worming its way into my skin, cracking into a hundred silver rivers.

Lucy knows that feeling. It's as familiar to her as the rise and fall of her chest. Jess has described the symptoms of aquagenic urticaria.

Confusion swirls through her.

She thinks of the clothes Jess favors—the high necklines, the billowing sleeves. The warren of tights and stockings at the bottom of her sister's cupboard. She had known, on some level, that Jess used clothes as a sort of cloak, a way of separating herself from the rest of the world. But she had always thought her sister swathed her body in fabric to tell people that she was different, that they should stay away.

But now Lucy sees that she was wrong. Jess hadn't been advertising her difference. She'd been hiding it, even from her own sister.

She thinks back to that weekend in Sydney. All those hours spent together, just the two of them. Had it not occurred to Jess to take Lucy's hand in hers, to tell her that she understood? To provide some sort of advice, some comfort?

On the contrary, she must have gone out of her way to conceal it.

Lucy looks down at her own body. Her legs are folded in the lotus position, and there's a lilac sheen spreading from behind her knees, grazing her inner thighs. She learned to set aside vanity a long time ago; learned that too much fabric caused sweating, which made things much, much worse. She dresses in linen and light cotton religiously, wears shorts at every opportunity, just like her parents always told her to.

Her mother's voice echoes.

No clingy material, Goose, and whatever you do, don't scratch. Your skin could get infected, and that might make you very sick, sweetheart.

In the trade-off between vanity and health, she had chosen health. It wasn't acceptance, not really. She had just learned to detach from her body, to see it as merely a tool, the implement of her mind.

It seems like that wasn't so easy for Jess.

Is that why no one has ever mentioned this crucial fact to her? Because of Jess's pride, her vanity?

Hot fury blooms in her chest. Lucy had always believed she was the only one in their family with aquagenic urticaria. The invalid, the freak.

She'd felt such shame, even as a small child, when her mother rubbed steroid cream onto her scabbed arms and legs, when her father worried about how to cool her down on a hot day, or what to do if it rained. And this whole time, they'd been through it all before, with Jess.

Why had they all lied?

She thinks of the timing of the diary entry: 1998. Over a year before she was born.

If her mother *did* have an affair, could it have continued right up until Lucy's birth? Would that explain why she and Jess both have aquagenic urticaria, while neither of their parents do?

But no. She can't countenance that; she won't.

She thinks of the baby pictures she's seen, the ones her parents keep in the faded black album in their bedroom. Lucy, pink-faced in her father's arms.

Even as a newborn, the resemblance had been clear. Something about the nose, the mouth. And the ears. Of course, the ears! Max's observation was right: Lucy, Jess, and their father all have a slight but distinctive peak to their ear shape. It's not possible that he isn't their dad. It's just not.

Googling it, she sees that there's considerable disagreement on whether or not the ability to roll one's tongue *is* a genetic trait: several articles from respected science journals even describe the theory as "debunked."

She takes a deep, shuddering breath.

OK. It's OK.

Jess was wrong.

She picks up the diary and rereads the entry. Now that her heart has slowed, she can see that, beneath the sophisticated prose, there's a sort of adolescent hysteria to her sister's words. A paranoia. Born, perhaps, of sleep deprivation, of the feeling that her body was no longer under her control.

A feeling Lucy understands all too well.

At least she has further evidence that Jess sleepwalks—or that she used to, at any rate.

The warmth of a hand in mine, a cold wind on my skin. A reflected face that wasn't my own.

Was she dreaming about the *Naiad* even then? Twenty years before she came to live at Comber Bay? She traces her sister's handwriting, as if there's some hidden meaning to be derived from the faded loops and curls of her pen.

There's something else about the diary entry that disturbs her, niggling at her brain.

Jess's art teacher, who'd offered to give her extra lessons. Mr. Hennessey. The name is familiar somehow—and then she remembers. The library book she'd found while cleaning up her sister's dining table—the one about surrealism—had last been checked out by someone called C. Hennessey. He must have given it to Jess when she was at school. Why has she kept it all this time?

Lucy frowns. Extra lessons and a book. She supposes that's not inherently inappropriate. But she still doesn't like it.

13

LUCY

THURSDAY, 14 FEBRUARY 2019

When dawn comes, Lucy's eyes burn with exhaustion. She'd staved off sleep with a combination of strong coffee and mindless scrolling through the true crime sub-threads on Reddit. She'd also read more of Jess's diary, frustrated to find no other references to sleepwalking or strange dreams, but relieved that Jess hadn't recorded any further suspicions about her parentage.

There had been more mentions of Mr. Hennessey, though. Jess had started one-on-one classes with him every week, and he'd begun teaching her art history and theory as well. Surrealism, expressionism.

Thinking of the lionfish drawing—the way it had been scrunched into a ball as if to be thrown away—Lucy feels a pang of sorrow for her father. How must it have felt, to know that Jess didn't need his help anymore? That she had reached a level of skill that he, older, and busy with the farm, would now never obtain?

Of course, there must have been a pride in that. But it would be painful, too. She's not surprised Jess didn't want to tell her parents about the extra lessons. Not to mention the fact that she was spending time alone with a male teacher. Though from what Lucy has read, Jess and Mr. Hennessey haven't so much as brushed fingers exchanging tubes of paint. Maybe she was reading too much into it, her interpretation of her sister's words colored by her own experience with men.

Not that there's been more than one. That's why it hurts so much. Ben had taken more than just her dignity; he'd taken her virginity, too. Did he know, she wonders now, that it was her first time? Did he realize what it meant for her to let him see and touch her naked body—a body that, most of the time, she pretended didn't exist?

When she'd taken that picture, she'd felt in control, like she was stepping into herself: confident and sexual. Not a girl any longer but a woman, at last. He'd woken that feeling in her, with his fingers and lips and tongue. And then he'd taken it away.

Shame and loneliness pull at her, a buckling inside, like she is collapsing in on herself. There is no one she can talk to about this. She'd tried, at first, with Em, who'd initially been sympathetic. But then she'd said: *I get that he shouldn't have shared the picture with his friends. But it's not like he actually put it on TikTok himself, is it? I dunno, maybe you two can find a way back from this.*

As if getting the guy was all that mattered. Like it would be a happy ending.

Her pain sours into anger. At Ben and Em, but at Jess, too. She was supposed to be here. She was supposed to listen, like a big sister should.

Passing through the living room, she forces herself to confront the canvas on the easel. The sisters walking into the sea toward the *Naiad*. The brushstrokes seem to move, transforming into the dark, leaping waves.

But it's the hands that draw her, the way they're interlinked. Like they'll never let each other go.

Haunted by her discovery of the *Naiad*'s sinking in 1801, Lucy spends the morning reading about convict transportation. Like every Australian, she knows the basics already—British and Irish criminals were exiled to Australia, then just a collection of colonies. She knows about Arthur Phillip and the First Fleet, the eleven ships that made landfall at Botany Bay on 26 January 1788, devastating the First Nations communities that had thrived there for millennia.

But she didn't know about that first night, after the female convicts were disembarked, when the male convicts were let loose on the women, so that shrieks and cries rang out in the dark. Or about the "female factories," where men selected women convicts to be their domestic servants, or their wives.

Nor did she know about the Female Register—the document created by Reverend Samuel Marsden, the settlement's most senior clergyman, dividing the colony's women into either wives or concubines, depending on whether or not they were married.

Whores. That's how these women—some of them mere girls— were seen.

Lucy's shirt sticks to her back in the heat, her skin fizzing and cracking with sweat. At her side, her fists clench and unclench. She's walking along Devil's Beach, far away from the water's edge, her sneakers slipping on the tussocks of grass that line the dunes. She can already feel the itch of sand inside her socks. It's windy today, the water a rippling, frenzied blue. Spray licks her face and she moves closer to the road.

From here, she can just make out the corrugated roof of Cliff House, glinting through the trees on the far side of the bay. The view is dominated by Devil's Lookout: the cragged rocks leading to the thundering sea, the winding steps. The caves like wide-open mouths.

The sight unsettles her, the story of Baby Hope still fresh in her mind. She turns away, looking for the memorial Jess photographed. She hopes that the monument will spark some realization, some epiphany. That it will unlock some clue as to how these convict women—women who lived and died centuries ago—have infected her mind, and her sister's, too.

She still feels that other world when she's awake, like a phantom limb. The clammy warmth of another body at her side, the gnawing hunger in her belly. The creaking of the ship as it founders on the waves.

She blinks the sensations away, focusing on the burn in her calves, the sun so bright that it hurts her eyes.

She doesn't see it until she's almost upon it: the granite stone glittering in the light. There's a park bench next to it facing the ocean, occupied by a man in a striped shirt and floppy hat. She considers turning back but he raises his arm in greeting, the sort of country wave you'd get at home. She's curious, she realizes. It might be good to meet another local. She can ask if he knows Jess, can try and get some more insight into her life here.

She nods at him as she approaches the memorial.

"Beautiful morning," he says, and she smiles in agreement. He's slightly younger than her parents, small and wiry, a dark cowlick beneath the floppy hat. Flecks of gray in his thick eyebrows.

She turns her eyes back to the memorial, reaches out a hand to trace the letters.

The loss of approximately 100 lives.

"Sad, isn't it?" the man offers.

"Yeah," she says. "Not a nice way to go."

"Might've been a mercy," he says, and she can't help wondering if he's right, given what would have awaited the women if they'd lived. "The ship's captain was infamous. They held a parliamentary inquiry after the voyage he'd captained before. Neglected the convicts, crammed them in too closely to make room for the rum he wanted to sell along the way. Fifty died in the crossing from Ireland."

"You know a lot about this," she says, offering her biggest smile. "Are you the local history buff?"

He heaves himself slowly from the bench, and for the first time she sees the walking stick on the ground. Instinctively, she starts toward him to help.

"You're all right," he says, grimacing. "Nah, not me. My dad. He was a member of the local historical society—I mean, society's some word for it, it was him and two other blokes. The memorial was his pet project. He liked sitting here. Passed away a couple years ago."

"Oh, I'm so sorry."

"Thanks," the man says, after a pause. Is she imagining it, or is there a glint of suspicion in his eyes? "I'm Ryan, by the way. You here on holiday? Not seen you around before."

"Lucy," she says, shaking the hand he offers. His palm feels weathered and calloused. "Yeah—sort of. I'm staying with my sister. Jess Martin, in Cliff House?"

"Ah, of course," he says, a smile transforming his face. "Lovely Jess. Well, she must be an expert on the *Naiad* by now, with all her painting. I gave her one of Dad's old files. Think he'd have liked that, one history buff inspiring another." He scans her face. "She didn't mention a sister, but I can see the resemblance. How is she? Haven't seen her about this week."

She pauses. She doesn't want to tell him that she's gone away, that Lucy doesn't know where she is; but she doesn't want to lie, either.

"Um—busy, I think," she says, which she supposes is true. "Preparing for this show."

Ryan nods.

"*The Sirens*, right? She gave me an invite. Sweet of her, but a bit difficult with my leg."

So, Jess had invited this man to her exhibition, but not her own sister? She hadn't even told him that she *had* a sister. Just like she hadn't told Melody.

"Do you think many people from the town will go?" Lucy asks. If she can find out who Jess spends her time with, then maybe she can find someone who knows where she is.

Ryan's brow furrows.

"From the town? Her neighbor, Melody, maybe. I think they're close. But I'd be surprised if anyone else showed up, to be honest."

There's an odd hesitancy to his tone. She takes a breath, decides to be bold. "I guess Batemans Bay is a long way to travel for an art show."

Though they both know it isn't, not really. It's only half an hour away.

Something shadows Ryan's eyes.

"I think it's more the subject matter than the distance, if you know what I mean."

Lucy is surprised. "Because it's about the shipwreck? But that was hundreds of years ago. And they put up this memorial, didn't they?"

Ryan adjusts his hat, looks out to sea and sighs.

"Let's just say that the memorial was . . . controversial. People are a little superstitious, around here. There are some funny stories connected to the *Naiad*. And then to have an out-of-towner come in, staying in Cliff House and wanting to dredge everything up . . . you can see how it would get people's backs up. Locals don't want reminders of that stuff."

"What stuff? What stories?"

Ryan puffs out his cheeks.

"I'm not saying I believe it. But I know people who say they've heard it, standing on the beach at night." He pauses, looks back at her. "Voices, coming from the waves. Women's voices."

She remembers now that this was mentioned in the first episode of the podcast. *Some townspeople believe that there's a supernatural explanation for the disappearances*, the host had said, skepticism barely disguised. *Two hundred years ago, a ship was wrecked on the reef off the bay's coast. The more superstitious locals say that if you stand on the beach at night, you can hear the voices of the drowned, carrying over the waves . . .*

It had been one thing hearing that in her car, miles and miles away from Comber Bay itself. Before she knew about the *Naiad*, before she'd connected the shipwreck with her dreams. But it feels different now, standing on this cliff, the blue turmoil of the waves below.

She swallows. Lucy understands the mindset of small towns, the mythology that a community weaves like cloth. A story repeated so many times that every local knows where to draw breath in the telling. Dawes Plain has its own ghosts. She thinks of the abandoned gold mine near the reservoir, the kids who say you can still hear the echo of metal on rock, even though the mine's been closed for a century.

She'd never believed the stories. But that was before.

"Look," he says, mistaking her expression for one of incredulity. "I was a fisherman here, a couple lifetimes ago. I never heard women's voices out there at sea. But I assume you know the town's history. That's why people come here. Bloody tragedy tourists.

"Eight men over almost four decades. And yeah, maybe some of those men drowned. Maybe there's some natural explanation. But I know that water like the back of my hand, and I never saw anything like a whirlpool. All I've got is my senses. My ears, my eyes, you know? And I've seen things myself that I can't forget. That, all these years later, I can't explain."

Something darkens his face as his gaze drifts back to the water. She waits for him to continue, her confidence returning. She's good at this, navigating the terrain of a conversation. Knowing when to push, when to ease off. People like to reveal themselves to Lucy. Girls with drunk glittering eyes at house parties, whispering about the boys they want, the lies they've told. If you create a silence, people want to fill it.

Funny. For the first time, it occurs to her that this—listening, asking the right questions—is a skill she shares with her mother.

Sure enough, Ryan takes a breath. "My dad used to say, *The sea gives, but it also takes.* Exactly the sort of thing an old fisherman would say, I know. But it's true."

Lucy wonders if she's imagined the catch of tears in his voice, but when she glances up she sees his eyes are shining.

"Sorry." He smiles sadly, catching her looking. "It's hard, remembering. Dad was in a nursing home in Moruya. I was working in the mines, down in Broken Hill, before my accident, and so I didn't see him as much as I should have. And by the time I moved back—well, let's just say he was pretty far gone."

"I'm sorry," Lucy says.

"It's all right," he says softly. "I just wish I'd been here more. Tried to understand him. He loved it here, even after everything that hap-pened. Anyway"—he sighs—"that's my reflection done for the day."

"I'd better get back, too," Lucy says quietly. "But it was nice to meet you, Ryan . . ."

"Smith," he says. "Ryan Smith."

It's only as she's walking back toward the house, following the spine of the cliffs, that she remembers where she's heard the name before. Ryan Smith is the brother of Daniel Smith, who disappeared in 1981.

And he was on the fishing boat that discovered Baby Hope.

The sea gives, but it also takes.

14

MARY

Mary did not know how long they'd been at sea. She seemed to have lost her grip on time, like it was a stitch she had dropped.

"It has been a week," Eliza whispered to her. "I have counted the meals, scant as they are."

She tapped seven times on Mary's palm, soft as a butterfly's wing.

When they first heard the juddering approach of men's footsteps, the whistling and the laughter, some of the women thought they were already there, that they had reached the great southern land with all its threat and its promise. Such foolish hope made Mary want to weep. She did not know why they were being taken up on deck, but she sensed their journey was far from over.

They climbed through the ship's decks, a chain of women sobbing and talking and laughing. The oil lamps lit their faces a greasy yellow: Bridie with her flame-red hair, thick and matted now; Aoife with her skin worn as threadbare cloth; Sarah and Annie with their matching dark eyes and wan faces. Eliza squeezed Mary's hand tight, so that her fear lessened, even as they rose higher and higher through the warren of the ship.

On deck, the light seared everything white, like the time in winter when it had snowed and ice folded itself around their little cottage, stealing away the color and the warmth.

Mary felt a pang then, remembering how Da had kept the fire burning high, had blown on their fingers to warm them. He'd allowed each sister one sip of *poitín*, the liquid traveling like fire into their bellies. Now, Mary blinked, and Da and the snow-bright cottage fell away.

She gritted her teeth, swallowing her tears. It was no use wishing things were different, that she was back at the cottage, safe and sound. She had to be brave, for Eliza. That was what Da would want. But despite her resolve, the fear returned. She had thought the ship so large when they first set eyes on it at the dock. It had seemed monstrous, like a challenge to God. Now, she saw that it was dwarfed by the sky that stretched overhead and the gray sea that spread out around them. The mast looked needle-thin, the sails fragile. Mary could even see great black holes in them, like the time Eliza had stood too close to the hearth and scorched her dress. It was hard to imagine that it might see them safely to the other side of the world.

As the women were shepherded into place, they passed rows of men lined up on the deck. Some of the sailors looked younger even than she and Eliza; others had weary faces, hardened by all they'd seen.

For all the bodies crowded onto the deck, the only sound was the roar of the wind through the sails, the slap and suck of the waves on the hull and the screeching of seabirds above.

Eliza gripped Mary's hand tight. Suddenly, the rows of men parted and the captain stepped forward, along with the clergyman in his dark robes. Mary was struck by the contrast between the captain and his officers and the sailors. The former were slick as berries in their rich uniforms, while the others looked to have been plucked from the streets with their ragged trousers and dirty mouths. Some of them couldn't have been older than twelve: one wiped snot from his nose with his sleeve, like a little child.

But now others were making their way through the crowd, carrying something wrapped in the faded canvas of an old sail. The men heaved the object onto the deck before the captain, and Mary's breath caught in her throat as the sail curled away, revealing the pale gleam of a foot.

Mary tried to listen to the clergyman's words as he led the ship in prayer, but they were foreign, flat-sounding. God's word stripped of its magic, its beauty. How it would shame Da, to know that Protestant prayers fell on his daughters' ears.

He had striven so hard, all the while they'd lived in Armagh, to see to it that they kept the proper faith. Other families in their village had converted over the years, Mary knew, so that they might escape the brunt of the English laws. Laws that also meant they could not own land or vote, that they could not even own a horse. Every month, Da had been forced to hand over the rent and the tithe to Byrne— Byrne with the long, tapered fingers and the black glint in his eyes— knowing that it would go to the upkeep of St. Mark's, the Protestant church with its walls of shining stone. Meanwhile, their own church was little more than ruins, reeking of animals and damp leaves, their worship there furtive.

But still, Da had stood firm. He taught his girls the rosary, taught them to love the Virgin and the saints. Even though, Mary knew, a part of him also clung to the old ways, the ancient beliefs in fairies and selkies. She did not dare ask if he believed in merrow.

In any case, all his teaching had been for naught. Da was not here now to stop their ears. The clergyman droned on, the words settling like a pall over the gathered crowd. Mary could not keep her eyes from the bluish foot that poked out from beneath the sail. The toes were wrinkled and covered in wiry hairs which moved in the sea breeze. Some dark substance shadowed the nails—dirt, or perhaps blood.

She wondered who the sailor had been, and how he had died. How did his body look, underneath its makeshift shroud?

The captain coughed and the clergyman's speech faded to an indistinct rumble. Mary saw how his Adam's apple bobbed in his neck, his nervous sideways glance to the captain. She couldn't imagine having that kind of power, so that even a man of God feared you. The captain was small, finely built, with girlish curls escaping from his peaked hat and a youthful glow to his face. But he had a way of drawing each eye, moths to a lamp, caught even as they burned.

Before they were taken down below—all of them gasping at the fresh air, as if they might carry it back to the prison deck—Mary felt a prickling pain across her scalp, a tightness in her chest.

Suddenly she longed for the dark.

After the bright day, the prison deck seemed blacker than ever before, as if they were inside a closed eye.

The women were noisy, going over what they'd seen—the endless sky, the dead body, the captain with his fair curls. Reliving the moment of freedom.

"I saw his head when they tipped him over," said one woman. "It was all bent and bloody. Someone must have killed him. And yet they call us criminals."

"It was a fall that killed him, you eejit," said another. "Working the rigging, or the crow's nest. I ought to know, my husband being a sailor all these years. Besides, you'd be foolish to kill someone on a ship, so you would. They'd walk you from the plank."

"I don't like to think of it," Sarah muttered in their corner. Mary heard Annie's yelp as her mother pulled her closer. "That there might be a murderer in their ranks. And us, exiled for stealing cloth and the like."

Mary said nothing. She could hear the soft tide of Eliza's breathing, and—she fancied—the bright snap of her sister's thoughts.

She wondered what Eliza remembered of that night by the stream, what moments haunted her. Whether she recalled the wet *thwack* of the rock against Byrne's skull, the soft gurgling sounds he'd made.

What would the others think, if they knew how close they'd come to taking a life?

Now, Eliza's fingers tapped softly on Mary's hand.

"I smell bread," she said, low in Mary's ear.

Mary sniffed the air, the stink of women's bodies, ripe with sweat and urine. But then, there it was. The smell of flour clenched her stomach with wanting.

It wasn't the sweet, golden scent of the farls that Da had taught them to make, the soft wet cakes of potato and flour that had sizzled on the pot over the hearth. But nor was it the dusty smell of the biscuits they were given for their ration.

"But where is it coming from?" Mary murmured to Eliza.

"It is Bridie. Her jaw clicks when she chews."

It occurred to Mary then that Bridie had been quiet since they'd been taken down below. This was odd, for normally she filled the deck with her ribald stories or the rich song of her laughter. Though they were only in the berth beneath her, Mary had not noticed. And then Mary heard it, too, the small, furtive sounds of chewing.

A bright ribbon of fury passed through her.

Bridie must have stolen the food somehow, when they'd been brought up from the hold. Many times they'd been told what penalty awaited them for theft: all the women would be punished if the culprit couldn't be found. They might be taken on deck to be whipped, or placed in leg irons. There was even a rumor of a wooden box—tight and dark as a coffin—where an offender might be placed for days on end, until the captain was satisfied she had learned her lesson.

"Bridie," she hissed. "How did you get that? What have you done?"

There was the hasty sound of the other woman swallowing.

"I earned it. Fair and square."

"How?"

Next to her, Eliza tensed. "Oh, Bridie," she said, a hint of sorrow in her voice.

"'Oh, Bridie' what? I'm the one with food in my belly. You could be, too, if you were quick enough to sell your wares."

"I do not understand," Mary said. "What does she mean, Eliza? What wares?"

Eliza said nothing. Mary felt a shudder pass through her sister's body.

And then she knew.

15

LUCY

THURSDAY, 14 FEBRUARY 2019

The night air is a cold hand on her face.

At first, she thinks she's still there. Submerged in darkness, the pound and crash of the sea all around. But where there had been women's voices, their warmth wrapping around her like cloth, now there is silence. Only the lonely tick of her own pulse.

She opens her eyes and her heart stills in her chest.

She is staring into a dizzying drop.

In the moonlight the rocks below glimmer like teeth. The sea shreds itself over them, dark waves foaming white.

Her blood pounds. She forces herself to stay calm.

She is not falling. She can feel the creak of wood beneath her feet. She reaches out her hands and finds the rough-hewn barrier. At last she places herself: she is on the deck of Cliff House.

Her wristwatch reads 3:20 A.M. How long has she been standing here? Her bare feet feel numb, frozen. Her mind stutters with panic.

What if she'd fallen?

Inside, Lucy switches on the light and is startled anew by the chaos of the living room. The tarp covering the hole in the floor balloons with wind, as if huge fingers are trying to push their way inside. The walls, with their blistered orange wallpaper, seem to close in on her. Avoiding the gaze of the women in the paintings—those wide, milk-white eyes—she heads to the kitchen. She forces herself to catalog her senses—the rumble of the kettle, the blinking neon of the microwave clock, the hot scald of tea on her tongue. But still it takes a few moments for her to accept that she has stepped out of that dream world and back into this one.

She remembers something she read as a child, in a *Lonely Planet* book, about sunken cities. Homes and churches drowned by governments to create reservoirs. Whole villages beneath murky water, chimneys and spires shadowing the surface.

That's what the dreams are like. Unseen, but always there. Waiting.

It frightens her, how much more she remembers with each one. How vivid they are, how *real*. She can still feel the phantom brush of matted hair against her face, can still hear the murmurs in her ear.

Her scalp prickles as she sits at the kitchen table. What if she hadn't woken when she did? She closes her eyes, sees herself plummeting over the edge of the cliff. A small figure in the darkness, her scream buried by the ocean's fury. The shatter of bone on rock.

She opens her eyes, shakes the image away. Stares into the mug of tea, watches the steam curling into the air. Her neck and shoulders ache, and she realizes that she has no memory of going up to bed, no memory of locking the window, of barricading the bedroom door. She must have fallen asleep here, at the kitchen table. Papers are strewn everywhere, along with empty wrappers of chocolate, the packaging from the fish and chips she'd bought yesterday evening.

She had been going through the file that Ryan Smith gave to Jess—the one that his father had collated on the *Naiad*. It had taken her hours to find it in the squalor, hidden in a stack of papers she'd moved when clearing the kitchen table. An ancient manila folder, held together with a bulldog clip, *Bernard Smith* written in faded pencil on the cover.

She'd read the bulk of the file before falling asleep, including letters to the local council about funding for the memorial to the wreck, the response from the council giving the go-ahead.

There are also articles from a local paper, the *South Coast Examiner*, including letters to the editor from 1981. *I have lived in Comber Bay my whole life*, one reads, *and am devastated at the thought of our beautiful town gaining notoriety for its part in distant historical events.*

Another claims that it is *offensive to erect a monument to drowned convicts—whores and thieves—when no such memorial stands for the men who have disappeared . . . Where is their monument?*

She pulls out a newspaper interview with Bernard Smith, dated November 1981, after the monument's erection. There's a photograph accompanying the article, and the face staring out at her in grainy pixels isn't at all what she'd expected from the chair of the Comber Bay Historical Society. She'd imagined someone thin and owlish, but Smith has the burly presence of a sailor. The age of the photograph doesn't hide the wrinkles around his eyes, the sun-spots on the hands knotted at his desk.

There's a strange expression on his face, written into the set of his jaw, the lines on his forehead. An odd mix of defiance and regret.

One might wonder whether the project has been a welcome distraction for Smith, whose son Daniel vanished earlier this year, the latest in a line of disappearances off Comber Bay's shores, including William Goldhill, Bob Ruddock, Pete Lawson, and Samuel Hall.

She thinks of the melancholy set of Ryan's body as he watched the waves, knowing his brother Daniel went to that beach and never returned. And then, only a year later, he witnessed the rescue of Baby Hope. He has been touched by two of Comber Bay's mysteries.

When asked why he campaigned so passionately to commemorate the victims of the shipwreck, Smith looks away. "I'm not a churchgoing man," he says finally. "But I believe in God, and doing what's right. Over a hundred lives were lost that day. Every soul deserves a proper resting place. A marker." An admirable sentiment. One can only hope that Smith's missing son will one day be afforded the same dignity.

That's the last newspaper clipping in the file.

The remaining papers are just yellowed scraps; their edges are ragged, as if they've been torn from a notebook. Their contents seem irrelevant to the memorial, and Lucy wonders whether they've ended up in the file by mistake.

She holds one of the scraps up to the light so that she can more easily read the scrawled handwriting. The paper is delicate with age, translucent as onion skin.

1960 1966 1973 1977 1981.

The years that the first five of the Eight went missing.

Another piece of paper is covered with a messy diagram, arrows snaking between the names of the men; on the reverse is a list of professions, the names of schools and churches. One list divides the missing men into "tourists" and "locals." It's obvious what this means, and the realization chills her. Bernard Smith was looking for connections between the vanished men, like a detective building a victim profile.

The final scrap of paper has just one, haunting, scrawled line.

Make it stop.

None of it makes sense to her.

Why, if Smith thought his son had been murdered, did he devote so much time—so much of his own money—into a memorial for a long-ago shipwreck, rather than to finding justice?

She looks at her watch again: 3:33 A.M. She doesn't want to go up to bed, to risk slipping back below the surface and returning to that dank world of tangled limbs and gnawing thirst.

Panic needles her. For a moment the blackness of the ship returns, threatening to swallow her up. Her fingers tremble as she takes another sip of tea, willing the dream away.

Being in Cliff House has left Lucy with more questions than answers about who her sister is. About her connection to this place, to the *Naiad*. To Mary and Eliza. And until she returns, Jess's diary is the only window into the mystery of why she is here, in Comber Bay.

Legs trembling, Lucy makes her way slowly up the stairs. After locking the window and wedging the chair under the door, she sinks into Jess's bed, grateful for the warm curve of Dora Maar atop the covers. Just as she picks up the diary from the bedside table, she hears a sound.

Singing. For a moment, she's sure of it.

But then it fades, and when she strains to catch it again, there's only the whoosh and suck of the sea on the rocks.

16

JESS'S DIARY

1998

10 July

I never thought I'd love Sunday evenings.

I used to spend them curled up in bed, the fan brushing my hair over my face, the muscles in my jaw tightening at the thought of school the next day.

Now, the week is like this:

Tuesday feels like grief. Like I've lost something I'll never have again. That feeling stretches into Wednesday, Thursday. I sit in class looking out the window at nothing, the chatter around me inconsequential as the buzz of flies. Not even Max can get through. At the greenhouse, he offers me a puff of his joint, his new AFI CD, but nothing works. I can't think how to explain it. It's like I'm trapped behind a pane of glass, the world and everyone in it blurred and fading away from me.

And then I wake up on Friday morning with a tiny golden seed in my belly.

In English, I pay attention to Mrs. Clark, about what Ariel signifies in *The Tempest*. I even take notes. I laugh at Max's jokes, tell him I think the lead singer of AFI sounds like he has a fence post up his

116

bum. Walking home from school, I look up at the huge sky and feel like the world's been cracked open just for me.

At dinner I smile as I eat whatever Mum's concocted—chicken laksa, lamb tagine, or pork larb—without complaint.

"Can you help me feed the ewes tomorrow?" Dad asks, and I say, "Sure!"

My parents grin at each other across the table.

I'm a changed girl, an angel sent to replace the old Jess.

The golden seed grows and grows over the weekend, a plant curling and quivering inside of me.

I feed the sheep and notice their strange beauty. I want to draw their weirdly human faces, their dark wet eyes. I read somewhere once that sheep can recognize people and I feel a rush of affection when I reach out and pat their soft, sweet-smelling wool. Afterward I find Mum doing the washing up, iridescent soap bubbles clinging to her hair. I come up behind her and put my arms around her and at first, she stiffens at my foreign touch but then she smiles, leaning into me. In those moments I almost think I can forgive her for all the things she doesn't say.

On Sunday night I dream.

But it's not like the other dreams. He's there with me, his hand on mine, and it's like he's followed me there, into that world of darkness, and shone a way out. Last Monday, we were focusing on narrative art—how pictures can tell a story. He showed me a painting of Orpheus and Eurydice, by Carl Goos. Eurydice is looking at Orpheus, her body wreathed in shadows. She's falling backward, into a world of nightmares. But he's reaching out his hand—his body gold and good and strong—and he's going to save her. He won't stop until he does, you can see it in his face.

That's us, I thought, when he showed it to me.

"How does it make you feel?" he asked, and I kept my eyes on his hands when I answered. Strong hands, those little moons of color under his nails.

"Hopeful," I said, not daring to look up.

He chuckled, moved his hands away.

"You know she dies, right? He doesn't save her."

"Oh." I felt the blood rise to my cheeks. I looked at the painting again and couldn't believe I hadn't seen it: the backward lean, the fear in her eyes. She was falling out of his grasp, back into the underworld.

I lifted my chin.

"Whatever," I said. "I like my version better."

He laughed again, a proper laugh this time, rich and throaty, the wrinkles round his eyes creasing. I wanted to take the sound with me, to keep it with me always.

This morning when I woke up, the seed that had been growing inside me had burst. I was fluttering inside, made up of a million writhing things.

The day stretched on like a drought, moving sluggishly from English to history to lunch to math. Finally, the bell rang and my heart jolted, my palms cracking with sweat.

Today, the large table in the art room was bare when I came in, but for a sheaf of paper and a stack of charcoal. Every other time there has been some sort of clue as to what I'll be learning. Once, he had me draw a sheep's skull, practicing until I got the curves of bone and shadow just so.

He was standing at the window, gazing out at the quad. The last stragglers formed little clusters; two girls skipping, a bunch of guys kicking a battered football. A couple kissing against a brick wall, thinking they wouldn't be seen.

The light was silky on his face, making him look softer, younger. He's only in his midtwenties, I think, but in that moment, he could have been a little boy, staring out into a world he didn't understand. I wanted to put my hands on his face, ask him what he had lost and how. But then he turned and saw me, his body straightening and his mouth settling into adult lines again.

"Jess," he said, nodding at me. "Sit down. We're going to try something different today."

I sat at my usual stool, feeling clumsy and exposed in my school uniform. I had an undershirt on, as always, but the Flakes had crept down my wrist, licking at my palms. I put my hands flat on the table so that he'd only see the rough silver of my knuckles.

The blank paper in front of me was so intimidating that my mind emptied.

"I want you to close your eyes," he said, "and then draw whatever it is that you see."

It was him that I saw when I closed my eyes, the way he'd looked when I came into the room. The mystery and vulnerability of him.

But when I pushed the image of him away, *she* was there, waiting.

She's always with me. Even when I'm awake. Like she's my own shadow, my own Eurydice.

I bent over the desk, pressing the charcoal hard onto the page so that my hand ached. She emerged in feathery black strokes. The grim set of her mouth, the gaunt cheeks. The thin lines of her wrists. Her eyes, empty in the darkness.

I'd never drawn her until today. I think I'd felt afraid to. As if giving her a physical form might conjure her into being, draw her out of the dream world and into this one. Those eyes staring into my soul, tethering me to her side.

But with Mr. Hennessey there, I felt brave.

By the time I'd finished, my hands gleamed with charcoal, a mark I'd chosen for myself. I felt exhausted, but satisfied.

There she was on the page. Exactly as she is in my dreams. The dreams that have haunted me now, for months and months.

Mr. Hennessey got up from the other side of the table, putting down the stack of essays he'd been marking. As he walked around the table, I felt each of his footsteps in my body. Finally, he was standing behind me, his long shadow falling over the paper.

For a while he said nothing, and fear and excitement raced through my veins.

"I like it," he said at last. "Who is she?"

I paused for a moment, my mouth dry. I haven't told anyone where I go, when I close my eyes at night; where my dreams take me.

I have barely been able to bring myself to write about it here, in my diary. Like I was scared that doing so would make it real.

But it is happening, it is real. Ignoring it hasn't made it go away.

I used to have night terrors when I was little. Sometimes, I'd sleepwalk. Once, when I was in kindergarten, Mum found me in the bath with the taps at full blast, water spilling onto the tiles. My skin wasn't right for weeks afterward, hardened into a blue-gray crust. It was so bad that I couldn't go to school.

As I got older, the sleepwalking stopped, and the night terrors faded.

But now they're back, and they're much, much worse. Now, I dream I'm someone else; wake to find myself wading into the dam, dark water rippling all around me, my skin shrinking and cracking. A little further out, a little deeper, each time. I thought about asking Dad to put a lock on my bedroom door, but then he'd just ask questions. Instead, I've been tying my wrist to my headboard with an old dressing-gown cord. In the morning, my skin is a raw, shiny pink as if I've been struggling, as if the water has been calling me.

But that's impossible, isn't it?

I could feel Mr. Hennessey's breath, warm on the back of my neck. I didn't want him to move away and was afraid that if I told him this truth about me, this wrongness, that he would. That all of it—the companionable scratch of his pen on paper, the way he hums to himself sometimes under his breath, the new ease with which we greet each other—would end.

Then I'd lose it, the tiny seed of hope that drives me through the days and sees me through the nights. For a moment, my throat closed, and I thought that I wouldn't be able to get the words out, anyway.

But it was the way he looked at me. Like he really wanted to know something about *me*.

"I think her name's Eliza," I said slowly, my tongue fumbling the words. "I—I dream about her. She's on a ship, a convict ship, with her sister—in the dream *I'm* her sister, I think, but it's Eliza that I can see. I dream that the ship is sinking. The water's rushing in, and it's so cold that it's like it's cutting my skin open. The other women around us are screaming, crying. Some of them are singing . . ."

My voice thickened with tears and I stopped, horrified.

He didn't say anything at first, just let me recover. I wiped my eyes and they burned with charcoal dust.

"The surrealists believed that our dreams could help us find our true creative selves," he said. I felt the hairs on the nape of my neck move in time with his breath. "Maybe you should make more art about these dreams, these nightmares. It might feel . . . cathartic."

I nodded. "Like an exorcism?"

"Yes," he said, and though I didn't turn around to look at him, I heard the smile in his voice. "Exactly like that."

I wondered if he'd ever had a nightmare he'd needed to exorcise. I was going to ask, but then I felt his gaze on my hand like heat, and when I heard his mouth open I knew what was coming next.

"I've been meaning to say—your skin . . ."

I scrunched my hand into a fist, hot shame spreading through me.

I've lost track of the number of teachers who've asked me about my skin. Who've made appointments with the school nurse, phoned Mum and Dad, sent letters home. They leave it alone eventually, once they realize the truth. That it can't be cured, only managed.

But I still hate that that's what they see when they look at me. Something that needs to be fixed.

"Sorry," he said. "It's just—I find it so interesting. Do you ever feel that impulse—when you see something that you want to paint, to capture?"

I thought of how he'd looked when I came into the art room. My heart squeezed.

"It reminds me of something, the color." He put his hand on the table, his fingers edging closer to my curled fist. He traced my knuckles with his index finger and then spoke so softly I had to strain to hear him. "That pinkish blue, the way it looks silver in the light. It's like the inside of a shell."

But the inside of a shell is beautiful, I wanted to say.

Does he—he can't possibly—think I'm beautiful?

We stayed like that for a moment, his finger resting on my knuckles. My heart was hammering so hard it was like a wild animal in my chest.

Then he cleared his throat, moved his hand away.

"What happens to her—this Eliza—in your dream?" he asked.

I kept my hand still on the table. Maybe if I stayed still long enough he'd touch me again.

"Oh," I said, reluctant to be pulled back into that world of slimy darkness, of hissing waves. "I don't really know. I normally wake up before the ship sinks completely."

I didn't tell him the truth.

That each time I have the dream, I wake up later and later. I feel the water course down my throat, feel it curl around my limbs. Dragging me under. A brightness dazzling ahead.

That I'm worried that one day, my improvised restraint won't be able to hold me. That caught in the dream, I'll sleepwalk into the dam.

And I'll drown with them.

17

LUCY

FRIDAY, 15 FEBRUARY 2019

It is after midnight when Lucy finally puts down the diary.

She stands at the bedroom window, watching the silver play of the moonlight on the waves. The scene is beautiful, like one of Jess's paintings, and yet dread worms inside her. She can't get that image out of her head—her older sister, younger than she is now, holding hands with a grown man. Part of Lucy longs for it to be false; a story that the teenage Jess—flush with hormones and infatuation—has told herself. But she knows it's true, feels it within her bones.

For most of her life, Jess has been a riddle to her, and now that the answer is here, in these very pages, Lucy can't bear to read on. Perhaps it would be better to close the diary for good, to put it back inside the eaves and out of sight. To throw it into the sea. Then she won't have to know, she won't have to read about what this man did to her sister.

And anyway, how would Jess feel if she knew that Lucy was reading her teenage diary? Guilt shifts inside her stomach. She would be furious, Lucy knows, at such an intrusion.

What will Jess say, if she finds out what Lucy has done? She doesn't have the words for it: the desperation to feel close to her sister, the longing to peer inside her mind as if she, Lucy, will find herself reflected there.

Sighing, she opens WhatsApp on her phone, returns to her conversation with Ben. She can't help but think about him, after reading what Jess has written about Hennessey. Her sister's words hum with the exquisite torture of first love. Lucy herself felt that way, not so very long ago.

Had Ben known, she wonders now, the strength of her feelings for him? Had her desire been as obvious in her text messages as it is in Jess's diary, burning bright in every word?

Had he ever felt the same?

She decides that it doesn't matter. He never deserved her in the first place.

She's scrolled up far enough in the WhatsApp thread to reach the picture she sent. A woman in a dark room, light falling across her vulnerable, open body. Her eyes wide, almost pleading. A woman she no longer recognizes.

She inhales, steeling herself, and deletes the conversation.

Lucy sits on the sand dunes at Devil's Beach. It's a little after eight in the morning; the sun on the waves is an apocalyptic red.

The email arrived an hour earlier, the notification waking her from a fitful sleep. Since then, Lucy has read it at least twenty times. It's as if she has fallen through a trapdoor into someone else's life.

Now, she murmurs the words aloud, as if doing so might make them feel real.

On Monday, 11 February 2019, the University received a complaint that you entered the accommodation of a fellow student without permission and assaulted him (the Complaint). Following the Complaint, the University attempted to contact you on several occasions but did not receive a response. Accordingly, pursuant to the Student Conduct Rules, you have been suspended from the University for a period of two (2) weeks while an investigation into the Complaint is conducted. You are not per-

mitted to attend campus or access the University's online facilities during this time. Should you wish to appeal the suspension, you may do so according to the procedure enclosed . . .

Her pulse slows to a surreal thud, the sound of it filling her ears. Suspension, with expulsion likely to follow.

She tries to summon details of her life at Hamilton Hume, the life she's worked so hard for and which now seems in jeopardy. She's dreaded this moment even as she has, in some ways, hastened its arrival. All those calls from the student welfare office, all those voice-mails. She never answered, she never phoned back; too seized by inertia to even attempt to defend herself.

But really, what could she have said? There is no question that she attacked Ben. There will be CCTV footage of her opening his door; there will be the testimony of Nick, who heard Ben cry out and saw Lucy leave his room.

Not to mention the fact that she had fled.

She opens the second attachment: the appeals procedure. Requirements and deadlines wash over her. She could, she supposes, see a doctor; try and get a diagnosis for her sleepwalking condition. Perhaps with a medical report, she could demonstrate that she'd had no control over her actions, that she hadn't *intended* to hurt Ben.

But hadn't she?

The more she thinks about it, the more she feels that something subliminal had directed her to his room that night. She had known, after the meeting with the student counselor, that he'd face no consequence for what he did to her. She knew that he would hide behind his wealthy background and his lawyer father.

And perhaps something inside her had cracked. All her life, she'd taken for granted that doing the right thing—being conscientious and kind and considerate—would be rewarded; that official procedures and processes could be relied upon. That there would always be a number to call, a person to report to, an answer to every question. That facts would always, inevitably, prevail.

But she'd been wrong. When she sought help through the proper channels, the *procedures*, no one gave her a gold star or thanked her for asking nicely. Instead, they wanted her to keep being nice, to put Ben's feelings—*his* reputation, *his* future—above her own. They wanted her to go away.

Though she'd been sleepwalking that night, in a way, she'd also woken to some essential truth. For the first time, she'd experienced the world and its injustice; the way the cards are stacked against her, just because she's female. (She doubted anyone had implored Ben to think of *her* future.)

With this awakening, there'd been something else, too. A new awareness of her power. Freed from her prior inhibitions—from the compulsion to be nice, to be a good girl—she'd become something she could never have imagined being. She'd become . . . dangerous.

Suspension. In some ways, it is a strange relief. There is no more waiting, no more uncertainty. Here is her fate. Something loosens inside her, and with it there's the realization that she doesn't miss Hamilton Hume the way she thought she would.

She doesn't miss the claustrophobic press of her neat dorm room, she doesn't miss the jostle of bodies in the university bar, the male students with their misplaced confidence. She's not even sure that she misses Em, especially after the last conversation they had.

It's not like he actually put it on TikTok himself . . . maybe you two can find a way back from this.

The only thing that had mattered—that now fills her with longing—was the work. That's what she has missed over the last week: the satisfying yield of the keyboard under her fingers as she constructs precise, careful sentences; the throb of excitement as a story takes shape.

But if her time in Comber Bay has taught her anything, it's that she never needed university to hone her journalistic instincts. They've been there all along, driving her forward.

She considers the existential doubt that has plagued her since fleeing university. Her fear that her life's ambition—to uncover the truth, through careful reporting—is naïve; a fool's errand.

And yes, sometimes, people look away from inconvenient facts—just like the student welfare officer did when Lucy told her what happened with Ben. Most people just want an easy life. It's unsettling when someone starts pulling apart the stories we've stitched together, the things we tell ourselves for comfort.

As a mother of a son myself . . .

The counselor hadn't wanted to accept what Ben had done to Lucy, or the idea that countless other young men—even, perhaps, her own son—might be capable of doing the same thing. It was too distasteful, too frightening, and so she'd turned away from it.

But just because other people are frightened of the truth doesn't mean that Lucy has to be. She can choose to be brave.

Lucy stares out at the horizon, at the billows of sand that give way to slick gold near the water's edge. The mud-colored seaweed, strewn with gleaming bluebottle jellyfish. Today is overcast and the water is gray beneath the blind white sky. Muscular waves shimmer and roll toward her, kicking foam skyward.

When she'd arrived three days ago, and first seen the familiar image on her sister's canvas—the two girls, the *Naiad* with its mermaid figurehead—it had been easier to dismiss it all as a coincidence. To doubt her own memory, her own senses. Perhaps she'd known of the *Naiad* already, perhaps her sister *had* told her about her latest project, on that last, brittle Christmas visit?

But there's no denying it now she's read Jess's diary and seen the ghosts of her own mind captured in her sister's handwriting, twenty years ago.

I think her name's Eliza. I dream about her.

Lucy doesn't know where Jess is, or why she was drawn to this town, with its drowned women and disappeared men. She doesn't know why they share such disturbing dreams or why they're lured to water in their sleep.

But there's that taste on her tongue, chemical-sweet: the heady rush of mystery, of a puzzle to solve.

She knows how to do this. How to investigate a story, how to pull together disparate threads and find the truth. And no one—not Ben, not Hamilton Hume—can take that away from her.

Besides, until Jess returns, it's all she can do.

Possible explanations for Jess and I having the same dreams, she writes, then underlines.

One: Folie à deux, i.e., a shared delusion. Seems unlikely as two people need to be physically together to participate in the delusion.

Two: Genetic memory. Again, seems unlikely as not scientifically proven. Speak to Mum and Dad about convict ancestors?

She frowns at the last sentence. She'd read a Wikipedia article about genetic memory—a traumatic memory that somehow becomes embedded in the human genome, passing through the generations like a disease. But the theory is controversial, and in any case, it would presuppose that someone survived the shipwreck.

She stares past the breakers to where the rocks jut out from the gray sea, hunched like human figures. She imagines the *Naiad* splintering on those rocks. Two girls, one blind, dragging themselves to shore, feet raw with cuts, hair in great wet ropes down their backs.

She looks to her left, to the cliff that juts into the sky. Devil's Lookout, its cratered face turned to the waves. How many lives has it watched slip away, over the years?

The prisoners of the *Naiad*; the eight missing men; even, perhaps, Baby Hope's mother . . .

It's as if there really is something devilish at work here.

The need to understand, to find her own place in the puzzle of Comber Bay, burns inside her. It's all she has.

Lucy stands, giddy with purpose. She knows where to go, where to begin her search for the link; for the thread that will unravel the knot of this place.

But first, she kicks off her shoes so that she can feel the sand beneath her feet. She sidesteps gleaming lobes of shell, tangled cauls of seaweed. She can feel the moisture working its way into her skin, changing her, but something pulls her forward, prevents her from turning back.

The waves drape themselves like lace over the sand, and she's so close that she can feel tiny droplets of spray landing on her skin.

Lucy closes her eyes, savoring the sensation. Somewhere, a seagull cries. All the while, the ocean pulses steadily against the shore.

Who else has stood here, in her place?

For a moment, she's certain that if she reaches out a hand, she'll find someone standing next to her. The girl with the unseeing eyes. Eliza.

Deirfiúr.

Sister.

She opens her eyes and finds she is alone. But the feeling remains.

Lucy climbs down from the bus, grimacing at the smells of petrol fumes and old rubbish. The depot at Sydney's central station has seen better days: the signs are vivid with graffiti and she can feel a wad of chewing gum sticking to her shoe. It's 3 P.M.—not trusting herself to drive, she'd caught a morning bus from Batemans Bay and, six hours later, heat has settled like a thick cloud over the city.

She hasn't been to Sydney since she visited Jess in 2017. Walking down George Street, she passes bookshops they'd browsed in, a gelato place where Jess had bought them ice cream. They'd grinned, realizing they shared the same favorite flavor—pistachio.

Where had it all gone wrong?

Blinking the memories away, she lets herself be propelled forward by the crowd of office workers, students, and tourists, swept along in a current of sneakers and tote bags. After the quiet of Comber Bay, the city seems to blare with noise and color: cars screaming past, the tick-tick-tick of the traffic signals, even the distant caw of the seagulls set her pulse rising. She feels a brief burst of longing for Dawes Plain, for the open sky. The city makes her feel both exposed and claustrophobic.

She adjusts her backpack, wincing with each step. It's been hours since she stood on Devil's Beach, but she can still feel the sting of saltwater on her toes.

The State Library of NSW rises in front of her, a sandstone behemoth. With its sweeping entrance and ionic columns, it brings to mind an ancient temple, erected to honor the gods. Inside the foyer, the atmosphere is suitably reverent. The spines of countless books glimmer from the shelves, catching the sun that pours in from the skylight. She breathes in the smell of dust and old paper, draws strength from it.

She walks across to the registration desk, wincing as her trainers squeak on the tiled floor. The tables are filled with students and professionals, tapping fluidly at their shining laptops. One woman in particular draws her eye—her hair is short and blonde, like Lucy's own, but cut into an elegant pixie style. She wears headphones and a lanyard around her neck. Lucy fancies that she's a reporter, transcribing an interview with a source.

The man at the registration desk gives Lucy a visitor's pass and directs her to the microfilm collection in the Governor Marie Bashir Reading Room. Once she's settled at the computer, the library's archive of digitized newspapers on her screen, she takes a breath and opens her notebook, double-checks the names and dates.

1960—SAMUEL HALL, PRIEST, 65
1966—PETE LAWSON, VETERAN, 28
1973—BOB RUDDOCK, TRADESMAN, 44
1977—WILLIAM GOLDHILL, CHEF, 54
1981—DANIEL SMITH, UNEMPLOYED, 21
1986—ALEX THORGOOD, TEACHER, 34
1990—DAVID WATTS, SOLICITOR, 39
1997—MALCOLM BIDDY, UNEMPLOYED, 37

There they are, the Eight.

They represent a range of ages and occupations, and while she knows from the podcast that some of the men—Ruddock, Lawson, Smith, and Goldhill—were local to the area, the rest were visiting from out of town. Thorgood was from Melbourne, on holiday with his sister after the loss of his wife and child in a house fire earlier in the year. Biddy was an unemployed itinerant traveling around Australia. Watts was a Sydney-based barrister, visiting the area with a view to purchasing a holiday home.

She thinks of Bernard Smith's frenzied diagram, the mess of names and arrows. No wonder he hadn't been able to find a link between the men. They're missing, and they're male—that's it, as far as Lucy can see.

She decides to start with the most recent disappearance, in 1997. Malcolm Biddy, thirty-seven, unemployed. She plugs his name and the year into the search bar.

An article from the *South Coast Examiner* dated 5 October 1997 announces his disappearance. He was last sighted in the early hours of the morning, it says, walking along Bay Road, in the direction of the shore, a kilometer from where his campervan was parked. But there's scant information about Biddy himself, beyond what she's already learned from the podcast. *Mr. Biddy*, the article reads, *of no fixed address, had arrived in the area only weeks before. Locals describe him as a "quiet but friendly" man who kept to himself.*

Lucy clicks out of the article and navigates to the next result, from the *Sydney Morning Herald*, dated January of the following year.

INVESTIGATION LAUNCHED AFTER GRISLY DISCOVERY IN MISSING MAN'S CAMPERVAN

NSW police were called to Batemans Bay Depot last week after a Eurobodalla Shire council worker reported finding suspicious materials in the vehicle of Malcolm Biddy, 37, who has been missing for three months. Mr. Biddy's vehicle, a yellow and white Dodge A100, was towed from Bay Road, Comber Bay, on Friday. A spokesman for the council says that a letter was sent to Mr. Biddy's sister, the vehicle's registered owner, but when no reply was received the van was removed.

A worker then phoned police after noticing weapons, including a rifle which the Herald *understands to be unlicensed, in the van's backseat. A police spokesman said yesterday that an investigation has been launched after a search of the vehicle unearthed further unlicensed firearms, as well as material depicting child sexual abuse. The spokesman refused to comment on whether the material might be linked to Operation Fern, revealed yesterday when Australian Federal Police announced that 10 arrests had been made in relation to an alleged nationwide pedophile ring.*

Mr. Biddy has not been seen since 5 October last year, when he was sighted walking in the direction of Devil's Beach in the early hours of the morning. Police have said that they are keeping an open mind as to the circumstances surrounding Mr. Biddy's disappearance. They did not comment on whether Mr. Biddy's case is thought to be connected to other disappearances in the area, including David Watts in 1990 and Alex Thorgood in 1986. Police have asked that anyone with information about Mr. Biddy's whereabouts contact Crime Stoppers at 1-800-333-000.

Lucy feels the creep of disgust at the horrifying words. *Material depicting child sexual abuse. Pedophile ring.* The picture of Malcolm Biddy accompanying the article is small and blurred, but she makes out long tangled hair, a grimy bandana. He looks hippy-ish, benign, which makes his alleged crimes somehow worse.

But it feels like a starting point. Is *this* what links the Eight? Had someone decided that the world would be a better place—a safer place—without them? Like any true crime devotee worth her stripes, she's familiar with vigilante killers. The most famous is Pedro Rodrigues Filho, who was apparently the inspiration for *Dexter.* Maybe someone has been doing something similar in Comber Bay all these years, luring his victims to the shore before disposing of them, the sea providing the perfect cover . . .

But she's getting ahead of herself. She has no evidence that any of the remaining seven—she thinks of Ryan Smith's brother Daniel with a twist of guilt—were involved in criminal activity.

She needs to be cautious, meticulous; careful to eliminate confirmation bias.

Next, she searches for David Watts, the solicitor. There's an effusive obituary from a trade publication called *The Lawyer*. There's also a hit from *The Australian* from 1989, but when she opens it she sees it's not an article at all, but a correction. Had the paper printed something that David Watts—a successful lawyer—hadn't liked?

Lucy's pulse climbs as she begins to read.

The Australian published an article on 7 August 1988 about solicitor David Watts and the death of his girlfriend Christine Cara that year. In it, we made several accusations about his character. We spoke to people we now accept were not informed about the case and failed to include evidence that Mr. Watts was not involved in Ms. Cara's death and that it was likely a suicide. We accept we failed to properly inform Mr. Watts of what the article contained and as such denied him a proper right of reply to its contents. The Australian accepts the story was rooted in inaccurate statements, given by third parties who had reason to target Mr. Watts with misinformation. We apologize wholeheartedly to Mr. Watts, undertake to never repeat the allegations, and have agreed to pay him damages.

Christine Cara. She knows that name. A quick Google search refreshes her memory: the doe-eyed model with coiffed hair and slender good looks. The daughter of Italian immigrants, she'd taken up modeling to put herself through nursing school. She'd just become the face of David Jones, Australia's premier department store, when she died after falling from the balcony of her high-rise Bondi apartment in 1988. Her boyfriend, Sydney lawyer David Watts, was the only witness to her fall.

The same David Watts who disappeared at Comber Bay two years later.

Cara's eyes—wide black orbs—stare out at Lucy from the computer screen. At the inquest into her death, Watts had given evidence that she was unstable, a drinker. That he'd wanted to end their relationship, and that she'd responded with a threat to take her own life. It hadn't mattered that Cara's Catholic parents had sworn that she would never commit suicide; that it was against their religion. Allegations that she may have been pushed were never substantiated and never pursued. The coroner's ruling had been suicide.

She rereads David Watts's obituary in *The Lawyer*.

David had struggled with his mental health in recent years, following a tragic personal loss.

Out of eight missing men, that's two—so far—who are connected to alleged criminal acts. Specifically to violence against women and children.

She checks her notes from episode one of the podcast. Watts had purchased a six-pack of beer and fishing bait from the general store at dusk. He'd told the owner he was going to fish from the rocks at the base of Devil's Lookout. The owner had warned him not to fish alone at dusk; Watts had said he was meeting someone, but Lucy can't find any details of who that might have been.

She thinks again of the twisting stone steps at the back of Cliff House, of the network of caves that form Devil's Lookout. Even though she's miles from Comber Bay, surrounded by the whirr of computer monitors and the clack of keyboards in the State Library, her skin tightens, as if brushed by sea air.

After finding little on the other missing men—though the South Australian priest, Samuel Hall, had at one stage worked at a church which faced abuse allegations thirty years later—Lucy turns the page of her notebook.

There's a heaviness in the pit of her stomach, a reluctance.

It has been invigorating, somehow, to read about the disappearances; to comb through old newspaper articles and draw connections between them. Her brain has felt sharp and clear, doing what it does best.

Immersed in research, she'd forgotten about the dreams. Forgotten that someone else's memories, their fears and thoughts and hopes, seem to have become entangled with her own. The Eight—they're only half of the puzzling whole, the first part of the riddle.

She shivers, remembering the words from Jess's journal.

In the dream I'm her sister, I think, but it's Eliza that I can see. I dream that the ship is sinking . . . women around us are screaming, crying. Some of them are singing . . .

Lucy places the *Sydney Gazette 1800–1820* microfilm into the reader.

She squints into the lens as she scrolls through issues of the *Gazette*. She knows that the *Naiad* sank in 1801 but doesn't have an exact date. Her eyes begin to water as the cramped print blurs past. She scans for mentions of the South Coast area, but so far there's just a report of a drowning near Batemans Bay in 1816, a suspected shark attack in 1811. The words *ship* and *fleet* jump out at her, but she zooms in only to find reports of the progress of Lord Nelson's fleet in the Mediterranean. Nothing about a local shipwreck.

And then. Monday, 5 May 1801.

Calamitous shipwreck.

She scrolls down to read the article, the blood throbbing in her ears.

It is our melancholy duty to report the loss of the female prison ship NAIAD, wrecked off the coast of New South Wales on or about 11 April 1801, with the estimated loss of over 100 lives.

The NAIAD departed the Cove of Cork in October last year, bound for Sydney, carrying 83 female convicts and 22 crew. She was commanded by Capt. R. Barker, who had prior sailed the barques **ANDROMEDA** and **RELIANCE**, also from Cork, to New South Wales with no incident, though it is to be noted that a good number of the convicts perished on the latter journey.

At about 3 o'clock in the morning on 11 April, a ship was sighted a mile out to sea, impaled on the reef and sinking rapidly. Later that morning, a native woman discovered five bodies washed to shore.

Since the tragedy, some twenty bodies—the majority of the male crew—have been recovered ashore and interred at the settlement in Batemans Bay. A search is underway for survivors, after several women were sighted in the vicinity the vessel was last seen.

She reads the next edition and the next, but Lucy can't find any further mention of the shipwreck, or whether any female survivors were ever located.

But it could be a possibility. An answer.

She kneads her temples, as if to untangle the mess of her thoughts. To separate fact from conjecture and fantasy. She thinks of the mermaid figurehead that she's seen through Mary's eyes; the same figurehead in the etchings of the *Naiad*.

She traces a circle on the back of one hand. She has *felt* Eliza's fingers in hers, the damp heat of her skin. Mary's memories have become her own: the rich gold smell of farls cooking above the hearth fire, the bite of wet rock against her cheek.

Lucy runs her fingers through the bristles of her hair. She studies her hand on the computer mouse, the knuckles with their silvered streaks.

There is no logic to this, no reason. The potential explanations she's written so carefully on the lined paper of her notebook stare up at her, mocking.

Her palm on the mouse is sweating. She looks about her: the desks closest to hers are empty, reality receding. As if other people sense her, an interloper in time. The glare of the overhead lights, the humming machines, even the books stacked silently on their shelves: all of it feels as temporary as mist.

She scrolls through the subscription resources on the library intranet until she finds the one she's looking for, the Convict Record Database. She navigates to 1800 and scans the names of the ships that left for NSW that year. The *William Pitt*, the *Tellicherry*.

There it is, the *Naiad*. She finds the list of passengers.

Jane Adams
Margaret Black
Elizabeth Dean
Catherine Fitzpatrick
Bridget Foley
Sarah Hagarty
Anne Hagarty

Her pulse thuds as the names roll past.

Eliza Kissane
Mary Kissane

There they are, as inevitable as the next beat of her heart.
They are real.
The edges of her vision flicker, and she is aware of her body growing soft and jellied, then the juddering impact of the floor.

18

MARY

Mary had been asleep—or in the strange place between sleep and wakefulness—when a new sound woke her, joining the groan of timber, the cries and murmurs of the women. The heavy tread of a sailor, cursing as he encountered the stench of the prison deck, the yeast and blood and sweat. A female smell. Mary liked to imagine it as a sort of force, a power in and of itself. A protective circle.

But now she heard clinking and rustling as women cringed away from the sailor's path. The oily glare from his lamp lit up wan faces and furious eyes.

Only Bridie seemed to welcome their visitor. She leaned over her berth to him, her pale body unfurling in the dark. The sailor put out his hand and helped her down, her curls glinting like flames.

When the bulkhead gate shut behind them, the silence that had fallen lifted.

"Whore," said Sarah, the word sharp as a blade.

"Fool, more like," Aoife murmured.

Mary said nothing. She could hear Eliza chewing her hair, and she wished suddenly for the return of the sailor's lamp, so that she could see her sister's face. So that she would no longer be alone with her memories, a child left in a forest.

———

Samhain. The night their lives changed forever. Bonfires burned in the darkness, heralding the coming of winter, warding off the spirits that watched from the Otherworld. The air was thick with *poitín* and smoke; men cradled fiddles as if they were babes, plucking cries from their throats.

Da had told them to stay inside the cottage. They were to eat the stew that hung in the pot over the hearth, to block their ears to the sounds of merriment. He gave Eliza his rosary for safekeeping, the corners of her mouth lifting as she clicked the beads through her fingers. Together they made a den of their blankets, like animals in a burrow; eating the stew straight from the pot.

"Leave it," Eliza had said, when Mary brought her candlestick under the blankets, frowning at the lick of heat on her face. "You don't need that."

And so Mary had joined her sister in the darkness. Eliza asked if Mary wanted a story, and Mary squeezed her hand to say yes.

"In Kerry, where the sea creeps up the shore, there once lived a merrow," Eliza began. "She had a tail the silver of fish scales, and hair the ruby red of dulse weed. Her voice was the sweetest thing anyone ever heard. One morning, she saw a fisherman—a handsome fisherman, with his own sweet voice—and the two fell in love. He made her his wife and—"

"Stop," Mary said.

"But don't you remember it? The story Mam told us, before Da took us away."

"She never told any story," Mary said. "You have heard it somewhere else, you have invented it."

She hated it, the way that Eliza clung to the memory of Mam. What good did it do Eliza to long for her so? She was never coming back.

The older she got, the angrier she was at Mam, for leaving them so carelessly. What had been in her mind, the day she went down to the shore and took off her cloak, throwing herself on the sea's mercy? Had she not thought of Mary and Eliza, and how much they needed her?

Da had told her it was a blessing that Mam hadn't taken Mary and Eliza with her that day, for then all three of them might be lost. Da had also told them that they must try not to think of the shore at Ard na Caithne, of the white waves on the sand, the sea that tingled on their skin. They must try not to remember the way their mother had endangered them.

And so Mam had become only an absence, a scar on her heart. Mam was not warm arms holding her close, or the sweetness of a lullaby. She was the cold space by the hearth, the ache of watching the village women hug their children tight. She was Da, hunched on the shore, turning the cloak over and over in his hands.

But Eliza kept going with her story.

"The merrow and the fisherman loved each other so much that they made two children, twin girls—"

Mary could not bear it. Anger burned fierce in her belly, as bright as the bonfire flames outside.

"Why do you do this—talk about her as if she were some magic thing? She didn't care about us, Eliza. She let the sea take her away."

Eliza fell silent. She turned her head, as though in anticipation of a blow.

"She might have come back," she said softly. "If we had waited. Da should not have brought us to Armagh. We don't belong here, so far inland."

"Come back? Eliza, she is dead," Mary said, standing so suddenly that the den of blankets collapsed around them.

"What if she is not?" Eliza pressed. "What if we were wrong? Perhaps she did not drown, perhaps she went to the *tír fo thuinn* . . ."

Mary coiled her hands into fists, the nails cutting into her palms.

"Just because you cannot see what is in front of you," Mary said, "does not mean that you see things others cannot. It does not make you special. Only broken."

The words fell heavy between them, and at once, Mary wished she could take them back.

"Eliza . . ."

There was the rustling of blankets. Eliza stood, and before Mary could react, darted toward the door and out into the night.

Mary followed her to the stream, her voice hoarse from calling her sister's name. Twigs snapped loudly beneath her boots, her breath misting in the autumn air. In the distance, a bonfire glowed, split into two watching eyes by Mary's tears. As she ran deeper into the woods, the sounds of Samhain—the fiddles and the shouts and the songs—faded, until there was only her own breath coming loud and ragged in her ears, her own desperate voice calling for Eliza.

She should never have said those things to her sister. She should never have driven her away, into the threat of the Samhain night.

By the time she reached the stream, Mary saw that Eliza had broken her promise not to touch the water: she had waded in so deep that it rose to her waist. Mary's breath caught. It was so cold—cold even for autumn—and the reeds that curled from the banks were sugared with frost.

Mary struggled out of her boots, lifted her shawl over her head. She did not think of the night air and how it needled her skin, nor the stinging bite of the stream. She thought only of Eliza.

She waded into the center of the stream, her frenzied movements sending white plumes into the air. The water pulled at her with hands that were icy but gentle, and something sparked inside her, something still and buried curled suddenly into life. Her arms, silver with bubbles, sliced through the water. A figure swam ahead, dark hair moving as if in a breeze. And in that moment, Mary felt herself slipping, felt the temptation to give herself over to feeling, to memory. To Mam.

Somewhere, an owl hooted, bringing her back to herself.

"Eliza!" she called. "Eliza!"

But it was as if her sister could not hear her, as if she had passed to some other plane, some other world. As if she had been lured to the water by some spirit or ghost, or perhaps even by an *each-uisce*, the shapeshifter from Da's stories.

She caught Eliza around the waist, her sister struggling in her grasp. One pale fist struck Mary in the cheek.

But Mary was the stronger sister—had always been the stronger sister. She dragged Eliza to the rock in the middle of the stream and pushed the wet tangles of hair from her face.

"What were you doing?" she hissed, fear turning to anger in her veins. The skin between her toes and fingers burned. She needed to get Eliza home, to get her away from the water and into the dry of the cottage. Her heart pounded at the thought of Da, if he learned what they had done.

"I was looking for it," Eliza said. "For the *tír fo thuinn*. The land beneath the waves."

As if she might find Mam there, like the merrow from her childish story.

Pain bloomed in Mary's heart, and she traced the glittering drops of water that clung to her sister's cheek. So many times, Mary had thought Eliza the wiser sister: the one who could read anger in silence, sorrow in a sigh. But in that moment, she seemed so innocent, naïve to death and its meaning.

The girl who sings but does not see.

It reminded Mary of her duty, as the first-born twin. To protect her sister, to guide her.

"I'm sorry for what I said," she whispered. "I didn't mean it."

"I know," Eliza said. "I know you didn't. And I know it isn't true."

But then, her features tightened, like the string of a fiddle.

"Hush," she said. "Someone is there."

Byrne, moving through the reeds toward them.

When the bulkhead gate scraped open again and the sailor Wright brought Bridie back inside, the women fell silent. Once the footsteps had sounded away and the light from the oil lamps had faded, the murmurs swelled.

Next to her, Eliza cringed in disgust.

"It's all right," Mary whispered. "He's gone."

"But he isn't," said Eliza. "I can smell him on her."

Mary caught it too, a new note among the female musk. Something sour-sweet, like old milk. A male smell.

She heard the berth above creak as Aoife angled her body away from Bridie's. "Don't touch me," she spat. "I won't share a bed with a *Sasanach* whore."

"What did you call me?" Bridie said, her voice low and dangerous.

"She called you whore," Sarah said from the berth across. "And she's right with it. Haven't we given the English enough? Our land, our men. They would even take our God from us. And now you'd give your virtue, too?"

There was a rustling then, the impatient sound of Bridie clucking her tongue.

"It's not my virtue I'm concerned with," she said. "But my belly. Would you not take it yourself, if it was offered? Extra meat for your *leanbh*?"

Sarah said nothing.

"I can smell food, Mammy," her child murmured. "I'm so hungry."

"Take it," Bridie said now. "For your girl."

There was the smell of biscuit then: the meaty brine of salt pork. The berth creaked as Bridie reached out to Sarah.

"I—"

"I won't be offering twice."

"I don't know how to thank you."

"Just see that your girl gets there alive."

Mary curled up tight, trying to banish the sound of little Annie's jaws moving. Her own stomach writhed with hunger.

And there was something else: something that struck fear deep in her belly, Da's warnings echoing inside her. A new pain in her toes, on the soles of the feet, where the bilge water had lapped at her, as if the skin was lifting and peeling away. She remembered the time as a child when she had plunged her hand into water and watched it turn white, the way the stream had burned on her skin.

Da had tried so hard to protect them from the water, from the sea that had taken Mam away.

And now they were at its mercy.

19

LUCY

FRIDAY, 15 FEBRUARY 2019

A hand on her shoulder, milk-sour breath on her face.

Lucy flinches, her body jerking backward. She gropes behind her, reaching into the stream for a rock, something that she can use as a weapon.

But her fingers brush carpet, then the cool of a tiled floor.

She opens her eyes to find a man—young, with a lanyard and round, rimless glasses—staring down at her. Sun pours through a sky-light, gilding his ears and nose.

The space comes into focus. The rows of desks, the book-lined walls. The humming computers. There's a pause in the air, as if the room has taken a collective breath. Heads crane over screens, around shelves. A dozen pairs of eyes are trained on her.

"Take it easy," says the man, his hand tight on her shoulder. "My colleague's calling an ambulance now."

"Ambulance?" For a moment the word feels foreign in her mouth; she has to dredge up its meaning. Then, a hot surge of shame in her cheeks. "No, please—I'm fine, really."

She shifts away from his hand, climbs giddily to her feet. The light is so blinding in the room, she doesn't understand how anyone can bear it. She grips the computer desk for support, nudging the mouse so that the screen flickers into life. The *Naiad*'s passenger manifest is still open on her screen.

Eliza Kissane.

Mary Kissane.

"Really, I have to insist," the man is saying. "You collapsed—I saw it myself. It's a health and safety issue, we have a duty of care . . ."

"I'm fine," she says, her pulse fizzing. She shuts down the computer, shoves her notebook into her bag and slings it onto her shoulder. "Forgot to eat lunch. I'll get a sandwich from somewhere."

"Look, could you just—"

"Thanks for your help," she says, pushing past him. She stumbles into a run, her sneakers slapping against the marble floors, dozens of eyes on her but she doesn't care. She passes the reception desk, the metal detectors, and bursts out of the foyer and into the bright heat of the day.

She cringes away from the sun, her breathing ragged. Her backpack knocks painfully against her spine. It is after 5 P.M., she realizes vaguely. She hasn't eaten since that morning, but the thought of food brings only nausea.

Their names loop through her mind, a sick mantra.

Eliza Kissane. Mary Kissane.

She is walking back down George Street; a tram shudders past. Shopfronts blare. Her legs are moving almost of their own accord, and it's not until she sees the concrete sweep of the railway line that she realizes where she's headed.

She passes Circular Quay station with its tourists and ice-cream vendors, its prowling seagulls. At the railings, she leans her elbows on the rusted iron. A ferry horn blasts, water lapping at the yellow-and-green boat. On her right, the white sails of the Opera House; on her left, the elegant curve of the bridge.

But Lucy doesn't see any of this.

Instead, she stares into the water, the shifting mirror of it. The light sparkles on its surface, belying its murky depths. A slick of rubbish, an ice-cream wrapper, a bloated chip, the flotsam and jetsam of modern life.

Lucy imagines broken pieces of history lodged in the harbor's seabed. The green glass of a rum bottle, a rusted length of chain. The cracked halves of oyster shells.

The present is nothing more than a tide, drawing away from her.

Could they have lived, Mary and Eliza? Did they survive the shipwreck, make their way somehow to Sydney Town, eke out a life on its newly cobbled streets? Did they change their names, leave their origins behind in the *Naiad*'s rusting hulk? Or did they die there, their bones long dispersed into tiny grains of sand?

She takes a breath, sucking in the briny air. In a buried room of her mind, there is a recognition that the sea is calming her, is slowing the pound of her heart. The nearness of the water is a balm. Why is it that her body seeks out the thing that would hurt it?

Eliza and Mary must have lived, they must have survived. Mary, at the very least. Long enough to bear children, to pass her memories down the centuries with her genes, to fill Lucy's brain with ghosts.

But then she thinks of Jess's journal.

I'm worried that one day, I'll get caught in the dream. And I'll drown with them.

Had Jess seen an ending that Lucy has not yet reached?

The dreams—or memories—are beginning to slot together now, like beads on a necklace. She thinks of a rosary, the wooden beads worn to silk by many hands, the click of them through her fingers. But she has never held a rosary, has never said a Hail Mary in her life. This is not her memory.

Another ferry is departing; the horn blasts through Lucy's thoughts, pulls her back to Sydney Harbour, 2019. She lifts a hand to her neck. The skin there feels bruised, tender.

She checks her phone: 5:20 P.M. Her bus leaves in half an hour.

She doesn't know how any of it fits together. Jess. The missing men. Mary and Eliza.

But she now feels certain that the answer is in Comber Bay.

20

JESS'S DIARY

1999

1 January

Happy New Year, diary.

I'm writing this in Max's bedroom, while he sleeps next to me. It's 5 A.M., and his curtains are open a tiny crack, the sun catching his eyelashes. He looks so peaceful. Almost too peaceful. If it weren't for the slow rise and fall of his chest, the occasional dart of his eyes beneath their lids, he might be dead.

I envy him, being able to sleep like that.

I tried to draw him but I couldn't get it right—I couldn't capture the calm of him, the way he looked so peaceful in his body. I kept drawing his eyes open instead of closed, open and tunnel dark. His skin scaled, his fingers webbed. I realized then that I was drawing *her*.

It's like I'm infected. Possessed.

I do the thing Mr. Hennessey taught me, the last time I saw him before the summer holidays. We were having our final lesson for the year, and I felt as if a sinkhole was opening inside my chest. I was copying a Derain self-portrait, but really it was him—Hennessey—I wanted to capture. *Capture.* It's the perfect word, isn't it? You paint someone and it's like you own them, like you've taken their soul from their body and put it right there on the canvas.

I was thinking about the long stretch of days that lay ahead, days that would be hot and dust-filled, which would smell of wool and sound of all the things my parents wouldn't say. Eight long weeks until I saw Mr. Hennessey again.

My hand began to shake and sweat, smudging my palm blue.

I didn't think he'd notice—he often sits at his desk while I work, marking papers with one long leg folded over the other—but then his soft voice was breaking through my thoughts, asking me if I was OK.

I nodded, but I couldn't stop trembling. He got me a glass of water from the art room's clanking metal sink, and while I drank he put his hand on my shoulder, just for a moment. I was wearing a long-sleeved top under my school uniform, stiff and probably stinking of sweat, but I still felt an almost electric charge, as if his bare skin was touching mine. Then he took his hand away.

"I get panic attacks sometimes," he said. "They started when I was a kid. My dad . . . he wasn't the easiest man to live with. I saw a therapist for a while, and she taught me how to deal with them. Think about your body—from your toes to your fingertips—and focus on how it feels. Breathe in, then breathe out."

I try this now, sitting in Max's room.

I feel the cold floorboards beneath my toes, the itch of the rough skin on my shins and knees, my thighs and stomach. I press my lips together, feeling the tenderness, like a bruise. I breathe.

In, out.

What would Mr. Hennessey think, if he knew what I'd done?

Max and I always spend New Year's Eve at his place. When we were younger, his mum would let us stay up until midnight to watch the Sydney fireworks on TV. We'd drink so many cans of Coke and Sprite that we'd form a little pyramid out of them. Max used to call it the Eighth Wonder of the World.

I could hear the soft burble of the TV from the living room as I was getting ready—Mum and Dad were settling in to watch the coverage from Sydney Harbour—and I felt desperate, suddenly, to be safely at Max's and away from them.

The atmosphere had felt heavy since Christmas lunch. As if the things I'd said then had swelled and swelled until they sucked all the air from the house.

Something had broken in me that day. I'd looked around the table, at the turkey and ham and smoked salmon and so many brightly colored salads that it looked like we'd robbed a delicatessen. Far more food than three people could ever eat.

Mum had been in the kitchen for two days, and her cheeks were still pink from the stove, her skin still shining with sweat.

I don't understand what made me so angry. She had merely done something nice—something she enjoyed, not just for the sake of it, but for the pleasure she hoped it would give us.

I think it was this odd feeling I sometimes get with her—like when she calls me "sweetheart," or tells me I'm beautiful, or reaches out to brush my hair from my face—that the love she feels for me is somehow tinged with guilt.

And in that moment, I couldn't take not knowing anymore. I found I couldn't swallow, as if the words would choke me unless I released them.

"Do you think we're having the smallest Christmas of anyone in Dawes Plain?" I said. I saw Mum's face buckle under my words, but it was too late now. I couldn't stop.

"Jess, don't speak to your mother that way," Dad said.

"Seriously, though. How can it be just the three of us? No grandparents, no aunts or uncles, no *siblings* . . ."

"Jess!" Dad's fist came down on the table hard.

"No, Mike, it's all right," said Mum. When she turned to me, her hazel eyes shone.

"We wanted to give you a sibling, sweetheart. More than anything. But—it just wasn't possible. Things weren't straightforward for us, in that area."

I should have shut up then, but I couldn't stop myself. I swallowed my mouthful of turkey and then said, "Why couldn't you adopt?"

Mum flinched at the last word and an awful silence settled over the table.

It was Dad who spoke first.

"We looked into that, love, but it wasn't an option—"

I pushed back my chair, so roughly that it scraped on the kitchen tiles.

Later, I kept thinking about Mum's face, when I'd said that word. *Adopt.* The way she'd jolted backward, her eyes wide. She hadn't looked angry, or even hurt.

She'd looked scared.

Maybe I was wrong, about the affair? Maybe there's another reason why I'm different.

I waited until they had gone to bed, when I could no longer hear Mum's crying, and the gentle murmur of Dad comforting her, filtering down the hall. The sounds made my heart twist with guilt.

But I had to know.

I went into the study, closed the door before I turned on the light, hoping it wouldn't wake them. The desk was messy, covered with paper and dust from Dad's pastels. He'd drawn Mum a rosella for Christmas, serene in pale pink. I didn't know where all our official documents were but decided to start in the drawers. There wasn't much. A faded sepia photograph of a man standing in front of a boat—Dad's father, maybe?—and an even older picture of a stern-looking couple I didn't recognize. The drawer creaked as I rummaged through old paperclips and yellowed newspapers, making me wince. My fingers brushed a stiff piece of paper, and I pulled it out, thinking it might be something official.

It was a drawing. One of Dad's, I could tell right away. Not a bird, like he normally draws, but a fish. A poisonous-looking fish, bristling with great banded spikes.

I heard footsteps coming quickly down the hall, and before I could react, Dad burst through the door.

His eyes were pink, like he'd been crying too, not just Mum. All because of me.

"Give me that," he said, pulling the paper from my hands so hard it almost ripped. Before I could stop him, he scrunched it into a ball and threw it in the wastepaper bin.

"Dad, what—"

"Go to your room," he said, gripping me around the elbow and marching me out of the door. "Can't you see you've done enough?"

I apologized and he sighed. "Come on, Jess," he said. "It's been a long, emotional day. I just want everyone to get some sleep, OK?"

I got under the covers, but once I'd heard the soft thud of their bedroom door closing, I snuck back to the study and rescued Dad's drawing from the bin.

It's beautiful. Why would he want to throw it away?

The day after Boxing Day, the two of them went for a drive together. They said that it was to get milk, but I wonder if it wasn't really to get away from me: Mum's eyes were red and she avoided looking at my face as she said goodbye.

Part of me hated myself, but I knew I might not be alone again for days. Back in the study, I spent an hour rifling through the contents of Dad's desk, flinching every time I heard the pop of the corrugated-iron roof expanding in the sun.

But there was nothing—the odd tax file, more of Dad's art supplies, Mum's old editions of *Birdwatch* magazine.

By the time I remembered the filing cabinet in their bedroom, there was the sound of car tires crunching up the gravel driveway.

I scurried back into bed and curled into a ball, listening to my Walkman.

I should have known then that the dreams would come. They—the girls—are like sharks. They sense it when you're weak.

New Year's Eve was normal, at first. When I arrived, Max stared at my face—I knew I looked pale, that there were shadows under my eyes—but he didn't say anything. He seemed to know, without being told, that I didn't want to talk.

His mum was out. She'd started dating someone in Bourke and was going to stay the night, so we had the house to ourselves.

We sat on the beanbag in Max's room and drank cans of lager, listening to The Cure. I wondered when the cans of Coke had been replaced by alcohol and felt kind of sad, like one day I'd stopped being a child and hadn't even noticed.

We watched the fireworks on TV, talking about what our lives would look like when we left school and moved to Sydney. Me, a student at the College of Fine Arts, and Max a musician. It all seemed bright and real, as if we could reach into the television and grab hold of the future right then and there.

I don't know what time we went to sleep. Maybe 2 A.M. Max gave me his bed and he slept on the floor.

When I woke up, I couldn't breathe. Everything was cold, neon blue. I was in water, drowning. My eyes were open and I could see the flail of my own limbs, ghost white, like I was already dead.

And then there was an arm around my waist, pulling, the pain of air rushing into my lungs and the scrape of gravel on my skin.

Only then did I realize where I was, what had happened.

As I coughed up the water, shivering in the night air with Max panting next to me, saying, "What the fuck, Jess," over and over again, I remembered the dream. The black jaws of splintered wood. White water, pulsing toward me. Somehow, it had pulled me into Max's pool. It had tried to drown me.

Max wrapped me up in a towel, delicately, like I was a child. He led me inside—I could feel my fingers pruning against his, knew that soon my skin would crack and peel—and made me toast and warm milk.

"Do you want to tell me what happened?" he said, leaning over the kitchen counter, watching me as I took tiny bites of my toast. His eyelashes were still wet, jeweled with drops of water. I wondered what it would have been like, to have a brother like Max. If I was adopted, then maybe I *did* have a brother, somewhere out there.

I shook my head.

"It was just a bad dream," I said. My teeth were chattering a little. "I sleepwalk, sometimes."

He looked at me for a while, his eyes scanning my face. Like he was trying to decide what I needed from him in that moment.

And then he grinned.

"You sleep-talk, too. And once when you stayed over here, you farted."

I laughed, the sound of it surprising me.

"You liar!"

"I swear," said Max, laughing, too. "It smelled like cow shit."

And then I was laughing so hard that I was crying, my tears mingling with the chlorine from the pool, and then I wasn't laughing anymore, only crying, and Max had crossed the kitchen and put his wet arms around me.

"Oh, Jess," he said into my hair. "Shh, it's OK. I've got you."

I let him hold me, enjoying the feel of it, the safety of his skinny body against mine.

And then his hand was on my chin, tipping my face to his, and his lips were on mine, soft and warm, and he was kissing me and kissing me and—

Part of me was shocked. But another part had always known that this moment would come. That one day there'd be this fork in the road, friendship on one side and something else on the other.

I didn't think, I didn't choose. Or maybe I did.

It was a relief to have another person touching my body, tethering me to the here and now, to the bright kitchen with its smell of buttered toast and warm milk. Maybe I thought Max's hands and mouth would keep me safely in this world and away from theirs. Away from the sound of wood splitting on rocks and women screaming and the sea roaring. Of men with milk-sour breath.

And it wasn't just that.

It was the new energy that had grown between us, crackling in the silences. It was the way he looked, leaning against the greenhouse, the adult slant of his jaw. The heat in my skin when he touched my ear.

It was the way he always knew what I needed.

The way he had saved me.

And so I kissed him back, followed him when he led me into his room, lay down with him on his bed, where our bodies made the sheets damp and chemical-smelling. I let him see me: the ravaged landscape of my skin, cratered as the moon, along with the part of me that wants to drown.

Now I wish I hadn't.

21

LUCY

SATURDAY, 16 FEBRUARY 2019

Rain rattles the windowpanes.

Cliff House feels vulnerable, on borrowed time. Lucy thinks of the soil beneath the house's foundations, imagines it growing thick and viscous, taking the house with it over the edge of the cliff. The rocks below littered with splinters of wood, bright strips of torn canvas.

It's Saturday, her self-imposed deadline, six days before the exhibition. She'd told herself that if Jess wasn't back by now, she would start making calls, to her parents, to the police.

The clock on the bedside table reads 7 A.M. It's early, still. Jess could be on her way, could be planning to return this very evening.

What should she do? Make the call now, or wait a few more hours? She feels paralyzed with indecision.

To distract herself, she sits up in bed and reaches for her laptop. It doesn't make sense, this feeling that the past has somehow taken her sister, that the dreams hold her hostage even now. And yet, she can't shake it.

The girls are like sharks. They sense it when you're weak.

Sisters who died centuries ago, but who somehow live on, in Jess's mind and in hers.

She doesn't know where her sister is, but she knows how to look for Eliza and Mary.

Opening her laptop, she types *historical births deaths and marriage records Australia* into the web browser. The most promising result is from the National Library of Australia, which informs her that most of the states and territories have records dating back to the end of the eighteenth century.

She takes her laptop downstairs and puts on the kettle.

As it boils, she decides to start with the NSW records first. If Eliza or Mary *had* survived the wreck, presumably they'd have stayed reasonably close to Comber Bay. Victoria had not yet been colonized and getting to Tasmania—then Van Diemen's Land—would've meant another sea voyage.

Lucy stirs milk into her coffee, sitting down at the kitchen table, moving a stack of Jess's papers. But when she looks for records relating to Mary Kissane, from the period 1800 to 1850, she's greeted with only one line of text.

Your search has returned no results.

Grimacing, she searches for Eliza Kissane instead, but there's nothing. Even though she knows it's a long shot, she checks the Victorian and Tasmanian websites, too.

Your search has returned no results.

Lucy sighs, stretching her arms out in front of her, wincing as she cracks her knuckles. The skin between her fingers feels tender, inflamed, as if her hands have been submerged in water.

If they survived, then they must have changed their names. It stands to reason, doesn't it? They could have reinvented themselves, masqueraded as free settlers rather than convicts. Slipped through the records like ghosts.

She broadens the search terms, trying *Comber Bay* and *shipwreck* and *survivors*. But the only results relate to the child discovered at Devil's Lookout in the early eighties. Baby Hope.

According to some theories, the sole survivor of another, smaller shipwreck.

She pauses, her fingers frozen on the keyboard.

She thinks of the water's surface, the way it changes from deepest blue to dullest gray, hiding its secrets of wood and bone. The ship-wreck of the *Naiad*. The remains of Malcolm Biddy, of David Watts, and Daniel Smith. Perhaps even Baby Hope's family.

Outside, the tide pummels the shore. She imagines it reaching white fingers over the cliff, searching for her. As if it knows that Lucy is here, looking for answers.

She could start at the other end. Comb through her parents' ge-nealogy chart, search for a female ancestor who arrived at the right time—one who doesn't appear on transportation registers or ship manifests. But then, Jess's words echo in her mind.

No grandparents, no aunts or uncles . . .

It's true that Lucy has scant knowledge of her parents' back-grounds. She's never seen a photograph of another relative, let alone a family tree.

The only time a grandparent was ever mentioned was a long-ago birthday. She'd begged to go on a camping trip, and so her parents had borrowed a tent from one of Mum's work colleagues and set it up out on Paddock Two. Dad had built a little fire and Mum had toasted marshmallows. As the three of them looked up at the stars glowing in the sky, her father had pulled out his acoustic guitar. Lucy had braced herself for a creaking rendition of Paul Kelly or Cold Chisel, but instead he sang something slow and haunting as he strummed the strings, a song of sailing to a foreign shore and leaving those you love behind. By the time he'd finished, there was a thickness in his voice, like he was close to tears.

"Oh, my love," her mother had said, but under her breath, as if she didn't want Lucy to hear.

"What was that song?" Lucy had asked. She wanted to tell him it was beautiful, but felt tongue-tied, worried she might embarrass him.

"An old song," Dad had said. "A sea shanty. My father taught it to me."

"What happened to him?"

But no one had answered her question. There had been only the whirr of the cicadas, and the strangely ragged sound of her father breathing, before her mother had suggested that perhaps it was time they all slept.

All her life, Lucy has prided herself on her passion for the truth. And yet she had never sensed what her sister had known all along: that her parents were hiding something.

Or had she felt it, deep down? Perhaps it actually led to her childhood thirst for puzzles and mysteries in the first place?

Lucy wonders now if she's spent her entire life distracting herself from the reality that there were too many gaps in the story of her family. A hollowness where the truth ought to be.

Over the last few days, she's tried so hard to ignore the suspicions Jess wrote about in her journal; her sister's fears that she was adopted. It is incomprehensible, that they might not be related. After all, people have always commented on the resemblance between them. She clenches and unclenches her fists, the fragile skin stinging. She needs Jess here, to reassure her, to offer up some explanation to assuage her fears. Her sister—Lucy cannot let herself entertain the possibility that Jess is anything other than her sister—is the only one who can help.

She thinks of the painting downstairs on the easel. The delicacy with which Jess has rendered the two figures, their hands clasped tight as they face the floundering ship.

Lucy is certain that Jess knows what connects their family to Eliza and Mary Kissane. And why they haunt her so.

There has to be *someone* who knows where she is.

Someone her sister confides in.

Max.

Could Jess still be in touch with Max? Her one-time best friend, to whom she lost her virginity?

She scrolls through the phone's contacts and there, just above "Melody Neighbor," is "Max Murphy."

But when she makes the call, there's no answer.

Later, when her own phone rings, she swears at the caller ID on the screen.

Shit. It's her mother. Lucy feels a pulse of fear—perhaps the university has contacted her parents—mingled with a burst of homesickness.

She stands, frozen, unsure whether to answer or let it go to voicemail. Eventually, it rings out, only for her mother to phone again. God, if her mother knows about the suspension, she won't stop calling until Lucy picks up.

Perhaps it's time to come clean, to tell her parents where she is. And to tell them that Jess is missing.

Fear ticking in her throat, she answers.

"Hello?"

"Lucy?"

She can picture her mother so clearly. It's still early, so she'll be getting ready to head to her weekend shift at the outreach center. Her gray curls tied back, a Breton stripe T-shirt tucked into her favorite pair of jeans. Before she leaves, she'll put some seed into the birdfeeder in the garden, then she'll wave at the small blurred shape of Lucy's father out in the fields. Lucy can hear the drone of his tractor over the phone, the sound of it bringing tears to her eyes.

"Hi, Mum."

"How's it going, love? Uni OK this week?"

Lucy's heart rate slows. Her mother doesn't know about the suspension, about what Lucy did.

"Oh, you know," she says. "The same."

"Are you sure? I had a voicemail yesterday from a woman at the student welfare office asking me to give her a call—is everything OK?"

Blood beats in her ears.

"Sweetheart?"

"Yes—yes. Everything's fine," she says, the words coming in an unrehearsed, garbled rush. "There was just a bit of a mix-up yesterday—I overslept and missed a lecture, and my phone wasn't working.

My friend Em was a bit worried, she told someone at SWO. But it's all sorted now."

She picks at the skin of her ankle as she talks, watching it come away in lacy webs.

"OK, so I don't need to ring this woman back?"

"Nope."

She closes her eyes, allowing herself one precious moment of relief.

"Great, thanks, love. So, how is everything going? Are you eating enough?"

"Yep, I'm OK. Actually, Mum . . ." She pauses. "Have you heard from Jess lately?"

"Not for a while—maybe a month or so? Why do you ask?"

"I, ah . . ." She scrambles for a lie, hating herself. "I messaged her the other day, but she hasn't replied."

"I'm sure she will in good time, Goose. You know how she gets caught up in her work. You mustn't take it personally."

A bird wheels past the window, close enough that Lucy can see tawny feathers shining with rain. A curlew with its scythe-like bill, its distinctive high-pitched call. *Who-wee, who-wee.*

"Lucy—what was that noise? I thought I heard—"

"Just a bird," she says. "I'm in the common room. Someone opened a window."

"Really? Strange, it sounded like . . ."

"What?"

"Nothing. It just reminded me of something. Anyway, darl—I'd better get on, they're expecting me at the center. Love you."

"Love you, too."

The rain has eased now, the clouds pearl-bright with sun. Gum leaves crunch underfoot, releasing their sharp fragrance, as Lucy walks down Malua Street.

On Bay Road, she looks out to the sea, at the breakers whipped by the wind. A lone surfer curling through the blue. She wonders if he feels safe out there, with that dark unknowable world beneath him. The *tír fo thuinn*. She looks away.

The pavement gleams, the shops' awnings dripping with rain. She checks, first, that the general store is empty before she goes inside. Melody is behind the counter, pasting price labels onto tins of soup. The radio is playing the cricket; she whoops as Australia scores. The bell chimes as Lucy crosses the threshold.

She's nervous, remembering the time they met at Cliff House, the way Melody had looked at Lucy like she was a secret Jess had kept. But now Melody smiles, her face warm and open with curiosity.

"Hello, love," Melody says. "I've been meaning to see how you're getting on. Dora looking after you?"

"All good." Lucy smiles. "But I wondered if I could talk to you?"

Melody is silent for a moment, her eyes searching Lucy's face. She nods to herself briefly, as if deciding something.

"Of course," she says, switching off the radio. "Let's go up to the house, have a cup of tea."

"Oh, no—I don't want to interrupt your work. I can come back later, after you've closed up?"

"All good," says Melody, plucking her woven handbag from a hook on the wall behind her. "Ryan's been in for his eggs and Beth's got her milk—I'm only expecting Bob Shepard later, and to be honest, he could go without his Violet Crumble. Diabetic." She grimaces at Lucy's confused face.

Melody's front porch is alive with the tinkling of wind chimes—just like the one that Jess has on her veranda, only dozens of them. They look homemade: twirling green fragments suspended from rough-hewn planks of wood.

"Sea glass," Melody says as she catches Lucy looking. "Amazing what washes up around here. Although maybe not, given the history.

Some of it might even be from the *Naiad*, I reckon. That's where the bay gets its name: from beachcombers, like me."

Lucy's heart catches at the mention of the ship, at the thought of the *Naiad* at the bottom of the seabed, slowly giving up its secrets.

"Here we are," says Melody, jolting her back to the present. "My humble abode."

She leads Lucy down a narrow corridor, past a coat rack slung with rain jackets and hats, a jumble of gumboots and sneakers, into a light-filled living room. A leather sofa is covered with crocheted throws, shelves overflow with paperbacks. A Georgia O'Keeffe calendar hangs on one wall. There's an enormous framed print above the mantelpiece, all delicate ochre and soft blues, a gum tree sloping elegantly toward a mountainous horizon.

"I love that painting," Lucy says, as Melody ushers her to the sofa.

"Gorgeous, isn't it? Albert Namatjira. Jess likes it, too. How do you take your tea?"

When Melody disappears into the kitchen off the living room, Lucy looks at the photographs on the mantelpiece. In pride of place is a faded photograph of a grinning couple who must be Melody's parents: the woman has the same dark eyes, bright behind round glasses; the man shares Melody's delicate jaw. Lucy recognizes the blue slice of the sea behind them.

"My parents," Melody says, reappearing in the doorway with a tray laden with a teapot and biscuits. "I took that picture on Devil's Beach when I was ten. They're both long gone, now."

"Oh," Lucy says, springing back from the mantelpiece. "I'm so sorry."

"Thanks." Melody sets the tray on the coffee table. "They used to love coming here, before all the disappearances became too much. Not sure they'd be thrilled about me moving here."

"You're not from Comber Bay originally, then?"

"Nope. I grew up in Sydney. Mum was a Wiradjuri woman, from Orange. She met Dad at teachers' college in Camperdown. They came here on their honeymoon and fell in love with the place—Mum used to say the sky was bigger here than anywhere else on earth. She had a real way with words."

Lucy smiles as Melody passes her a mug of tea, but there's an ache in her chest. There's a softness in Melody's eyes as she talks about her parents—it's clear how much she loved them—that makes Lucy long for her own.

"Some years we spent the summer holidays in Orange with Mum's mob, but mostly we came here. Long, golden days on the beach—collecting driftwood and playing cricket with Dad, reading with Mum. I loved it."

"It must have been hard," Lucy says gently, "to stop coming."

"Yes," Melody nods, staring into her mug. "It was such a special place for us, before."

Before what? Lucy wants to ask, but she can't bring herself to intrude on the other woman's memories, her grief. Silence pools between them before Melody looks up, features rearranged into a smile.

"Anyway," says Melody. "What did you want to talk to me about?"

Lucy takes a breath.

"I'm probably overthinking it," she says. "But I wanted to double-check that Jess definitely didn't mention when she'd be back? I guess I'm just a little worried, not to have heard from her. And, you know, she didn't take her car, or her phone . . ."

Melody nods slowly.

"It must hurt, to think that she'd forgotten you were coming to stay."

"No," Lucy says, her mouth dry. "It's not that. I just—I wonder if she's OK."

Melody reaches over to squeeze her hand.

"She'll be back, love. She's worked so hard on these paintings—she wouldn't do anything to risk the exhibition. I think she was just stressed." Melody takes a breath. "I know it sounds odd, but I think people can underestimate the effect a place like this will have on them, beautiful as it is."

"How do you mean?"

"Well, the history. The shipwreck, the disappearances, Baby Hope—all of that. And Jess has been immersed in it. She was obsessed with the *Naiad*. You know, some people reckon there's a supernatural explanation for the missing men. That it's the women from the shipwreck. That's the story Jess wanted to paint—that she wanted to *capture*, she said. But maybe it all became a bit too much."

Lucy remembers seeing the *Odyssey* among the books heaped on Jess's dining room table, and thinks of Charybdis and Scylla, female nymphs who became monsters of the sea. The sirens, luring sailors to their deaths.

"Is that what people believe, in the town? That Comber Bay is haunted?"

"Enough of them to matter. It's like a stain; you can't rub it out. I remember what it was like here, when I was younger. It was a busy little place, those early summers. I suppose not many people knew about the older disappearances. Although I remember my parents talking about Bill Goldhill, who went missing in '77. He used to own the fish-and-chip shop with his wife. Not a nice man."

"In what way was he not a nice man?" Lucy asks, but she thinks she's guessed the answer already.

Melody sighs. "Everyone knew how he treated his wife. She was always black and blue. Poor woman. No one did anything—it was different in those days. Anyway, most people thought it was just an accident, when he vanished. That he'd had one too many before going for a swim. It barely made the local news. But then Alex Thorgood went missing in the eighties, and David Watts *and* Malcolm Biddy in the nineties—"

"And Daniel Smith," Lucy interrupts. It strikes her as strange for Melody not to mention him, given that Ryan is one of her regular customers—possibly even a friend, from the number of times she's mentioned him.

"Yes, and Danny—of course," Melody says. She pauses, and Lucy catches the way her eyebrows crease together, the hard set of her mouth. She flushes, feeling thoughtless: perhaps Melody had been close to Daniel. Danny.

"Anyway, by the late nineties the place had become a ghost town," Melody continues. "I mean, surfing is a pretty male pastime, isn't it? And men were afraid to come here. Hell, they were afraid to live here; that's why I own the store."

"Who owned it before?"

"Mack Burton, but he sold it to me a couple years back. He was the last person to see David Watts alive. Sold him some bait. Don't think he ever really got over it."

"Yes, I read that. And didn't Watts say he was going to meet someone?"

Melody nods.

"Yep. Eerie, when you think of the stories. When I was a teenager, we used to say that if you stood on the shore after dark, you'd hear the drowned women, singing. Like they were calling to you."

Lucy's hands twitch in her lap. The skin between her fingers itches; she suppresses the urge to pick at it, to peel it away. Again, she feels worlds colliding: Melody is talking about long-dead women, but they're women that Lucy knows. She knows the timbre of their voices, the smell of their hair, the way their breathing comes ragged and small in the pitch dark of the hold. Their lives have become as real to her as her own.

Her heart lurches. She swallows, grits her teeth. She needs to detach herself, to step back.

"Hang on," she says suddenly. "What do those stories have to do with David Watts meeting someone before he went missing?"

That hard look returns to Melody's face when she speaks.

"Well, that's the thing," she says. "Apparently Watts said he was going to meet a woman. I have an old newspaper clipping about it somewhere, actually." Melody eases herself from the sofa. "Mack gave an interview not long after Watts disappeared. Back in a tick. Eat one of those biscuits, won't you?" She gestures to the Tim Tams arranged on the china plate on the tray.

But Lucy can't bring herself to eat. She clenches her fists, trying to ground herself in *this* world, *this* life. She focuses on the scratch of the blanket against her skin, watches dust motes dance in a shaft of light through the window. She counts the different shades of blue in the painting that hangs above the mantelpiece.

She's relieved when Melody comes back into the room at last, bearing a battered shoebox.

"It's a bit dusty, sorry," says Melody as she clears space for it on the coffee table. For a moment, Lucy is comforted by the familiar scent of old newspaper. She lets Melody's chatter, the sound of rustling paper, wash over her.

"It's here somewhere—oh, look at this, an article about Judith Wilson. She and her husband adopted Baby Hope. Did Jess mention them? They used to live at Cliff House. It fell into ruin, after they left—until Jess bought it, really. Awful, the way they were treated. All those rumors. Here, take a look."

Melody hands her the crumpled front page of a tabloid from April 1982. The headline is enormous, taking up most of the page: BABY HOPE MYSTERY: DID SOUTH COAST WOMAN ABANDON OWN BABY? Accompanying the blaring text is a small black-and-white photograph of a woman, dark hair in a neat chignon, one hand lifted protectively to her face.

But it doesn't matter. It doesn't matter that her face is half covered, that the photograph is old and creased and black-and-white.

Lucy would know that face anywhere.

She knows it almost as well as she knows her own.

PART TWO

22

MARY

Mary's skin was burning.

She opened her eyes, gasping at the pain. Her feet stung where the water had licked at them for so many long weeks, the flesh rough and thickened. She tried to wriggle her toes and winced.

Oh, how she longed for light, to escape the dark heat of the prison deck, the other bodies pressed in around her. She closed her eyes and saw Da's face at the courtroom. What was he doing now? She imagined him alone in the cottage, his head in his hands, shoulders shaking as the goat nickered, unfed, in the corner. Smelling of stale sweat and unwashed clothes and too much drink.

A stirring next to her: she had woken Eliza.

"Mary?" Her sister's voice, soft and low in her ear. "Are you hungry? You must stay strong—they will feed us soon."

It was worse, somehow, that Eliza could remain so calm. That she was at home in this blackness. But Mary could not mark it. Was it not a greater torture for Eliza, who Da joked could hear a man whistle all the way from Dublin, who could tell you whether some mammy had burned her farls in the next county? How could she bear it, the heat that pressed against their bodies like sticky hands? The bilge water, teeming with rotting food and human waste and the soft

171

corpses of rats? The sounds of four score women crying and muttering and praying to God above for their deliverance?

"It is not hunger," she whispered, for it was true that her stomach had shriveled, that it had learned to accept little. "It is the pain," she murmured, forcing the words through dry lips. "In my feet, my hands."

"I feel it, too," Eliza whispered back. And then she took Mary's hand in hers, unfurling her fingers and tracing them over the winged flesh between her own. Mary gasped at the feel of her sister's skin, sharp and crusted as if with scales.

"Yours is the same," Eliza said. The two sisters were quiet a moment, hands clasped together tight.

Mary thought of Da, the hunched curve of his back as he keened to the waves, the twist of Mam's cloak in his hands.

She thought of Mam, who had given herself to the mercy of the sea, and what it had done to her.

She wanted to ask Eliza what was happening to them, but she could not find the words. Her fear was so great that it had stolen her voice.

The days seeped together like mud. The air was still, too, and without the howl of wind and waves they could hear seabirds for the first time. They did not sound like the birds from home; the jays and the robins and the finches with their pretty songs. Instead, their calls were harsh and eerie.

The women were quiet, the stifling heat sucking their energy. Above deck, it seemed a different story: the timbers shook with frenzied steps, shouts and laughter slipping through the cracks. More than once they heard screaming, the scuffling of a fight. When the men came to deliver their rations, they carried with them the sweet stink of rum.

"The doldrums, they call it," Bridie said. "When the sea is flat and the wind dies, so the sails cannot fill. Wright told me it sends men mad."

Aoife clucked her tongue. She often ignored Bridie for days at a time, after Wright's visits.

"He's not so bad," Bridie would say. "He wants to be here as little as we do. Press-gang got him when he was a lad, took him off to fight the Yankees. He went back home last year to find his mam but she'd long since died. He doesn't know how to do anything else, he says. After he finishes, he likes me to stroke his hair. Once he wanted me to sing him a lullaby."

"Ugh," Aoife would spit. "I don't care how much he misses his fucking mammy. He's still English, a *jackeen*."

"Doldrums," Eliza said now, rolling the word around her mouth. "A perfect name for such a thing. Like the tolling of a bell."

"What kind of bell?" Sarah asked, her voice thin. "A church bell, like a funeral?"

"Not mine," said Bridie, loud and somehow jaunty, as if they were not in a ship's hold but some crowded Dublin tavern. "They won't be burying my body at sea. I'll die an old matron, with hundreds of acres and gold rings on fingers so fat that no one will be able to get them off. All that gold, lost to the worms."

Little Annie giggled. "Can I've a gold ring, Mammy?"

Sarah shushed her. "Greed is a sin," she said to her daughter, though Mary knew the words were meant for Bridie.

"Tell that to the judge who sentenced you," Bridie said. "Half a yard of linen, was it? You're lucky you didn't swing from a rope."

"Hush now," said Aoife. "I won't have this talk of death and funerals. It's bad luck, so."

The winds returned, and with them a lightness to the men's steps when they came to deliver the rations.

"We'll be stopping soon," Bridie murmured, returning from one of her visits with Wright. "The men are giddy with waiting for it."

"Stopping?" Mary asked, failing to understand. "You mean, we've reached New South Wales?"

Bridie laughed.

"Not New South Wales, you eejit. We've got months more to go still, Wright said. No—he told me the name of the place. *Rio*, he called it."

"Rio? I've never heard of it," Sarah said grandly from the opposite berth.

"Well, it must be purely a sailor's fancy," Bridie scoffed. "I shall tell Wright to advise the captain not to sail to Rio; Sarah Hagarty thinks it does not exist."

The days stretched on, the ship cutting through the waves, and Mary forgot about what Bridie had said. There was too much else to crowd her mind: the flesh between her fingers was beginning to thicken, and there was an odd ache under her jaw, as if something were budding there.

But then Eliza woke her, tugging frantically at her hand.

"The air," said her sister, as Mary opened her eyes to darkness. "The air is different."

Around them, other women were stirring and talking, voices hissing and rumbling. Mary tasted the air, as Eliza had taught her. There *was* something else, mingled with the familiar brine of the sea. A green, animal smell.

Land.

Rio de Janeiro. Another name that was strange on Mary's tongue.

The women were briefly brought on deck, allowed to watch the throng of colorful little boats dance in the harbor. The sky seemed to have grown in the time since Mary had last seen it: her mind could not fathom so much blue. Beyond the dock, she could make out buildings lining the jungle's mouth like pretty teeth. Mountains rose in the distance, green and lush. One of the sailors gave them oranges: they peeled back the bitter skin and sucked the sweet juice from the tender flesh. It was the best thing Mary had ever tasted.

Later, the men removed the casks and barrels that were stored with them in the prison deck, straining and sweating in the heat.

"Rum," said Bridie as one of them passed, grunting and wincing under the weight of a barrel. There was a wistful note in her voice.

"What will they do with it?" Sarah asked.

"The captain will be wanting to sell it," said Bridie. "The king doesn't pay him much for transporting the likes of us. Wright says it's a racket, that His Majesty's government would arrest the captain if they knew. But none will risk their skin to tell."

Mary was glad that the captain was selling the casks and barrels, for surely their absence would mean more room in the prison deck. There'd also be less rum for the men to drink, or to offer Bridie and the other women who'd followed in her footsteps. There was a new, glassy look to Bridie's eyes that she didn't like, and sometimes she heard her teeth chatter, though it was never cold in the prison deck, in that warm fug of breath and bodies.

But after only a few days, the sounds of men cursing and grunting filtered down to them. As their lights approached, Mary sat up, her hand groping for Eliza's. When the bulkhead gate opened, she saw that it was the sailors bringing back the casks and barrels of rum.

"Wright says the captain couldn't sell them," Bridie told them later. "He'll be wanting to make his coin some other way."

After they left Rio, the sea grew rough and cold, the rations fewer. Mary had thought that there might be fresh food now, remembering the sweetness of the orange on her tongue. Surely the purpose of such a stop would be to purchase more supplies? But if there was anything fresh to be had, they never saw a morsel: the sailors brought them gruel and the dried husks of biscuits, fleshy-tasting with maggots. Sometimes, they were given only water, blood warm and paltry.

Bridie said that the captain must have kept the king's coin for himself rather than spend it on more rations.

"Didn't I tell you," she said, "that he'd need some other way to make his funds?"

The hungrier and thirstier they were, the harder it was to brave the storms. Thunder and lightning tore the air, and the ship groaned as she climbed the waves. Icy water rushed into the prison deck, and one of the casks burst, flooding the bilges with rum. Mary's ears rang with screams of terror, and her own heart galloped in her chest, keeping time with the bucking waves.

She thought of Mam, and for the first time in years let herself wonder what her final moments had been like, in the gray fury of the sea. Did it hurt, to drown? Or had it been like the strange memory Mary had, of silver bubbles and darkly drifting hair?

23

LUCY

SATURDAY, 16 FEBRUARY 2019

Something cold makes its way over Lucy's toes, lapping at her ankles, her calves. It burns; she shivers. At first the world is just a haze of blue. Then she hears the roar and hiss of the waves. Gasping, she jerks upright, pulling her feet from the water's touch.

She is on the beach, sitting right at the lacy edge of the sea. Next to her, her backpack is soaked. The sun is high in the sky, its heat pressing down on her. It's 11 A.M.; the tide has come in. How long has she been sitting here? Her breathing grows panicked, shallow, as she scrabbles for details.

But then she remembers.

Everything she believed about her life is a lie.

She gets slowly to her feet, brushing the sand from her legs, grimacing at the sting of tiny grains on her skin. Skin that is already burning and tightening from the water's poison kiss.

She had come straight from Melody's. She'd practically run, as if somehow the sea had called to her, exerting its own magnetic pull. She remembers sitting down on the soft sand, the water still meters away. She'd watched the minute movements of a crab, the click of its pincers. And she'd cried, her thoughts wheeling in all different directions, like the flock of gulls cawing in the distance.

She'd closed her eyes, grinding the heels of her hands into her eye sockets, as if to rub away the memory of the newspaper article, that face.

Her mother's face.

Then the darkness had washed over her, sucking her back in time. She remembers the burning blue dome of sky, the citrus burst of orange. The insistent gnaw of fear.

Her phone buzzes in the pocket of her shorts. No, not her phone—*Jess*'s phone.

Oh God.

Jess.

Jess is Baby Hope.

She knows, doesn't she? She must have known for years. That's why she's here, in Comber Bay.

Jess's phone is still ringing. It's Max.

A gust of wind hurls sand into Lucy's eyes. She blinks. Her mouth is dry, claggy. She doesn't know what to say to him. How can he help her, this stranger?

But he's Jess's friend. Someone she cares for. Someone who might know the truth, who might know where Jess is. She answers.

"Jess? God, it's been so long—are you OK? I've only just seen—"

"Sorry, Max?" Lucy takes a breath. "It's actually Lucy here, Jess's"—her mouth struggles to form the word—"sister?"

"Oh. Right. Hi, Lucy—are you with Jess now?"

"That's why I tried to call, actually," she says. "I—um—I came down to see Jess a few days ago but she isn't here. Her car's here, and her phone—obviously—but her neighbor said she was going away for a while. I was hoping she might be with you. Or that you might know where she is?"

"No," Max says, drawing out the word slowly. "No, she's not, and I don't. We actually haven't spoken for a while. I assumed she was ringing about—ah . . ."

"About what?"

"Listen, it doesn't matter. I'm sure she's fine. Trust Jess to leave her phone behind." He attempts a laugh, but it sounds brittle. "But when she gets home, would you tell her to give me a call? That I'd really love to speak to her?"

"OK," Lucy says, her lips cold and numb. "But are you sure you don't—"

"I'm sorry, Lucy," Max cuts her off. "But I really have to go. I'm sure Jess is fine. Bye now."

He hangs up before she can say anything more. She grips Jess's phone tight in her hand, resisting the urge to hurl it away. There was something that Max wasn't telling her. She could hear it in his voice.

Anguish thrums in her veins. All of her senses are raw, as if her skin has been filed away.

Her mother isn't Maggie Martin, but Judith Wilson. Her father isn't Michael Martin, but Robert Wilson. The man who found Baby Hope at Devil's Lookout and offered her to his wife, as if she was some treasure he'd dredged up; a pearl or an abalone shell.

And Jess is Baby Hope.

Which means Jess is not her sister.

All these years, her family has been nothing more than a story. A collage of half-truths and lies.

Fragments from the podcast swirl through her mind, the scrutiny the couple—*her parents*—faced in the wake of the adoption, the bitter tabloid rumors.

Mrs. Wilson might have given birth to the child and then, suffering from postpartum depression, left it in the cave before confessing her actions to her husband. In this version of events, Mr. Wilson was not a hero but an accomplice who had sought to cover up his wife's crime by staging the dramatic rescue from Devil's Lookout.

She can't bear to even countenance the possibility of that being true. But then—it's the only version of events where she and Jess are sisters.

The waves froth and roil, reflecting the maelstrom of her thoughts.

But Jess *is* her sister: Lucy feels it in every cell. It's not just the physical resemblance—their shared skin condition, or the matching whelks of their ears, bestowed by their father.

It's the dreams, their shared world, the link between them that defies rational explanation. Jess has left her very fingerprints inside Lucy's brain.

How can they not belong to each other?

24

JESS'S DIARY

1999

3 January

I've imagined so many times how it'd feel to lose my virginity. I used to think of it like a snakeskin that I could slip off, revealing a shiny new layer beneath. Strong and beautiful and . . . adult, I guess. I didn't know quite how exposing it would feel. How terrifying.

When I woke up this morning, I thought for a moment that I was still there, in Max's bed. The sheets smelling of chlorine, his hair bright in the soft lamplight. Outside the window, the night fading, taking with it the old year. People in town—in towns and cities all over the world—were still partying, throwing back vodka shots and toasting the new year.

It would have been perfect. The whirr of the cicadas outside, the soft lamplight falling across my body, making me beautiful. My heart was still trembling in my throat after waking up in the pool, my nostrils stinging from where the water had forced its way into my sinuses. But I also felt something else. The tingling on my skin—harbinger of the Flakes—felt different, this time.

Like I said. It would have been perfect.

He traced his fingertips lightly on my stomach. I gasped from the

181

thrill of it, but then he stopped, as if afraid to touch the thickened white landscape of the rash. There was a hitch in his breath, and his fingers hovered above my skin. A coldness spread through me. He was reluctant, I realized. Repulsed.

"Um," he whispered, "do you want the light off?"

Such a simple question: just six words. But they said so much.

For a moment I couldn't speak, the pain of it lodging in my chest.

Then I said, "Sure," reaching out to flick the switch, leaving us in darkness. It stung, when he was inside me, and the tingling feeling on my skin went away, leaving me cold and shivering.

How could I have thought he would find me beautiful, once he saw me as I really am?

But I don't want to think about Max. Not now.

At last, Mum and Dad are out. Mum's driven to see a friend, and Dad's out putting fence posts up in one of the paddocks.

It's been a week since Christmas lunch, since they flinched when I said the word *adopt*. I feel like I'm holding the truth in my hands—I just have to bring it to the light, to look at it. To see.

Ten paces to their bedroom. To the filing cabinet. I'll open it, I'll find my birth certificate. And then I'll know.

Later

Dad got home twenty minutes ago, the whine of the screen door interrupting me. I was sitting on the floor of their bedroom, the file spread out around me. All the names and places—they don't make sense.

"Jess, are you here? Jessica?"

Dad's voice boomed through the house. The familiar mix of weariness and love brought a lump to my throat, the prick of tears to my eyes. The floorboards began to creak under his step, and I heard the kitchen tap, then the click of the kettle.

I had to get out of there. I couldn't let him know what I'd found. Not yet.

Still, I felt like Pandora in the John William Waterhouse painting, peering into the box that once opened could never be closed. The strange phrases and fragments churned inside me. I pressed my hand to my mouth as if to swallow them down, but there was no going back.

I needed to take the file.

I shoved it down the inside of my shirt and ran back to my room, crouching to hide it under the bed. I'd just stood up again when there was a knock at the bedroom door. Without waiting for an answer, Dad pushed the door open with his foot, bearing two cups of tea.

"If it isn't God's gift," he said, a slow grin spreading over his face. *God's gift*—one of his nicknames for me. Apparently, it's what Jessica means, why they picked the name. "I thought you didn't believe in God?" I used to say, a joke between us. "I do when I look at you," he'd reply, with a big cheesy Dad wink.

Now I could hardly bear to look at him.

"Hey," I said. He needed a shave, and there was a smear of dirt on one of his cheeks. He was wearing his favorite T-shirt, the one Mum keeps threatening to throw in the bin because there's a hole in one sleeve and an old curry stain down the front. It says *Dragon* in big stupid seventies letters.

Dad.

But he's not my dad.

He's Robert Wilson, a stranger. And I'm . . .

Name at birth: Unknown.

"How about a chat?" Dad said, taking a noisy slurp of tea. "We could watch some TV together, until your mum gets home. Or we could sit and draw, like we used to? I could get a head start on next year's drawing. I'm thinking: currawong."

If things were normal, I'd have said, "Don't be an idiot, Dad, you did that three years ago. It's hanging on the wall outside the laundry."

But things weren't normal. Nothing would ever be normal again.

"Sorry," I said, finally. "Headache."

Before he could respond, I shut the door in his face. There was a pause, and then, after a time, the slow, defeated thud of his footsteps retreating down the corridor.

I sank to my knees in front of the bed, my hands shaking. I didn't want to look, I didn't want to know. But I had to.

I pulled the file out from under the bed with shaking fingers. There were three certificates in the file and a thick wad of legal papers. Two were deed poll certificates, changes of name.

Once, my parents were other people. They weren't Mike and Maggie Martin, but Robert and Judith Wilson.

But the third certificate was the worst.

"Certificate of Adoption," read the fancy scroll of script on the top.

Adoptive parents: Michael and Margaret Martin
Child's name after adoption: Jessica Judith Martin
Child's name at birth: Unknown
Child's date of birth: Unknown
Parents at birth: Unknown

The only detail was a place. Comber Bay, NSW. It was on their certificates, too. *Place of residence: Comber Bay.*

I've never even heard of it. Mum and Dad never mentioned it.

Mum and Dad.

Now I know why they never talk about their lives before Dawes Plain. Because the legal papers were even worse.

There was a letter from a firm of solicitors, addressed to Mr. and Mrs. Robert Wilson of Cliff House, 1 Malua Street, Comber Bay, NSW, dated 1 August 1982.

Dear Sir and Madam, it read. *Please see final copy of the agreement with* Yes! Magazine *enclosed, together with our invoice for your kind attention . . .*

I flipped the yellowed page over to find a deed. And there it was, wrapped up in legalese, like the last layer in a game of pass the parcel. The truth.

Settlement agreement between Wilson and Yes! Magazine, it read. *29 July 1982.*

My parents had sued a tabloid magazine for publishing an article about them. It alleged that my father's rescue of a newborn baby from a seaside cave—a baby my parents later adopted—had been staged, to conceal a crime. That my mother, ill with postnatal depression, had given birth there in secret. That she'd tried to abandon the child.

That she'd tried to abandon *me*.

Everything around me—the green glow of my lava lamp, the hum of the cicadas outside, the rumble of the pipes as someone runs a tap—has melted away. As if none of it was ever real in the first place.

Nothing exists now, except for that word, the fattening horror of it in my heart.

Abandon.

Really, it doesn't matter who put me in that cave. Whether it was Mum or some stranger.

Either way, I was unwanted.

———

4 January

My hand holding the pen looks wrong, foreign somehow.

The split nails. The new, thickening flesh between my fingers.

It's like some cord has been severed between my brain and my body. I'm watching my hand move across the page, watching the words spill out, but none of it—not my hand, not even my life—belongs to me.

I had one of the dreams last night. I *felt* the press of dank wood against my nose and mouth, saltwater soaking into my skin. The rhythmic pounding of the waves in my skull.

It makes a strange sort of sense now, doesn't it? The water holds some part of me still.

I drew a self-portrait earlier. My eyes wide and dark as a seal's, the unruly tumble of my hair. I even drew the Flakes, the creep of them from underneath my shirt collar. Delicate as scales.

I asked Dad if I could use the phone. I said I was going to call Max.

"Sure," he said. He was sitting on the couch, the TV flickering bright but with the sound turned so low he can't have been watching it.

I never noticed it before, how haunted he looks. How lost.

For a moment I felt guilty, and wondered if I should get out our sketchbooks and pencils and *Birds of Australia*, like the father and daughter we used to be.

But then the guilt shifted inside me, turning to fury.

You lied.

Instead, I took the portable phone from its cradle and went to my room and shut the door. I'd written down the number from the list Mum keeps pinned to the fridge. They're all on it—Mrs. Clark, my English teacher, Mr. Webb, my math teacher. And, of course, Mr. Hennessey. Cameron.

My palms began to sweat as I dialed, as the phone rang and rang. I almost hung up—I wasn't even sure what I wanted to say to him; all I knew was that there was no one else I wanted to tell—but then there was the mechanic *click* of someone picking up the receiver.

"Hello?"

My tongue swelled in my mouth at the sound of his voice. For a moment, I couldn't speak.

"Hello?" he said again, impatient now.

"Mr. Hennessey?" I wanted to use his first name, but somehow couldn't bring myself to.

"Jessica! This is a surprise."

He recognized my voice. My body thrummed, a plucked string.

Everything bubbled up to the surface. The certificates. The legal papers. That awful word: *abandon.*

A sob caught in my throat.

"Jessica? Is everything all right? Has something happened?"

"I—" Another great, shuddering sob.

"It sounds like you need someone to talk to," he said.

"Yes," I said, the word trembling out of me.

"Look, I'm a little tied up today, but are you free tomorrow? Do you want to meet at school, at the art studio? You can tell me what's been going on. How does that sound?"

"OK," I whispered, relief flooding through me. I'd lost my parents, I'd lost Max. But I still had him. "Thanks, Mr. Hennessey."

"Please," he said. "Call me Cameron."

I thought, then, of the way that he'd touched my skin.

The inside of a shell.

He sees something in me, I know he does. He's different than everyone else, than Mum and Dad and Max. He sees my flaws and thinks they're beautiful. A warmth unfurls inside me, and it's like I'm already there, looking into his green eyes, soft and bright with understanding.

I feel like I've been given a life raft. A tiny chink of hope.

Somehow, I know that he will make everything OK.

25

LUCY

SATURDAY, 16 FEBRUARY 2019

Lucy's hands shake as she puts the journal down, her stomach churning. When did she last eat? She can't remember.

She is sitting on the sagging couch in the living room of Cliff House. Cliff House, where her parents had once lived. Had her father sat at the worn kitchen table, pencils and paper spread out around him? Had her mother chopped vegetables in the tiny yellow kitchen, humming as she looked out to sea?

It was her mother's bird-feeder that hung from the tree outside, her mother's magazines she'd found dust-choked in the eaves.

She closes her eyes to stem her tears and sees the tabloid headline, neon bright on the canvas of her eyelids.

She imagines her mother, white-faced and pregnant, struggling down the treacherous steps to Devil's Lookout. Imagines her crouched in the cave's red womb, alone and terrified as she pushed a child from her body . . . a child that mental illness drove her to abandon . . .

She cannot bear it. She cannot bear to think of her mother like that, helpless and prone and ill. But she cannot bear the alternative, either: that her mother never birthed her sister at all.

That her sister isn't her sister.

Oh, Jess.

188

A thundercloud glowers over the sea, a gray crouched creature. The first drops of rain hit the windowpanes, gunshot loud. The house creaks in the wind, low and mournful. She thinks of all the pain it has witnessed over the years.

Jess's pain.

Was this why she had always kept her distance from Lucy? Had she feared that Lucy would reject her, once she learned that they were not biologically related?

That they weren't really sisters?

Tears sting at the thought and she realizes that she can't accept it. It doesn't matter to Lucy that they didn't come from the same womb, that they didn't journey into the world from the same place. They might not have grown up together, but they were raised in the same home, by the same parents, with the same rules and rituals. The same mysteries.

She closes her eyes, focusing on her memories of Jess, as if doing so might summon her home. Sitting on her knee as a small child, listening to the soothing rhythm of her heart. A warm, gentle hand over hers, guiding bright crayons over paper. The harmony of their voices, singing nursery rhymes and Disney songs, and later, Nick Cave . . .

My sister.

She thinks now of that night at Jess's flat in Sydney, the taste of hot chocolate laced with alcohol and the soft murmur of the record player. The question she'd asked so clumsily, the way that Jess had seemed to shut down.

It must have brought all of it back. The year she'd lost her virginity was the year she'd discovered she wasn't who she thought she was, that she wasn't from Dawes Plain but a sea-swept cave, mere meters from where Lucy sits now. That she'd been abandoned, unwanted. And then, she'd had no one to turn to. No one except Hennessey, who had sowed poison seeds of trust in her young mind, and waited for them to bloom.

What had he done to her?

How she wishes she could return to that moment in Jess's flat, that she could approach the conversation with the experience and insight she's gained since. She could tell Jess that she understands. That she knows how it feels, that need to be wanted. How vulnerable it makes you.

"I'm so sorry, Jess," she whispers to the empty room. "I'm so sorry."

Lucy's words are lost to the rain, now so loud it might be falling on her body, great big drops clattering against her bones, breaking her open.

She cannot bear to read on, but she must. She must know the truth.

But then there's the hammering of a fist on the door. Lucy climbs from the couch, nervous as a child. She can see the front door from here, the blur of dark figures behind the glass panel.

"Hello?" comes a stern voice, barely audible over the lash of the rain. "Police. Open up."

26

LUCY

SATURDAY, 16 FEBRUARY 2019

"Police!"

Lucy is frozen, pinned in place.

She knows, in some distant part of her brain, that she must walk across the room, that she must open the door and talk to the police. But her body seems to have forgotten the precise order of movements necessary. Her lungs empty of air.

Dora Maar is scratching at the door, tail rigid and ears flat against her skull.

To steel herself, Lucy imagines what will happen next: greeting the officers, offering tea or coffee, a place to sit. She imagines folding her hands into her lap as they speak.

Your sister, they will say, *Jessica Martin. We have found a body and we have reason to suspect it is her.* She imagines her sister, a pale spread of limbs at the bottom of a cliff. Washed up green and gleaming on some distant beach. She imagines that the sea has taken her again and spat her out, an animal rejecting its young.

The knocking comes swift and hard, the door rattling with it. The officers are growing impatient; she can hear snatches of their conversation. The words *warrant* and *reasonable cause* and *suspect*. Oh God, what if they suspect Jess has been *murdered?* That foul puddle of urine

191

in the toilet. Perhaps Cliff House is a crime scene and Lucy has been here for days, touching things, polluting evidence. What if Jess did not leave voluntarily, what if she *was* missing—and Lucy did nothing because she was too consumed by her own problems, by what she did to Ben?

Nudging Dora Maar aside, Lucy takes the chain off the door, then flings it open, letting the storm pour in.

The two officers—a man and a woman—wear fluorescent rain jackets, their hats marked with the insignia of the NSW police. A radio crackles in time with the storm.

"Miss Martin?" says the woman, and Lucy nods. "Can we ask you a few questions?"

But they're already moving inside, Lucy pressing herself against the wall to make way. They smell of rain and stale coffee.

She knows she should say something but her tongue seems to have swelled, her brain emptied of everything but: *my sister. My sister is dead.*

"Can we sit?" asks the male officer. He's older than the woman, her father's age.

Lucy ushers them to the couch, moving aside Jess's diary, a blanket covered in Dora Maar's hair. She sees the way they look around the cluttered room, at the tarp-covered hole in the floor, the mold-patterned walls. She sees the raised eyebrows, the shared glances.

Lucy stands opposite them, head bowed, readying herself for the blow.

The woman shifts forward, crossing one leg over the other and clearing her throat. More static comes over her radio: she silences it.

"So, Miss Martin . . . can we call you Jessica?"

Lucy's head snaps up. Her lungs reinflate, her tongue shrinks in her mouth. Brain is reconnected to body.

Jess isn't dead. Jess isn't dead. The police are looking for Jess. What has she done?

"I'm not Jessica," she says quickly now. "I'm her sister, Lucy. Sorry—I thought you were here because something had happened to her. Is Jess OK?"

The woman's eyebrows lift in surprise. She adjusts her body on the sofa, writes something in her notebook.

"I see," she says. "And I take it your sister isn't here right now?"

Lucy shakes her head.

"Right. And when did you last see her?"

Lucy's mind races. Why are they looking for Jess—what do they want? She searches their facial expressions for clues—the male officer has a nerve pulsing above his eyebrow, the woman stares at her, impassive, waiting. She barely seems to blink.

"I don't understand," Lucy says. "Is my sister in some kind of trouble?"

"Why would you ask that?" The female officer waits, patient.

Lucy chews at the nails on her right hand. Her heart is beating faster now.

"Well . . . I guess I'm a little worried, given that you're here asking about her."

"Do you normally live with Jessica?"

She looks at her hands, at the silver web between each finger. She notices, distantly, that the rash is getting worse. She wants to stretch the moment out, wants the opportunity to *think*. She should have offered them tea or coffee, bought herself a little time. It's too late now: it'll just seem like what it is. Evasion.

"Not normally, no," she says, keeping her voice low, a whisper.

"So, you're just staying here, then?"

Lucy nods.

"I'm going to ask again. Can you tell us when you last saw your sister?"

Her thoughts wheel like birds. What does Jess need from her, in this moment? Does she need her to lie, to invent some kind of alibi? If only Lucy knew.

But it doesn't matter. That instinct for the truth is still inside her, beating hard as another heartbeat. She takes a breath.

"I haven't seen my sister for over a year," she says quietly. "I arrived on Tuesday morning and she wasn't here."

The officers exchange a glance.

"You had an arrangement and she broke it?" the female officer clarifies.

"No," says Lucy quickly. "No—she wasn't expecting me. She didn't know I was coming. Her neighbor—Melody, in number two—told me she'd gone away."

"Thanks." The woman nods. "We'll speak to the neighbor."

"Do you mind"—Lucy breathes hard—"please, could you tell me what's going on? Has something happened to Jess?"

The male officer leans forward.

"Does the name Cameron Hennessey mean anything to you?"

Lucy is sure that they'll be able to see the jump of her pulse in her neck, the new flush to her cheeks. A cold certainty sweeps through her body: now she has to lie. She fights to keep her face blank.

"No," she says, furrowing her brow. "Should it?"

She is horribly aware of the books stacked on the table, *A Wave of Dreams* at the top of the pile. His name on the inside cover.

"Jessica never mentioned him to you?"

Lucy shakes her head. This much, at least, is true. She only knows about him because she read Jess's diary.

"We urgently need to ask Mr. Hennessey some questions in relation to an ongoing investigation. Now, we understand that Miss Martin and Mr. Hennessey were previously in an intimate relationship—had been for several years. His car was found by a member of the public at a nearby location. So with your sister being unaccounted for, you can see why we have to investigate the possibility that they're together."

"Sorry—an investigation into what?"

"I can't disclose that."

Lucy's mouth is dry, her skin prickling with panic.

"Did he hurt someone? Could he have hurt Jess?"

The officers look at each other. The female officer turns to her, and for a moment Lucy is sure that she wants to say something, to provide some kind of reassurance. But then, thunder, the kind that sounds like the sky is being zipped open. Dora Maar darts under the sofa in fear.

The house trembles, and Lucy sees the male officer glance nervously toward the window. The clouds are dense, veined and greenish, like some great creature's wings.

The female officer closes her notebook and stands, brushing down her trousers as if to remove any trace of the house.

"Right," she says. "Well, thank you for your time. I'm going to leave my card here." She puts it on the table, right on top of Hennessey's book. Lucy's heart thuds. "And if your sister comes home, please ask her to call me."

When, at last, the crunch of tires on gravel has faded, disappearing under the weight of the storm, Lucy sits down again, trembling. She looks at her feet, notices that the skin between her toes is thicker, almost webbed. She scratches at a scaly patch on her big toe and pulls it off. The layer underneath is bluish and shining.

She thinks of what the officers said, that Cameron Hennessey's car was found nearby. And she thinks of how she'd found Cliff House when she arrived. The hardened washing-up in the sink, the dirty plate on her sister's bed, the urine in the toilet bowl.

Like Jess had run away from—or with—someone.

27

MARY

Days—or perhaps weeks—passed before they were taken on deck again.

As the women struggled to their feet in a chorus of groans and clanking chains, Mary wondered if there had been another death. Despite her constant hunger, her stomach churned at the thought of the dead man they'd buried at sea all those weeks ago, the pale blue of his foot.

But once on deck it was clear that they had not been summoned for a funeral: instead, the mood was one of celebration.

Mary closed her eyes at the touch of fresh air on her face, savoring its briny tang. It was dusk, and when she opened her eyes she saw the first glimmer of stars appear in the pink sky. The sea stretched around them, dark as a bruise.

An iron smell reminded her of the times she'd helped Da slaughter chickens, and as her eyes adjusted to the thin light, she saw that rivulets of blood seeped across the deck. Through the throng of sailors, she could not see where it was coming from.

Panic gripped her: Had they killed someone?

Around her, the men drank and danced and sang, their feet

stamping in time to the words, and through their shifting bodies she saw that a carcass hung from the mast.

Aoife was in front of her, patches of scalp shining through her hair. She stiffened, so that Mary bumped into her. The older woman's whole body was trembling, and her rasping words struck fear into Mary's heart.

"What have they done?" she was saying. "Dear God, they have killed us all!"

Mary squinted to make out the gruesome sight. Her fogged brain had assumed that they had slaughtered some pig or sheep, but of course none had been brought on board; not at Cork and not in Rio. That was why their rations were so paltry.

"Please, Aoife . . ." she said, her lips numb with fear. "In God's name, please tell me that isn't a person?"

But Aoife only trembled harder. Beside her, Eliza made little noises of frustration, her fingers clinging desperately to Mary's own. Mary knew how much Eliza hated these moments—moments when the keenness of her other senses could not fill the gap left by blindness—and her heart ached with guilt. Eliza counted on her to make sense of what she couldn't see. But there was nothing she could do, no reassurance she could give, when her own eyes could not comprehend the sight before them.

It was Bridie who answered.

"It's a shark, you eejits," she said, turning to face them, then sighing when she saw their blank looks. "A giant fish with great big teeth, that's all. They've caught it and hauled it up on deck."

Mary's pulse slowed, but it was a shock to see Bridie's face after so long in darkness. Her cheekbones were sharp, her eyes shadowed; her red mane of hair was matted and alive with fleas. Mary shuddered to think how she herself must look—she could hardly bear to look properly at her twin—but it was somehow worse to see Bridie brought so low. Even Wright's payment couldn't keep the flesh on her bones.

In front of her, Aoife was still trembling and sobbing.

"Hush, now," Mary said. "Did you not hear Bridie? It's a shark—a fish—not a person."

But Aoife only sobbed harder, cursing the captain and his men for bringing bad luck down upon them all.

"I think she knows what it is," Eliza said, her voice low. "She is from the Blasket Islands, remember? She must know each fish in the sea. But will you describe it for me, Mary? The shark?"

Eliza's voice was heavy with concern for Aoife, but still Mary caught the relish with which she sounded out that new word—*shark*. It was so like Eliza to take pleasure in the learning of something new, even amid all this terror. Her hunger for the world and all its workings was never sated. Not for the first time, Mary wondered if God had made some sort of mistake when he took her sister's sight. He ought to have taken Mary's instead. She'd always been so dreamy—Da used to say her head was so far up in the clouds that she never saw what was right in front of her. It was Eliza who brought Mary back to the world, to how it really was.

She strained forward, eyes narrowed as she inspected the strange creature. She saw bright teeth, sharp rows of them, like a weaver's loom. Fins that made her think of wings, a shimmer of scales. The dead glint of an eye.

She imagined the creature gliding through the deep. Perhaps, beneath the waves, the shark took human form; became the ruler of the *tír fo thuinn*. She thought she understood why Aoife railed against what the men had done.

How to tell Eliza all of this?

"It is the loveliest—and the most frightening—thing I ever saw," she said. "They should not have killed it."

When the shark had been butchered, they were taken back below. The smell of cooking meat filtered from the galley all the way down to the prison deck, turning Mary's stomach. When the sailors unlocked the bulkhead, bearing buckets of charred, bloodied flesh, Aoife began to sob again. Some of the women gagged, but most ate the pungent meat.

When a sailor flung a scrap into Mary's hands, she shuddered at the feel of it. The flesh was veined with blood, and she could not help thinking how only hours before, it had throbbed and pulsed with life, propelling the shark through the sea.

How many times had she swallowed mutton stew, or gnawed on the bone of a chicken? Had she not eaten the fish that Da had caught, when she was a small girl back in Ard na Caithne?

But this felt different. Even as she tried so hard to push it from her mind, she could not stop thinking about Eliza's story, about the merrow woman with her shining silver scales. The story she said Mam had told them, the story Mary could not bring herself to remember. When she closed her eyes, she could still see the shark's carcass before they had carved it away; the elegant sweep of its tail, the silver gleam of its flesh. Bile rose in her throat.

But she needed to survive. She pushed the cold, jellied meat into her mouth and swallowed.

Mary could not sleep.

The prison deck seemed tighter around her body after their brief glimpse of the stars. Her stomach contracted around the shark meat. The other women stank: the tang of roasted meat added to the sourness of urine and sweat, of body parts too long slicked together.

Next to her, Eliza slept, strands of her hair tickling Mary's nose. Mary breathed in, searching for the smell of her sister, the smell of nights spent safe and loved in their father's cottage; the must of old blankets and the sweet rise and fall of breath. But there was only the lingering smell of cooked flesh, black and tarry in her nostrils, like the bonfires from Samhain.

It was harder, then, to keep the memories away.

She could not say when she'd first become aware of Byrne. For as long as she could remember—ever since they'd moved to the north and into the little cottage with its plot of flax, its spinning wheel and loom—he had come to collect the rent and tithe.

He spoke, as all the villagers did, differently to them; the vowels were somehow smaller, sharper, in his mouth. His hair and eyes were the black of turf, his clothes fine with the wages he earned from the Big House.

It was Eliza who first learned to predict his visits. Da would draw into himself, would become sullen and quiet, fingers reaching more often for the *poitín* bottle than for the fiddle. "The tithe," she would whisper to Mary in the warmth of their blankets. "He'll come for it tomorrow. That's why there are no stories. No songs."

And sure enough, morning would come, bringing with it the rap of knuckles on the cottage door. Byrne, smiling with all his teeth, blessing their health as he took Da's earnings from his hands.

At first, his eyes had glazed over Mary—Eliza had always hung back, a sheep scenting a wolf—but as her body changed, so did the tone of these meetings. He would look not at Da but at Mary, at the new swells of flesh beneath her dress. She began to drape her shawl over her shoulders when the knock came at the door, even in summer when the cottage grew thick with heat. Before, she had always smiled hello when she saw him around the village, or at the market, frightened that any rudeness might hold some consequence for Da. But she began to keep her eyes to the ground when she caught sight of him cutting through the crowd.

Still, she'd put him out of her mind for the most part, busying herself with her daily tasks. The give of the vegetables under her knife when she prepared the evening meal, the dough for the farls sticky on her palms. The dreams that sustained her: of growing up and falling in love, of bearing children and keeping them close. When Da fell asleep, she'd walk with Eliza to the stream, her sister's hand firm in hers as if to tug her away from those dreams and back to earth, to the grass beneath their feet and the brush of insects on their skin.

"I wonder where you go, sometimes," Eliza had said to her, softly in the warm dark of their bed one night. It was summer, and Mary's skin itched with straw, and with the too-close heat of her sister's body. Each time she rolled away, pressing herself against the coolness of the wall, her sister moved with her.

"What do you mean?" she said, though the question pricked like a splinter on her finger, an intrusion.

"When you're quiet like this, but your breathing is shallow. I know you're not asleep, but you're not here, either."

"Nowhere," Mary lied, pressing her cheek against the wall. She could not tell Eliza of these longings: longings for love and children. Of a family, complete rather than fractured, the way theirs was.

She loved her sister—though love was not a strong enough word for the sensation that Eliza's heart thrummed in time with hers, that if one of them ceased to draw breath, the other would, too. But she did not know how to fit her sister into these dreams.

Perhaps Byrne had smelled it on her, the longing for something else.

Perhaps that was why it was her that he singled out. Why it was Mary that he chose, instead of Eliza.

Samhain. The burn of the water on her skin, the rush of the stream around her. The new tightness in Eliza's face.

Hush. Someone is there.

He came upon them so quickly that Mary had felt unable to move, fear weighting her down like stones. Eliza had thrown herself from the rock, but Mary had lain frightened and twitching, a gutted fish. He swore as he waded through the icy water, his hands reaching for her, calling her *his love, his beauty.* His breath touched her before his fingers did, reeking of drink, of something sweetly rotten.

Then, his shadow on her, a bat blotting out the moon. Around her, the night sounds swelled, as if this—a man pushing a girl against the jagged face of a rock—was but some ordinary occurrence of nature.

Still she could not move. One hand clawed at her breast, the other reached for her skirts, his breath a ragged wheeze in her ear and then—

The soft, wet *thwack* of rock on bone; his body slumping over her; lips slack and drooling in her hair. She could see the moon again, and in its yellow light Eliza, reddened stone trembling in her hand.

Blood sweetened the air, and Mary saw them hang—their bodies swaying on the rope, Da stooped in mourning clothes—before Byrne groaned against her ear. Eliza helped her struggle out from under his weight. Mary gasped as the air forced its way into her lungs.

"It was my fault," Mary said later, under their den of blankets in the cottage, hiding like foolish children. The men's shouts were getting closer and though she did not yet know the words *assault* and *exile*, she knew they would be punished for what they had done. "I was clumsy, I led him there, and then I did not . . ." The words clogged her mouth. "I *could* not fight. I am weak. Not like you."

"No, Mary," Eliza said. "No. You must not think that. It was the water that protected me. It's the water that makes us strong."

The wind grew loud and furious, blowing high and fierce as a woman's voice. Mary began to wonder if Aoife was right, if the sea sought vengeance for what they had taken from it. The tide lifted them with great gray hands and the sailors' shouts of work turned to screams of terror. Down below, the women held hands and closed their eyes.

When the lightning came through the cracks between the boards, her own body looked strange and otherworldly; her toes greenish and webbed. Her skin seemed to shimmer, as if covered with tiny scales, like the shark's had been. But then, in the next burst of light, the illusion was gone.

28

LUCY

SATURDAY, 16 FEBRUARY 2019

Lucy is standing alone in the kitchen, the house trembling around her.

The storm still rages: lightning comes blue through the blinds, patterning her body, the thunder as regular as a heartbeat.

She looks down at the alien spread of her hands. The nails clean and pink rather than torn and black. She is holding Dora Maar's ceramic bowl, and her wrists ache with the weight of it. Dora Maar winds herself around Lucy's calves and she yelps in surprise, the cat skittering away in fright.

There is the smell of cooking flesh in her nostrils, oily and sweet. She feels off kilter, off balance, as if missing the rocking motion of the ship. The room presses in on her, then recedes. She is here, but not here. It feels as if she's been hallucinating. How much time has she lost?

Shaking, she crouches to the floor, opening the tin of cat food and spooning it, fishy and gelatinous, into the bowl. The smell makes her want to gag.

She squeezes her eyes shut, tries to remember, to draw the lost minutes toward her like a skein of thread. The police had been here.

The police. The police are looking for Jess. For her sister who is not her sister.

Names and images blur across her mind. Her mother's face in the newspaper, the delicate, futile lift of her hand. The shock hits all over again, like cold water in her lungs.

Cameron Hennessey.

Cameron Hennessey is missing. Jess is missing.

And Lucy is losing her grip on time, on herself. On reality.

What had she done, after the police came? She remembers tearing through Jess's room—upending drawers, sending showers of loose coins and hair pins and pens clattering to the floor, pulling her sister's clothes from the wardrobe—for some clue as to where she has gone. But she found nothing.

She'd sat for a while on her sister's bed, watching the lightning vein the clouds until the sky turned black. She remembers picking up her phone, her fingers hovering over her parents' number. She remembers that voice in her head saying: *Make the call. End this.*

But what would she say?

That she finally knows the truth, that their family is as imagined as a fairy story? That she, Lucy, keeps slipping into another world entirely, a world of chained women and sea and songs? That Jess is missing? That the police are looking for her, along with the man who was once her teacher, then her lover?

The cat had come to her rescue, mewling for food. Lucy had gone downstairs and into the kitchen and picked the ceramic bowl up in her hands and—

Everything had fallen away.

She looks down at her legs, bare in her old pajama shorts.

The rash on her legs is peeling, coming off her in great pale strips, like the discarded skin of a snake. Below it, the flesh isn't pink and raw, or dotted with blood. Instead it glimmers, changing color with the light of the storm. Green then blue, then the pinkish white of mother-of-pearl. Iridescent as scales.

Lucy is in Jess's bathroom, rubbing her medicated cream into her shins, her pulse a sickly thud. But even through the greasy layer of ointment she can see the new strangeness, the *wrongness* of herself.

Her mind clings to facts and logic, to the solutions offered up by her frenzied internet searches. Plaque psoriasis; some kind of fungal infection. But none of the images match the new bluish sheen of her skin. The strange beauty of it.

Instead, her mind returns to the dream. To Mary.

Her skin seemed to shimmer, as if covered with tiny scales.

She remembers a detail from one of Jess's paintings.

Walking down the stairs, her hand grips the banister, and her legs shake so much she fears they'll give way. The storm has died down now, the wind a ghostly song on the waves, and in the silence she can hear her own panicked breath in her ears.

In the living room, she stares at the painting on the easel. Two women holding hands as they face the sea. The storm has stolen the sun from the sky, and even with all the lights on, the house is too dim for her to make out the painting's finer details. She switches on the flashlight of her phone and shines it over the women's legs. She reaches out her trembling fingers, touching the paint that is somehow both coarse and fine as silk.

A flash of childhood memory. Her parents had once forbidden her from playing outside after they'd seen a brown snake under the azalea bush, but Lucy had disobeyed them, fingers combing the undergrowth until she'd found her prize. She'd held it in her hands, light and sheer as gossamer, watching it catch the sun, trying to understand why something so beautiful might be unwanted. She'd kept it, in the secret place beneath her mattress, saving it until her sister's visit. She had given it to Jess and not thought of it again until now, as she feels its texture under her fingers, embedded in the canvas of the painting.

A snakeskin.

—

When she again hears knocking at the door, Lucy's pulse hammers.

Can the police be back already? She doesn't want to let them in, doesn't want to hear whatever new discovery they've made. There's a numbness to her thoughts, a slowness. An unwillingness to accept what is happening.

She won't answer the door, she decides. She will stand here, her hands on Jess's artwork, as if she can soak up her sister's thoughts.

More knocking, and then: "Lucy? It's Melody."

"One sec," Lucy calls, turning from the painting. She's about to unlock the door when she looks down at her legs, at the shimmering surface of her skin, the crusting flesh between the toes.

Fuck.

"Sorry, just getting dressed!"

In Jess's bedroom, she tugs on an old pair of leggings and thick socks. The soft fabric grates on her skin, her body resisting constraint.

Only when she's raced back downstairs again, taking the stairs two at a time, does she realize that the socks are mismatched.

You look mad, she thinks to herself. But she doesn't care. She *is* mad.

"Hi, love," says Melody when Lucy finally opens the door. "Think I'd better come in." The hood of her jacket glitters with rain, her eyes are narrowed with concern. She steps inside without waiting for an answer, smelling of laundry powder and a medicinal hint of eucalypt. The smell of her house. Suddenly, Lucy longs to be tucked up on Melody's sofa under one of her soft crocheted throws, listening to the wind chimes tinkle in the breeze. For a time before the arrival of the police, before the arrival of this new knowledge: that Jess really is in danger.

She trembles, watching as Melody wipes her shoes on the mat and hangs her raincoat on the hook next to the door with practiced ease.

"I'll put the kettle on," Melody says, clattering mugs onto the counter and rooting around in the pantry for teabags. "You sit down, try to relax." She gestures to the sofa as if she is the host and Lucy is the guest.

The bustle of activity in the kitchen and the hum of the boiling kettle drift over her in a comforting fog. For a moment, she forgets where she is, feeling nothing but the exhaustion that threads itself through her bones.

Her eyelids droop, and that other world—the one that waits below the surface—beckons, banished only when Melody places a cup of tea in front of her.

"So," she says as she sits down, dark eyes scanning Lucy's face. "The police came round, asking when I last saw Jess."

When she speaks again, her voice is softer, as if she's addressing a child.

"I know you must be very worried about her, sweetheart."

Lucy nods as she takes a sip of the tea, the liquid scalding her tongue. She takes a breath.

"Did you know about him, Cameron Hennessey? Did Jess tell you about—about what happened between them?"

For a moment Melody's expression is unreadable, and then she nods, once.

"Yeah. Yes. She did."

"You know they found his car nearby? I don't know why they're looking for him, or what he's done. But now he's gone, and she's gone, and—"

And I'm scared that she's in danger. That he's hurt her.

The sob bursts from her throat, and she buries her head in her hands.

But then Melody is moving closer to her, fingers lightly stroking Lucy's back.

"I'm going to tell you something," she says. "And you're going to sit and drink your tea, and you're going to listen.

"I should have told you this before," Melody continues. "I did think about it. But I didn't know how to say it in a way that would make sense. That you'd believe."

She sighs.

"I still don't know how, to be honest. But Jess is the only other person I've ever told. And I think she'd want me to tell you, now that this has happened.

"When we spoke earlier, you mentioned Daniel Smith. The man—well, I suppose he was more of a boy—who went missing in 1981. Ryan's older brother."

"Yes," Lucy says slowly. She remembers how Melody's face had shuttered at his name, as if she was fighting to keep something locked away inside her. Now, as she talks, Melody stares into the middle distance, or at her hands that work and worry in her lap—anywhere but at Lucy's face.

"I knew him, when I was a teenager. I mean, I knew everyone around here, coming as I did every summer. But he and I, we were close. I was seventeen." She smiles sadly. "I thought we were in love. God knows what he thought. Not that.

"He was older. He'd left school already; there was a glamor to that. He used to take me out in this little dinghy. We'd scare ourselves, listen out for the shipwrecked women singing, but we only ever heard the waves, the gulls. Mostly we'd just lie in his boat and kiss.

"He wanted to go all the way. I wanted it, too, but there was something in me, something that felt . . . uncertain. Unsafe, maybe, looking back on it. So, he'd put his hands on the button of my jeans, and kiss my neck and beg for more, and I'd say no, even though sometimes I felt like it'd be easier to say yes. Just give in, I'd think. Get it over with. It can't be that bad. But still, there was that little seed of fear."

Lucy nods, too scared to speak in case Melody stops talking.

"The cave in Devil's Lookout, the cave where they found Baby Hope," Melody continues, and Lucy suppresses a flinch at the name, at the tangled thoughts of her parents and Jess. "Bloody dangerous to get to. But it was another thing kids did back then, part of the local lore. Like a dare. Who was willing to go to the beach in the middle of the night, to listen for the voices? Who was brave enough to go and drink in the cave?

"It was January: we'd come up after New Year's. I was so excited to see Danny again, and when he asked me to go to the cave with him, I agreed. I waited until my parents were asleep, and then I snuck out to meet him. I remember he was carrying a backpack, clinking with beers.

"I was nervous—sweating. The tide was coming in, and we argued about whether it was safe. But Danny grabbed my hand and pulled me along. We inched around the headland, trying not to slip on the wet rocks. When we got to the cave, I was so exhausted, so afraid of how we'd manage to get back, that I almost forgot what we were there to do.

"It smelled like rotten seaweed and it was dark. He kissed me, pushed me to the ground, and I remember thinking *gross* at the slimy feel of the rocks, when I should have been thinking about how to get him off me, how to get away. His hands moved to my waistband and then inside my trousers. It hurt and I told him to stop, to get off me.

"He did stop, but I don't think it was because of what I said. I don't think he even heard me. He said: 'What's that sound?' At first I didn't know what he meant, but then I could hear it, too."

"Hear what?"

When Melody speaks again, Lucy thinks the note in her voice is pain, or fear. But then she looks at her, at the brightness of her eyes, the softness around her mouth. No, not pain nor fear, Lucy realizes. Wonder.

"Voices. Women's voices, like in the old ghost stories. But they weren't screaming, crying as they drowned—they were *singing*. This beautiful, lilting music—I couldn't make out the words but I remember it sounded almost like a folk song. It comforted me, made me feel safe, somehow.

"It was different for Danny. His whole body froze. I could smell the fear coming off him. But there was something else, too. A kind of . . . desire."

Lucy thinks, but doesn't say, how intertwined those things are. Fear and desire. How one can become the other so easily. All it takes is the tightening of a hand on your wrist, your throat.

"He sat up. I kept saying his name—*Danny, Daniel*—but my voice was soon drowned out by the singing; it was growing louder and louder. It seemed to be alive, somehow—an organism that had wrapped tentacles around him.

"Danny started moving toward the mouth of the cave, as if something was drawing him closer. It was a bright night, a lot of moonlight. He was almost silhouetted. I remember his whole body hunching forward as he crawled to the edge. And then . . ." Melody looks off to the side before meeting Lucy's gaze. "And then, he was gone."

"Gone?"

"He fell. Or jumped. I remember thinking"—Melody's tongue darts out to lick her lips, and her hands in her lap look rigid, but her eyes still have a faraway sheen—"that it was odd that he didn't scream. It was one of those slow-motion thoughts, the type you get when you're in shock."

"What did you do?" Lucy breathes. She can picture Melody as she would have been at seventeen: her dark eyes even larger in her face, her legs long and slim in denim shorts. Just a kid, all alone in a dank cave, watching a man fall to his death.

"I couldn't move. Not at first. My breathing was so loud—that's what made me notice that it had stopped. The singing. And then I immediately felt calm. Decisive. I knew I had to get home, that I couldn't tell anyone I'd been with Danny. I threw his backpack into the sea. It was funny—I'd been so frightened, on the way there. But on the way back, it was like my feet knew exactly where to go.

"When I got back to the beach, I put Danny's towel there, on the sand. To make it look like he'd just gone for a midnight swim and drowned."

"How come you didn't tell anyone what had happened?"

Melody sighs. "Well, they'd have blamed me, of course. They'd have said I led him to the cave, that I pushed him. I mean, everyone knew Danny had his issues. But he was a local." Her hands clench into fists. "And I was an outsider. Which is fucked up, when you

This morning, I told Mum I was meeting Max. Dad had ridden out on his tractor at daybreak, and Mum was driving into work, so with any luck neither of them would be home if Max called.

"Do you want a lift?" Mum asked, as I hoisted my backpack onto my shoulder and made for the front door.

"Nah," I said. "I'll cycle. We're going to ride to the old reservoir—Max wants to swim."

Mum raised her eyebrows. It was a stupid lie—Max would never have been so cruel as to suggest I watch him swim—but Mum bought it.

"Are you taking a hat?"

I nodded, lifting Dad's Akubra from the coat rack and cramming it onto my head.

"Don't tell," I said, bringing a finger to my lips, and Mum laughed.

By the time I'd wheeled out my bike from its position next to the shed and closed the front gate behind me, my face ached from the effort of smiling.

It took two hours to cycle to school. It was thirty degrees, and after only five minutes my breath was coming hard, sweat collecting behind my knees and on the inside of my elbows. But I enjoyed it, the hot dusty air on my face, the landscape whooshing past as if I was leaving it for good.

I cycled past the reservoir on the way, and there were loads of kids from school there, the colorful squares of their towels brightening the scabby grass. Someone had rigged a rope to an ancient gum, and they were taking turns launching themselves into the muddy water. Their whoops of laughter, the splash of their bodies breaking the surface, followed me like a taunt.

I cycled harder. *Let them have their reservoir*, I thought. It's little better than a glorified puddle, a slick of mud in the cracked land.

I could almost feel it then, the place where I'd been found. The salt rush of the sea, as powerful as the blood in my veins.

By the time the squat buildings of the school came into view—the gray concrete dingy against red earth and blue sky, the noticeboard with its peeling letters wishing me a *restful break*—I felt like I was seeing it with new eyes. I've been coming here since I was five and for the first time I was noticing the shabby smallness of it.

I've never belonged here.

I chained my bike to the fence, then cut through the empty quadrangle to get to the greenhouse. There, amid the smelly tangle of old sports equipment and my memories of Max, I slipped off my long-sleeved top and jeans. I pulled two water bottles out of my bag, drank one and poured the other over my head, feeling my skin tighten and tingle. I'd stolen one of Mum's dresses from her wardrobe: it was long and V-necked, made of a soft green jersey, the kind that clings to every curve. Sleeveless. I slipped it over my head and then looked at myself in the compact mirror I'd taken from her dresser.

My wet hair framed my face in black tendrils; the dress showed the silvered skin of my chest and arms.

Good, I thought. *Let him see me as I am.*

As I walked to the art block, I couldn't help but savor the air on my bare skin. I tilted my face to the sun and watched as a flock of galahs flew overhead, candy pink in the blue sky.

I was like a snake, shed of its skin. New and perfect and free.

Mr. Hennessey was in the art room already, sitting at one of the high tables, paper spread all around him, his hair bright with sun.

"Jess, hi."

I felt his eyes on me—on my bare skin, my damp hair—and then his gaze flickered away, uneasy. He cleared his throat and gestured to the chair opposite.

I draped my bag over the back of the chair and sat down. His eyes returned to mine and I thought how young he looked.

"Are you OK? I was worried about you yesterday. Has something happened?"

His hands were resting on the table, his knuckles speckled with think about it. *They* were the outsiders, not me. What's two hundred fucking years to more than sixty thousand?"

It's the first time Lucy has heard Melody swear. She doesn't know what to say: nothing feels adequate. All she can do is listen.

"They never found his body," Melody continues. "What happened to Danny spooked my parents. They knew we used to spend time together—not that they approved of him, Dad said he didn't trust him as far as he could throw him—but I guess it felt too close to home. Sometimes I wonder if Mum sensed it, that I was involved somehow. That she worried I'd be blamed. Anyway, we never came back again."

"But you did," Lucy says, trying to read the expression on Melody's face. The twist at the corner of her mouth, the flickering muscle of her eyebrow. "You came back."

"Yes, eventually."

"Why?"

Melody reaches for her own cup of tea, takes a long sip, her eyes trained on Jess's painting.

"Like I told you before—it was a special place for us, as a family. After Mum and Dad died, there was no one else to remember the time we spent here together. Coming back—it made me feel closer to them, kept them alive, somehow. But there was another reason, too."

Lucy waits.

"I came back," Melody continues, "because I felt safe here. I *feel* safe here. I know that doesn't make sense. I should be traumatized by what Danny almost did to me, by what happened to him. But something protected me that day, Lucy. Something—someone—kept me safe."

"You mean whoever—or *what*ever—was singing?"

"Maybe." Melody pauses. "I've thought about it a lot over the years. Maybe it was the ghosts of the drowned women, like in the stories. I guess if I were Christian, I might call it God, only it didn't feel like any God I'd ever been taught about it. I'm only sure of two things. One, it was of the sea—not the land, *my* land. And two, it felt . . . female."

Lucy doesn't know what to say. The two of them sit in silence for a while, listening to the rain gently falling on the roof. She thinks of the men who've disappeared from Comber Bay over the years. David Watts, who'd been suspected of his girlfriend's death, but had never faced justice. Malcolm Biddy, whose disappearance had led to the discovery of a nationwide pedophile ring.

And Danny Smith.

She remembers what Ryan said about his father. About how he'd become obsessed with the *Naiad* after Danny's disappearance, how people had called him mad. It did seem mad—devoting all that time, all that money, to erecting a memorial for the *Naiad*'s victims, when your son was still missing.

She thinks of the paper with its desperate scrawl, of dates and names and possible connections. The sentence written on the back.

Make it stop.

What if Bernard Smith had known what his son was really like, had guessed what he'd done? What if he hadn't been trying to commemorate the *Naiad*'s victims, but to appease them?

Melody puts her mug of tea on the coffee table, places her hand on Lucy's knee. Lucy tries hard not to flinch at the contact, at the press of the fabric of her leggings on the raw layer of skin beneath.

"What I'm trying to say," Melody murmurs, dark eyes staring into Lucy's, "is that we don't need to worry about your sister. There's something about this place, something different. It keeps its women safe."

29

JESS'S DIARY

1999

10 January

The dreams were the worst they've ever been last night.

When Mum knocked on my door to tell me dinner was ready, I told her I still had a headache.

"Oh, poor love," she said, opening the door a crack. I buried my face in the pillow so that I wouldn't have to look at her, this stranger. "Can I get you something? Painkillers, water?"

"No," I said, gritting my teeth. "I'm just going to sleep it off."

"All right, sweetheart. Let me know if you need anything, OK? Love you."

I didn't say it back.

An hour later, another knock on the door. It was Dad, this time.

"GG," he said. "Jess. Max is on the phone for you."

My gut lurched. I could picture Max in his room, the phone cradled between his ear and his shoulder as he sat in the chair by his desk, bare feet resting on his bed. The bed where we'd—

"Tell him I'm sick," I said, even though I wanted to hear his voice more than anything. I needed my best friend.

Shame flushed through me when I remembered what we'd done.

213

The way his fingers had hesitated on my skin. How he'd wanted to turn the light off. Like he couldn't bear to see me as I really am.

How could we be friends—how could we be anything to each other—after that?

"All right, love," Dad—or the man who pretended to be my dad—said, shutting the door softly.

I lay there for hours, unmoving. I didn't get out of bed. Not after I heard the hiss of the tap running as Dad did the washing-up, the soft burble of the television from the living room. Not even after I heard the floorboards creak as they went up to bed, turning off the hallway light so that everything was black.

At some point I must have fallen asleep, because the next thing I was aware of was the groan of timber all around me, the bite of icy water on my skin.

When I woke up, I was sitting on the edge of the bath with the tap on full blast, white water thundering over my toes. The lights were off and in the slice of moonlight through the window, the skin of my legs shone blue. I turned off the tap so violently that my palms burned. I sat, heart pounding, listening for any noises coming from the master bedroom.

But there was nothing. Just the house breathing silently around me.

After I'd dried myself, I sat cross-legged on my bed with the lava lamp on, watching myself change. First, the webbed flesh between my toes began to itch. When I touched it, the skin came away in white ribbons, revealing a shining blue layer beneath.

Abandoned by the sea.

That must be why this happens. Why I'm drawn to water, to the thing that hurts me. Dawes Plain is almost one thousand kilometers inland. Mum and Dad—or Robert and Judith Wilson—took me as far from the sea as they could.

Why?

To protect me, or to stop me from learning the truth?

———

This morning, I told Mum I was meeting Max. Dad had ridden out on his tractor at daybreak, and Mum was driving into work, so with any luck neither of them would be home if Max called.

"Do you want a lift?" Mum asked, as I hoisted my backpack onto my shoulder and made for the front door.

"Nah," I said. "I'll cycle. We're going to ride to the old reservoir—Max wants to swim."

Mum raised her eyebrows. It was a stupid lie—Max would never have been so cruel as to suggest I watch him swim—but Mum bought it.

"Are you taking a hat?"

I nodded, lifting Dad's Akubra from the coat rack and cramming it onto my head.

"Don't tell," I said, bringing a finger to my lips, and Mum laughed.

By the time I'd wheeled out my bike from its position next to the shed and closed the front gate behind me, my face ached from the effort of smiling.

It took two hours to cycle to school. It was thirty degrees, and after only five minutes my breath was coming hard, sweat collecting behind my knees and on the inside of my elbows. But I enjoyed it, the hot dusty air on my face, the landscape whooshing past as if I was leaving it for good.

I cycled past the reservoir on the way, and there were loads of kids from school there, the colorful squares of their towels brightening the scabby grass. Someone had rigged a rope to an ancient gum, and they were taking turns launching themselves into the muddy water. Their whoops of laughter, the splash of their bodies breaking the surface, followed me like a taunt.

I cycled harder. *Let them have their reservoir*, I thought. It's little better than a glorified puddle, a slick of mud in the cracked land.

I could almost feel it then, the place where I'd been found. The salt rush of the sea, as powerful as the blood in my veins.

By the time the squat buildings of the school came into view—the gray concrete dingy against red earth and blue sky, the noticeboard with its peeling letters wishing me a *restful break*—I felt like I was seeing it with new eyes. I've been coming here since I was five and for the first time I was noticing the shabby smallness of it.

I've never belonged here.

I chained my bike to the fence, then cut through the empty quadrangle to get to the greenhouse. There, amid the smelly tangle of old sports equipment and my memories of Max, I slipped off my long-sleeved top and jeans. I pulled two water bottles out of my bag, drank one and poured the other over my head, feeling my skin tighten and tingle. I'd stolen one of Mum's dresses from her wardrobe: it was long and V-necked, made of a soft green jersey, the kind that clings to every curve. Sleeveless. I slipped it over my head and then looked at myself in the compact mirror I'd taken from her dresser.

My wet hair framed my face in black tendrils; the dress showed the silvered skin of my chest and arms.

Good, I thought. *Let him see me as I am.*

As I walked to the art block, I couldn't help but savor the air on my bare skin. I tilted my face to the sun and watched as a flock of galahs flew overhead, candy pink in the blue sky.

I was like a snake, shed of its skin. New and perfect and free.

Mr. Hennessey was in the art room already, sitting at one of the high tables, paper spread all around him, his hair bright with sun.

"Jess, hi."

I felt his eyes on me—on my bare skin, my damp hair—and then his gaze flickered away, uneasy. He cleared his throat and gestured to the chair opposite.

I draped my bag over the back of the chair and sat down. His eyes returned to mine and I thought how young he looked.

"Are you OK? I was worried about you yesterday. Has something happened?"

His hands were resting on the table, his knuckles speckled with paint. Mine were just inches away. I remembered his fingers, feather-light on my skin.

I told him about Robert and Judith Wilson. About Cliff House, about Comber Bay.

He listened, his eyes never leaving mine. Something changed in the set of his body; there was a new weight to him, as if he could see that my burden was too heavy and so had shouldered it himself.

By the time I finished, my cheeks burned with tears. He produced a folded wad of tissues and placed it on the table between us.

"I thought you might need these," he said softly and I imagined him putting those tissues in his pocket and thinking of me. Some of the heaviness inside me lifted.

"Thank you," I said, and the words sat between us, inadequate. The sun poured through the windows, and despite the whirr of the fan, the air was hot, close. I could smell his breath, with its hint of peppermint.

He waited until I had dried my tears before he spoke again.

"I can't imagine how it feels, discovering something so important has been kept from you," he began, then paused. "I loved my dad, when I was a kid. Really hero-worshipped him. Until one day I came home from school with a painting that the teacher had given a gold star. He ripped it in half. 'Only faggots like art,' he said."

"That's awful," I said.

He shrugged, like it was nothing.

"Yours is an extreme example," he went on, "but we all go through it. That realization that your parents aren't who you thought they were. Bigots in my case—liars in yours. But not everyone in your life is going to hurt you, Jess. I promise you that."

"Would you? Hurt me, I mean."

He looked away, then back again.

"No," he said.

I moved my hand so that my fingertips touched his.

The silence swelled. I could see the jump of his pulse beneath the gold stubble of his jaw. My own pulse thundered in my ears, and I wondered if our hearts were beating in time.

It seemed we might sit like that forever; other students' artworks staring down at us like saints in a church. The moment unbroken as a spell.

And then, the sudden warmth of his hand on mine. Changing everything.

I don't want to write about what happened next. I don't think I could do justice to any of it. Words can never quite capture everything, can they?

Maybe one day I'll paint it. The tender shine in his eyes. Our hair—mine dark, his blond—tangled together.

I keep thinking about that painting he showed me of Orpheus and Eurydice. But instead, he's saving me. Taking my hand and pulling me away from the dream world into this one.

He gave me a book to borrow, before I left. *A Wave of Dreams*, by Louis Aragon. It's old, the letters on the cover peeling, the spine cracked.

"It made me think of you," he said, his body framed in the doorway to the art block.

I've been reading it since I got home. There's a passage about how when we sleep, we summon our dreams; like we're communing with ghosts. A lightness spread through me as I read. He understands. He understands what it's like.

But that isn't even the best part. The best part—I've traced it again and again with my fingers—is the borrower's slip on the flyleaf, where he's written his name in neat, sloping letters.

If I sleep with it under my pillow, it'll be like he's here.

30

LUCY

SATURDAY, 16 FEBRUARY 2019

Lucy closes the diary, unable to read any more.

Melody left a couple of hours ago, promising to return the next day.

"You will eat something, won't you?" she'd said, placing her hand on Lucy's knee. "I don't like the look of that fridge. What's in there—one egg and half a carton of milk?"

Lucy had laughed, which had somehow made the tears fall. Melody had drawn her into a tight hug, and Lucy had let herself be cradled, breathing in the other woman's clean and comforting scent.

Melody had drawn back, fixing her dark eyes on Lucy's.

"She's all right, wherever she is. I know it."

The house had been eerily still after she left, and Lucy found she longed for the tumult of the storm. It had kept her inside, ensured that there was nothing she could do to find Jess. Now, she felt restless, useless. She opened the windows, hoping the fresh air would calm her, inhaling the smell of rain-washed eucalyptus. Myna birds chirped, a currawong trilled.

It reminded her of a rainstorm—years ago—that had broken a months-long dry period in Dawes Plain. It had drummed so loudly on the corrugated roof that Lucy had worried it would buckle, that their house would be washed away.

She'd watched it come down in shimmering waves out of her window. Her father had dressed in waterproofs to check on the sheep and she was anxiously waiting for his return. For ages and ages, he didn't come, and fear bubbled inside her.

Then she saw him, a dark figure in the shifting light, almost a stranger in his long coat and peaked hat. She'd waved, but he hadn't seen her as he trudged toward the house, head bent forward against the downpour.

But then he'd taken off his hat and tilted his face up to the sky, letting the rain thunder over him. There'd been something about the stance of his body—the slope of his shoulders, the outstretched fingers of his hands—that even as a child, Lucy had recognized as longing.

Whatever had happened before—whether or not her parents were telling the truth about how their eldest daughter came into their lives—they had given up everything for Jess. To keep her safe.

Now, the journal heavy in her hands, thoughts of Jess and Hennessey clouding her mind, Lucy knows that she can put it off no longer.

They were *in an intimate relationship*, the police had said.

But Jess had been just sixteen when it began. A child. He'd groomed her. She has to talk to her parents, find out what they know.

She has to tell them Jess is missing.

The phone rings and rings, so that Lucy begins to hope they're not home, that the conversation can be avoided for a little longer.

But then her mother answers.

"Martin residence."

Lucy's eyes burn. She can almost see her mother standing in the kitchen, her graying hair piled on top of her head, weathered hands chopping vegetables, her wedding ring resting in the ceramic dish shaped like a shell. She'd be humming a song—the Beatles or the Kinks, maybe. Every so often, she'd reach for her favorite wineglass, the one with the frosted stencil reading *Mum* that Lucy bought her one birthday. Outside, the fields would be vast and pink in the dusk. The scene is so vivid that Lucy almost feels as if she might reach out and touch it.

And yet it feels exactly that—a scene. For almost forty years, her parents have played at being other people. And for her whole life, Lucy has been the only one who didn't know. The only one in the dark.

"Mum," Lucy says now, and the word is a desperate plea, as if somehow her mother can change the past, edit it to remove the gaps, the lies.

"Goose, is that you?" And then, when there's only silence: "Lucy, sweetheart, what's wrong?"

"It's Jess. She's gone." The last word comes out strangled, partially formed, as if her mouth cannot bear to utter it.

"Gone? Gone where? I don't understand."

Lucy takes a breath, trying to slow her heart. She has to tell the truth. Her parents' idea of her—the easy daughter, with the good grades and ambition—is a mask she must take off.

"Mum, I lied when we spoke on the phone the other day. I'm not at uni. I'm at Cliff House. In Comber Bay. But Jess is gone."

A sharp intake of breath, then silence.

"Sorry—you said *Cliff House*? You're at Cliff House?"

"Yes."

"What has Jess told you?"

"No, you don't understand—Jess hasn't told me anything. I haven't even spoken to her, she's not here. I got here a few days ago and the house was empty. Her car's here, and her phone . . . and now the police have been here. Looking for someone called Cameron Hennessey."

Another intake of breath.

"Mum, do you know who Cameron Hennessey is?"

"Dear God, I hoped I'd never have to hear that name again. Lucy—look. There are some things your father and I need to tell you. But I think it's best if we do it in person—"

"I already know everything, Mum. I've been reading Jess's diary. I know that Jess is Baby Hope."

"Lucy. Don't read any more of that diary, please. I'm going to call your father now and we're going to get in the car and drive down there. We'll be there the day after tomorrow—sooner if we can. All right?"

"All right."

"And Lucy? Luce?"

"Yes?"

"I love you. Both of you. Please, remember that."

Lucy knows it's true. She *is* loved, and so is Jess. Their parents left everything behind to protect her.

But they also lied.

Don't read any more of that diary.

What else are they hiding?

31

MARY

Mam's lips were warm against Mary's ear.

"Come, *a linbh*," she said. "Follow me."

Mary opened her eyes to darkness. There was the long-buried smell of home—not the smell of the cottage in Armagh, with the hearth that she had yet to sweep and the stain of *poitín* in the air. Instead there was the briny tang of the sea, the sweet rot of fish guts. Her mother's scent, sun-baked sand and the gritty insides of shells.

Mam lifted her from the bed, and Mary buried her face in the damp tendrils of her hair. They passed Da's sleeping form, her mother stepping lightly over the coils of rope at the threshold and into the pearled morning.

Eliza was waiting on the shore, her eyes on the foaming waves as if she could see them. She turned at the soft fall of their footsteps in the sand and smiled.

See, her face seemed to say. *Didn't I tell you?*

Mam took their hands in hers, and together the three of them walked toward the water. Spindrift raked back Mary's hair with gentle fingers. She was afraid to look at Mam, afraid that if she did, the tall, elegant figure—pale and thin as if she'd been whittled from scrimshaw—would disappear.

They passed bloated bodies of jellyfish, red ropes of dulse, and then the water frothed and bubbled over Mary's toes. Already it began to sting, and the fear started up in her. She hung back, pulling at Mam's fingers, but Mam and Eliza strode on, white water rising to their chests.

Mary looked back to the shore, to the little stone cottage squatting on the shingle. Somehow, she knew that if she kept going—if she followed Mam and Eliza—she would never see it again. She would never see Da again.

"Come, *a linbh*," Mam said again, and for the first time Mary allowed herself to look upon her mother's face.

Fleshy wings, like the gills on the herring Da caught in his net, beat beneath her jaw. Her cheeks were crusted gray with barnacles, and there were raw pink holes where her eyes should have been.

"Come, *a linbh*," she said once more, as if those were the only words she knew. Mary knew then that this was not Mam but some copy of her, that Mam was dead, a corpse eaten by the sea.

Her own scream woke her to the groan and pitch of the ship. Her breath came fast in her chest, and she raised fingers to her neck, checking that the skin there was smooth. It was tender to the touch, so tender that she ripped her hand away, not wanting to feel it, not wanting to know.

Already, the water was soaking into her, pulling her into its maw. She imagined it reaching inside the ship and dragging her to the seabed, the way it had done with Mam, the flesh lifting from her greening bones—

"Mary?" Next to her Eliza stirred. "What is it?"

She could not answer, her mouth was too dry and swollen with thirst. How cruel that water raged around them, that it seeped into her very dreams, and yet there was still not enough to drink. She wanted to cry but the tears would not come.

Instead, she folded herself small as she could in the berth, gagging on the stink of rotting blankets and her own unwashed flesh. She wished there was some way she could stop her ears, some way she could drown out the sound of terrified sobbing around her, the awful boom as the ship rose and fell.

At first, she thought she was imagining Eliza's voice, that it was part of the dream that lingered still. But then the sweet notes grew louder, and she knew that her sister sought to soothe and comfort her. She felt Eliza's hand grasp hers.

Join me, she seemed to say. *It will help.*

It was a strange song that Eliza had chosen, with its eerie echo of Mary's dream. She wondered if her sister had seen inside her mind, had seen the specter of Mam that had haunted her, so different from Eliza's beloved merrow with shining scales. Perhaps she wanted to vanquish Mary's nightmare, to paint in her mind the image of Mam as she, Eliza, remembered her.

But Eliza was right about one thing, Mary realized. Singing would calm her, and so she tilted back her head and pushed the song out through her lungs. It was one that Da had taught them, when they were small enough to sit at his knee before the jumping flames of the hearth. It was about a maiden who waits on the shore, luring a sea captain with her voice, before robbing him of his coins and his sword. Da had sung it with such passion—Mary remembered feeling the notes quivering from his chest—that she had believed he'd composed it himself.

But that could not have been so, for the other women began to join in until their voices grew so strong that it seemed they might lift the ship above the waves, away from the savage sea to safety.

> *You should have known me before*
> *I sang you to sleep, and I robbed you of wealth*
> *And again I'm a maid on the shore.*

Mary wondered if the captain could hear it. The beauty they made of his prison.

32

LUCY

SUNDAY, 17 FEBRUARY 2019

Her voice carries on the dawn air, echoing against the rocks.

Lucy lifts her fingers to her mouth as if to grasp hold of the song and examine it in her hand. But there is nothing—only the hush of the waves on the shore, the thrum of her own blood.

She does not scream or flinch this time.

It feels almost inevitable to be standing halfway down the cliff's sandstone staircase, body tilted like a diver's. Dawn bloodies the horizon, and in its pink light Lucy sees the plunge of the cliff below.

Her pulse rises. Her toes cling to the edge of the rough-hewn step; one wrong move and she will fall.

Breathe. She has to breathe.

In. Out.

But the breaths come quick and ragged; her heart begins to pound in her chest. Her voice finds the song as if she has only just set it down, and her lungs and diaphragm expand and contract.

> *"Well, I'll sing you a song," the fair maiden did cry,*
> *And the captain was weeping for joy o.*
> *She sang it so sweetly, so soft, so completely,*

226

She sang captain and sailors to sleep o,
She sang captain and sailors to sleep o.

She knows the lyrics from deep within her bones. It's the same song that Jess used to sing to her when she was a little girl.

It's like her sister is there with her.

Her heart slows. She can feel the sweet rush of oxygen to her brain, her thoughts sharpening into sense.

It's then that she remembers the rope she saw on her first day here, flapping limp in the wind against the staircase. If she can find it, she can use it as a guide and pull herself back up the steps. She reaches to her right, and her fingers brush something coarse and wiry. She leans further, groping over grass and jagged rock. A cloud passes over the moon, leaving her in darkness.

She curls her toes around the step, gripping tight, calves burning with the effort. She can hear the rope moving in the wind, she realizes: can hear the gentle *thwack* of it knocking against the cliff.

When she finds the rope at last, she breathes hard, every muscle screaming as she pulls herself upward. She climbs, each step sending pebbles raining below. Her breath comes hard and fast as she wonders how on earth she made it down so far, how her unconscious body navigated this terrain.

The house comes into view, jutting out from the rock like a tongue. Her eyes burn with tears of gratitude and exhaustion.

She is gripping the veranda's edge when she feels something hard digging into the sole of her foot. A shell, she thinks at first, but it is smooth rather than jagged. One hand gripping the balcony rail, she reaches to retrieve it.

It is a gold ring, cold and heavy in her palm.

Under the weak kitchen light, she can see it is a man's wedding ring. The gold is a little scratched, but it looks relatively new. She doesn't like the way it feels in her hand. The significance of it. She puts it down on the table and unlocks her laptop, the webpage she'd been reading earlier still open on the screen.

Cameron Hennessey's LinkedIn profile.

The most recent position—one he's held since 2012—is head of the art department at a Sydney private school, Marsden College. Googling the school, she sees that there's an article in the *Sydney Morning Herald* from 11 February. Monday. The day before a flustered Jess knocked on Melody's door to say she was going away for a while.

PROTESTS ROCK SCHOOL AFTER ALLEGATIONS, reads the headline.

Police have confirmed they are investigating an allegation of sexual assault after claims circulated online about a teacher at a prestigious Sydney private school.

On Friday, pupils at $30,000-a-year Marsden College—an independent, coeducational school in Sydney's leafy North Shore—staged a mass walkout and protest over the claims.

Now, NSW police have told the Herald *they are investigating "a number of allegations of sexual offenses" from between 2012 and 2019.*

The Herald *understands these accusations relate to one teacher, whom the paper is not identifying for legal reasons, but who has been named in a Google document cataloguing female students' experiences of sexual harassment and assault. It is understood that the teacher has not been seen in school since the protest.*

School principal Dr. Matthew Turner declined to comment. But shortly after the protest, alumna Emma Caulfield, the youth activist who created the online document detailing the accusations, posted to Instagram: "I stand in solidarity with the brave students who have come forward, and call on Marsden and the police to take immediate action. It's bad enough that girls face sexual harassment and abuse from their male peers. For someone in a position of authority to do this is unthinkable. Enough is enough."

Many comments on this post named the accused teacher, prompting a police warning that doing so could result in criminal charges.

Lucy easily finds the activist's Instagram account and the relevant post. There are over 9,000 likes, 700 comments. She scrolls through them, hands trembling.

I went to Marsden, reads one. *He was always a fkn creep.*

Hennessey taught my sister. He asked her if she'd model for a life drawing . . . ugh. So sad for the victims 💔 .

Say his name. Cameron Hennessey. He doesn't deserve anonymity.

Of course the cops want to protect an abuser. Prob too busy hiding their own to investigate. ACAB.

I personally witnessed him ask a girl if the ladder in her tights was a "stairway to heaven" 😨 .

Shock drops like a stone into Lucy's stomach.

She thinks of the things Jess wrote about Hennessey in her journal: the way he'd stroked the skin on the underside of her wrist, the way he'd placed his hand over hers.

I don't want to write about what happened next. I don't think I could do justice to any of it.

She picks up the ring from the table, looks at the dull metal shining in her palm.

On the inside of the band is an inscription. *C & N, 8.11.15.*

She types *Cameron Hennessey Sydney marriage* into Google, and on the second page of results, she finds what she's looking for. An old post on a wedding photographer's website, titled *Cameron and Nicola, 8 November 2015.*

Cameron and Nicola.

She's holding Hennessey's wedding ring.

The police were right. He *was* here, at Cliff House.

The photographs on the website fade in and out of focus. She finds she cannot bear to look at him—his fair hair, the face that might once have been handsome, now blurred with age and fat. He embraces his bride, a slim redhead in an ivory gown, the sun falling across her cheek. They gaze at each other lovingly.

You would never know, she thinks, to look at him.

Had there been signs? she wonders now. Evenings where he came back late from school, furtive glances at his phone? Had this woman—Nicola, with her pale eyes and freckled nose—lain in bed beside her husband, unease ticking in her gut? Or had she lived in blissful ignorance?

Lucy is seared by a new, awful clarity.

Because an unspeakable possibility is unfurling in her mind. She cannot name it, not even to herself. Not until she knows for sure.

She remembers her mother's voice on the phone, frightened and pleading.

Lucy. Don't read any more of that diary.

She leans forward, deposits the ring on the coffee table in front of her with a dull clink. She wipes the palm of her hand on her trousers, as if to remove any trace of him. For a time, she sits, staring at the diary, its pages bloated with damp and age, the stupid pink swirls of its cover. As if nothing a teenage girl might write could be of any importance.

Her phone chirps with a message.

Mum: *Any word from J? Have driven through night—should be there 10ish.*

It's 6 A.M. now.

She could wait for them to arrive, for them to try and explain.

A sudden image of herself, the younger Lucy. The sandy bowl cut, the skin pale with creams and bandages. Notebook in hand, writing her little lists. Her facts. Even then, she'd felt it. That yearning for truth, for something solid she could hold on to.

Lucy picks up the diary, swallowing as she skims the final lines of the last entry she'd read.

I don't want to write about what happened next. I don't think I could do justice to any of it.

She considers again the timing of it all.

January 1999.

She turns the page to read the next entry and finds not words but a drawing: ink cross-hatched violently so that it is darkest in the center, like a cave. The next page contains a similar drawing, and the next, but still there are no words and soon there is nothing, only blank pages under her fingers.

Her skin prickles with panic. Could an entry have been ripped out?

She closes the journal, runs her finger across the inside edges of the pages, searching for a gap, the tatter of torn paper. Then she notices a thickness, a bulge.

A folded photograph, wedged tight into the journal's spine. She retrieves it with shaking fingers. The weightiness of the paper, the lamination of it. She knows. Already, she knows.

It's her mother's face that comes to her. The bright hazel eyes, the easy smile. The crooked incisor.

The folded paper trembles in her hands. She opens it.

The image is murky, as if it's been taken underwater. She supposes, in a way, that it has been. In the darkness, a pale form. The globe of the head, the amphibian curve of a spine.

An ultrasound.

The column of text on the left-hand side reads:

20 April 1999
Martin, Jessica

PART THREE

33

JESS

19 SEPTEMBER 1999

Jess unfolded the ultrasound furtively, tilting it away from any curious passengers. She liked the photograph, the way the baby seemed so content there, in the ocean of her womb. The perfect fit of her, a mollusk in its shell.

If only she could stay there. If only Jess did not have to go through with it—the labor that blanked her mind with terror. She refused to imagine it, nor to imagine a life afterward; as if it was not birth that loomed, but death.

Folding the ultrasound up small, she wedged it back inside her diary. She turned the pages to the last entry she'd written in January. The final line glimmered cruelly back at her.

If I sleep with it under my pillow, it'll be like he's here.

Something rose inside her, and she uncapped her pen, in case it was a sentence. But the words would not come, just as they had not come for the long swell of time since she had last seen Cameron Hennessey.

Instead, when she put her pen to paper, she drew. The shuddering motion of the bus jolted her hand, so that her pen veered across the page in wild loops. Still, it took form. The lines dark and undulating, a hollow, shadowed space.

It looked like a mouth, or maybe a womb, but Jess knew it was a cave. She had begun to dream of it, ever since she'd felt those first, furtive movements. She knew how the sun crept inside it, glinting off the stalactites that hung like fangs. She knew the texture of the stone, the warmth of it, the wet slick of lichen. She knew the smell of salt and iron and things growing and dying away.

She knew, somehow, that it was safe.

She did not know exactly how she'd find it. But she knew that it must be near the house where her parents had lived, before they became her parents. The address she'd seen on the lawyer's letter, now committed to memory.

Cliff House, 1 Malua Street, Comber Bay.

This was where she was going. This was where the bus was taking her.

When she had finished drawing, the page swallowed by darkness, she looked out the greasy window at the passing landscape. It was dull and brown, flecked with the flat silver roofs of houses. Just the sight of it made her thirsty. She ached for a glimpse of the coast, a blue slice of sea, even though they had to be miles and miles away, still.

It was as if someone had cast an invisible wire across the land, had caught her between the ribs and pulled.

The sea was in her veins, calling loud as a song.

Jess wondered how long it would take her parents to notice she'd run away. Perhaps two days, when she failed to return from the school trip to Canberra she'd invented, the lie bolstered by a form with the school letterhead, painstakingly constructed on the library photocopier. Perhaps sooner, if Max told them, which she feared he would.

Poor Max. He didn't deserve any of this.

She'd told him three months ago, no longer able to ignore the notes slipped into her locker, increasingly desperate in tone. He was haunted, he wrote, by the thought that he'd done something wrong on New Year's Eve. That he'd upset her somehow. He'd been so nervous, he'd explained. So frightened of hurting her, of making her uncomfortable. He'd wanted it to be perfect, like she deserved. She hadn't known what to say, confronted with how wrong she'd been, how she'd misjudged him.

But even this felt trivial against the silvered swell of her body.

They had met at the greenhouse, and when she told him, the look on his face scooped her out with shame. His gaze was earnest beneath the knot of his forehead, like they were discussing a piece of schoolwork Jess couldn't quite get the hang of.

"I'll help," he'd told her. "It's my responsibility, too."

She'd felt, then, an awful impulse to get away; to cement her ugliness in his heart. To say something that would repel him forever, for his own sake.

"Actually," she'd said, the words ferric on her tongue, "it isn't."

For years afterward, she would lie awake at night, seeing the look on his face. The eyes wide and the mouth slack with shock. He'd said nothing for a moment, unable to translate thought into speech, as if she'd damaged some fundamental mechanism inside him.

And then:

"It's him, isn't it? Hennessey."

She wanted the conversation to be over, she wanted to get away. After all, she was so tired. Tired of the dragging pain in her belly, the new weight to her limbs. The effort of concealment. And so it seemed easiest to say nothing.

There had been no question of telling Hennessey—or Cameron, as she still thought of him. He was long gone by the time she knew.

"It's not safe for me," he'd said, one day in late January, just weeks after that sunlit afternoon in the studio. "I can't stay."

The librarian, he'd told her, had noticed her bike leaning against the art studio block that afternoon, had heard the sounds coming from inside. She had reminded him to keep the studio locked, lest other students "rendezvous" inside.

Jess had scratched at the skin of her wrist, inflamed by worry, and she'd seen him flinch and look away, repulsed. He no longer saw her as beautiful, as precious as the shells on some imagined beach.

Perhaps he never had.

When the announcement of a new art teacher came at assembly, all Jess could do was marvel at the speed with which he'd erased himself so completely from her life.

She hadn't had the energy to mourn his loss: her days were swallowed up by the work of denial, of concealing the secret that swelled inside her. The lonely effort of it, vomiting quietly into the toilet. Taking the bus to Bourke for a pregnancy test, hoodie pulled down over her face, and later, the ultrasound. Combing charity shops for the loosest, baggiest clothes. The constant fear that the truth was written in the new, sloping lines of her body; in the shadows under her eyes.

For months, she'd sat across the dinner table from her parents, knowing their secret and waiting for them to guess hers.

The easiest way to lie to someone, she learned, is to lie to yourself.

And how she'd lied. She ignored the baby's twists and turns inside her, avoided mirrors, avoided looking down at the pale moon of her body when she dressed.

Except at night. At night, when there was no sound in the house but the soft tide of her parents' snores, she had taken to locking the bathroom door and running the bath, the water blue in the moonlight from the window. Robing herself in the cool silk of it. Later, in her bedroom, she would feel her skin burn, watch as the dome of her stomach cracked and hardened like a sea creature's shell. It was better to do it this way, when she was awake, than let the water draw her in her sleep. This way, she could be careful: to lock the door, to wipe the tub down afterward, to remove the strands of her hair from the plughole.

It was like a great thirst had overtaken her, had become the ruler of her body. Even as she slept, she was at its mercy.

———

Sydney. In the dark, the harbor was studded with the lights of small boats, as if the sky had fallen in. The bridge reminded her of a sheep's carcass she'd seen once with Max, the great arc of it like an exposed rib cage. Her fingers itched to draw it, but there was no longer enough light.

A bus interchange. Cigarette butts on the pavement, the crumpled remnants of a takeaway food container. An addict stared at her with bottomless eyes. The smells of tarmac and fuel and drink and the sharp, metallic scent of the city itself.

Another bus, the seat upholstery worn and tinged with ancient sweat. A beer can rolled around on the floor, clanging every time the bus braked or turned. There were only two other passengers: a teenage boy with glassy eyes, redolent of alcohol, and a woman with a suitcase. Neither took any notice of her.

Jess put her headphones on and leaned against the window, but the battery on her Walkman was dead.

Hours passed, blurring together. The sun came up, gilding the land. Things were greener, here; she opened the window and smelled eucalypt. There was a mineral smell, too; Jess inhaled it deep into her chest. It was the sea. They were close.

The bush crackled around her, leaves and twigs brushing at her skin, urging her onward. She saw, as the ground sloped, flashes of blue through the trees.

Cliff House rose up ahead—a sunken roof, a veranda thick with debris. One window broken, the other boarded up. She climbed the stairs, stumbling over a beer bottle. The door swung open, the lock smashed and useless. Inside, there was an underwater smell; the walls were bloated with damp. More bottles, an abandoned sleeping bag. In the kitchen, fragments of pottery that she recognized: blue-patterned shards in the sink a match to the cereal bowls they used at home. All her life there had been only three. There were a few other signs of her parents: a faded apron on a hook on the kitchen door, old magazines yellowing in the living room.

Clinging to the banister, she hauled herself up the stairs to the bedroom. The floor glittered with condom wrappers and ring-pulls. At one stage the window—now closed—had been left open and rain had soaked through the mattress, so that it now bloomed with mold. But Jess had not slept for twenty-four hours and so she did not care.

She lowered herself onto the bed and closed her eyes. Before sleep hit her—quick and brutal as a punch—there was time only to think of her parents, sleeping on this very bed seventeen years ago. To wonder whether she had been conceived here, before she was abandoned, or in another bed, by another couple entirely.

For the first time in months—years, even—her sleep was black and dreamless. It was night when she woke, the moon painting the ceiling white. The pain had woken her: a bright, clenching pain, radiating from her pelvis in rhythmic waves.

Such pain she'd never felt, such fear that there was no room for anything else in her mind. She watched the shifting of the moonlight and screamed.

At first, she thought she had imagined the sound: women's voices, singing a song that, somehow, she knew.

> I sang you to sleep, and I robbed you of wealth
> And again I'm a maid on the shore.

She crawled from the bed, and suddenly her thighs were slick, water gushing from between her legs and onto the broken floorboards. The waves of pain came closer together now. She knew that she had to keep going, that she had to follow the source of the song. That she had to find the women and join them.

She sobbed as she made her way down the stairs, thighs shaking with the effort, and opened the back door onto the veranda. She found the beginning of the staircase, the rope that danced in the wind, waiting for her to take it in her hand.

The sea beckoned. The hurl of the white waves, the rippling spread of blue, winking with light. It was so beautiful that it hurt her throat.

The cave held her close. The water lapped its way inside, as if in greeting. She was comforted by the cool lick of it against the burn of her skin, against the pain that coursed through every cell of her. The song swelled on the waves, growing louder and louder as she pushed, an encouragement.

They were waiting, she knew. She had to hurry. She had to join them. It was what all of this had been leading to.

The rocks cut into her hands as she pushed, the smell of blood in the air. She breathed in rich brine, and as the space between her legs opened, so did other parts of her. There no longer seemed a barrier between herself and the sea.

She was part of it, she had become the thing she'd feared. She was the white foam on the waves, she was the pink shell on the seabed. She was the great leathery weed drifting in the current; she was the fleshy bristle of coral.

Pain bloomed between her fingers and her toes, at her neck where her pulse drummed. She brought a hand to her throat; the flesh felt hot and ribboned. When she took her hand away, she saw that it was webbed.

Another wave of pain, now; her body rushing ahead of her, a dance to which she did not know the steps. She ground her palms and the soles of her feet into the jagged floor of the cave and pushed and screamed and pushed one more time and then—

The child.

A miracle formed by her own body. Slick and perfect in her hands, jellied white. The child opened her mouth, a velvet darkness, and Jess wondered if it was not, after all, the cave that she had dreamed but this. The baby cried, a piercing wail that should not have been musical, but was. Jess felt as if there had never been sound before this, as if the world had been dead and quiet before her child had woken it.

She pressed the tiny body to her chest, felt the tide shudder through them both, in harmony with the beat of their hearts. She whispered her name.

She began to crawl toward the lip of the cave, moving toward the women's voices, toward the water. It was only then that she realized the singing was gone, that it had been replaced by a new sound, a wrong sound. A manmade sound, cutting through the drift of sea and sky. A motor.

She will not remember this part well.

There will be only snippets, only flashes.

Rescue workers, their uniforms so bright they hurt her eyes. Hands, pulling at her. The baby screaming. The blood still seeping from her, dripping into the rockpools of the cave. A stretcher.

A boat, rocking in the shadow of a cliff. And there, bundled in a lifejacket and leaning over the prow, looking so incongruous all these miles from the bare sunburned earth of the farm—her father.

Later. How much later, she could not tell.

The harsh press of neon against her eyeballs and the industrial scratch of a hospital blanket against her skin. A monitor beeped. There was a pulling sensation in her belly and in her breasts, her body aware of the lack before her mind.

Someone was squeezing her hand; she opened her eyes to see her mother's face, looking strange and tight, the features arranged in a way Jess had not seen before.

"Hi, sweetheart," her mother said, barely breathing the words.

"Where," Jess tried, but her mouth was too dry to speak. She was thirsty, ever so thirsty. She licked her lips and tried again. "Where am I? Where is Lucy? Where is the baby?"

Her hand fluttered past her aching breasts to the tender spot beneath her jaw. But it was smooth, the ridges gone. The webbing, too, was gone from between her fingers, leaving only white, crusted flesh.

She became aware of another person in the room with them, sitting near the door, behind her mother.

"Dad?"

"He's gone for a cup of tea," her mother said, squeezing her hand. "He'll be back in a minute."

But she did not want to see her father. He should not have brought her—should not have brought *them*—here. She longed for the beat of the tide, for the feel of her baby against her chest.

Panic burst inside her.

Lucy. I need Lucy.

"This lady needs to talk to you, sweetheart," her mother said. A plastic chair creaked and a woman stepped into the light. "It won't take long. You need your rest. And then, I'll ask the nurse to bring the baby—Lucy—in. All right, sweetheart?"

Jess nodded. She kept her eyes on her mother's face, as if the woman would disappear if Jess did not look at her. A fairy story. If only all this were a fairy story.

"Do you like it?" she whispered. "Lucy."

"Yes," her mother said, her eyes full and bright with tears. "Lucy," she said the name again, as if tasting it. "It's beautiful, sweetheart. It's perfect."

The woman had a narrow face, the features drawn together in a point like a snout. She clutched a clipboard tight in her hands. A lanyard around her neck read "Visitor," as if Jess had invited her there.

"Hello, Jessica," she said, reading from her clipboard. She did not look Jess in the eye. "I'm from the Department of Communities and Justice. I'm here because, owing to the circumstances of the birth of your daughter—"

"Lucy," Jess interrupted. Her heart began to race.

"Owing to the circumstances of the birth of your daughter, Lucy, the department has concerns about your ability to parent her. The circumstances of her birth being as follows: you told no one you were pregnant. You attended only one scan, failing to provide your contact details so that medical staff were unable to contact you. You ran away from home and, when your labor commenced, you made your way not to a hospital but to a location that was extremely dangerous, owing to its isolation and its exposure to the elements. You did not seek medical attention for your daughter, nor for yourself after the birth. You were discovered, and provided with medical attention, purely because your father—who I understand to be familiar with the area—managed to locate you.

"If he had not found you before the tide came in, then the consequences for you and your child might have been very severe indeed.

"As such, your actions placed your child at risk of serious harm. Accordingly, the department intends to file an application for an emergency care and protection order with the Children's Court of NSW, placing Lucy into emergency foster care for fourteen days, after which time the department will seek to renew the order—"

"No," said Jess, the word swallowed up by the blood roaring in her ears. In the plastic chair next to the bed, her mother lifted her hands to her mouth.

"You can't do this," her mother said, rising from the chair. "Let me get my husband—we'll help her, we'll help her. You don't need to do this!"

The woman from the Department of Communities and Justice turned to address her mother. Jess noticed the fleshy arrows of skin at each eye, the downward turn of her mouth. The woman glanced at her watch, and Jess wondered if she had another appointment to get to, another heart to break open.

"As the child's grandparents," the woman began, "you can apply to be named as carers on the ECPO. This would mean that the child would live with you rather than with emergency foster carers. Is this something you would like to explore? If so, I can arrange for the application to be amended, subject to the necessary checks."

Her mother swallowed. She took Jess's hand and squeezed it tight.

"Jess? Is that what you want us to do?"

Jess felt a cavity open up inside her, a vortex. She was nothing but longing: longing for the tiny, glimmering hands, the wide, dark eyes. The cry that rang like a song in her blood.

The words *foster care* hovered in front of her. She imagined faceless beings lifting her child away, taking her to some distant place she could not follow.

She nodded, tears running into her mouth.

"I didn't mean to hurt her, Mum," she whispered. "I didn't mean to put her in danger."

"I know, sweetheart. I know."

34

MARY

In the dark of the prison deck, there was little to distract her from the pain. From the whoosh of blood in her ears, the ache of thirst in her throat.

Sometimes, Mary wondered if there was a world beyond the ship at all.

It had been some other girl, some other Mary, who had seen the stars blink through the clouds at night; who had watched starlings write their messages in the sky. Even the girl who had shivered in the cart from Kilmainham to the port, passing through the green countryside still scabbed with war; even that girl was a stranger to her now.

Mary's world had shrunk to contain only her own body. Her hunger, her thirst. And the new, strange pain: the feeling that something was pushing through the soft skin on her neck, that her fingers and toes were knitting themselves together.

They had been told that they had only four weeks left now. As hungry as Mary was, and as much as the smell of the slop buckets and the gnawing of the rats made her want to retch, fear wormed in her chest. When they had the energy to talk, the women began to wonder what awaited them in New South Wales.

A woman called Lizzie with a Northern accent spoke of a girl from her village who had been transported several years before. The girl had found someone in Sydney Town to write a letter home to her mother and Lizzie had read it aloud for her.

"She wrote that she'd been taken to a place called *the female factory*," Lizzie told them, whispering the final words for effect. "Where settlers would come and pick out the girls they wanted for servants or wives. Her mammy was beside herself, thinking her precious girl might have to marry a Protestant, or bed someone out of wedlock. The poor woman couldn't decide what would be worse."

Mary had imagined a man plucking her from a line as if she were a cow, taking her away from Eliza. She had felt for her sister's hand and squeezed it tight. Perhaps it would not be so bad, she told herself. A man might be kind, like Da. But he might be like the sailors, or like Byrne.

That was the problem. There seemed to be no way of telling the difference.

One morning, after the rations had been delivered, Mary lifted her hand to her neck, wanting to soothe the stinging pain she felt there. She gasped as her fingers touched the flesh; the wet smoothness of it, like a membrane.

"Eliza," she whispered now. "Move your hair aside."

"What? What's wrong?" Eliza's fingers fluttered to her chest, brushing at her smock. "Is it a rat?"

"Hush," Mary hissed. "I don't want the others to see. Just—I need you to show me your neck. Move a bit closer to me." Eliza shuffled forward, to the space where light snaked from the upper decks, and held back her hair. Mary covered her mouth with her hand so that her sister would not hear her gasp.

Two slits had appeared on Eliza's neck, at the exact spot where her pulse flickered.

She watched them move in time with her sister's breathing. At first, her mind was too blank with horror to comprehend them. But then she remembered the herring Da had caught back in Ard na Caithne, the nightmare she'd had of Mam. The beat of those fleshy wings.

"Come now," Eliza said, catching Mary's shaking fingers in her own. "There's no need to be frightened."

"But these wounds," Mary breathed. "This sickness—"

"It is not a sickness," Eliza said. "But you know that, you remember. That night, the things Mam told us . . ."

Mary rolled away from her sister, pressed her body against the curved wall of the berth, with its stink of sweat and tar.

She closed her eyes, but instead of blackness, she saw a face. Mam's face, that terrible face from her dream, with its scaled skin; the raw pink of its empty eyes. Eliza stroked her back, murmuring softly, but Mary pulled away, burrowing tighter into herself.

She would not listen to Eliza's whisperings, her imaginings borne of grief.

And she would not remember. She could not bear to.

35

JESS

MONDAY, II FEBRUARY 2019

Jess lifts a hand to her neck, feeling the race of her pulse beneath her skin. Slowly, the room comes into focus. The gray light moving through the billowing curtains, the cat curled at the end of her bed.

What has woken her? Have they come for her, at last?

The digital clock on her bedside table reads 6 A.M. Outside, there is the rush of the tide against the shore, but no other sound.

She sighs, flopping back against her pillows.

It has been six months since she bought Cliff House, six months since she packed the meager contents of her life into her old Ford and made the journey down from Sydney. The house had stood mostly empty for forty years, the realtor said: the man who'd bought it in 1982 had tried to turn it into a holiday let, and the couple he'd sold it to in 2001 had tried and failed to do the same. The damp, he explained, and the noise. The wind, coming off the sea. It unsettled people, kept them up at night. He hoped she was a heavy sleeper.

She had spent the first two weeks clearing the place out: the house clearly held an allure for local teenagers, and Jess had filled a dozen garbage bags with sticky beer cans and pizza boxes. At some stage, part of the floor had caved in, but Jess couldn't afford to repair it—the purchase had taken all her savings—and so she'd covered it with a

249

tarp that now filled and slackened with the breeze. She'd planned to remove the wallpaper, but had thought better of it after one section revealed a forest of mold.

But at least the house was clean now. She had half hoped to find some of her parents' things, but the realtor told her that any remaining items—those that were not stolen—would have been thrown away, or else put into storage. The scratched dining table is, as far as she knows, all that remains of them. Of the life from which they'd fled.

They hadn't wanted her to come back. Her mother had cried on the phone, her father swearing in the background.

"What good will it do to go back there?" her mother had said.

"I can't explain it," she'd said. "It's just something I need to do."

For the first few weeks, she'd barely slept, sitting on the back veranda at night and watching the waves, listening and waiting. The dreams had returned, lifting her hopes, but when she was awake she heard nothing, only the rush and roar of the sea.

And so she decided to paint them, the women. As if to let them know that she was there. That she was ready. It would be the opposite of an exorcism. A summoning.

She had intended to avoid the townspeople, to avoid starting new friendships. Though she had sought out Ryan, about whom she'd long been curious. He had been on the *Marlin* that day, thirty-seven years ago. She wondered if he recognized her; whether he saw a flicker of the infant she'd been in her adult face, though if he had, he'd given no sign of it. Mostly she'd kept to herself, alone but for Dora, the stray who'd nosed her way inside the house in Jess's first week of living there and then refused to leave.

She hadn't counted on Melody, her shopkeeper neighbor. One morning in September, her least favorite month, she'd gone to the store to buy tuna (for Dora) and a bottle of wine (for herself). This would be the third bottle of wine in as many days. Two days previous, she'd bought a postcard for Lucy in a hungover haze, and later, at dusk, walked down to the postbox, drunk on Chardonnay and memory. Already, she regretted sending it.

"You all right, love?" Melody had asked when Jess paid, counting out the coins in her hand (Melody suffered neither fools nor card machines).

"Fine, sorry." Jess had sniffed, attempting a smile. "Bit of a funny day today."

"Yeah? Why's that?"

Jess had felt the full glare of Melody's curious gaze, bright as a searchlight. She looked around her, even though she knew the store was empty.

"An anniversary of something."

"Ah." Melody had nodded, placing the change in Jess's palm like a gift. "I'm sorry. Someone close?"

Jess realized the woman thought she was talking about a death.

She'd thought no more about the conversation until later that evening, when Melody had appeared on her doorstep cradling an enormous ceramic dish which turned out to contain lasagna, a bottle of wine tucked under one arm.

"Soakage," she'd said, stepping inside.

In the end they'd had the entire bottle, Jess talking more than she had in weeks. Melody knew a lot about art, had even done a bit of sketching here and there. They talked about their favorite artists: Cossington Smith and Namatjira (Melody); Werefkin, Carrington, and Kahlo (Jess).

"I like that," Melody had said, nodding at the canvas on the easel.

"Thanks," Jess had said, feeling a flush of pride, followed by the familiar vulnerability, a sense of being exposed. "It's not finished, though." She thought she'd captured the sea quite well: the shimmering hues that changed depending on the time of year, even the time of day. Aqua and violet and green and pink. She was happy, too, with the movement of it; the muscular waves, the bursts of spray that almost seemed to touch your face. It was the figures she couldn't get quite right. She'd spent most of the previous day mixing paint with all manner of materials: beeswax paste, even sand. But still, the texture of the skin—those iridescent scales—eluded her.

The failure haunted her. For it meant the painting was unfinished, that she hadn't *captured* them. This, she reasoned, must be why they stayed away.

"Who are they?" Melody had asked, and Jess felt the conversation being pulled in the direction she'd been avoiding, inevitable as the tide.

"Well, one is me," Jess said slowly, and as she spoke the words she realized that, in a way, they were true. She'd started painting one thing and ended up painting something else entirely. "And the other is . . ."

She paused.

"It's all right," Melody said, leaning forward to refill Jess's glass. "You don't have to say. I understand. I've lost people, too."

Jess didn't know how to explain it. How gaining someone could also mean losing them.

Now, as she watches pale morning light bloom through the window, she remembers what Melody told her the last time they'd seen each other. Her friend had seemed in a strange mood: she'd eaten less and drunk more than usual. A few times, Jess caught the twitching of her mouth, the muscles of her throat working, as if they were trying to push something free.

"Is something wrong?" she'd asked, and that was all it had taken for Melody to talk. It had been hard to hear about the cave. The cold slime of the rocks digging into her friend's back, the lap of the sea. It had been hard to listen, hard not to remember.

Funny to think that they were linked by that place. That they had both lain on those sharp rocks and felt their lives change forever.

But still, Jess hadn't been able to tell Melody the truth. Just as she still hasn't been able to visit the cave. Perhaps if Lucy were here with her, she might be braver. She might lead her down the rocky steps, their hands clasped—just like the painting—and show her.

But of course, Lucy is not here.

She thinks back to the phone conversation she'd had with her mother on Lucy's eighteenth birthday. The deadline they'd set all those years ago—the deadline for telling the truth—had finally arrived.

"It bothers me, this idea she has of being a journalist," her mother had said. "I worry—about what it might lead to."

I'm worried she'll discover the truth.

"If she thinks being a journalist will make her happy, then she should do it," Jess had said. And then, more quietly: "I want her to be happy."

And she did. She wanted that more than anything.

"So do I. Which leads me on to . . ." Her mother took a deep breath. "I know we said we'd tell her, once she turned eighteen. But I'm scared, Jess. I'm scared of how she'll take this. What it will do to her."

Jess had said nothing. She was sitting on the balcony of the tiny flat she rented in Sydney's Inner West. The flat that Lucy had visited, not so many months ago. It was dusk, and flying foxes swooped low overhead. The faint meow of a cat carried from the rubbish bins below. Suddenly, Jess longed for something—someone—to hold on to.

"I see," Jess had said. "OK. Well. You're her mother, really. You know what's best."

"Jess—" her mother protested.

"It's fine," Jess had said, even as the emptiness spread through her body. "It's what's best for Lucy, isn't it?" She paused. "Can I ask one thing, though?"

"Of course, sweetheart. Anything at all. And darling, *you're* her mother. You always will be. We don't have to decide anything right now. All I've ever wanted is to make this easier for you. For both of you."

"Then let her be happy," Jess had said. "Let her study journalism, let her do whatever she wants. Just, please. Let her be happy."

"Oh, sweetheart—"

"I've got to go, Mum."

And then, Christmas: the little farmhouse smelling of plum pudding and her parents' fear. Lucy, sitting there cross-legged, scratching absent-mindedly at a silvered patch of skin on her knee. A fork in one hand, her phone in the other, eyes wide as she read out excerpts of the *New York Times* piece on Harvey Weinstein to their parents. Jess leaned against the kitchen counter, keeping herself separate. If Lucy noticed this, she said nothing.

"Guys—listen to this," Lucy had said, before reading out a quote. "Fuck, this would make a good podcast. That's what I want to do, I think. Make podcasts."

Her cheeks were flushed, her short hair sticking up from her scalp in gold bristles. Her whole body seemed to thrum with the future. It shone from her like light.

And suddenly, with searing clarity, Jess saw that her mother was right. To tell Lucy now—it might destroy all those hopes and plans, all those dreams for the future. If Lucy knew that the story of her life was a lie, she might lose her passion for seeking the truth.

And Jess couldn't do it. She just couldn't take that away from her.

After all, she'd felt such anger, such betrayal, when she'd stumbled on her own truth all those years ago. Anger at the façade of a life her parents had so carefully constructed. But now, looking at Lucy's innocent, ignorant face, she finally understood their choice. Now, she had her own façade to maintain.

It was then that she thought of Cliff House and wondered who owned it. Whether there was a way she could go back there, back to where it had all begun. Perhaps by understanding where she came from, she'd be able to bear it: letting Lucy go.

And perhaps she'd hear it again. The women's voices, calling to her. That sweet sound of belonging.

Her phone buzzes, and she frowns as she picks it up from the bedside.

There's a missed call notification from Cameron, and a voicemail.

Why would he be calling her? They haven't seen each other for months—not since before she left Sydney, at the same hotel where they'd had their first meeting after running into each other at a gallery. It had been ten years, then, since the art room in Dawes Plain, since he'd stroked the skin on her knuckles like it—like *she*—was beautiful.

She didn't tell him what had happened after he left. He seemed to understand that anything that had transpired in that time was off-limits. A sealed part of her.

From there, they met every few months—less regularly, after his marriage, his children. He'd call her from a private number, so that she couldn't call back and surprise him at an inconvenient time. Mostly, everything was arranged via one of those apps that automatically deleted messages after six minutes. It felt like they were spies.

Jess wasn't sure exactly why she did it. Sometimes, she wondered if perhaps she was trying to travel back in time, to unravel their knotted history.

She sucks in a breath and plays the voicemail.

"Jessie," he says, and she flinches at the old nickname, the reach for familiarity. "I'm in a bit of trouble, babe. A misunderstanding at work. Nothing that won't sort itself out, with a bit of time. Anyway— look, I'd like to see you. Be good to get away for a bit. Reconnect." Another breath. Jess can hear that he's driving: there's the tick of the indicator, the whoosh of another vehicle passing. "I'll come to you, see the new place—Malua Street, isn't it? Probably stop overnight somewhere, so be with you tomorrow. All right. Ta for now, love."

Jess types Cameron's name into Google, dread already pooling in her gut. For a moment, she's reassured by the lack of results, but then she searches *Marsden College*, where he's just been promoted to head of the art department. There's an article from the *Sydney Morning Herald*, published yesterday.

Protests rock school after allegations.

The letters on the screen blur together, forming impossible, inevitable words.

Allegation of sexual assault.

She thinks of what happened between them, all those years ago. The memory of it—his hands, his mouth—has been buried under more recent encounters. Now, she tries to focus in on it, and all she can remember is asking: *Would you? Hurt me, I mean.*

And his answer. *No.*

Had it been assault, what he did?

You were old enough, she tells herself, and the words have the rhythm of a mantra, something she's said to herself before. So this doubt has been there, all along.

She'd been almost seventeen—a young woman—and he'd been just twenty-four. Seven years separated them. What's seven years? It's hardly more than the age gap between her parents.

But she'd been a particularly vulnerable young woman. Insecure, confused, and reeling. She'd just learned that she was adopted, that her home was not her home. That the two most important adults in her life—her parents—had lied to her.

All she had wanted was someone to look up to. Someone she could trust, who would make everything better.

You were old enough.

But she wasn't, was she?

Not for any of it.

The memories—the memories of the worst year of her life, the memories she tries so hard to tamp down—rise to the surface.

The time in the Sydney hospital. The hushed voices outside the room, the click of pens and the rustling of paperwork. Her parents in their Sunday best, kissing her on the forehead before departing to a courthouse that, in Jess's mind, imposed on the landscape like a castle. Her parents asking who the father was; her mother saying that Max had told her about the teacher, and that if Jess would let her, she would contact the police, the new school he taught at, anyone who would listen. She would make him pay. Jess had said nothing. Her father had placed a hand on her shoulder and Jess had turned away to face the wall.

She remembers the thin wash of watercolor on paper, her frustration that she could never capture the cave as it had looked, as it had felt. The dreams dwindled, along with her milk.

Around Lucy, she had felt frozen with fear, the social worker's words ringing in her mind.

Your actions placed your child at risk of serious harm.

She began to wonder if she was cursed, if being abandoned had broken something fundamental inside of her, had made her unworthy of being Lucy's mother. She was frightened to go near her daughter, frightened that her touch would hurt her, infect her in some way.

When she did try to hold Lucy, her arms shook, as if they no longer recognized her weight.

Back in Dawes Plain, she had hidden in the dark of her bedroom, like an animal burrowing away to die. Lucy's cries had echoed through the house, Jess's body aching in answer. Lucy slept in her parents' bedroom. Jess covered her head with the duvet so that she couldn't hear her mother's coo as she lifted Lucy from the cot, or the lullaby she sang as she gave her a bottle.

While her mother crooned "Twinkle, Twinkle, Little Star," Jess whispered her own lullaby into her pillow.

> *I sang you to sleep, and I robbed you of wealth*
> *And again I'm a maid on the shore.*

When even this hurt too much, Jess reached for the new Walkman her father had left outside her bedroom door. The old one had been lost to Cliff House, along with the schoolbag that contained her journal. He had put a CD in there for her—Nick Cave's album *The Good Son*. One of the tracks was called "Lucy," a song she listened to again and again. She wondered what her father meant by this. Perhaps it was a rebuke, a reminder that her baby daughter needed her. Or perhaps he was saying that he understood: that he knew Jess would love Lucy forever, just like the song said, and that until Jess was ready to show that love—to care for her child—he would do it for her.

"Stay," her parents said when she told them she'd enrolled at the College of Fine Arts, only a semester later than originally planned. "Be a part of her life. Please." But she'd left as soon as she could.

She had needed that feeling again: the feeling that she could make something beautiful, even if her heart felt withered and ugly.

Jess deletes the voicemail. She spends the morning at the kitchen table, sketching. She sketches Mary and Eliza, the sisters who haunt her dreams, whose pale forms glimmer at her already from the canvases on the walls.

But now she draws them differently. With scaled skin and pulsing gills, with webbed hands and sinuous tails.

She pauses to touch her throat, remembering the way her skin had split itself into ribbons, the webs of flesh that had sprouted between each finger. Sometimes she wonders if she imagined it all, the way her body changed, the singing. If it was merely the delusion of a vulnerable teenage girl, bewildered and in pain.

But when she thinks of what has happened in this town—the catalog of the drowned—she's not so sure. It's as if she carries some kind of strange knowledge, in the base of her spine, in the tender flesh beneath her jaw. What Melody told her about her own experience in the cave has only made her more certain.

Eight men since 1960. For the theory to work, there need to have been more. It needs to have gone on for longer. She needs to look at the town records, somehow, all the way back to 1801. Look for any instances of drownings or disappearances in the area. But she has no idea how to go about doing such a thing, no idea how to trawl old records and newspaper articles.

Lucy would know.

Lucy.

As always, the thought of her sits heavy as a bruise.

Jess remembers her as a child. Coming home at the end of each university term was like meeting a new little girl each time. Lucy had been inquisitive from the first: once, she presented Jess with a snakeskin she'd found in the back garden. She still remembers the papery feel of it in her palm, remembers Lucy asking why the snake had abandoned something so beautiful.

"Well, snakes grow, just like humans do," Jess had said. "But their skin doesn't grow with them. So when they're ready, they shed it, and there's a nice new glossy skin underneath."

Lucy had chewed her lip, her eyes wide, scratching at the inside of her wrist.

"Can I grow a new skin, too?"

Jess wishes she could go back in time to that moment, draw the little girl into her arms and hold her close.

Yes, she'd say. *You can. Because you're special. Because you're mine.*

Jess drops her pencil, abandoning her drawing. She scrapes back her chair, the noise startling Dora Maar from her favorite position on the couch. She takes the stairs two at a time and flings open the doors of her wardrobe. She sinks to her knees, scrabbling for the cardboard box amid the detritus of tights and socks. But there it is.

She opens it and lifts the yellowed tissue paper out carefully. The snakeskin shimmers inside.

Jess spends the whole day at her easel.

It's almost midnight by the time she's finished incorporating the snakeskin into the canvas. Her back aches and her stomach growls with hunger, but her heart feels so light and buoyant that it might lift her into the air.

She had known that it wasn't quite finished. She hadn't yet responded to the emails about the logistics for the exhibition, the exhibition that her gallerist—alarmed by her sudden sea change—had pressured her into having. How could she, when the centerpiece was incomplete?

Raising the hem of her skirt, she compares her own skin to that of the painted figures. It's perfect. The snakeskin is translucent, shimmering with pink and violet and blue. All the colors of the sea.

She makes herself a piece of toast, carries it up to her bed.

Her head and heart are so full of the joy of her work, of capturing the essence of something so exactly, that all other thoughts are pushed from her mind.

Only as she begins to fall asleep does she think of Cameron. But in the dark—with the sea murmuring outside and the warmth of Dora Maar purring beside her—he feels like a specter, a ghost story.

He won't come here, she tells herself. The police are investigating—surely they will catch up with him quickly. She won't have to be involved. There will be no need to confront the things she did, the things that were done to her. She can stay here in Cliff House, clinging to the edge of the world like a limpet to a rock.

Alone, and safe.

36

MARY

It was Bridie who first suggested that they break into one of the rum barrels on the prison deck. They were all so thirsty. Some of the women had tried to drink the bilge water, only to add the contents of their stomachs to the mess that swirled and frothed around them.

Mary would never have thought that she would hanker for rum, for the drink that fouled the sailors' breath and yellowed their teeth. But she had begun to crave something that would dull her mind, turn her thoughts from her memories of Mam. From the changes to her body and what they might mean. The webbed flesh between her toes, the new shine to her skin, the tender ridges on her neck. She had become a creature she did not know.

It took three days and nights to prize a nail from the barrel, the women taking it in turns with pruned fingers.

At last, they yanked the nail free and a ribbon of liquid burst from a tiny crack in the wood. They lapped at it with their tongues, desperate as cats. Bridie tore off a strip of her smock and pressed it tight against the hole so that the fabric turned dark. She leaned over Aoife and squeezed the fabric so that a few sweet drops might fall onto her lips. Mary never thought she'd see the day when Aoife would accept a gift from Bridie, the woman she'd called *Sasanach whore*. But the long, dark weeks had smoothed away the roughness between them, like water carving rock.

When it was Mary's turn, she coughed as the liquid burned through her. The rum took her mind to a place she had not been before, but somehow recognized. It might have been the future, or a past so old it was not her own. There was a cave, the walls dark red and curved in the shape of a woman's body. She was wet and in pain, frightened. But there was magic, too: the sound of a child crying, a warm bundle pressed to her chest. She looked into eyes as dark as the kelp on the shores of Ard na Caithne; tiny fingers clasped her own. Her breasts—her whole body—ached.

She slipped in and out of the dream, so that some moments she clung to emptiness, or woke not to the child's cry but to the keening of the waves, a longing pulsing through her.

She thought of the day she'd got her first blood, how Da had said she was a woman now. She remembered the village women, the way they carried their swollen bellies in front of them. How she had longed to join them one day, to bring a babe of her own into the world.

The gouges in her neck burned, the strangeness of her body taunting her.

If she lived—if they made it to New South Wales and were not punished for their oddness, their unnaturalness—would she one day have a child? Was her body, with all its changes, even capable of such a thing? Perhaps the child would be sickly, malformed in some way. Poisoned by her womb.

And what kind of mother would she make, she who had no mother of her own?

Even if she were to have a child, she would first have to marry and take a man into her bed. When they arrived in New South Wales, she knew, they would be taken to the female factory, where a settler would pluck them from a line as if he was buying an animal at market. She would be wife or servant, perhaps both.

It would not be like Da, meeting Mam by the shore.

She did not tell Eliza of these thoughts, of how the future frightened her.

After all, her sister would not understand.

She already knew how to be different.

They drained the entire barrel of rum before they were discovered. It was Wright who realized, bringing their rations for the first time in two days. She saw him pause after he unlocked the bulkhead, the lantern swinging from his fist, tasting the new sweetness in the air. His eyes traveled over the women, some of whom slept soundly for the first time in weeks, cradled by the rocking of the waves; some of whom smiled and sang, as if they no longer knew where they were.

He stepped over the sleeping bodies and began to check the barrels. Soon enough he came to the one they had split open and sucked dry like a summer fruit. Mary felt Eliza begin to shake beside her.

Wright left and returned with two officers and the captain, whose cheeks were flushed with rage. When he spoke, his voice was so loud that the sleeping women startled awake, and the drunken singing died to whimpers of terror. Mary was surprised that such a strong voice might come from such a small man.

"Who is responsible for this?"

The bunk above her creaked, and she squeezed her eyes shut, not wanting to hear Bridie's confession, not wanting to think on what might become of her friend.

"I am. I am responsible."

But the words were too thin—too frail—to come from Bridie. It was not until Eliza dug her nails hard into Mary's palm that she realized who had spoken.

Aoife.

37

JESS

TUESDAY, 12 FEBRUARY 2019

It is 5 A.M. and Jess's heart pounds in her chest, so loudly that the whole house seems to shudder with it. But no—it is not her heart she hears but something else. Someone is knocking at the door. Jess sits up in bed, groping for the light, before she thinks better of it.

It must be Cameron. Who else could it be?

She sits, barely breathing, hardly daring to move. As though if she stays very, very still, he'll simply slink away, like a monster in a film.

"Jess!" Though his voice is muffled by the wind, she can hear the desperation in it. She imagines the shock of it ringing out into the bush, the leaves of the gum trees bristling, tiny lizards and rodents scuttling away in fright.

Will he have woken Melody, driving down Malua Street? Her bedroom window faces the road; she might have seen the beam of his headlights. Jess knows she often sleeps with her curtains open: she likes to be woken by the sun.

She swallows, her mouth sour. Thinks of the words from the article.

Sexual assault.

She doesn't want Melody—doesn't want Comber Bay—mixed up in this.

On her bedside table, her phone bursts into life. He's calling. He can probably hear the phone ringing from outside the house. There's no pretending she's not home, not now.

Jess creeps from her bed, wrapping her long dressing gown tight around her body. She gropes her way down the stairs, not wanting to turn the light on and reveal herself. In the living room, the moon breaks through the curtains, her canvas shimmering with it. She allows herself a burst of pride at the completed painting, as if a part of her already knows it will be a very long time before she holds a brush in her hand again.

Her gaze falls to the sketches she'd made earlier in the evening: Mary and Eliza, their hands webbed and their skin crusted with scales. For some reason, she doesn't want him to see them.

She folds them up, secretes them inside a kitchen drawer.

Then, she takes a deep breath and crosses to the front door, her feet light on the old floorboards. Dora Maar winds around her legs, meowing.

"Jessie, thank God," he murmurs through the door. "Please, Jess. Let me in."

Her fingers on the bolt are damp.

She slides back the lock and opens the door.

The first thing she notices is how small he looks. He's wearing tracksuit pants and an old T-shirt, stained yellow under the arms. His belly pushes against the fabric. Even in her pajamas, her hair falling unkempt down her back, she seems to tower over him.

He's unshaven, and there's a smear of something—ketchup, maybe—on one cheek. He smells of petrol stations and sweat and unbrushed teeth.

He doesn't meet her eyes.

She moves some papers and magazines aside on the couch, motions for him to sit.

In the kitchen, she fills the kettle. As it boils, she picks up two dirty mugs from the counter. She washes one but not the other, and when she carries the mugs of tea through, she gives him the one with the crusted rim of dirt in the bottom.

"Thanks," he says, taking a long sip of the tea. "I'm sorry, Jess. For showing up like this. I have been wanting to see you—I wasn't lying about that. But, you should know—Nicola kicked me out."

She hasn't sat down. She feels better standing over him, noting the new sparseness of his hair, his raw scalp.

"I've read the article," she says simply, "in the *Herald*. About the school."

She's setting him a test—something the old Jess would do. He flushes as he gulps his tea, his knuckles whitening around the mug.

He looks up at her, and for the first time their eyes meet. His pupils are dilated.

"It wasn't like that, Jessie," he says, pleading. He stands up, puts his mug down on the coffee table and takes a step toward her. "It wasn't like with you and me. What we had—that was different. We were both young. Kids. This is just some silly girls with the wrong idea. Teenage hysterics. A witch hunt."

His breath is rancid in her face. There are tiny burst veins in his eyes. He smells disgusting.

"*I* was a kid," she says now. "But you weren't, Cameron. You were twenty-four."

"Hey." He puts his hand on her wrist. "Don't tell me you've forgotten what it was like between us? I can still remember the first time I ever saw you." He's panicked now, beseeching, the words tumbling over themselves in their rush to leave his mouth. "This scrappy little thing with your black hair and your long-sleeved shirts in that heat. So unsure of yourself, of your talent. But I remember I complimented you on your drawing and you looked up at me with those big eyes of yours, like I had all the answers."

His voice catches.

"No one had ever looked at me like that before. You know what my father was like, how he beat me. Called me a faggot because I liked fucking Monet. I left behind everything I knew to go to art school and then the only job I could get was working at some shithole school in some shithole town in the arse end of nowhere. I spent all my life feeling small and then I met you and I felt . . ."

His hands are digging into the soft flesh of her arms.

"I felt big."

Jess wants to take a step back, to turn her head away from the staleness of his breath. Her mind is whirring, picking over the past like the teeth of a loom.

All this time, she had thought he believed *she* was special. That he saw a young woman with strength and talent and ambition, instead of a little girl with her sleeves pulled down to her knuckles, desperate to cover the mess of her skin, the wrongness she felt inside.

But all he had seen was his own ego reflected back at him. Her admiration made him feel like the man he was desperate to become.

It was never about her at all.

"Please, Jess," he says, fingers gripping tighter now. "Tell me you don't think that I took advantage of you. That I"—he takes a breath, but the next word still comes out strangled—"*assaulted* you. Because I couldn't bear that. I couldn't."

The last time their bodies had been this close was at the Sydney hotel, just after Jess had decided to move to Comber Bay. Cameron had accepted she was leaving easily enough, promising he'd visit. But they'd both known he wouldn't, that Jess was just a distraction to him, a distraction he no longer had time for. He'd been promoted to head of the art department just as his wife had gone back to work after their second child.

But now he has come here, to Comber Bay. The police might follow him here. Someone will have seen his car.

She's part of this, now.

"Jess? Please, just say something."

"I don't think that," she says. "Of course I don't think that."

She keeps her voice, her breathing level; lets him hold her. Her mind works furiously. This is Comber Bay. Australia's Bermuda Triangle, with its own catalog of mysteries.

A plan begins to form.

"What am I going to do?" Cameron moans into her hair. "What am I going to do, Jessie?"

38

MARY

Afterward, Mary wondered if that awful sound—the kiss of the whip on Aoife's back—would echo through the rest of her days.

Aoife's blood had run down the mast, staining the deck. The captain had ordered twenty lashes; the surgeon watched, face tight with disapproval. Even some of the sailors had looked away.

"It's wrong," she heard one of them say, gruff voice carrying on the sea breeze, "to whip an old woman like that."

Mary had not looked away. She had borne witness. It seemed the least she could do.

They had been ironed for the spectacle, the metal around their wrists and ankles reminding them of their captivity. As if, confined in the blackness below, they might have forgotten.

Bridie's sobs carried on the wind, pitched high as a bird call. Sarah pressed Annie into her side, covering the child's ears with her body. Eliza stood silent, her skin greenish-pale. Her hair hung in filthy clouds about her neck, but Mary, knowing where to look, could still see the pulse of movement at her throat. Their legs, at least, were covered in filth, cloaking the skin that was somehow rough and smooth. She curled her own hands into fists, so that no one would see the

269

webbing between her fingers. Strange, to think the light—something she had once longed for so fiercely—had now become a threat.

Thwack. Thwack. The whip tore through the air.

Mary's eyes blurred, but still she did not look away from the pale figure of Aoife clinging to the mast, the skin of her back blooming red. She wondered if this was why the sight of the shark's carcass had tormented Aoife so. If it had been some portent of her own suffering.

Later, in the prison deck, Aoife swam in and out of consciousness. Together, the women had lowered her gently into a berth.

Mary did not know why Aoife had offered herself up to the cat-o'-nine-tails. They had all stolen the rum; even little Annie had pressed her mouth to the crack in the wood and drunk. Why had Aoife—the frailest—taken the blame?

Bridie knelt over her, combing her fingers through the dry wisps of the old woman's hair, braiding it as if she was a maiden on her wedding day. Her tears fell onto Aoife's back where the skin was split, revealing the red gleam of flesh.

"Why, Aoife?" Bridie said, the words heavy. "It was my fault. Mine."

She bent her coppery head and kissed the other woman's wounds.

Silence throbbed in their corner of the prison deck. Sarah hushed Annie, told her to say her rosary for Aoife. Next to Mary, Eliza cried softly.

For a time, Aoife did not answer Bridie's question, and fear squeezed Mary's heart. There had been so much blood over the deck. Even now, it hung in the air, coppery sweet on Mary's tongue.

Aoife was so still, so small on the berth. Mary thought of her dry, rasping voice, the skin that was veined as a fallen leaf. All the years she'd seen, all the rest she'd earned. And instead, this torture in its place.

"Why?" Bridie murmured again, and when still Aoife did not answer, Eliza gripped Mary's hand tight.

She is already dead, Mary thought. *Eliza knows it, she can feel it.*

But then: a tiny, miraculous rise of the furrowed back, a slight movement of the head.

"It makes no difference to me," Aoife said, thin and faint. "I will not see another winter, and certainly not one in the colonies. You"—she took a long, shuddering breath—"might be godless, and whorish. Sleeping with a *jackeen*." She laughed softly, the sound of it breaking Mary's heart. "But you're young. You have a chance."

"So do you," Bridie murmured. "We've come this far, Aoife. You can't give up yet. You can't."

"You would not understand," she said. Her breath came in little shudders now, and Mary realized that she was crying.

"Perhaps we might," Eliza said softly. "If you told us."

She knelt, groped for Aoife's hand, then clasped it to her chest. Mary crouched next to her. Aoife smelled strangely sweet, like flax left out to rot. Mary thought of the air in the prison deck, thick with the soil of their bodies. She imagined that grime working its way into Aoife's flesh, sending poison fingers to her heart.

"We should wash the wounds," she murmured to Eliza, though she did not think they had enough water to do so. There was barely enough of it to drink.

"Wait," Eliza whispered in response. She lifted Aoife's papery hand to her mouth and kissed it.

"Please, Aoife," she said. "Help us to understand."

The older woman let out another hiss of tired breath.

"Those first days," she murmured, "those first days, you told stories. Why you were here, what you had done. I did not. I did not want to confess."

They waited. The ship rose on the crest of a wave, then fell again. Mary, Eliza, Sarah, and Bridie held Aoife's limbs gently in place so that she would not tip from her berth. Annie nestled her straw doll—now a wet, stinking thing, but still the girl's most treasured possession—in the space between Aoife's neck and shoulder.

"We are all criminals, Aoife," Bridie said, with something of her old humor. "Even Sarah, though she doesn't care to admit it."

Aoife shook her head; the movement made her whimper in pain.

"It was not bread I stole, or lace. It was a life. They would have hanged me, but for my age. My husband, he was cruel. I had"—she struggled for breath again—"no choice. Foxglove. It was growing on the cliffs . . . a sign . . . purple as the bruises he gave me. I have felt safe here, with all of you. I want to die feeling safe."

"You are safe, Aoife," Bridie murmured. "We will keep you safe." Sarah said a prayer, and Eliza kissed the woman's hand again.

Mary struggled inside herself for some words of comfort, but found nothing. Only fury, building in her like a song.

39

JESS

TUESDAY, 12 FEBRUARY 2019

Sweat sheens Cameron's forehead, his unshaven chin quivers. Jess feels a pulse of revulsion. Had she really let this man touch her, hold her?

"I'm only going to say this once," she says, keeping her voice low and fierce. "And so you'd better listen. The police are going to look for you, if they aren't already. Maybe your wife will lie for you, invent a family emergency, an illness—if you're lucky, which you have been until now. But the police *will* come."

She lets the possibility of what might happen next sink in: a criminal investigation. A trial.

"You can't stay here. Once they know we have a history, this is the first place they'll look. And if they do charge you, they'll want me to talk. They'll twist things, you know they will. I don't want that to happen. For things to be . . . misconstrued." She pauses for impact. "I'm going to hide you," she continues, once she sees the fear written on his face. "Until everyone comes to their senses and realizes this is all a big misunderstanding, like you said. I've got a friend with a boat; I'll call him. He'll help us lie low for a bit. But he won't be able to pick us up from the marina; people will see." She takes a deep breath, as if the idea is just coming to her now. "I've got a plan. Another place

273

we can meet him. A secret place. But for this to work, you're going to have to do everything I say. OK?"

He nods, then reaches toward her, catching her hand between his own. She resists the urge to flinch at the dampness of his skin on hers.

"Thank God," he whispers, closing his eyes, fingers tightening on hers. "I knew you'd believe me, Jessie. I knew that I didn't imagine what we had."

She says nothing. There's a clawing sensation inside her chest. *In, out.*

He brings her hand to his mouth, kisses it.

"Thank you," he says.

Jess drives down Malua Street, gravel crunching under her tires. She checks her rearview mirror to make sure that Cameron has kept his headlights off as instructed. It's getting lighter now, the sky gold and pink through the canopy of trees.

As they drive past Melody's, she fights the urge to pull over and jump out of the car, to knock on her friend's door and tell her everything. To ask for help. Instead, she keeps driving.

She's relieved to see that the beach is empty. She'd worried that a surfer would be out early, or that Ryan Smith would be sitting on his usual bench by the memorial. But it's early enough that she's safe.

After five minutes of driving, they turn down a dirt track leading into the national park. It is, she calculates, within walking distance of Cliff House.

She pulls under a low swoop of gums, a spot not easily seen from the road. The sort of place someone from out of town would think to hide their car. Of course, someone from out of town might not notice the depression in the grass, the smooth logs gathered in a circle. This is a picnic spot, one that locals love. Someone will come here, eventually. Someone will see. She *needs* someone to see; to think that Cameron has tried to cover his tracks in coming to her house, the house of a potential witness in the case against him. That he planned to hurt her all along—this woman with the power to destroy him.

She rolls down her window. "Leave the keys in the ignition," she says. Cameron hesitates, half in and half out of his car. "Remember what we agreed."

He sighs, then slams the door behind him. He walks toward the passenger door of her car and gets inside. This close, the smell of his sweat is sour and she leaves the window down as she drives, letting the morning air inside.

They do not speak.

Her pulse quickens as they pass the beach and she sees what she hadn't noticed before: the black comma of a surfer cutting through the waves. But with any luck, the car is too far away for him to notice.

Once they're parked outside Cliff House, Jess gives Cameron a list of things to pack. "Water," she says. "As many bottles of it as you can fill. There are some energy bars in the cupboard—bring those, too. Any medication you need. We might have a while to wait for the boat. My friend says he can't come right away."

Cameron nods.

"What about my phone?" he says, fingers twisting at his wedding ring. "Should I turn it off?"

Fuck.

"Yes, good thinking. But bring it—I don't want anyone finding it at my place," she says quickly, getting out of the car. "Hang on. I'll be back."

"Hey." Melody's eyes widen as she opens the front door. "You're up early—is everything OK?"

Her friend is dressed for work, her hair tied up with a colorful bandana, a denim apron around her waist. Jess checks her watch: it's almost 6 A.M. She's got to make this quick.

"All fine," she says, forcing a smile. She can feel that it doesn't reach her eyes. "Look, can I ask a favor? I need to go away for a few days—would you mind feeding Dora, from tomorrow? She's sorted for today."

Melody's eyebrows lift.

"Of course not. Is something wrong? Where are you going?"

"Nope, all good," she says. "Just need to escape for a bit, you know? A bit of a breather before the show."

She knows that it doesn't make sense. Where would she escape to? Comber Bay is where people come to get away, after all.

But Melody nods slowly.

"OK, hon. Whatever you need. Do you have a spare set?"

"What?"

"Of keys."

Damn. She hasn't been thinking straight; she's left her keys on the hook next to the front door.

"Forgot—sorry, been running around. Packing. I'll just leave the door unlocked. No one's going to steal a few paintings, are they?"

"Course not, love."

"Thanks," Jess says, turning to go. But Melody lingers in the doorway.

"Were you out late? Thought I saw headlights, just before sunrise."

"Oh." Jess's mind races. "Just, you know, couldn't sleep. Thought a bit of a drive would help."

"OK," Melody says, her eyes searching Jess's face. "Well, you'll let me know, won't you? If you need anything else."

"Will do."

Before Melody can reply, Jess sprints back up the road, the heat of her friend's eyes on her back.

The stairs are even worse than she remembers.

The sandstone is slippery with lichen and spray, and the rope is frayed and thin against her palm. Below, the rocks loom up at them like jagged teeth. The sea seethes.

"Fuck," Cameron grunts behind her. Looking back at him, she

sees that his cheeks are pink, his chest heaving. The morning is cool but already wet patches have formed at his armpits.

"Are you OK?"

"Yep." He blows his cheeks out, and she sees the effort he's making not to look down. "Just—my wedding ring's gone. I must have dropped it. I fiddle with it sometimes—stupid habit, Nicola's always telling me not to—"

He chokes down a sob.

"We've got to keep going."

"Yeah," he says, puffing out the words. "But what if they find it? It's engraved; they'll know I was here."

Good, she thinks.

"They won't look," she reassures him. "Not here. Hardly anyone knows about these stairs."

"OK," he says, but it sounds forced, like he doesn't quite believe her.

She turns to look back at him again, then smiles.

"I got you. OK?"

Her heart thuds as she approaches the sea, the lip of rock that curves around the cliff to the cave. Twenty years have passed and yet it is unchanged. The morning shimmers in the rockpools, and she imagines the creatures lurking beneath. Starfish, crabs, the furling tentacles of a blue-ringed octopus. She presses a hand to her abdomen and remembers the weight of her child inside, those final precious moments they shared together before the cut of the motor through the air, the hospital. The woman with the narrow features, the faceless horror of her words. *Foster care.*

"Are we almost there?"

She's stopped and Cameron has caught up with her, panting, his breath hot on the back of her neck.

"A few more steps," she says. This is the hard part, she remembers. There is a narrow gap between the rocks and the ledge that leads to the cave. They are still high up, the sea meters below. A wave hits, the spray soaking through the leg of her trousers. Her skin tingles.

"Just do what I do," she calls, yelling over the noise of the surf.

She leans forward, her hands scrabbling for a hold on the ledge. The rock is slippery and sharp with barnacles. She clenches her jaw as she pulls herself forward, over and above the lick of the sea.

"OK . . ." She kneels on the other side, wincing at the rocks digging into her knees. "Give me the backpack, then I'll help you up."

Cameron's eyes dart nervously to the waves frothing below.

"Is it safe?"

"It's safer than a police station."

He hands her the backpack, and she tests the weight of it in her hands, hoping he's packed everything. She puts the backpack on and reaches out her hand.

When his palm is in hers, she thinks: *I could let go. I could let the sea take him now, pull him to his death.*

But she doesn't. Instead, she pulls him up, so that they are both kneeling on the ledge, soaked and breathing hard.

The cave is smaller than in her memory, dark and wet as a mouth. Tears burn in her eyes at the familiar smells of brine and seaweed. Below, the tide whispers. *Hush*, it says, *hush*. Like a mother's lullaby.

It feels wrong to bring Cameron into this space; a female space, with its scent of iron and milk. She has him crawl in ahead of her, and even in the dark she feels his body tense, smells the fear on him, acrid and male.

She can see the phone in his back pocket, the oblong shape of it. Her heart thuds as she reaches, easing it out as gently as she can manage.

"Fuck," he says, and she pauses, frozen. The phone is in her hand, halfway to her own pocket.

"What?"

He has stopped moving, stopped crawling forward.

"Just—cut my hand on a rock."

When they stop, huddled under the cave's daggered roof, she hears him scrabble for it, turning out his pockets, opening the zipper of his backpack. He swears again, his voice rising in pitch.

"What's the matter now?"

"My phone. Jesus Christ. My phone is gone. I must have dropped that, too." He has found the flashlight and turns it on, yellow light slicing across his face.

"Where did you last have it?" she asks, angling herself away from him so that he cannot see the bulge in the pocket of her jeans.

"I don't know. It was in my pocket. Fucking hell—the ring's bad enough, but my phone . . ."

"I'll go back and look for it."

She crawls toward the light, where seafoam licks at the entrance. When she reaches the cave's lip, she pulls the phone from her pocket and switches it on.

The background image is his family: Nicola and the two children. They both have their mother's red hair, but the girl has Cameron's green eyes. She waits until the reception bars appear, and then, after a few seconds, throws it into the sea.

"Sorry," she calls back. "I can't find it."

She crawls back to Cameron, who looks frightened and sickly under the flashlight's glare. She looks up at the cave's roof, at the glistening teats of rock. She feels held close, safe.

"Now what?" Cameron breathes, the words souring the air.

"Now we wait."

40

MARY

At some stage Mary must have fallen asleep, lulled by the movement of the waves and the murmurs of the other women's prayers. She woke to darkness, solid against her skin: no light filtered through from the upper decks. There was nothing but the burn of the water on her body, the heave and creak of the ship as it bucked and fell. The hush of four score women breathing, the occasional whimpered cry and prayer.

And then, another sound. One soft, high note followed by another, rising and rising.

Eliza, singing a *caoineadh*, a lament.

It could not be true, could it?

Mary reached over the sleeping bodies of Bridie, Sarah, and Annie, searching for Aoife's hand. It was cold and limp. With her other hand she reached for Eliza, joining her own voice to her sister's song.

Aoife was dead. The captain had killed her.

When morning came, they turned Aoife gently onto her back, smoothing the hair from her face. The thin blades of light made her features look younger, and Mary wondered if perhaps she wasn't quite so old as she had thought. Perhaps, if she'd led a different sort of life, the forehead would always have been so unclouded, the mouth always so unlined.

A trembling rose through Mary's body, all the way from her toes to the very tips of her fingers. It was the first time that she had touched the dead body of someone she had loved.

But she knew what ought to be done.

If they had candles, they would be lit. If there were curtains, they would be drawn. They would wash the body, dress it in fine linen. Decorate it, even, with garlands of flowers. Aoife deserved all of this, and more.

But here, in the prison deck, they had nothing, not even a proper shroud to cover her. She would be wrapped in an old sail, and sent to the blue deep of the ocean. Aoife, who had so feared the sight of the shark strung from the mast, who had cursed the captain for bringing bad luck down upon them all.

They did what they could. The five of them pooled what remained of their water, tipping the rust-smelling dregs onto Aoife's face and body, gently brushing the grime from her skin. Bridie closed the older woman's eyes, revealing the lids, thin and blue as eggshells. They folded her arms over her chest, the limbs moving stiffly now, as death took its hold.

The cold yield of Aoife's skin beneath her fingers, the soft murmuring as the women worked together, made Mary think of Da. Da, who had two score years already, she knew. She closed her eyes for a moment, trying to summon his face: the ripe brown health of it, the white, even teeth. But all she saw was the slight stoop to his back that had worsened in recent years, the way he had begun to squint at the distance, the new clouds to his eyes.

One day, she knew, Da would die. Alone, in the cold dark of the cottage they had left.

Who would perform this ritual for him? Who would wash his body, who would sing the lament, with his daughters exiled from the land?

She pushed the thoughts from her mind. She could not think of Da when it was Aoife whose body lay small and shrunken in the berth.

"I wish we had some flowers," Bridie said. "Flowers, and a proper shroud."

"What flowers grow on the Blasket Islands?" Sarah asked.

Mary thought of foxglove—the purple bells of it, curved and fleshy as a woman's parts.

Purple as the bruises he gave me.

There was some justice in that, Mary thought. That nature had given Aoife such a weapon, and shaped it in the image of herself.

They took Aoife's body away when they delivered the day's rations. It was Wright who came, him and one other. And though Bridie clung tight to his legs like a child to its mother, though she cried and begged that they be allowed on deck to watch the body meet the waves, he only shook his head, teeth gritted.

But Mary saw the pulse of a vein at his temple, saw the way he did not meet the other sailor's eye. The tenderness with which he cradled Aoife's skull, as though she was sleeping and he did not want her to wake.

They had no way of knowing when she was given to the sea. They could not hear the clergyman's English prayer, could not see the small body in its sail-cloth shroud, could not hear the *splash* of it entering the water, the current bearing it away.

They said their own prayers, the prayers of Ireland.

But as they murmured, heads bent over the berth that was now empty, Mary wondered at the words they spoke. The truth of them.

She thought of the ruined church where Da had taken them to worship, the altar home to a nest of sparrows who left offerings in white clumps along the pews. The priest—O'Sullivan—wore a cassock that fluttered with moths, stored in the hollow space behind a broken rock, along with the tin cup and plate for the Eucharist. He seemed so sure of the things he said, having risked everything to say them.

When he'd spoken of good and evil, of righteousness and sin, he'd made it sound easy to tell the difference between the two. As clear as sorting flax stalks from their seeds.

But where did that leave Aoife, who had killed her husband to save her own life?

And where did that leave her and Eliza?

41

LUCY

Lucy sits on Jess's sofa, the diary resting next to her. Dora Maar flits from underneath the coffee table to the kitchen, a growl emitting from deep in her chest.

Her mouth tastes stale, metallic.

She looks at the ultrasound in her hand, at the ghostly capture of her own newly forming limbs. At her sister's name.

Images of her childhood flash before her eyes, like the jumping reel of a film. Her mother holding her hand on the first day of school, her father teaching her to drive, singing loudly along to the radio. Smiling shyly before her school formal, her parents on either side.

All of it a lie.

She thinks of Jess. The longing she'd felt for her as a little girl, as if some part of her had always known.

She finally understands the dark shapes that shifted beneath the surface of her childhood. Who had first uttered the word *sister*? Who decided that this was what Lucy would be? Had it been Jess? Had she wanted to give her up?

She thinks of Jess's distance, the way she kept herself apart from

Lucy. She thinks of her childhood gift of a snakeskin, kept for all these years, now glittering in Jess's painting; her masterpiece. She thinks of the passcode on Jess's phone.

20 09 99.

How had it felt for Jess, to key those numbers into her phone countless times a day? The date she gave birth to the child she surrendered? The rush of pain she feels is as much for Jess as it is for herself.

She does not let herself think about the man who might be her father, about the ring that shimmers on the coffee table. At least, she will not think of him in those terms.

She slots the facts into place, cold and hard, as if she is loading bullets into a gun.

Jess had an affair with Cameron Hennessey.

Cameron Hennessey has been charged with assault.

Cameron Hennessey's car was found nearby. His ring was on the staircase leading to the sea.

Cameron and Jess are missing.

They must be together. Is she sheltering him, protecting him? Or has Hennessey been keeping her prisoner? Lucy thinks of the staircase where she found the ring. Where could they have been going? Had they taken a boat somewhere?

She tries to visualize the cliff face as she's seen it from the opposite end of the bay. There is no dock or jetty, no place for a boat to moor.

And then she remembers: Devil's Lookout. The dark maw in the sandstone.

The cave.

She scours the kitchen for a weapon, pulling a serrated knife from the knife block. Only then does she realize: another of the knives is missing.

Outside, the sky is thick with clouds, heavy and purple as fruit. There is a sensation as if her body, or perhaps the whole world, is preparing to burst.

She shivers as she stands at the precipice of the staircase. Either side of her, the tussocks of grass flutter in the wind, and the music of the wind chimes grows frenzied, almost violent.

Her heart drums with fear as she looks down, at the dizzying fall to the sea. The white waves tongue the rocks, the tide rising and rising. She has to go now—if she waits, then the swell will be too high. She needs to get to Jess as quickly as she can.

Lucy takes a breath, touches the flat shape of the knife in her pocket.

She begins her descent.

42

MARY

A month after Aoife died, the men brought buckets of seawater down to the prison deck.

"You're to wash," said Wright, raising his lantern high so that he could see their frightened faces. "And then we're to bring you on deck, where you'll be checked over for lice."

Some of the women scoffed: lice itched everywhere, from the hair on their heads to the fur between their legs. But fear wormed in Mary's gut. The captain was trying to make them presentable, as if they had not been left to molder in the ship's bowels all these long months. That could only mean one thing: they were almost at New South Wales.

Blood hummed in the ribbed flesh of Mary's neck. She thought of the scaled skin of their legs, the pearly webs between their fingers and toes. How would they hide such disfigurement from the surgeon's inspection, let alone from the men in New South Wales?

The men handed out more buckets of seawater: the prison deck was alive with the splash and shriek of women washing. She did not know how much time they had before the men returned with the fetters, ready to take them on deck.

She nudged Eliza forward, to the barrels that rolled and slammed against the hull, forming a narrow gully where they could hide. Rats had made their nest here, and Mary cringed at the smell of their waterlogged bodies, the mulch of shredded cloth and droppings beneath their hands and knees.

The timbers creaked and shuddered with the footsteps of the returning men.

Mary's mouth was bitter with terror. Eliza's shallow breathing filled her ears.

The sailors yelled for quiet as they took the women on deck, leaving Mary and Eliza behind. Relief flooded Mary's body: her plan had worked; they had avoided the surgeon's inspection.

But they could not hide forever. Sooner or later, someone would see their difference. Their wrongness.

The prison deck hummed with one word as if it were a prayer.

Land.

When they had embarked so many months before, Mary could never have imagined how the word would toll in her heart like a gong. The women's excited description of what they had seen above deck— the distant flank of a coast through the mist—brought no comfort, only terror.

Mary imagined bone-white cliffs looming ahead, the snap of irons around her wrist. Eliza's hands wrenched from hers. Medical men with sharp eyes and sharper fingers, prodding and pulling at the mystery of their bodies.

There had been a lamb, she remembered now, born with two heads sprouting from its neck. The villagers had called it an abomination, a sign from the devil. Da had bade them stay away, but Mary had heard from the other children of the tongues that lolled in twisted mouths, the stalk neck that sagged with the weight of two skulls.

The farmer who owned the lamb had put it to death, crushing each skull with a rock. He had burned the carcass rather than risk the curse of eating or selling the meat.

Now, Mary thought of the delicate bones of Eliza's face, the petals of her eyelids. Her sister's hair, shrinking and crackling in flames.

That evening's rations came with a quart of wine, and the sailors opened the hatches and launched the windsail, so that fresh air sighed against the women's faces. Moonlight poured in like milk.

"The first thing I'll do," said Bridie, "is try to get home."

She had barely spoken for days, and when Sarah scoffed at the words, Mary knew that tenderness lay behind her smirk, that she had longed to see Bridie return to herself.

"How?"

"A Cornish lass made it all the way back to England, I heard."

"That's shite."

"I swear it! She stole a currach and sailed it home."

"The English don't make currachs, you fool."

"You'll be the fool when I'm sitting pretty in some Dublin tavern!"

"I can smell *earth*!" someone shouted, and a cheer went up, so loud it might've launched the ship into the air.

Mary could smell it, too. A tang that might have been peat but wasn't, not quite. It made something tighten in her chest.

The sea grew rougher now that they were close to land, as if it was unwilling to let them go. One morning, a wave curled over the ship just as the hatches had been opened, soaking the women through. Bridie laughed: she seemed to have become giddy with her pain at Aoife's loss and the relief that their journey was almost at an end.

For days, she had refused Wright's entreaties: rejected rum, port wine, even the golden promise of an orange. But after a time, as the frenzy of curiosity in the hold built and built, she gave in, as if selling herself for information was some way of making amends.

Mary wished she wouldn't. The toll was written on her face, in the deep-set lines of it.

"Two days of sailing left," Bridie said, after Wright had ushered her back through the bulkhead. She passed the segments of an orange around: it burst, sweet and miraculous, on Mary's tongue. "Can you believe it? Two more days and I'll be standing on dry land." Bridie spread her arms wide, ragged smock clinging to the outline of her ribs, before bending so low that her hair brushed the wooden planks.

"I will kiss the land!" she said. "Even if it's filled with monsters as they say!"

"Jesus, Mary, help you," Sarah muttered.

The ship keeled, knocking Bridie into Sarah's lap.

"Oh, I'm sure they will!" Bridie said, kissing Sarah's cheek. "I'll put in a good word for you and the others."

Sarah laughed, and Mary saw real mirth flicker across Bridie's face, almost as if she was herself again. She could not help but smile with them. She nestled closer to Eliza, pretending just for a moment that it would be all right, that she'd find a way to keep them safe.

43

JESS

Jess does not know how long they have been in the cave. She thinks it has been three days, but cannot be sure: she left her phone in Cliff House, and Cameron's is long submerged. The flashlight's batteries have run out, as has the water they brought from the house. They drink rainwater, now, collected in the plastic bottles. There is enough left, she thinks, for two more days, if that.

Twice a day, the tide floods in, forcing them to scramble up the sides of the cave. On these occasions, they huddle in an alcove formed by a jagged column of rock. Water churns below them, runs in milky drips from the stalactites that graze their heads.

The tide draws in and out, like a creature's breath. Six tides and she has not heard a single note of song. She is running out of time.

Where are they?

During the day, the light is dim, reddish. But now it's night, and there is nothing but the slick rocks beneath her body, the *shush* of the sea and Cameron's ragged breathing in her ear. He has brought a flask of whiskey with him—he must have concealed it in the pocket of his jeans before they dumped his car—and the smell of it sours the air.

He, too, has tired of waiting.

Sometimes he yells, makes threats; she has to talk him out of leaving the cave, of making the perilous climb back up the cliff face. But most of the time he begs and whimpers, childlike and afraid.

"I don't understand," he is saying now, again. "The boat—where is it? Jess, it's been days. Shouldn't it be here by now? Please—there has to be somewhere else we can go. I don't like it here, Jess."

The cave seems to terrify him. He complains of the constant damp, the way that his fingers have become pruned by the water. Sometimes she hears his teeth chatter, as though a fever grips him.

It is different for Jess. Moisture has soaked into her body, her skin tightening and fizzing. She runs her fingers over the rippling surface of her shins, thinking of her painting. She touches her throat and it is furrowed, as if her skin is parting, opening to something.

"I've been here before, you know," she says, more to herself than to Cameron. "I ran away."

And she is there, heaving the swell of herself through the crackling bush; she is gripping tight to the rope at the stairs, the coarseness of it stinging her palm. She is climbing down, lower and lower, the sea pulling at her with the pain.

She is there.

She is here.

Cameron swears, startling Jess back into the present. The sea is growing rougher, just as it had the night that Lucy was born. A plume of spray bursts into the cave's mouth, soaking them. Jess inhales, savoring the smell. The smell of seaweed, of the secret things that dwell beneath the surface.

"I can't stand this," Cameron says. Jess can hear his teeth chattering. "I really can't. I'm cold and I'm wet and I'm tired and I want to go home."

"They tell ghost stories about this place, you know," Jess says, the words light in her mouth. "A lot of people have died in these waters. A ship sank, full of convicts, women. But the story goes that some of them survived. They'd spent so long tied up in the ship's hold, weeks without fresh air or sunshine, so that by the time the ship ran aground on the rocks, they'd become something not quite human. Something monstrous."

"Stop it, Jess."

"Then, of course, there are the men who went missing."

Cameron says nothing.

"Eight, at least, that we know about. I think there are more, but people started paying attention too late. You must have heard of them. Everyone has. Eight unexplained disappearances, eight men drowned. No bodies."

"I'm not in the mood for this, OK?" Cameron says, raising his voice. "It's been days and we're just stuck in this cave. Where's this fucking boat, huh? Some plan of yours. We probably couldn't get out even if we wanted to. I'm about ready to fucking give myself up. I want—I want . . ." He takes a shuddering breath. "I just want to see my wife again. My kids. I want to go home."

"I wanted to go home too, you know," Jess says now, her voice sharper. "That day in the art studio. I liked it, at first. Your hand on mine. It was comforting and safe. I felt . . . anchored by it. I wasn't sure of anything anymore. I didn't know who my parents were. Who I could trust. But then . . . you kept going."

"Stop it, Jess. You're rewriting history. You wanted it, practically *begged* me for it—"

"You kept going," Jess continues, "and it wasn't what I thought it would be. It hurt."

The burn of his fingers inside her. She had told herself, all those years ago, that she was protecting him by not writing it down. But really, she was protecting herself. She hadn't wanted to remember.

"Oh, shut up," he spits, the venom of it surprising her. "It wasn't like you were a fucking virgin. And we didn't even have sex!"

In the dark, every sense is heightened. The splitting of her flesh in the water, the roar of the waves on the rocks. She strains, her mind sifting through the sound, searching for the sound of voices, of singing.

Where are they?

"You're a liar," Cameron is saying now. "Just like the others. Fucking manipulative. Acting like you want it, then pretending that you didn't, because you feel ashamed. Ashamed of being a fucking slut. Well, I don't care. I'm getting out of here. I'm going to get out and I'm going to get a fucking good lawyer and I'm going to tell the police you held me here against my will."

He is moving, scraping himself over the rocks.

"No," she says, grabbing hold of him, and then they are tearing and scratching at each other, their bodies edging closer and closer to the mouth of the cave, until Jess feels the cold touch of air at the back of her skull; the sting of a blade on her throat.

44

MARY

The night before they were due to make landfall at New South Wales, Mary woke to a strange sound. A violent tearing, like the rending of time itself. Then, as if clasped by great hands, she was wrenched from her berth, her skull cracking against the wall opposite.

She tried to grab hold of something, to scramble upright, but the ship tilted forward and there was another great ripping sound. Mary realized that it was the splintering of wood, the bursting of casks and barrels. The sea was lapping its way inside the ship.

All around, the women were screaming, crying, praying. A terrified chorus.

"God help us!"

"I cannot see, I cannot see!"

"Pray for your souls!"

"Holy Mary, Mother of God, pray for us sinners . . ."

"The floor! The floor!"

Mary looked down and saw that the wooden walkway between the berths was gone—in its place rose black, jagged rocks, the sea swirling around them, vicious white.

She cried out in pain as the gouged flesh of her neck began to widen. She pressed a shaking hand to her skin. It felt warm and slick, like the inside of her mouth.

She heard Eliza's voice, calling to her in the dark. Around her, women retched and screamed in fear.

The ship pitched again and she took her chance and leaped back to her berth, the sea licking at her feet. She felt Eliza's hands reaching out to her, pulling her to safety.

"We need to go," Eliza said. "Now."

"Where?" Mary asked, though she knew the answer. Her lungs already burned for it.

"You must believe, Mary," Eliza said, her voice urgent and trembling. "You must believe and you must remember. Remember how the sea felt back in Ard na Caithne, how it felt cold and good and sweet. Remember Mam, swimming ahead of us, leading us to the deep."

Mary trembled. She gulped at the air, and yet could not slake her thirst for it.

Eliza squeezed Mary's hand, placed it on her own throat so that she could feel the desperate beating wings there.

"Remember, Mary. Please. The water makes us strong."

The hole in the deck was widening, the planks disappearing into the water. She thought of the ship as they had first seen her: the proud swell of her sails, the mermaid figurehead with her painted eyes. She had never been a match for the waves, for the ocean's fury.

Mary could hear Annie screaming, Sarah trying to comfort her with ragged words. "Do you remember what Mammy told you about heaven? The place you'd go if you were a very good girl? You've been such a good girl, *a linbh*. Such a very good girl."

Bridie's laugh rang out, brittle and brave. "Cruel, isn't it? For us to be almost there and it to come to this!"

A boom, and the ship sagged further into the waves. Mary looked up: for the briefest of moments, there was a great hole where the roof had been, and she could see the night, spangled with stars.

The mast.

The impact was so loud that Mary felt it, juddering in her bones and teeth. The rigging, torn and knotted, fell over them like a net.

"Now," Eliza hissed, her breath hot and ragged on Mary's skin. "Now, or we'll be trapped."

The sea rose around them.

Mary thought of the stream back in Ireland, the way the water had felt like gentle hands on her skin. The hands had returned. It was time at last to give in to them.

The sea wrapped itself around her, cold and sweet, as Eliza had promised. The gills on her neck opened like flowers, the water singing on her skin.

She was no longer freakish, no longer stunted. Blooming into herself, at last. She felt her spine burst through her dress in spiked fins. Her hands, when she held them to her face, were strangers: her pulse beat in the webbing between her fingers.

She remembered now.

Mam, taking her gently by the hand and leading her to the shore. Her face—not crusted and gray but glittering pale. Laughing at the tickle of the water over her toes, and then the hardening of her skin all over, the strange pressure in her throat. Gills blooming beneath Mam's jaw, velvet red as roses. The three of them diving down deep, their bodies weightless.

How would you like to stay in the sea? she had said that night, the night before she left. *For the three of us to be together forever, with the dolphins and the seals?*

She remembered how she had cried, how she had dug her toes into the wet sand, calling out for Da. Mam had knelt, silhouetted against the moon and the white spray and held her close. Then she had lifted them—one child on each hip—and taken them back to the stone cottage, her tears running into Mary's hair as she told them the story. The story of the merrow who longed for the sea. Who loved her girls but could not part them from each other. Who hoped that, one day, they might choose her world for themselves.

And now Mary was here, a thousand leagues from the coast of Kerry, in a different ocean. But that forgotten taste from childhood had returned: salt and weeds and the minerals that make up the sea-bed, floating toward her in a glorious dust. And it felt then that per-haps Mam was not so far away, that perhaps the same water that had combed Mam's hair from her face now gently brushed Mary's cheek.

At last, rightness in her body. At last, the knowledge that Mam lived, that she had not wanted to leave them behind. That she had loved them.

Her small surge of peace was soon swallowed by horror.

The ship fell to pieces around them, a broken cage. There were bodies, too: men, wreathed in crystal bubbles, their eyes bulging as their lungs filled. Mary looked for the captain, hoping to see the fear in his eyes as he drowned. But she saw no officers, only sailors, their shirts billowing like shrouds.

Eliza swam ahead, and Mary followed her past sinking barrels and lengths of chain, past sails that rose like ghosts. The sounds—the screams and the cries and the great shuddering as the ship broke apart—were muffled by water. Mary heard only the rush of the sea, as right and rhythmic as the thrumming of her heart.

Her eyes filmed with tears, tiny drops that floated away from her.

She remembered Bridie's farewell, Sarah's whispers of comfort to her terrified child. She turned back for one last look.

Don't.

She felt, rather than heard, Eliza's voice, the way she'd once felt her breath on her skin.

She turned back. Eliza swam next to her, eyes wide and pale as moons.

You can see me?

No. Feel you. Your movements. It's too late. We cannot help. Please, Mary—I can't lose you. Please.

Mary remembered Aoife. How they had all stood and watched on the deck, as the whip sliced through the air toward her fragile fresh. How she had done nothing. How she had been weak, just as she had been when Byrne had reached his foul fingers toward her.

But she was different now. Changed.

Half-merrow, half-fisherman.

The *tír fo thuinn*, the land beneath the waves, belonged to her, just as it had belonged to Mam.

Was it any wonder men had feared it so?

She reached out and grasped Eliza's outstretched hand one final time.

Mary, please.

But Mary turned away from Eliza, back toward the sinking ship.

The *Naiad* listed on its side, a drowning animal. The hull gaped where the reef had torn its flesh. Curious fish darted in and out, glinting in shafts of moonlight.

Mary swam toward the mermaid figurehead, placed a hand over its painted eyes. She looked at the pert wooden breasts, the fish's tail with its chipped paint, then down at her own body. Her smock rose around her, a pale membrane. There was no tail, only her legs, the pinkish webs of skin between her toes.

She scanned the dark shifting water, saw only the graceful turn of sinking bodies. Time seemed different, under the sea, slow and sinuous. And perhaps it was now, for her, and for Eliza. But not for the others.

She swam toward the jagged hole on the side of the hull and paused. There was a prickling sensation along her spine, in her fingers and toes. Her gills fluttered. She slipped inside.

The ship closed around her, coffin-dark. Mary pushed herself along the passageways, passing the quarterdeck and the store decks, the officers' sleeping quarters. Something sharp tore at the skin of her arm and she screamed, the sound swallowed by water.

Her lungs squeezed. Fear burned through her veins, her gills beating so hard they made tiny currents around her.

She groped forward, searching for the prison deck, her palms brushing jagged wood, the coarse hair of a rope; once, something cold and soft that she didn't like to think about. Moonlight poured in through the hole that had been left by the mast and she jerked backward when something flickered ahead. Then she saw that it was the suspended body of a rat, tiny hands clawed and snout tilted upward, tail moving with the current as if it were alive.

She thought of Bridie, her red hair drifting with the tide, her lungs still and swollen with the sea.

What a coward she had been, leaving them behind.

But she was almost there. All she had to do was swim down the hatchway and through the bulkhead, and then she would be at the prison deck.

The bulkhead gate was slightly open, thrown off its hinges when the ship had broken apart. Mary swam through sideways, the splintered bars nipping at her like teeth.

Her vision was beginning to adjust, the shapes in the prison deck forming with awful clarity. She tried hard not to look at the berths. At the clouds of hair, the ragged blankets that drifted upward to reveal vulnerable feet, ridden with sores. Here and there, a pale hand lifted from a berth, grasping at nothing.

Here, locked in the ship's bowels, they had never had a chance.

Mary swallowed a sob. She should be here, lying bloated and silent with the others.

But instead, by some divine trick she did not understand, she had been spared.

She willed her body to swim on, to find the corner of the prison deck that had been theirs. To retrieve the bodies of her friends and bear them up to the moonlight, where the night sky could touch their faces one last time.

Bridie, with her rich bawdy laugh. Sarah, holding Annie close and humming in her ear. And Annie herself, pushing her doll—her one treasure—into Aoife's berth.

All of them, gone.

But then. Some dappled movement, which might have been nothing more than moonlight through the hatches, caught her eye.

She closed her eyes, feeling the sea move around her. Waiting. Then, there it was: something fluttering through the water, like a kick.

Mary swam toward the sound, her arms outstretched as if she might feel her way toward it. In sinking, the ship had turned on its side, so that one corner of the prison deck—*their* corner—pointed toward the surface. It was there that Mary saw the glimmer of treading feet.

Hope surged in her lungs, a glorious bubble of it, lifting her upward.

Someone was alive!

She blinked, again and again, for surely it was not possible, surely it was just that her eyes could not yet make sense of this new underwater world.

But it was real. She could even see the dull red of Bridie's hair.

Two women, one child. Their legs working furiously, sipping from an air pocket that clung to the arch where the ship's joists met the hull. Sarah pressed Annie to her chest, and even as Mary looked up at them from below, wreathed in shadows, she could see the exhaustion trembling in their muscles.

She did not know how she would get them to safety. She would have to take them one by one—perhaps she could take Annie first, have the child cling to her back. But there wasn't time for them all—there wasn't air.

Whoever she left would drown.

Eliza, she thought, focusing on the word with all her might. *I need you.*

45

LUCY

SUNDAY, 17 FEBRUARY 2019

Lucy breathes hard as she climbs down the staircase, stones skittering to the deep. The muscles of her calves quiver. Below her, the sea shimmers and ripples like skin.

Ten more steps.

She clings tight to the rope, which is frayed and damp, blistering her palm.

As she gets closer to the water, she has the strange sense that she is being pulled by something, a fish with a hook through its gut.

Then she feels it in her bones; in the patches of skin that tingle at the water's touch, in the place where her pulse beats in her neck.

She has been here before.

Her fingers slip on the rocks as she pulls herself over the ledge. The sea is louder now, thundering around her; the cling and push of strong white hands. The wind moans through the rocks, whipping the hair from her face.

She can see the cave up ahead, a dark gash in the rock.

"Jess!"

She screams, but the wind whips her voice away.

A wave curls toward her, an animal ready to pounce. She grips the rock tight, driving her fingers into the sharp grit so hard it hurts. Bracing herself.

But when the water comes it is soft and gentle. Soothing.

She feels her grip on the rock loosen, the temptation to let go, to float away, seizing her.

"Lucy?"

A face, pale and wild, peers over the lip of the cave. It's Jess, her eyes wide and full of sky; her hair tangled with the sea. There is something wrong with her neck; it blooms pink and ragged beneath her jaw, opening and closing in time with her pulse.

"Take my hand," says Jess. Lucy does not hear the words so much as feel them, a song humming in her bones.

Jess grasps Lucy's hand—her skin feels moist and smooth and strange—and pulls.

I have been here before, Lucy thinks again as Jess leads her into the cave. They crawl on their knees, the rocks making indents in Lucy's skin. The sea's roar is quieter here, musical. Above her, daggers of rock glisten like teeth.

When they are inside, Jess stops, turns to face Lucy.

"You came," she says, putting her arms around her.

Lucy rests her head on Jess's shoulder. Her skin does not smell of linseed and vanilla as Lucy remembers, but of something sharper, animal. A smell that might come from Lucy herself.

The sound of Jess's heart beating fills her ears. She feels her breathing slow, the blood settling in her veins.

She would know it anywhere, that sound. The first she ever heard.

Jess's skin is grimed and crusted, her hair plastered to her forehead. There is a cut against one sharp cheekbone, vivid red. The wounds on her neck flutter.

"You're hurt," Lucy says, reaching out a hand. Panic fizzes through her body. She needs to get Jess out of here, to a hospital. "What happened? Where's Hennessey?"

Jess swallows, her eyes bright as coins.

"How did you—"

"The police," Lucy says. "They found his car."

Jess closes her eyes, takes a breath that sounds to Lucy like relief.

"OK," she says. "OK."

"Where is he?"

"Gone," says Jess. "Drowned."

Lucy's breath catches in her throat.

"You didn't—"

"No. No, it was an accident. We struggled. He—he fell."

Lucy swallows. She thinks of Hennessey's face, the age-softened jaw. Imagines it greened by the sea.

"Was he"—Lucy trembles as she forms the words in her mouth—"my father?"

Jess shakes her head violently, and Lucy closes her eyes with relief.

So it must be Max. Max, who is gentle and kind. Who had pulled Jess from the water and put his arms around her. Who had loved her.

"Did he do this?" Lucy says, tracing the frills on Jess's neck. There is something familiar about the sensation of the skin beneath her fingertips, the pulsing heat of it.

"No," says Jess, placing her own hand on Lucy's neck.

There is a stinging pain, so sharp that Lucy winces. Jess is drawing something from her flesh, some ancient thing stored in her cells. Then the skin of her neck splits; she feels it open, come alive, under Jess's fingers.

"You asked me once," Jess says, her voice breaking, "if you could shed your skin like a snake."

Lucy thinks of the painting—*The Sirens*. The two women, their scaled skin. She nods, eyes brimming with tears.

"And I said no. No, you couldn't. But you can, you have. We both have."

Tears run into Lucy's mouth.

"I've been here before, haven't I?"

Jess nods, and Lucy sees that she is crying, too.

"I carried you here, in my belly. I'd seen it, in my dreams. This dark, safe place; a place between land and sea. I was so frightened, Lucy. I had been for months. The fear grew and grew so that I worried it would choke me, kill us both.

"I got a coach to Sydney, another bus from Batemans Bay. I wanted to see it—Cliff House, Devil's Lookout. The place I started from. I was in the house when the pain began. That's when I heard them for the first time, singing. Like they were calling me. And then I was here, with the rocks cutting into my hands and the tide beating in my ears, and then I pushed and pushed and then you were here, too. The most perfect thing I'd ever seen. I remember your little hands"—she clasps one between hers now, squeezing tight—"they were so tiny, but they seemed to contain all of me. My whole heart. I called you Lucy. I wanted you to have the sea in your name."

An ache spreads through Lucy's chest.

"But why?" she says, the words small in the echoing space of the cave. "Why didn't you want me?"

"Oh, Lucy," says Jess. "I always wanted you."

She holds up one of Lucy's hands, stroking the webs of flesh between her fingers.

"I wanted to take you home, to the sea. I never wanted you to feel like I did, like you didn't belong. But then, they found me. I don't remember much of what happened next." She closes her eyes. "Only flashes—a hospital; your cries. The skin peeling from us both, my whole body thirsting."

She takes a breath, then continues.

"There was a woman from the government. The Department of Communities and Justice. She told me that I was unfit, that I had put you in danger, bringing you—birthing you—here. They were going to take you away from me.

"Mum and Dad stepped in. They applied to become guardians, and we decided—or it was decided—that you would be my sister.

"We were going to tell you the truth when you turned eighteen. But then . . . it wasn't so easy."

"But—I don't understand. What do you mean, you wanted to take me to the sea? Are you saying"—Lucy licks her cracked lips—"are you saying that you wanted us to drown?"

"It wouldn't be drowning," says Jess, stroking Lucy's cheek. "Close your eyes."

46

MARY

Bubbles streamed past her, whirling white.

Eliza. She was there, the fins along her spine shifting and bristling, striped like a tiger in a story from the East.

The air bubble was quickly getting smaller: Bridie and Sarah pressed their faces against the dank wood of the hull, their fingers white as they gripped the planks. Annie curled into her mother's chest, taking weak breaths of the dwindling air.

The women flinched as they approached, their feet treading the water in a frenzy of panic. They were afraid, Mary realized. She and Eliza appeared to them as monsters.

"Bridie," she said.

Her friend's lips moved in response, but it took Mary a moment to make out the words over the lap of the sea against the hull and the creaking timber.

"Mother of God, pray for us sinners, now and at the hour of our death . . ."

"Don't you know me, Bridie? Take my hand. You have to come. If you stay here, you'll die."

But still Bridie's eyes glittered with fear.

"Pray for us sinners, now and at the hour of our death."

"I'm not going to hurt you, Bridie!"

There was the *thunk* of the ship hitting the ocean floor. Cold fear bloomed in Mary's gut. The air bubble morphed, shrinking.

She had to find a way to reach them. To show them that despite the new strangeness of her body—the frilled flesh of her neck, the fins—she was still Mary. Mary who had bled and cried with them, who had sang with them in the dark.

"You should have known me before," she sang, the water turning her voice eerie. *"I sang you to sleep and I robbed you of wealth . . ."*

Eliza surfaced next to her, and together they sang the last line.

"And again I'm a maid on the shore . . ."

"God help me," Bridie breathed. "It is you. Both of you."

"Take a breath," Eliza said. "Take a breath and don't let go."

Bridie wrapped her legs around Mary's waist, as if she were a little child. Eliza took Sarah's weight, Annie tucked safe between their bodies, her mother stroking her hair to soothe her whimpering. "You've just got to be my very good girl for a moment longer, *a linbh*," she gasped.

Checking that Bridie's arms were tight around her rib cage, Mary slipped beneath the surface.

The moon glimmered on the waves, debris crashing against the rocks. The coast rose behind them, a dark curve. Mary felt a power humming from it. She saw eyes burning bright in a great forest, faces framed by pale trees. The land had hidden her people in her belly for thousands of years, but now the English—men like the captain and his officers—had come to split her open. Mary would have no part in it, she decided. She would not venture beyond the rocks and cave in the cliffs. She would leave the land and her people alone.

She hooked her arm around Bridie's waist and swam backward, letting her friend feel the night on her face, the cool air in her lungs. Tears shone in Bridie's eyes as she took ragged, gulping breaths.

Mary leaned down and placed a kiss on her forehead.

Beside her, Eliza floated on her back, Sarah and Annie tucked under each arm.

"Look at that, *a linbh*," Sarah whispered, lifting her hand from the water to point at the spangled sky. "All those stars. Aren't they grand, so? Aren't they beautiful?"

While the others clung to a floating barrel, Mary and Eliza gathered as many planks of wood as they could find, lashing them together with seaweed and torn lengths of canvas sail. By the time the raft was finished, the horizon was beginning to pale, the stars fading.

They lifted their friends onto the raft, the three of them clinging tight together.

"Do you think anybody else . . ." Bridie started but did not finish. The question hung in the air.

Mary thought of what she'd seen as she swam through the sinking ship. The limp flower of a hand; the strands of hair moving with the current.

Not even the sailors had been able to swim. What chance had the women had, locked in the prison deck?

"We should say a prayer for their souls," Annie said, her voice small in the night.

"Yes, *a linbh*," said Sarah.

Bridie reached forward, stroked Mary's gills with gentle fingers.

"I think we have the old gods to thank for this," she said softly. "And so I'm not much of one for praying, just now. Let us bid our friends farewell, instead."

Sarah nodded. She turned in the direction that the ship had sunk—there was nothing but black sea, silvered by the coming dawn—and trailed her hand in the water.

"*Slán abhaile*," she said.

"*Slán abhaile*."

As the sun rose in the sky, Bridie, Sarah, and Annie rested, their bodies curled into each other on the makeshift raft.

Mary and Eliza swam to the reef, to the jaws that had closed around the ship's body. They gathered supplies for the others—a bladder of water, any food that might have survived the wreck.

The reef reminded Mary of the forest in spring, teeming with color and movement. Bristles of pink and red coral moved gently with the current. Fish shimmered past. A dark shadow lifted itself from the seabed and floated away.

She had never seen so much beauty. Her eyes ached with looking and yet she hardly dared blink. It was as if, for all these years, she had been living with a great thirst, and at last was able to slake it.

She reached out a hand, stroking the fins that made their way down her sister's back.

I wish you could see this, she said.

Eliza turned to her, and there was something different in her face, something certain in her eyes.

I can, she answered. *I have always seen this. This moment. Us, changed by the sea. I spent so much time dreaming of it, longing for it. For the* tír fo thuinn. *The land beneath the waves.*

I know you did.

I wanted to find it. I wanted to find Mam.

Mary placed her hands on Eliza's arms. Energy pulsed between them.

I am sorry for the things I said. That night we were arrested. I am sorry that I didn't want to talk about Mam. That I didn't believe you. And that—and that I made us stay behind, all those years ago.

Eliza smiled, tears glinting in her eyes.

But you didn't, she said. *I was the one who was frightened, who did not want to go.*

I do not understand. Eliza?

I had told you that I didn't want to leave Da. But you knew I would not tell Mam; you knew how much I longed to please her. And so you pretended that it was you—that you were the one who was afraid. You did that for me.

Eliza begins to cry, and soon, Mary joins her. This, Mary understands, is why Eliza had wanted so badly for her to remember, why she had wanted them to talk about Mam. She had not wanted Mary to blame herself for Mam's leaving.

Perhaps we were both afraid.

Yes. Perhaps we were not ready—perhaps we would never have been ready, if not for the ship, and everything that led to it. But now we are here, and it is ours. The tír fo thuinn. *Unless you want to go back?*

Mary thought of the world above the water's surface. She thought of Byrne and his cruel, sharp fingers. She thought of the captain and the look on his face when he had ordered that Aoife be whipped.

But then she thought of Da. The comfort of his voice, his stories. The way he had tried so hard to protect them—from men like Byrne, but also from themselves.

But hadn't he taken them from the sea, from their birthright? Hadn't he deprived them of the chance to choose?

She knew that she would miss Da for every day that remained to her. The currents would change and the coral would grow and she would think of him and worry. Whether he was ill, whether he was warm and fed. Who would wash his body and light the candles after he died.

But even if she wanted to find her way back to him somehow—back to the little village near the stream—she could not. She was changed. She was free.

She prayed for Da, prayed to the God that he had taught her to believe in. And she prayed to the sea with all her power. In her mind's eye, she saw Da returning to Ard na Caithne, looking at the sun upon the waves and knowing in his heart that Mary and Eliza were safe.

As a girl, she'd longed for a husband to share her bed and fill her with a child. That, she had thought, was her purpose in this life.

But now another purpose hummed inside her. For while there were some men like Da, too many were like Aoife's husband, like Byrne. Like the captain.

The captain, like Wright and the other sailors of the *Naiad*, was gone, lost to the waves. She thought of his bones crumbling on the seabed, becoming nothing. There would be other men like him, she knew. Whole ships of them plowed the waves even now, bringing fear and violence to this unfamiliar land. Mary felt the strange new muscles in her body clench, felt the spines bristle on her back. Her blood sang with fury.

No, she told her sister. *I do not want to go back.*

"Where will you go?" Eliza murmured.

Bridie shaded her eyes, looking at the coastline. Mary followed her gaze. Close to the shore, the water was blue as a jackdaw's eye. The sand was strewn with seaweed and broken fragments of wood. Worse were the bodies, bloated and battered by the rocks.

There was a flicker of movement through the scrub.

"They will come looking for us soon," Bridie said, watching the shoreline. She turned to Sarah, who pulled Annie closer to her.

"And if they find us?" Sarah asked.

"The female factory," Bridie said, her eyes dull. "They will take Annie from you. A man will pick you out of a line, to work his field or his bed. If you marry, you can get a ticket of leave. But you won't be free. Not really."

Annie tilted her face to look at her mother's. Her eyes were so filled with fear that Mary had to look away.

Sarah sobbed, a broken, quiet sound.

"It's all right," Bridie said, her voice soothing. "We just won't let them find us. If an English girl can make her way back home, then so can we."

Mary felt Eliza's hand brush hers under the water, unseen by the others. The time for farewell had come.

Mary lifted herself from the water, letting each of them embrace her in turn. Bridie's hair crackled against her cheek, and underneath the reek of the prison deck, she fancied she could detect some other scent. Peat and flowers, the Irish earth she would never see again. Annie kissed Mary's forehead, and Sarah gripped her hands tight.

"Thank you," she said, eyes shining, as she reached out to touch Eliza's face. "Both of you. For saving her. For saving us."

Mary could only nod. Grief closed her throat. So many days and nights she had spent with these women, sharing their pain, their fear, their hope. But now they must say goodbye.

Their friends belonged to one world, and they to another.

A world where sharks glided in the deep, where fish swam in glittering clouds. A world where songs swelled and rippled, traveling for miles.

A female world.

Mam's world.

She remembered what Aoife had said, the day they'd been forced aboard the *Naiad*, terrified and in chains.

A woman on a ship. Bad luck, so.

She thought of the maid on the shore who lured the sailors with her song. Of the mermaid figurehead and her painted smile.

Again, she saw the cave. The girl with her swollen body and wide, scared eyes. And all the other girls who would come, before and after her.

Mary had thought that being a merrow meant she could never be a mother; that she'd have to choose between the two, the way Mam had done. But now, her mind full of the frightened girl in the cave, she felt an ache of certainty. She *would* be a mother. Yes, together she and Eliza would mother all the girls who came to this place, all the girls who needed protection and vengeance. She, Mary, would do this; until there was no more life in her body, whenever that time would be.

She pictured them again, that line of girls waiting.

We will keep you safe, Mary thought as she and Eliza watched the raft drift away, carried by the sunlit water.

I promise.

47

LUCY AND JESS

SUNDAY, 17 FEBRUARY 2019

Jess is holding her daughter's hand, feeling the beat of her pulse.

Her daughter.

For twenty years, she has not allowed herself to look at Lucy properly. She has turned her gaze away from her daughter's eyes, so like her own. The delicate bones of her skull. The fragile wrists. The skin with its angry thirst for the sea.

Twenty years, each a score on her heart.

In this moment, Jess knows only these things for certain. She knows that she cannot shed the past, the choices she made or didn't. Her failure to keep her daughter safe.

She knows that she loves her daughter, a love as vast and furious as the tide that, even now, seeps into the cave.

The sea is rising with the storm. Soon, the rocks that lead to the cave will be submerged.

"Take my hand," Jess says to Lucy now. The sea laps its way inside, weeds brushing against Lucy's skin. Darkness, but for the white curls of the water, the glimpse of sky beyond the cave, rent by lightning.

Lucy hesitates, looking at Jess's outstretched fingers with their shining pleats of skin.

Jess is asking a question, Lucy knows. Asking her to choose.

She takes her hand in answer.

In the water, Lucy feels herself bloom.

Her throat opens and she is breathing: she can feel the water nourish her, the sweet sting of the salt. She stretches out her hands in front of her, marveling at the webbed flesh. Her blood beats like a drum. She kicks her legs, feels the power in them, the beauty.

Ahead of her, Jess moves with the tide, her body at one with the sea, her hair a dark, drifting halo. Lucy sees the dance of the coral, throbbing pink and bright in time with the current. The silver dart of fish, the elegant shadow of a stingray.

Above, she knows, the storm rages: ashore, trees bend and sway, the leaves crackle with lightning. The wind picks up the sand in great billows, whips the waves white.

But here, all is peaceful, time slowed to the space between her heartbeats.

Jess swims by her side. Lucy can see herself in the way that Jess glides through the water. The scoop of her arms, the kick of her legs.

My mother.

For the first time, she allows the words to fill her heart.

Her mother turns to look at her and smiles.

This, Lucy thinks. *This is my place.*

What does she care for the world above? For green-gold light, the prickly warmth of a cat on her lap, the sweet drift of banksia on the evening air?

At first, Lucy thinks the shadow is the curve of a wave, or perhaps a reflection of the darkening sky.

But then she hears the whirr of the motor, cutting through the peaceful beat of the tide.

———

For a moment, Jess thinks that time is looping back on itself. That she is not moving through the sea with her daughter by her side, but crouched trembling in the mouth of the cave, baby cradled to her chest, the boat roaring toward her.

No.

Jess reaches out and takes hold of Lucy's hand, pulls her closer so that they swim as if one creature. They must go deeper, to the places the light can't reach.

They must keep the promise. Take up the mantle, take up their place in the ocean's trenches and tides. Cast the net with their song.

She thinks of Cameron, of his body drifting somewhere below.

She can still feel the kiss of the blade at her throat, can still smell his sweat, pungent with fear. He held her down so that she was half over the lip of the cave, the wind tearing at her. She was waiting for the siren call, certain it would come at any moment. The song that would wrap itself around Cameron's body and pull him to the deep.

But it had not come.

Desperate, she had sunk her teeth into his forearm and his grip on the knife had loosened.

It had been a simple thing, then, to wrest it from his hands and drive the blade into his gut.

Later, after she had rolled his body over the lip of the cave and watched it fall into the sea below, the blood spreading out around him, she had heard it at last. The singing.

It was coming from herself.

After, she'd lingered in the cave, hungry for the sea. Her body yearned for it, even as her mouth soured with the last of the biscuits they'd taken from the house, nothing to drink but plastic-tainted rainwater. But she'd been frightened to let go of herself, once and for all. Frightened that she would look up at the water's surface with its elusive glitter of sun, tortured by all she'd left behind. The feeling of a brush in her hands, the smell of paint and linseed. Melody's laugh; the gentle timbre of her mother's voice on the phone.

And, most of all, the chance of seeing Lucy again.

Now, with her daughter by her side, there is nothing in the world above that can possibly keep her.

She tugs on Lucy's hand, feels her blood drop as they go deeper, seeking darkness.

And then a new sound. The crack of fiberglass on rock. The motor cuts out, and there is the suck of a boat turning on its side, rolled by a wave, and then something is falling through the water, wreathed in silver and white.

A man, his oilskin jacket billowing around him.

Lucy feels the water ripple across her skin. Something has broken the calm. Ahead, fish scatter, registering an intruder.

She feels the twist of Jess's body next to her and follows her gaze. A man, drifting toward them, mouth open to the sea.

Her body shrinks to just one thought, one word.

Dad.

She lets go of Jess's hand and kicks, propelling herself toward him.

It's him. The man who stole her from this place, who pulled her from the cave like she was his to take. The man who took her child from her and raised her as his own.

That's who Jess sees, in the blank, open eyes, the blood lifting itself in ribbons from his head. In the hands, outstretched and limp, trembling with the current.

But she also sees her father.

Her father, who recorded her first word in a notebook that he treasures, even now. Who held her hand in his own when she took her first, uncertain steps. Who pulled her from the sea—twice—because he wanted to protect her, to keep her safe. Because he could not bear to let her go.

Her father who named her *Jessica*. A gift from God.

Her throat closes.

She swims.

Lucy is already there, one arm around his rib cage, the other flailing wildly for Jess to come, to follow, to help.

And Jess is kicking hard, catching him around his waist and pushing him up, up, up, toward light and air.

She had asked Lucy to make a choice.

But sometimes, there is no choice.

There is only love.

48

LUCY

APRIL 2019

Lucy looks in the mirror, running her fingers through the bristles of her hair. It's getting longer, now, the blonde strands wiry. She tilts her head to the side, watching the pulse beat in her neck. The flesh there is only faintly ribbed. She touches the tender skin with its light crust of salt. Out the window, she sees the blue thread of the ocean through the trees. Waiting for her.

She bends to the sink, splashes water on her face, closing her eyes with relief.

She lingers a moment before going downstairs, her fingers resting on the doorknob.

Her watch shows 10:28 A.M.—he'll be here any minute now. Sounds filter from downstairs: the rumble of the kettle boiling, the *plink* of someone chopping fruit. Melody laughing at one of Dad's jokes, the clatter of plates as Mum sets the table.

Mum. Dad.

Lucy catches herself.

It's hard to shake twenty years of habit. Harder still to accept the truth of her family.

They've all agreed to take things one day at a time.

There's a scratching at the bathroom door, and Lucy smiles when she opens it to find Dora Maar waiting outside. The cat tilts her head and meows, green eyes narrowed.

"Coming," Lucy says, scratching her behind the ears.

Her heart flutters as she walks down the stairs, her hand sticky on the banister. The scent of croissants and coffee drifts toward her.

"Goose!" Her father, standing at the kitchen bench, turns. She is not yet used to the uneven twist of his smile; or the stubble of his scalp, its failure to hide the jagged scar from the surgery. "What do you think—this enough for six?"

He moves aside—his left side following his right, like a clumsy mimic—so that she can inspect the fruit salad he's prepared. Amber cubes of rock melon, grapes, crisp slices of apple, rounds of banana. His fingers tremble on the knife, newly clumsy. She can see his pride in it, this task that would have been beyond him only weeks ago.

"Looks great," she says and he grins, flushing with pleasure.

"Don't go overboard," her mother says from the table. "The boy was always a whippet, barely saw him eat a thing."

"I remember." Her father laughs.

Lucy treasures the sound. It almost makes up for the waxiness to his face, the slight droop to the left corner of his mouth. She pushes aside the memory of how he'd looked in the water, haloed by his own blood. The little boat he'd hired had hit the reef, tipping him into the sea. He had knocked his head on the hull.

A traumatic brain injury.

He would have died, the doctors said later, if they hadn't reached him in time. If they hadn't dragged him to the shore, if Lucy hadn't run—her neck stinging as her gills closed, air burning her lungs—to Cliff House, where she'd found her mother pacing up and down the veranda, red-eyed and white-faced.

There had been an air ambulance, and then long, fluorescent-lit weeks in the hospital, when none of them saw the sun for days at a time. At first, her father just slept, his cheeks sinking into cavities, hands thinning on the hospital blanket. When he did speak at last, his lips struggling around the words, it had been Lucy he'd asked for.

"Goose," he'd said, the sound alien in his newly puckered mouth, "I'm sorry."

"It's OK, Dad," she'd said, even though he wasn't her father, and it wasn't OK, not yet.

But it would be. She believes that.

Lucy looks around for Jess. She's outside on the back veranda, elbows resting on the balcony rail.

There's a tension to her spine that Lucy has come to recognize as a sign of nerves. She's seen a lot of it, lately. Jess has told her a little of the interviews with the police. The detectives accepted her version of events—that Hennessey had abducted Jess after she threatened to report his whereabouts and held her hostage in the cave. That he had told her to tell Melody that she was going away, had threatened to harm her friend if Jess revealed the truth. He had taken a knife from her kitchen and, later, held it to her throat. The struggle that had resulted in him falling to his death had also led to the loss of the knife, but the wounds to Jess's face told their own story. As did Hennessey's phone records—cell phone triangulation placed him at the cave on the day Jess said he'd abducted her.

When the last interview was over, Jess had disappeared to the ocean for hours. When she'd emerged, her body gleaming as she hauled herself up the staircase, the gills closing and the webbing between her fingers receding, there'd been a new, clean look to her face. As if something had been washed away.

"Hey," Lucy says now, closing the back door softly behind her. "You OK?"

Jess turns to face her, smiling. She blows out her cheeks and then winds her hair into an unruly knot on top of her head.

"Yeah. Just, you know. Nervous."

Jess is still a little too thin, a little too insubstantial-looking. They've been sleeping in the bedroom together while the others have been staying downstairs, and Lucy finds herself waking in the night, as if to check she's still breathing.

"Do you miss them?" Jess asked once, as they watched the moonlight ripple across the ceiling.

"Miss who?"

"Mary and Eliza."

"A little," Lucy said, surprising herself. The first weeks, she hadn't noticed their absence—she'd been at the hospital with Dad, and sleep had been stolen in gritty snatches. It had dawned on her gradually, the feeling of wrongness. Like turning around and realizing you no longer had a shadow. "Yes."

"Why do you think they've stopped?"

"I don't know. Maybe because we don't need them anymore."

"We don't?"

"No. Now we have the sea."

"And each other."

"Exactly."

Now, Lucy rests a hand on Jess's back.

"It'll be OK," she says. "Anyway, if anyone should be nervous, it's me. I'm about to meet my real father properly for the first time."

Jess laughs, then frowns, turning back to look at the sea. The sky is cloudless, the water holding all its blue. In the distance, a seagull floats past. Lucy feels an ache for it, for the ocean against her skin. Later, she tells herself. When the others are asleep. They will wade into the water and let it change them.

Afterward, as the night air dries her skin, she will sit here, on the veranda, and she will write. Of all the things they see in the shifting depths, where the *Naiad* lies broken on the ocean floor. The rusted ribs of chains, the rotted planks of the berths. Here a rosary, there the brass disc of a coin. And all around, the green silt of bones.

Four score women, whose stories have not been told, whose names have been forgotten.

She has the passenger manifest, the archives, the facts. The loom to weave a story around. She will write them back into history. Bring them to the surface, the light.

It doesn't matter that she won't be going back to university; that she won't become a journalist. After all, there is more than one way to tell the truth.

She's not proud of what she did to Ben, the violence of her hands around his throat. But in a way, she's glad that it happened. It led her here, to this moment. To this new understanding of who she is, her place in the story.

"I'm sorry," Jess says. "That we lied to you. I know what it's like. Not knowing where you come from. Where you belong."

Lucy puts an arm around Jess's waist, squeezes tight.

"But you do know," she says softly. "You belong to me."

The crunch of tires on gravel. Lucy's heart jolts. She knows they should go inside. But she wants one more moment, standing here and looking out at the water, Jess's body warm against hers. Just the two of them.

There's the creak of the back door opening. Melody stands in the doorway, as if asking permission to break the moment.

"Girls?" she says. "Max is here."

EPILOGUE

COMBER BAY, NSW

THIRTY-SEVEN YEARS EARLIER

Before he was Mike Martin, before he had daughters to lose and so many secrets to keep, Robert Wilson woke in his bedroom at Cliff House and watched the moon rise over the sea.

He kissed the top of his wife's head. She murmured in her sleep, then rolled away from him, to face the wall. He could see that her hands had come to rest on the flat plane of her stomach.

Robert sighed as he folded back the cotton duvet and crept lightly from the bed. He stood for a moment, watching his wife's sleeping form, spliced by the moonlight that came through the blinds. He was struck by the beauty of her bare arm: the lightly muscled bicep, the slope of her shoulder blade. His wife had a strong body: sturdy ankles, even sturdier hips. Childbearing hips, you might call them, if you were cruel.

A waste, his mother had said before she died.

Robert agreed that it was a waste. His wife was born to be a mother. Not because of the width of her hips or the strength of her arms, but because . . . well, it was hard to put into words, and even if it hadn't been, there was no one to hear them. If there'd been anyone to listen, Robert would have said that his wife was like the grit inside an oyster, polishing the pearl. She brought out the best in all who knew her.

That was why he hated himself so much as he padded downstairs, as he changed into the clothes he'd left out the night before: fisherman's trousers, boots, a thick jumper, and a heavy waterproof. He closed the front door with a soft click. Judy wouldn't wake, he knew. She was a fisherman's wife and was used to him rising before the sun.

As he descended the stone stairs, the moonlit sea gleaming in the distance, the guilt gradually ebbed away, replaced by a thrill in his stomach.

The night was cool but Robert's skin was slick with sweat by the time he reached the cave. His jaw ached from clenching: every time he edged his way down the steep sandstone steps that led to the water, he imagined his skull splitting on the rocks below, Judy in her nightgown, opening the door to the police.

Sometimes, he wasn't sure why he kept coming back. But on certain nights he woke and dressed, his body acting almost of its own accord, dancing to some remembered song.

He had to stoop to enter the cave. He could tell already that she wasn't yet there: he'd come to learn the smell of her. A female scent, milk and fish and blood, but somehow pleasant. Now, the cave smelled of dank rock and lichen, of emptiness.

The first time, and the next few times after that, Robert had not believed what his eyes were telling him.

He'd been alone in the *Marlin*, early one morning. Ryan hadn't shown up—he hadn't been the same, since his brother's death—and it'd been hard work, hauling in the catch. He'd anchored in the shadow of the cliff, so that he could watch the sunrise. The catch stared, glass-eyed, from the net. He sat on a crate and poured a cup of tea from his thermos. His muscles ached. Fish scales glimmered on his hands.

A snatch of music, perhaps a woman singing, had drifted toward him. A radio from another ship, he'd thought (though none were around), or from the shore (though he was, surely, too far out to hear).

Then, a rippling sound, as though the water had swallowed something, and the music was gone. There was a tightening of his scalp, of the skin on the back of his neck. He turned, looking for the source. Just the shifting waves, pink with sun; the refracted light blinding him.

And then, out of the corner of his eye. A fin?

He'd tensed, watching the dark shifting water, the movement of something pale. And then she'd surfaced, the gleaming impossibility of her, resting her elbows on the side of the boat.

The myths did not do her justice.

Her scales glittered beneath his fingers, cold to the touch. When they kissed and his hands cupped her jaw, he felt the beat of her gills against his skin. Her voice, when she spoke, was musical but somehow wrong, like a poorly tuned instrument.

At first, when he asked, she would not tell him her name. Later, when she did, he had trouble making it out: her mouth could not form the syllables, as if it had been an age since she had uttered them.

Mare, she might have said. A word for the sea.

He could not decide if she was beautiful in spite of her monstrosity, or because of it.

"Where do you come from?" he'd asked her once, the tide sighing around them. She had smiled, showing the sharp rows of her teeth, as if she knew it was his way of asking: *What are you? Are you real?*

"Somewhere far away," she'd said, in her strange, lilting voice. "I'm a visitor here. Like you."

Over time, he learned her origins, her purpose. Of the fates of the men who had disappeared, though he had only known Daniel well. Judy had never liked him, he remembered. "The way he looks at me," she'd said once, simply.

"Will it happen to me, too?" he'd said, feeling the nip of her teeth against the soft part of his neck. "What happened to Daniel, and the others."

"No," she'd said, breathing the word against his skin. "You're different, aren't you."

He couldn't decide if it had been a statement or a question.

Perhaps it was an instruction.

He longed to take some piece of her home, to feel that she was with him, somehow. Once, returning from the cave with her briny scent in his nose and the memory of her scaly skin against his, he'd tried to draw her. But the furtive scribblings at the kitchen table (he was terrified, always, that Judy would wake) did not do her justice. He had never been good at drawing people. Perhaps because their faces changed so much, or because they themselves were always changing. That was their magic, a magic he could not capture. When Robert drew a human face he felt as if he'd pinned a butterfly for study. As if he'd taken something that flickered with life and beauty and killed it.

He would not do that to her.

And so instead he decided to draw something else to remind him, secretly, of her. Something that recalled the lustrous spread of her fins, the quivering spines. Something that was beautiful and vicious all at once.

A lionfish.

The tide brought water rushing into the cave, and there she was, her body wreathed in foam. Later, he would pick over his memory for signs. A curve to her stomach, a new heaviness to her shining breasts. But there had been nothing.

———

Months passed. One day, he came home to find Judy sitting at the kitchen table, hands trembling around a mug of tea. She looked at him with eyes so full of hope and fear that he had to look away. "Bobby—I'm pregnant," she said. She had waited longer to tell him, afraid that it was only a matter of time before she was curled on the bathroom floor, the beginnings of their child shuddering out of her.

When the inevitable happened again, something inside Judy seemed to die, too.

She moved away from him in bed. She said little and took long walks, her binoculars slung on a strap around her neck, preferring the birds for company. When she returned, her feet left shimmers of sand on the tiles. He wondered, half hoping, whether she had a place like the cave, a place she went to forget.

One morning he woke up feeling different. A strange pull, deep in his belly. Had it been like that before? He couldn't remember. He put the feeling from his mind.

On the water, the sun painted the waves red, like they were fishing in blood. The nets came up empty but for tangled skeins of seaweed. The men were twitchy, bleary-eyed. Ryan's breath stank sweetly of booze.

"Lift the anchor," said Robert, powering up the motor.

The feeling was back, a song humming in his bones.

"Want me to cast?" Ryan said when they dropped anchor in the shadow of the cliff, the *Marlin* bobbing gently in the current.

"Wait a sec," Robert said. His eyes scanned the waves. He wasn't sure if he was hopeful or fearful of seeing her. On the one hand he longed for it—hadn't he driven the boat to the cave based on the strange stirring in his gut?—but he knew it wasn't safe, not with the others here.

In the distance, something caught his eye. A flash of white. Probably just the crest of a wave, he told himself.

The waves slapped against the hull. There was a sound almost like a bird call, but strangely human, the notes of it touching his spine.

"Christ," said Ryan. "What the bloody hell was that?"

"Sounded like my baby niece," said Dave.

"We're at sea, dickhead."

Ryan and Dave started their usual sniping, but Robert didn't hear them. There was something inside the cave. Something pale and small and—

Before he was really aware of what he was doing, Robert was tugging frantically at his waterproofs and his boots. He climbed up onto the side of the hull, touching his toes like a diver.

"Mate, what the fuck—"

But the men's cries were swallowed by the rush of water in his ears, down his nose. He resurfaced, coughing and blinded. His muscles drove forward, propelling him through the churn and froth of the sea.

Afterward, in the back of the ambulance, Robert stared down at the damp bundle in his arms.

Her eyes were wide and so blue they were almost black, like the deepest part of the ocean. Her tiny hands curled open and shut, the skin between her fingers webbed. Silver shimmered around the lobes of her ears, her mouth.

She cooed, dark eyes looking up at him. Something burst open in his chest.

She was perfect, and he knew then that he would never let her go.

ACKNOWLEDGMENTS

Writing this book is one of the hardest things I've ever done. The first—and indeed, the second and third—draft of this novel bore very little resemblance to the story that you have just read. Before I found Mary, Eliza, Lucy, and Jess, I wrote—and deleted—almost 300,000 words in two years. That's how long it took to find *The Sirens*.

One very important person kept me going through that time—my wonderful agent, Felicity Blunt. I'm of course biased, but I really believe that Felicity is the best literary agent in the industry today. It was her guidance and encouragement that led me to this story. Thank you, Felicity.

I also can't imagine this novel existing without the input of my brilliant editors, Sarah Cantin and Amy Perkins. I've been a lucky author indeed to benefit from your passion, precision, and insight. Thank you so much, Sarah and Amy—I miss our Zoom calls already!

My huge thanks also to my US agent, Alexandra Machinist, for her wonderful support and encouragement. You and Felicity are the dream team!

I'm also very grateful indeed to Beth Coates and Jo Thompson for much handholding during the production process.

Thank you to my star foreign rights agent, Tanja Goossens, for helping my novels find homes all over the world. I so appreciate all your hard work.

Thank you so much to Flo Sandelson, Rosie Pierce, Georgia Williams, and Emma Walker at Curtis Brown, and to Katherine Flitsch at CAA.

At St. Martin's, I'm so grateful to Jen Enderlin, Drue VanDuker, Lisa Senz, Anne Marie Tallberg, Marissa Sangiacomo, Katie Bassel, Michael Clark, Mary Beth Roche, Robert Allen, and Emily Dyer. Huge thanks, too, to Michael Storrings and the rest of the brilliant art team at St. Martin's Press for my beautiful cover.

At The Borough Press and Harper Fiction, my sincere thanks to Jabin Ali, Maddy Marshall, Emily Merrill, and Emilie Chambeyron. Thank you to Claire Ward and the rest of the Borough art team for the gorgeous UK jacket.

And to everyone at The Borough Press and St. Martin's Press who has helped shepherd not one but two of my novels into the world— you have my deepest gratitude. Thank you for all that you do.

Huge thanks to my excellent copy editors, Amber Burlinson and Linda Sawicki, and also to my proofreader, Sarah Bance.

Thank you to Bianca Valentino for your generous guidance and insight.

I'd also like to take this opportunity to acknowledge some of the literary works without which *The Sirens* could not have been written.

Firstly, to the wonderful Charlotte Runcie: thank you for your beautiful book, *Salt on Your Tongue: Women and the Sea*, which was a source of such inspiration. Your work also led me to the discovery of the old folk song "The Maid on the Shore," the lyrics of which are woven throughout this novel. I'm so grateful to you.

I consulted my copy of *The Fatal Shore* by the late, great Robert Hughes so much while researching this novel that it is now literally falling apart. I would recommend this book to anyone looking to read more about Australia's history of convict transportation; it is meticulously researched and written with stunning beauty. Thank you, Robert, for your work.

I am also indebted to the wonderful scholarship in Deborah Oxley's *Convict Maids: The Forced Migration of Women to Australia*, Babette Smith's *A Cargo of Women*, and Deborah J. Swiss's *The Tin Ticket*.

I would not have been able to bring Mary and Eliza to life without, in particular, R. F. Foster's *Modern Ireland: 1600–1972* and Olive Sharkey's brilliant book *Irish Country Life*.

My sincere thanks to the Museum of Country Life in County Mayo, Ireland, where I spent a fascinating day in 2021, and to the Hyde Park Barracks Museum in Sydney, NSW.

To every bookseller who has championed *Weyward* and now *The Sirens*, thank you for making my dreams come true. Huge thanks, too, to Niamh and Mary O'Donnabháin, for your help with the Irish phrases used in this novel. All errors are entirely my own.

To my brilliant author friends, Lizzie Pook and Ally Wilkes: Thank you for your constant encouragement and advice. I don't know where I'd be without either of you.

My wonderful friend Cheryl O'Sullivan: thank you for reading so many different iterations of this novel, and for your generous guidance on Irish language and culture. I'm so grateful for our friendship. Thank you also to Bethan Mackey and Victoria Atkins, for sailing the high seas with me.

Thank you, Uncle David and Aunt Susan, for the precious childhood memories of Rosedale—I'll treasure them forever.

Mum, thank you for reading every draft and for your loving encouragement across the oceans. A huge thanks also to Brian, my wonderful stepfather, for your constant support.

Dad—thank you for inspiring this story with your tales of our family history, and reading many early versions of this book.

Thank you to my younger brothers, Adrian and Oliver, for all of your support—and for being such wonderful young men. I'm so proud of you both. Thank you to my stepmother, Otilie, for pressing *Weyward* into so many peoples' hands!

Fundamentally, this novel is about the ability of water—and sisterhood—to heal and transform. If anything inspired it, it was the love and support that my sister Katie showed me while I recovered from a stroke in 2017. Katie, I will never forget the day that you took me swimming at London Fields Lido. Thank you for helping me find myself again.

Last but certainly not least, Jack. Thank you for helping me craft realistic newspaper articles, for bringing me daily cups of coffee, for making me laugh when I wanted to cry. Above all, thank you for believing in me. I kept going because of you. I love you.

ABOUT THE AUTHOR

Sophie Davidson

Emilia Hart is the author of *Weyward*. She grew up in Australia and studied English literature at university before training as a lawyer. She now lives in London.